Dangerous NIGHTS

BETH CORNELISON
MERLINE LOVELACE

Two exhilarating, pulse-racing seductions that you'll never forget

G000144943

NIGHTS COLLECTION

July 2013

August 2013

September 2013

October 2013

Dangerous
NIGHTS

BETH CORNELISON
MERLINE LOVELACE

Mills & Boon, an imprint of Harlequin (UK) Limited, Eton House, 18-24 Paradise Road, Richmond, Surrey TW9 1SR

DANGEROUS NIGHTS © Harlequin Enterprises II B.V./S.à.r.l 2013

Tall Dark Defender © Beth Cornelison 2009
Undercover Wife © Merline Lovelace 2008

ISBN: 978 0 263 90734 6

025-0913

Harlequin (UK) policy is to use papers that are natural, renewable and recyclable products and made from wood grown in sustainable forests. The logging and manufacturing processes conform to the legal environmental regulations of the country of origin.

Printed and bound in Spain
by Blackprint CPI, Barcelona

TALL DARK DEFENDER

BETH CORNELISON

Beth Cornelison started writing stories as a child when she penned a tale about the adventures of her cat, Ajax. A Georgia native, she received her bachelor's degree in public relations from the University of Georgia. After working in public relations for a little more than a year, she moved with her husband to Louisiana, where she decided to pursue her love of writing fiction.

Since that first time, Beth has written many more stories of adventure and romantic suspense and has won numerous honours for her work, including a coveted Golden Heart Award in romantic suspense from Romance Writers of America. She is active on the board of directors for the North Louisiana Storytellers and Authors of Romance (NOLA STARS) and loves reading, travelling, *Peanuts'* Snoopy and spending downtime with her family.

She writes from her home in Louisiana, where she lives with her husband, one son and two cats who think they are people. Beth loves to hear from her readers. You can write to her at PO Box 5418, Bossier City, LA 71171, USA, or visit her website at www.bethcornelison.com.

To my wonderful editor, Allison Lyons.
Thanks for all you do!

Chapter 1

The lights weren't supposed to be off.

Irritation, tinged with a tickle of uneasiness, skittered through Annie Compton. She fumbled in the predawn darkness to jab her key into the lock at Pop's Diner. Her boss, Peter Hardin, was supposed to have left the outside light on to deter burglars and to illuminate the front door for the employee who opened the diner in the morning. Today, Annie was said employee with the unenviable responsibility of showing up at 5:00 a.m.

She grumbled under her breath as she groped on the shadowed door to locate the lock's slot. The door moved unexpectedly. Just a fraction of an inch, but enough to catch Annie's attention. A bolted door shouldn't have wiggled that much.

Annie pulled the handle, and the heavy glass door swung open. Her pulse spiked. Turning on the front light wasn't all her boss had neglected when he closed the restaurant last night.

Gritting her teeth, she entered the diner and flipped on the overhead lights. The cold bluish-white glow of the fluorescent bulbs flooded the dining room.

"Hello? Mr. Hardin?" She scanned the empty restaurant cautiously. Listened. Waited. "Is anyone here?"

When she heard nothing, saw no one, she released the breath she held and crossed the floor. Annie stashed her purse behind the lunch counter, wishing she could call grouchy Mr. Hardin on the carpet for his gaffes. Considering her boss had only criticism for her waitressing skills, she figured turnabout was fair play.

She huffed a humorless laugh as she plucked out a coffee filter and dropped it into the brewing basket. The man had left the diner unlocked, for crying out loud! Compared to exposing the restaurant to theft, her forgetting to refill the saltshakers was nothing.

Problem was, neglecting the saltshakers wasn't her worst mistake. Her gut clenching, she poured a carafe of water into the coffeemaker. She'd made her biggest blunder ever just a few nights before—a royal screwup that Hardin claimed had cost him two hundred thousand dollars. The amount seemed preposterous to her, but her boss insisted that was how much she'd lost him.

Annie's hands shook as she measured out the coffee grinds. She could never make up for losing Mr. Hardin so much money. She guessed she was lucky she still had her job, lucky he hadn't beaten her senseless the way Walt would have.

Thoughts of her violent ex-husband sent another shiver down her back. She rubbed the goose bumps on her arms and squared her shoulders. *Never again.*

If she had to work this dead-end waitress job the rest of her life, barely making ends meet for herself and her two young children, the price was worth her freedom from her abusive marriage. No man would ever hurt her or her children again.

Annie jabbed the power switch, and with a hiss and a waft of rich aroma, the morning java began dripping into the pot.

A glance around the diner showed numerous cleaning jobs that had been ignored at closing last night. She pressed her lips in a taut line of frustration. Perhaps this was part of her boss's plan to punish her for her colossal and costly mistake three nights earlier. Perhaps she deserved as much.

Two hundred thousand dollars. Acid bit her gut. How could she ever make up for that mistake?

Sighing her resignation, she took a clean rag from the cabinet and headed to the kitchen for a bucket of soapy water to start cleaning tables.

She noticed the foul odor as soon as she stepped through the swinging door from the dining room. Wrinkling her nose, she flipped the lights on and checked for some food item that might have been left out to spoil. But not even rotten milk smelled this bad.

Coupled with the unlocked front door, the putrid scent gave her pause. Too many things seemed off-kilter at the diner this morning.

A ripple of apprehension shimmied through her. Annie hesitated by the main grill, which still sported last night's grease.

"Mr. Hardin, are you there?" She heard the quiver of fear in her tone and pressed a hand to her swirling stomach. "Hello?"

She took a few baby steps forward, scanning the dirty kitchen. Rounding the industrial-size freezer, she crept into the back hall.

On the floor, a pair of feet jutted through the open door to the manager's office.

Annie gasped. Dear heavens! Had he fallen? Had a heart attack?

"Mr. Hardin!" she cried, rushing forward.

When she reached the office door, Annie drew up short.

Her breath froze in her lungs. Bile surged to her throat. Black spots danced at the edge of her vision.

Peter Hardin lay in a puddle of blood, his eyes fixed in a blank, sightless stare. Two bullet holes pocked his chest, and a third marred his forehead.

Annie stumbled backward, horror clogging her throat.

Numb, shaking, light-headed, she edged away from her grisly discovery.

Shock and denial finally yielded to terror. A scream wrenched from her throat and echoed in the empty kitchen.

Her boss was dead. Murdered.

And though she hadn't pulled the trigger, Annie was certain Hardin's murder was her fault.

Three days earlier

He'd stalked his prey long enough. Time to move in for the kill.

Over the rim of his coffee cup, Jonah Devereaux eyed the rotund, balding man across the Formica table from him.

Martin Farrout.

Everything Jonah had learned to date in his investigation told him Farrout was the muscle of the gambling operation, the gatekeeper. Getting past Farrout, rooting out the players up the chain of command was what the past six months had been about.

"Mark my words. Kansas will go all the way," Ted Pulliam, one of Farrout's lackeys, said, jabbing the diner's table with his finger for emphasis.

Jonah grunted and lowered his coffee. "North Carolina. They're a powerhouse with a winning legacy to uphold."

Pulliam scoffed. "All right, Devereaux, put your money where your mouth is." The wiry man with faded tattoos slapped a Jackson on the table. "Twenty bucks. And I'll give you five points."

Jonah schooled his face and divided a bland look between Pulliam and Farrout, sizing them up. Weighing his decision to push his investigation to the next level.

He drained the cold dregs of his coffee and shoved the mug to the end of the table. In seconds, their waitress had snagged the coffeepot and stepped over to refill his cup.

Lifting a hand, Jonah waved her off. "Naw, I'm done, Annie. Thanks anyway."

"Gentlemen, we close in ten minutes. Can I get you anything else?" the attractive brunette asked as she cleared away the dirty mug.

Sure. I'll take an order of inside information about the local gambling ring with a side of details on the money-laundering operation I suspect your boss is running. Hold the onions.

If only it were that easy.

Instead, he'd spent months investigating the illegal activities he'd traced to Pop's Diner, and he still didn't have the evidence he needed to resolve the case and turn his information over to the local police.

The evidence he needed to give Michael justice.

Pushing aside thoughts of his mentor, Jonah flashed Annie a quick smile. "Just my bill."

While posing as a paper-mill worker who'd recently moved to the area, Jonah had eaten enough greasy meals at the small diner to send his cholesterol count into the stratosphere—a lesser-known hazard of undercover work that'd take countless hours in the gym to rectify. At least the coffee was good. God knew he'd guzzled enough of the brew at Pop's to last a lifetime.

But over the weeks, his regular meals at Pop's had gained him the level of familiarity with the locals he needed to loosen a few tongues and open a door or two. Things were finally beginning to fall into place.

He shifted his gaze to Farrout and pitched his voice low. "I want the real action. Five grand on UNC to win it all."

Pulliam fell silent and sat back in the booth.

Farrout lifted a thick black eyebrow. One taut second ticked after another, the tension screwing Jonah's gut into a tight knot. Unflinching, he held the portly man's stare.

Finally, Farrout narrowed his eyes to slits. "Ten."

Jonah sighed, pretending to consider the higher stakes. He couldn't seem too eager or too free with his cash. The working-class stiff he was supposed to be wouldn't have ten thousand dollars to lose on a careless bet. Not that *he* had that kind of money to lose, either.

He rubbed his thumb idly on the handle of his spoon and glanced out the plate-glass window to the night-darkened street. "That's pretty steep."

Farrout shrugged lazily. "I gotta know if you're for real or if you're just wasting my time. First bet is always ten grand, minimum."

Pulliam twisted his lips into a taunting grin. "How sure are you of UNC now?"

Keeping a stoic face, Jonah drummed his fingers on the table in an intentional display of nerves. "I can go eight now, two more next payday."

Farrout's fleshy lips twitched. "Deal."

Annie returned with separate checks for the three men. When she reached for Farrout's plate, he grabbed her wrist with his meaty hand and squeezed. "Did I say I was through?"

Wincing, Annie gave Farrout a wide-eyed glance. "I'm sorry. I just thought—"

Fury burned inside Jonah, and he stiffened. "Let go of her."

The barrel-chested man returned a cold stare. "Butt out, Devereaux."

Jonah gritted his teeth. "Let. Go."

Annie's cheeks had drained of color, and her dark eyes rounded with apprehension.

A muscle jumped in Farrout's jaw, but he released Annie with an angry thrust. "Watch yourself, Devereaux. I don't like people sticking their nose where it don't belong."

Hell. He didn't need to blow his investigation by pissing Farrout off. But he damn well wouldn't sit by and let him rough up a woman, either. He'd done that too often as a kid when his dad was in one of his moods, and the guilt still ate at him.

Annie rubbed her offended wrist and cast a quick, curious glance at Jonah before hurrying back to the lunch counter.

Over the months he'd been working the case, he'd gotten to know all of the waitresses by name. Annie was the most reticent of the waitstaff, but she was also the most intriguing. Though attentive and polite to a fault, she was far less inclined to engage in good-natured banter and flirting the way the other servers did. An air of mystery surrounded her, partly because of her shyness, partly because she wore her silky dark tresses in a style reminiscent of the sultry movie stars of the 1940s—parted on the side with a curtain of hair covering one cheek.

Jonah had caught a glimpse of that hidden cheek once and seen the scars she was concealing. Those scars added to the enigma that was Annie but, in his opinion, didn't detract from her pretty face. Clearly she thought otherwise, or she wouldn't work so hard to hide the jagged pink lines.

As Jonah dug his wallet out of his back pocket, Farrout and Pulliam slid out of the booth and sauntered to the counter with their checks.

"Put it on my tab, doll face," Farrout said, tossing his ticket on the counter and turning to leave.

Pulliam added his bill and clicked his tongue. "Ditto."

Annie's brow furrowed, and she shook her head. "But...we don't—"

The men ignored her as they walked out, chortling to themselves.

From the booth, Jonah seethed over the men's rudeness. He studied Annie's crestfallen expression, her drooping shoulders and moue of disgust. She slapped the counter with the rag in her hand and huffed loudly.

When she raised her gaze to him, he quickly shifted his attention to his bill and pulled a twenty out of his wallet. He rose from the bench seat and approached the counter where she wiped up the day's mess with more vigor than necessary.

Extending the ticket and cash to her, he smiled ruefully. "Keep the change."

She glanced at the money and frowned. "But all you had was coffee."

He lifted a shoulder as he returned his wallet to his pocket. "Maybe I want to help your day end on a positive note."

Annie gaped at him as if she didn't know what to make of his kindness. As if she'd never encountered generosity before. "But—"

"Annie!" Peter Hardin, the manager of the diner and Jonah's key suspect in the money-laundering scheme, burst through the swinging kitchen door.

Jonah saw Annie tense as her linebacker-size boss stalked over to her.

"I need you to do an errand for me." Hardin slapped a bulky tan envelope on the counter.

Annie's face fell, and she glanced at her watch. "Now? It's almost midnight."

Jonah took his time putting on his jacket, unabashedly eavesdropping on the exchange. Annie's distress around her boss piqued his curiosity.

"Yes, now. This has to be delivered to Fourth Street in the next half hour. It's extremely important, so don't be late with it. Guard this envelope with your life."

Jonah clenched his teeth. Fourth Street was a notoriously bad section of town. This time of night, the area was downright dangerous. What was Hardin thinking, sending a woman on an errand alone in that part of town?

"But—" Annie hesitated, chewing her lip as if debating the wisdom of arguing with her boss. "If it's so important, why aren't you delivering it?"

Hardin glared at her. "I have my reasons. You want a job tomorrow, you deliver that package on time. Got it?"

Annie opened and closed her mouth in dismay, then nodded.

Her boss handed her a scrap of paper and hitched his head toward the front door. "That's the address and the name of the guy you give the package to. *Only* to him. No one else. Got it? Now, go on. I'll close up."

After fishing her purse out from under the counter, Annie tucked the package against her chest with a sigh.

Jonah watched her leave the diner and walk past the parking lot without stopping. He frowned. She didn't have a car? Walking Fourth Street alone at night could be suicide.

Without giving it a second thought, Jonah fell in step behind Annie. Peter Hardin might not care about his waitress's safety, but Jonah wasn't about to let Annie make that delivery unprotected.

Annie's footsteps reverberated in the dark shadows looming around her. Alone on the downtown street, she clutched the manila envelope to her chest like a shield.

She shouldn't be here. This part of town was dangerous, especially at this late hour. But how could she refuse her boss's order? She couldn't afford to lose her job. She only had a few more minutes left to make Hardin's delivery, and he had been emphatic about the deadline—and the dire consequences if anything happened to the mysterious contents.

Just make the drop and get out of there. Get home. Get safe.

The sound of her shallow breathing rasped a harsh cadence in the quiet March night, and her heartbeat drummed in her ears like a death knell. She slowed her frantic pace, closing her eyes long enough to gather her composure.

Keep your wits and don't blow this.

The drop-off address had to be close. She searched for numbers on the buildings, but the dilapidated storefronts and graffiti-decorated buildings bore no identification.

She gritted her teeth. Damn Peter Hardin for forcing her to do this dangerous errand! If she didn't need her job so much, she'd have told him where to stick his order to do his dirty work. She sighed in disgust, wishing she'd stood up to Hardin.

But she'd always been a pushover. Her ex-husband had known it and taken advantage of that truth.

Squaring her shoulders, Annie kept walking, realizing how this decrepit neighborhood was a reflection of her life. Lonely, scarred and struggling to survive.

She'd had the typical fairy-tale dreams for herself as a girl— love and marriage, happily ever after. Instead she'd found a nightmare—fear and abuse, divorce from a man now serving time for a laundry list of crimes. After six years of unhappiness, at least she was free of Walt. Her job as a waitress at Pop's Diner barely covered her bills, but her children were safe now. She was safe. That was all that truly mattered.

Yet as she searched for some evidence of where to take the package, she felt anything but safe. A prick of alarm nipped her neck. Though she heard nothing, saw no one, the uneasy sense that someone was following her crawled over her like a cockroach on her skin. She shuddered.

Annie drew a deep breath for courage, her nose filling with the stench of sewage, mildew and despair.

A scuffing noise filtered through the night from an alley just ahead of her. Her steps faltered. Her pulse jumped.

"H-hello?" she called, her voice cracking.

A hulking figure emerged from the black void. The man descended on her before a scream could form in her throat. He wrapped arms of steel around her, and a fleshy palm covered her nose and mouth. Lifting her as if she weighed nothing, her attacker pulled her into the dark alley and slammed her against a brick wall.

The collision knocked the air from her lungs. Shock and fear froze her limbs.

No! her brain screamed. *Not again!* Slow-motion images of her past flickered before her mind's eye.

"You call this slop dinner?" Walt's hand cracked against her chin in an upward arc.

Her assailant seized the manila envelope she'd sworn on her life she'd deliver only to Joseph Nance.

Panic surged inside her. Her fingers curled into the package, clinging to it for all she was worth. "No!"

"Give me the money, bitch!" he growled. His fist crashed into her mouth, and a metallic taste slid over her tongue.

Red smears stained the floor. Blood. Her blood.

Walt kicked her in the ribs, and crimson drops leaked from her nose and splashed onto the linoleum.

The man's beefy fingers bit her flesh. He shook her. "Give it to me, or I'll kill you!"

Past and present twined around each other. Numbed her. She did what experience had taught her was her best defense. She shut down. Drew into herself. Closed her eyes.

Just endure it. Survive.

Her grip slackened, and the package was ripped from her arms.

Chapter 2

With a frightened cry, Annie slid to the ground, raised her arms to protect her head. Through the haze of her terror, she heard the shuffle of feet. A grunt. A curse.

Opening her eyes a slit, she found a second man in the alley, brawling hand-to-hand with her attacker.

Touching her swollen lip, she scooted farther away from the men who battled in the shadowed alley. She cringed as the newly arrived man landed a solid blow to her attacker's gut. Her assailant responded with a resounding punch to the other man's jaw.

Annie curled into a ball, trembling as fists flew. She squeezed her eyes shut and plugged her ears. She'd seen and heard enough violence in recent months to last her a lifetime. Her ex-husband's abuse was an all-too-present memory that haunted her every day.

Hot tears leaked onto her cheeks, and she conjured a image of her children, Haley and Ben. She prayed she'd survive to see them again. *Please, God.*

Her kids were all that mattered. The reason she worked the exhausting waitress job at the diner. Her reason to persevere. Her reason for leaving Walt sixteen months ago, despite the horrifying weeks that followed as her abusive ex hunted her, terrorized her, nearly killed her.

A loud, pained shout jolted her out of her protective shell, and she peeked out at the scene unfolding before her. Her assailant was on the ground, the second man rubbing his knuckles. As he stepped back from his opponent, the second man moved through a shaft of light from a streetlamp.

And Annie glimpsed a face she knew from the diner. A regular. Her gasp drew the man's attention.

She searched her memory for his name. John? Jacob? No— *Jonah.*

"Annie, are you all right?"

In those few seconds of Jonah's distraction, her assailant snatched up the envelope and ran from the alley.

"The package!" Panic wrenched Annie's chest.

Jonah pursued the thief to the end of the alley but apparently decided against a footrace. Instead, he walked back toward Annie, wiping blood from his nose with the sleeve of his shirt. "Are you hurt?"

"He took the envelope," she said, her voice quivering. A sinking disappointment crushed her chest. Though grateful to be alive and to have had Jonah's help, she dreaded what Hardin would do when he discovered she'd lost his package. Peter Hardin was no gentleman, and she doubted he'd be forgiving about her screwup. She buried her face in her hands as fresh tears puddled in her eyes. "He's going to fire me. I know he is. Oh, God…"

Jonah crouched in front of her, and she jolted when he stroked a hand down her arm.

Raising a wary gaze, she scrunched a few inches farther away from him. He may have scared the mugger off, but she'd seen his skill with his fists. Experience had taught her to give violent men a wide berth.

"Hey, come on now." The low, soothing rumble of his voice lulled her. "You won't lose your job. It's not your fault you were mugged." His dark eyebrows drew into a frown, and his tone hardened. "If anyone is to blame it's that bastard Hardin for sending a woman into this neighborhood alone in the middle of the night."

Jonah flexed and balled his hand. Annie's mouth dried, the stolen envelope temporarily forgotten as she focused on the more immediate threat—the man fisting his hand before her.

Taking a deep breath, she eyed Jonah's clenched fist. "Wh-why are you here?"

He cocked his head slightly and lifted a corner of his mouth. "I'd have thought that was obvious. I followed you when you left the diner."

So her sense had been right. Her pulse sped up. "Why? What do you want?"

He raised his hands, palms out. "I only wanted to keep an eye on you. I figured something like this might happen and…" He sighed. "I'm only sorry it took me so long to catch up once the jerk grabbed you. I should have stayed closer, but I didn't want to spook you if you saw me following you."

Annie furrowed her brow skeptically. "So you were following me to…*protect* me?"

He grunted. "I heard Hardin tell you to make the delivery, knew the neighborhood…" He glanced away for a moment and swiped at the blood beading under his nose again. "I oughta wring the jerk's neck for putting you at risk this way."

"No!"

Her vehement protest snapped his gaze back to hers. "Oh, I won't. I'm not interested in being arrested for assault." He held his hand out to her. "Can I help you up?"

Annie hesitated, staring at his large hand. His knuckles were swollen and raw, his palm toughened by calluses. That hand had packed a powerful punch to her assailant.

"Annie?"

Her gaze darted up to his. In the harsh shaft of light from

the streetlamp, she studied his face. His bloody nose had a bump at the bridge, as if it had been broken before. A thin, silvery scar bisected his dark eyebrow, and a red blotch on his jaw hinted at a future bruise, courtesy of her attacker.

Yet despite all these visible signs of past and recent fights, his lopsided grin and warm green eyes spoke of a softer side to this man.

"Keep the change."

"Let go of her."

Did she dare trust him? He *had* come to help her. Or so he said.

"If you wanted to protect me…" She paused, second-guessing the wisdom of challenging him on his story. Challenging Walt had earned her more than one beating.

"Go on."

She took a fortifying breath. "Well, why not just walk *with* me? Why follow me?"

He rubbed a hand over his battered jaw. "Fair question." He tugged up the corner of his mouth. "If I had offered to walk with you or drive you to the drop-off address, would you have accepted?"

"I—" She lifted her chin. "Well…probably not. All I know about you is that you like lots of milk in your coffee—skim, not whole—and that you usually sit at the counter. First seat, facing the door."

His grin was a tad smug. "That's what I thought." He offered his hand again.

This time, after a brief hesitation, Annie placed her hand in his and let him pull her to her feet. The warmth and strength of his fingers, curled around hers, sent an odd shiver through her. How could a touch be both comforting and unnerving at the same time? The size of his hand, swallowing her smaller one, sent a tingling awareness through her. His height dwarfed her five feet four inches, and he had more strength in one arm than she had in her whole body. Like Walt had.

Jonah had the power and skill to crush her if he chose.

Her stomach did a forward roll. Snatching her hand back, she rubbed her arms, hoping to warm the chill that burrowed to her bones.

"Did he hurt you, Annie? I can take you to the emergency room if—"

"No! I—I'm fine. Really." *I've taken far worse.*

Uncomfortable under his scrutiny, she averted her gaze, tried to collect her thoughts. "I...I guess I should call the police. File a report."

Jonah's eyes narrowed, and he rubbed his jaw. "Uh, generally yes. But...I'd rather you didn't."

Her gaze snapped up to his. "Why not? He took Mr. Hardin's package. He said the package was important and—"

"The guy is long gone."

"But the cops need to know! I was attacked, and...maybe they can find the package before—"

Before Peter Hardin finds out the envelope was stolen. Fear seized her lungs, and she struggled for a breath. "Oh, God," she wheezed.

"Annie?" Concern knit Jonah's brow as she leaned against the bricks and gasped for air.

"H-Hardin...will kill me. H-he's...going to hate me. H-he..."

Jonah stroked a hand over her back. "Calm down, Annie. It'll be all right. Hardin can't blame you for this."

She angled her head to glance up at him and scoffed. "You don't know him very well." She bit her bottom lip to keep it from trembling. "I don't have a cell phone. I'll have to wait until I get home to report this... Unless you—"

Jonah was shaking his head. "Annie, I know you have no reason to trust me, but...I need you not to call the cops about this."

Annie frowned. "Wha— Why?"

"I have my reasons. I know that's not much to go on, but it's all I can say now." He scowled and ducked his head. "Please, Annie. I need you to trust me on this."

Trust him? She barely knew him. And trust was one thing she had little of when it came to men. Walt had destroyed what little trust she had. But to get away from him, to get out of this deserted alley and get home to her kids, she'd promise anything.

"All right. No cops." *Yet.* She reserved the right to change her mind once she was safe at home.

With his mouth in a grim line, he gave a tight nod. Jonah swept his gaze over her, then stepped back. "I can at least walk you back to the diner parking lot."

"I don't have a car. Can't afford one." Annie lifted her chin, determined not to feel any embarrassment for her financial woes. She had no reason to be ashamed.

"Mmm. That's kinda what I figured when you didn't drive here. How did you plan on getting home?"

She scooped her purse off the ground. "Same way I got here. Walking. Usually I take the bus home. But on nights when I work late, the bus is no longer running."

Jonah heaved a sigh. "Well, my truck is back near the diner if you'd like a ride."

Annie adjusted the purse strap on her shoulder, steeling herself for the long walk home. "No. Thank you."

He scowled. "You know I'm going to follow you, regardless."

Her heart gave a kick, and her muscles tightened. Walt had disregarded her wishes, too. Done as he damned well pleased, whenever, whatever. She'd felt powerless.

The last thing she needed was another controlling man dictating her life. Especially one who clearly was no stranger to violence. But how did she refuse without incurring his wrath? How did she impose her will on a man whose mind was obviously set?

With the flutter of ill-ease in her veins, Annie backed toward the street. She cleared her throat to steady her voice before replying, faking the confidence she hoped she projected. "I…appreciate your help earlier, but I can get home by myself."

He rubbed his hands on the seat of his jeans, shaking his head. "It's late, Annie. The streets in this part of town are dangerous—as you've discovered."

She shivered, remembering the instant terror when she'd been grabbed. Her arm still throbbed from her attacker's viselike grip. Defeat settled in her belly like a rock, followed closely by a surge of desperation. How would she explain the lost package to Hardin? Was she destined to be a victim of men's violence for the rest of her life?

Not a victim, Annie. You're a survivor. *Stay positive. Attitude is everything.* The mantras and platitudes Ginny, her counselor from the women's center, preached echoed in her brain. But on days like today, keeping a rosy outlook took more energy than she had. She'd dealt with grumpy customers, poor tippers and a demanding boss. She'd been on her feet since noon, spilled coffee on a customer who then threatened to sue and had had her life endangered thanks to a boss who would likely fire her for losing his package.

Annie shoved aside the sense of impending disaster and squared her shoulders as she faced Jonah. "I can't stop you from following me, but I prefer to get home by my own means."

Jonah ducked his head, his mouth twisted in a frown of disagreement. "Fine. I won't argue with you." He shook his head and huffed his frustration. "But if you change your mind, give a shout. I'll be just a block or so behind you."

The cocky lift of his eyebrow dared her to try to stop him from tailing her. He stepped back to let her pass, and she marched toward the street, squeezing her purse to her chest and giving the dark downtown avenue a wary scrutiny.

A queasy jitter roiled in her gut, knowing she'd disappointed him, upset him. Her innate need to please, an instinct Walt had exploited and pushed to an unhealthy extreme, caused her a moment's hesitation. She almost balked, almost relented.

When she'd risked her life to free herself from Walt, she'd vowed to never depend on a man for anything ever again. Rebuilding her life, her confidence, her inner strength was a daily struggle. Old habits and emotions, ingrained in her during six turbulent years of marriage, died hard. But she'd sworn to shed the debilitating attitudes and knee-jerk reactions from her marriage in favor of strength and self-empowerment.

One day at a time.

She could take care of herself and her children, no matter what. She hated that she needed the job Hardin gave her so desperately, but without a college degree, her employment options were limited.

She glanced behind her a time or two as she made her way home, and each time, Jonah gave a nod as if to say, "Yep. I'm still here."

She sensed Jonah's stare like a weight on her back as she crossed the parking lot and climbed the outside iron stairs to her second-floor apartment. On the grillwork landing, she lifted her gaze and found him in the lawn below. She flicked her hand, shooing him away.

Crossing his arms over his broad chest, he nodded to her door.

Sighing, she unlocked the door and pushed it open an inch. Again she flicked her fingers, sending him away. His lopsided grin flashed white under the bluish light of the security lamp, and he waved. Only when she turned to go inside did he finally amble off in the direction they'd come.

She parted the sheers on the kitchen window to make sure he really left, didn't loiter in the parking lot or try to come up the stairs to her door. His loose-limbed stride mirrored the relaxed confidence she'd come to know when she waited on him at the diner. He poked his hands into the pockets of his jeans, and for an instant, she admired the way his clothes fit his taut, muscular body.

"Miss Annie?"

The young voice jarred her from the intimate perusal of Jonah's physique, a side trip she had no business making. Clapping a hand over her scampering heartbeat, she faced her babysitter. "Rani, I... Sorry I'm late. My boss had me run an errand after I got off."

"It's okay. I was just watching TV. I—" Rani paused, wrinkling her brow. "Gosh, what happened to your lip?"

Annie touched her swollen mouth. She'd almost forgotten about the blow the mugger had landed, splitting her lip. "Nothing really. I'll be fine. Just a little accident," she lied out of habit.

She'd gotten good at making up explanations for the injuries Walt had inflicted.

She was a klutz. The baby had bumped her nose with his head. She'd tripped over a toy in the dark. Her babysitter frowned but said nothing else about Annie's injury.

"Come on." Annie hitched her head toward the back of the apartment. "Let's get you your check." She paused at the door to the kids' bedroom and peeked in.

Ben slept soundly in his crib with his diapered butt poking in the air, and curled in her bed, Haley clutched her stuffed cat, Tom, under one arm.

A tightness squeezed Annie's chest as love filled her heart to bursting. Quietly, she stepped into the room and adjusted Ben's blanket to cover his arms, then crouched to stroke Haley's long, dark hair. Her daughter stirred, and Annie held her breath, hoping she hadn't woken Haley with her motherly doting. She tiptoed back out the door and turned toward her bedroom where she kept her checkbook.

After scribbling out Rani's weekly payment, she walked the teenager to the door.

"You still need me at eleven thirty tomorrow morning?"

Rani Ogitani had graduated from high school the previous May and started babysitting for Annie the following summer. Now, ten months later, Rani claimed to be looking for a job, thinking about college, weighing her options, but seemed content watching Annie's children and living with her mother for the time being.

"Yeah. Eleven thirty. The kids give you any trouble today? I know Ben can be a handful."

Rani yawned. "They were okay. Mom says Ben's crankiness is just his age. Typical terrible twos."

Annie grinned. "This, too, shall pass."

"Hmm?"

"Something my grandmother used to say. Never mind." She held the door open for Rani and stood on the landing to watch as the teenager crossed the parking lot to her mother's first-floor apartment.

The March evening still held a nip of the winter just past, and goose bumps rose on Annie's arms. Before stepping back inside, she scanned the yard, the parking area, the street. Jonah was gone. Or at least she couldn't see him anywhere, if he was hiding, watching.

She shook her head. That was paranoia talking. Walt's legacy.

Or was it? Jonah had followed her when she left to make her delivery for Mr. Hardin. Was he really just being thoughtful and protective? Why had he asked her not to call the cops? Was he her guardian angel—or was Jonah hiding a dangerous secret?

Chapter 3

The next day, Jonah took his place at the lunch counter at Pop's Diner as he had nearly every day for the past several months. With luck, he'd only have to subject himself to the diner's menu another couple of weeks. As he followed through with the bet he'd placed with Farrout the night before, he hoped he now had an inside track to learn more about how the illegal gambling operation worked—how gamblers paid their debts, where the money went, who was involved at higher levels.

Follow the money.

He thought about the package Annie had been given to deliver last night, and tension spiraled through him. He'd bet anything Hardin's package had to do with the gambling money he was laundering through the diner. Whoever had been on the other end of that delivery was a key player in this operation.

Jonah gritted his teeth. He'd been so close to filling in another piece of the puzzle in this investigation before that bastard had jumped Annie and made off with the package.

It almost seemed as if the guy had been lying in wait for her. As if he'd known that package was to be delivered....

Jonah puffed his cheeks and blew a slow, thoughtful breath out through puckered lips. Who could have tipped the thief off? Where was the leak in the operation? Was someone gunning for Hardin?

Nothing about last night's turn of events sat well with Jonah, especially when he figured Annie into the picture. Hardin had drawn her into the dynamic. She could have unwittingly become ensnared in the sticky web of deceit Hardin and Farrout had spun.

Jonah mulled his next move, then glanced up from his ham on rye when Annie breezed through the front door at ten minutes until noon. She cast him a quick nervous glance as she poked her purse under the counter and rushed back into the kitchen.

Jonah swabbed another greasy fry through his puddle of ketchup, keeping an eye on the kitchen door. Waiting.

Moments later he heard Hardin's raised voice roll from the back of the restaurant like thunder announcing a storm. "You *lost* it? You idiot! I told you how important that package was! How could you *lose* it?"

Jonah craned his neck, trying to find Annie through the service window.

He heard the soft murmur of Annie's response, recognized the frightened tremble in her tone, and his gut pitched.

"Sorry's not good enough!" Hardin screamed.

A loud crash. Annie's frightened yelp.

In an instant, Jonah had jumped from his stool and barreled through the swinging door into the kitchen. He sized up the situation in a glance. Hardin's red face, balled fists and threatening pose as he leaned close to Annie. The young waitress had scrunched back against the wall, her face pale and arms raised defensively to protect her head.

"Is there a problem here?"

Hardin's glare snapped over to Jonah. "What are you doin'? Can't you read? Employees only!"

"Annie? You all right?" he asked, ignoring Hardin.

Frightened brown eyes lifted at his inquiry.

Hardin jabbed a finger toward the door. "This ain't none of your business!"

"I'm making it my business. I don't take kindly to any man threatening a woman."

Annie's brow furrowed warily.

"The bitch lost two hundred grand of my money!" Hardin growled.

Annie gasped, and her eyes widened. "Two hundred grand!"

Hardin narrowed a glare on her. "That's right. Two hundred grand. And it's comin' out of your paycheck!"

Her face blanched a shade whiter. "Mr. Hardin, I can't—"

"Shut up!" He slammed a hand on the wall beside her head, and she yelped, trembled.

Jonah's blood boiled, and he strode closer to Hardin. Grabbing the man's shirt, he yanked him around, then shoved him back against the opposite wall. "Back off! If I see you so much as breathe on her again, I'll tear you apart."

Hardin puffed his chest out and shoved back. "Don't threaten me! She's my employee and—"

"That doesn't give you the right to hurt or intimidate her," Jonah growled through clenched teeth. "Don't touch her. Ever."

"Jonah…" Annie said quietly. "Don't."

"If anyone is to blame for that money being stolen from her, it's *you*." Jonah poked the man in the chest with his finger. "You had no business sending a woman into that neighborhood alone, especially at that hour. What were you thinking? She could have been killed." He took a deep breath to calm the rage seething inside him. The urge to smash the guy's face was too strong. He needed to step back, cool off. He released Hardin's shirt and moved away, his hands still bunched at his sides.

Hardin's eyes narrowed, and his face flamed red. "Get out of my kitchen! Out of my diner!" He turned to Annie, aiming a finger at her. "And you! You're fired!"

Annie bit her bottom lip and squeezed her eyes shut.

Jonah moved between Annie and her hostile boss. "Not so fast, pal. Unless you'd like to explain to the cops what that two-hundred-grand delivery was about, where the money came from."

Now he had Hardin's attention. The man's eyes widened, and his face leeched of color.

"She can file a wrongful termination lawsuit whether she has grounds or not, and the delivery you asked her to make is sure to be called into question. You got an explanation ready for the judge about that two hundred grand?"

Tensing, Hardin glared darkly at Jonah, then cast his glower toward Annie.

Jonah held his breath, second-guessing his rash challenge. Tossing down the gauntlet with Hardin might not have been his wisest move if he wanted to keep a low profile as he worked his investigation.

But Hardin, in his rage, had spilled the tidbit about the huge sum that had been in the package. Hardin knew Jonah had been at the diner last night when Annie left to deliver the envelope. And Jonah couldn't help but wonder if his intervention now hadn't provoked Hardin to fire Annie.

Guilt pinched Jonah. He couldn't let her lose her job because of his temper.

"Fine," Hardin snarled, spittle spraying Annie's direction. "Consider yourself on notice. You screw up again, and you're gone."

With another scalding glance to Jonah, Hardin stomped into his office and slammed the door.

Annie pressed a hand to her chest and slid to the floor, shaking.

Pulling in a deep breath for composure before he approached her, Jonah studied Annie's trembling body and wan expression. He'd seen reactions like hers too many times in both his personal and professional life not to know what he was dealing with. If her fearful reaction to Hardin weren't enough, her scars and her distrust of him last night bolstered his assessment.

She'd likely been abused. Husband, father, sibling—didn't

matter who. The devastating legacy of violence and mental cruelty didn't differentiate.

Acid roiled in his gut, and he took another couple of seconds to cool off before squatting in front of her.

"Annie—"

"You shouldn't have gotten involved," she murmured. Raising her eyes to meet his, she shook her head. "He's my problem, and I have to learn to deal with him."

He frowned. "Annie, he had no right—"

"That doesn't matter! Right and wrong isn't the point." Annie hiked her chin up a notch and firmed her jaw in a display of moxie that sparked hope in him.

He held his tongue, giving her the chance to speak her mind. Her body language as she gathered herself and recovered from Hardin's intimidation spoke volumes to him. She was strong. A fighter. She had the mettle to overcome her past. Warmth swirled through his blood as he held her rich-coffee gaze.

Annie swallowed hard and squared her shoulders. "This was my problem, not yours. I have to learn how to handle these situations for myself, if I'm going to—" She tore her eyes away and shook her head again. "Never mind."

When she pushed up from the floor, Jonah put a hand under her arm to help her to her feet. She shrugged out of his grip. "I'm all right. I don't need—"

"Okay." He held his hands up and backed away one step.

Stroking her hands down her uniform apron, she angled a dubious look toward him. "Why have you decided to be my protector? You barely know me."

He shrugged. "How well do you have to know someone to want to help them?"

She ducked her head and didn't answer.

Jamming his hands into his pockets, he cocked his head and studied her bruised cheek and swollen lip, evidence of last night's attack. Even with the injuries marring her ivory skin, her beauty shone through. Annie was a curious blend of child-like fragility and womanly allure. She had a dusting of freckles across her nose that lent to her young, waifish appearance, while her bowed lips and thick-lashed brown eyes contributed to the seductive movie-star quality her hairstyle evoked.

He cracked his knuckles, working off the remnants of adrenaline following his confrontation with Hardin. "Look, are you all right?"

A pointed, dark brown gaze snapped up to his, half hidden by the curtain of hair she kept over her left cheek. "I'm fine. I appreciate your help, but—"

"But nothing. Forget it." He waved a hand in dismissal and pivoted on his heel. He'd made it as far as the swinging door before he reconsidered. "No, don't forget it." He marched back to Annie and drilled her with a hard gaze. "You want to learn to take care of yourself? To handle men like Hardin and that guy in the alley last night?"

Annie blinked her surprise. "What are you talking about?"

"You said you had to learn how to handle situations like this, guys like Hardin." He flicked a thumb toward the spot where Hardin had stood earlier. "Did you mean it?"

A deer-in-the-headlights look froze her face.

"I can teach you to handle yourself when a man attacks you. I can show you how to defend yourself, protect yourself."

She eyed him skeptically for several silent moments. "What about my children?"

"Kids?" Jonah fumbled, caught off guard by her question. "I…I guess I could teach them, too."

"No, they're too young. I mean, can you teach me to protect them from men like…" She paused, bit her lip, then lowered her voice. "Men like Hardin?"

Jonah held her gaze, moved by the depth of fear, the passion and motherly concern he saw reflected in her dark eyes. A degree of desperation shadowed her expression and tugged at dusty memories deep inside him.

"I can…if you're willing to trust me."

His answer seemed to douse her interest with a cold slap of

reality. She frowned and jerked her gaze away with a sigh. Trust was clearly in short supply for Annie. Not surprising.

Jonah twisted his mouth to the side as he thought. "May I have your order pad and pen?"

With a puzzled look, she took the items from the front pocket of her apron and extended them to him.

"What time do you get off work tonight?" He scribbled an address on the pad and clicked the pen closed.

Again she hesitated before answering, her gaze narrowed on him as if she could detect his motives, any ill-intent or hidden agenda if she studied him close enough. "Eight. Why?"

"That's my gym." He tapped the front of the pad. "I'll meet you there at eight thirty and give you a few pointers on self-defense, if you want. There are plenty of things a woman can do to protect herself, even from a man twice her size. I'll show you a couple of the most effective ones tonight."

He handed her back the pen and pad, and she perused the note he'd made. She worried her bottom lip with her teeth again and wound a strand of hair around her finger. "I don't know. I...I'd have to call my babysitter and make sure she could stay late. And I hate to miss the kids' bedtime. I see so little of them as it is." Her shoulders slumped a bit, and he heard working-mother guilt rife in her tone.

Seizing the opportunity to learn more about her and make her feel more at ease with him, Jonah grinned. "How old are they?"

Her head snapped up. "What?"

"Your kids. How old are they?"

Her expression softened, and warmth flooded her eyes. "Haley is five and a half, and my baby, Ben, is almost two."

Her obvious affection for her children needled a vulnerable place in Jonah, an emptiness he hadn't allowed himself to dwell on. The idea of having his own family stirred a complicated mix of emotions in him. He longed for the domestic ideal of home and hearth, but his memories of family left him in a cold sweat. Norman Rockwell dreams of a picket fence and two-point-five kids were a fantasy for him. Out of reach. Too risky.

His broken family, his only experience with home life, was a recipe for disaster.

Clearing his throat and shoving aside his own bitter memories, he flashed her another smile. "A boy and a girl. That's great. You have a matched set."

A corner of her mouth quirked up. "Hardly matched. They're as opposite as can be."

Jonah chuckled. "Funny how that happens, huh?"

Her mouth curved a bit more, forming the first hint of a grin he'd seen on her lips in weeks. "Yeah. Funny."

"I'd love to meet them someday."

Her smile vanished in a heartbeat, replaced by the damnable wariness again. "Why?"

He shrugged. "I like you. And I like kids. Stands to reason I'd like your kids."

Her brow lowered. "Mr. Devereaux, I'm not interested in—"

"No, you're right." He raised a hand to cut her off. "Too fast. I didn't mean to be pushy." He nodded toward the order pad still in her hand. "But please consider coming tonight. For your safety's sake." As he backed toward the door, he threw in a parting shot he knew was pure manipulation. But he didn't care. "Do it for your kids if not yourself."

Annie needed to learn to protect herself, to stand up to bullies like Hardin, to revive the spark her abuser had extinguished. Jonah wasn't above a little manipulation if it motivated her to make changes in her life.

The truth was, Annie had been the delivery person when a two-hundred-thousand-dollar transfer of funds was stolen. Had the thief intended to kill her to keep her quiet, stop her from identifying him? Would the party who'd expected the cash seek retribution? Could Hardin become more desperate and, therefore, more dangerous?

No matter how he looked at this turn of events, Jonah didn't like the crosshairs Annie had found herself in after last night. She needed more than just a few self-defense techniques if someone tried to keep her from talking. But his lessons would be a start.

Meanwhile, he'd be extra vigilant. Annie needed someone with his experience and training to watch her back.

Annie surveyed the last few diners who'd come in for a late meal, then faced Lydia, who was working the last shift. "Can you handle things if I go now?"

"Sure thing, honey. I got it covered." The older waitress smiled and jerked her head toward the door. "Get on home to those babies and give 'em a kiss for me, too."

"Thanks, Lydia." Annie untied her apron and stashed it under the counter. Grabbing her purse, she headed back to the kitchen, walking with careful penguinlike steps to avoid slipping on the greasy film that had accumulated on the floor through the day. As she neared Mr. Hardin's office, she heard his raised voice, and her heart beat a little harder.

"That's not enough time! I said I'd get it to you!" he ranted.

As Annie tiptoed past his half-open door to clock out, she caught her reflection on the stainless-steel side of the industrial freezer. The image rubbed a raw nerve.

How many times had she cowered around Walt, tiptoeing through their house in order not to wake him, or quietly keeping a discreet distance to avoid triggering one of his tantrums?

She'd thought her days of treading lightly around hostile men were past, yet here she was skulking past Hardin's office like a guilty child. Frustration and self-censure stabbed Annie.

She'd come too far and paid too high of a price to be free of Walt to fall back into old habits now. Habits born from fear.

Damn it, she didn't want to live in fear anymore! Annie jammed her time card in the clock so hard it crumpled in the middle. Spinning on her heel to leave, she marched back by Hardin's office, her chin up and her back straight.

"Annie!"

She froze, dread slowing her pulse and snagging her breath. *Please, Lord, not another errand like last night.*

Heart thumping, she turned toward Hardin's office and stepped to the door. "Yes?"

"Where do you think you're goin'?" he asked around a cigarette dangling from the corner of his mouth. His eyes mirrored the same dark resentment she heard in his tone.

"My shift is over. I was going home."

"Not if I say you don't."

A rock lodged in Annie's stomach. She dragged in a smoke-laced lungful of air, trying to steel her nerves and battle down the building panic.

And anger—the most dangerous of emotions.

Dealing with the repercussions of Walt's rage had been enough to teach her just how dangerous. But her own temper had led her to say foolish things at times that had only inflamed Walt's wrath. Fury over Walt's unfairness and controlling nature had seethed in her gut like a corrosive waste until she would throw up, so she'd long ago learned to suppress her temper, swallow the bile and deny the heat of anger that flashed through her blood.

Yet despite her best efforts to erase her ill-will and moments of irritation, she still carried a boatload of frustration and ire for the desperate circumstances of her life. She blamed Walt's abuse and her submission to his violence for the dark cloud his threats still cast over her. Now Hardin was doing his best to intimidate and control her, and she struggled to keep the poisonous emotion at bay.

"My shift is over, Mr. Hardin. I need to get home to my children." Her voice quivered with anxiety and barely suppressed indignation. She curled her fingers into her palms, and the pulse of rising adrenaline throbbed in her temples.

Her boss narrowed his eyes and stabbed out his cigarette in the overflowing ashtray on his desk. "Seems to me there's a matter of two hundred thousand dollars you either have to pay back or work off."

The flutter of fear taunted her, beating hard against her breastbone.

"Mr. H-Hardin, I could never work enough hours to repay—"

"Well, if you ain't going to work the extra hours, then maybe you could settle your debt with me…another way." Surging to his feet, he raked a lascivious gaze over her and smirked.

Annie fell back a step. Disgust slithered over her, and she shivered. Taking a slow breath, she searched for enough confidence to reply without her voice quaking. "No."

He crossed his arms over his chest, and his gaze continued to roam over her.

"I'll find a way to repay the money," she said, though the words were sour knots in her throat that she had to force out. "It will take me a while—" *Like forever.* She cringed at the thought of tightening her budget even further and scraping together small payments for Hardin. "But I'll find a way."

A muscle twitched in Hardin's jaw, and his flinty eyes drilled into her. "I want the money by next week."

The ice in his tone, his stare sent a deep chill slicing through her. Trembling to her marrow, Annie whirled away and hurried toward the dining room. Her feet slipped and skidded on the greasy kitchen tile, but she didn't slow down. She had to get away from Hardin. Get out of the diner. Get home to her children—the only place she felt even remotely safe anymore.

"I can show you how to defend yourself, protect yourself."

As she rushed out of the diner, Jonah's promise filtered through her head. Her steps slowed, and she reached into her pocket for the scrap of paper he'd given her with his gym's address.

If only—

Forget *if only.* Dreams and wishes were for other people. She had to deal in reality. In truths and concrete facts.

Her truth was she had to pay her hostile boss a hell of a lot of money.

Picking up her pace again, she jogged to the bus stop, still quaking from Hardin's chilling threat. No way could she find two hundred thousand dollars to repay him, even if she had a year to pay him. Much less a week.

Her bus rumbled up to the stop just as she reached the street corner. While she waited for an older man with a walker to board, she fished in her pocket for her bus pass.

Once more her fingers brushed the crumpled paper Jonah had given her.

"Do it for your kids if not yourself."

Guilt and fear squeezed her chest, tangling with irritation over Jonah's obvious manipulation of her love for her kids. She stared down at the address. What could it hurt just to go and see what Jonah wanted to teach her? He'd already proven he wanted to help, not harm her. And a gym was a public place. She'd be safe there. Right?

"You coming or not?" the bus driver called, jarring her from her deliberations.

"I—" Annie exhaled a deep breath of resignation. She had to at least *try* to protect herself from Hardin and men like the thief who jumped her last night. She was tired of living with this fear. She'd come too far to lose everything because she let a bully like Hardin intimidate her.

Annie raised her chin and met the bus driver's gaze. "Not."

With a puff of exhaust, the bus chugged away from the curb, and Annie headed toward Jonah's gym.

Chapter 4

The scents of body odor and rubber floor mats greeted Annie as she entered Jonah's gym minutes later. Wrinkling her nose as the unpleasant smells assailed her, she cast a wary glance around the cavernous warehouse.

When Jonah had invited her to his gym, she'd pictured an upscale facility where beautiful bodies jogged on treadmills, followed a perky blond instructor in aerobic dance or toned their muscles on expensive weight machines. This gym was a far cry from her vision.

Dingy and dark with nary a perky blonde in sight, the large room housed four boxing rings and numerous punching bags suspended from the bare rafters by steel chains. A litany of grunts and curses reverberated from the concrete block walls, while burly men in scruffy shorts and sleeveless shirts pounded the weighted bags—or each other.

Apprehension slithered through Annie as she crept deeper into the room. Like a brewing storm, the raw power and the brute violence on display filled the room with an ominous and suffocating energy. Struggling to pull air into her lungs, Annie scanned the men's faces for Jonah.

With every passing minute, she grew more uncomfortable and self-conscious. One by one, sweat-drenched men paused from their training to eye her with curious, even lewd, glances. Her discomfort spiked as a man in the nearest boxing ring caught a bone-jarring blow to the chin that sent him to the mat with a groan.

"That'll teach you to talk back to me!"

She pressed her throbbing cheek to the cool floor, not daring to get up before Walt stalked from the room. Getting up only gave him the opportunity to knock her down again.

The images before her blurred as tears pricked her eyes.

She staggered backward, edging toward the door. She shouldn't have come. Shouldn't have risked—

As she passed a different boxing ring where two men sparred while a third coached from the ropes, recognition slammed through her. She squinted at the face barely visible behind the protective headgear, and her heart tapped double time.

Jonah.

Stunned, she stared while Jonah exchanged jabs with the other man, shuffling his feet to dodge blows. Sweat glistened on his arms and glued his tank-style T-shirt to the flat plane of his abdomen. Well-defined muscles in his shoulders and chest spoke for the hours of training and conditioning Jonah had put in.

Annie gawked at his brawny build, and heat prickled her skin. An unfamiliar flutter stirred in her chest, and realization that his size and strength had piqued her feminine interest startled her. Had she learned nothing in her marriage to Walt? She'd been physically attracted to Walt when they married. He'd been especially handsome in his military dress uniform the day they wed. But all the sexual chemistry in the world didn't outweigh the suffering he'd put her through in later years.

Yet she couldn't help but stare at Jonah's toned and powerful physique, his smooth style as he moved around the ring. With practiced skill, he ducked a swing and landed a solid hook to his opponent's pad-protected jaw.

Shocked out of her gawk-fest by his potent punch, Annie gasped.

Jonah's gaze darted to her.

In that split second of his distraction, his opponent struck back with a blow to Jonah's ribs.

Annie felt the blow as surely as if she'd taken the hit herself. The air whooshed from her lungs, and tension screwed her muscles tight. Clapping a hand over her mouth, she fell back another step.

"Devereaux, what the hell are you doing?" the silver-haired man by the ropes shouted. "You gotta keep your eyes in the ring!"

Grinning through a grimace, Jonah raised his boxing gloves. "Time. I've got company."

She sidled toward Jonah as he climbed through the ropes and jumped down to meet her.

"You came." Equal measures of pleasure and surprise colored his tone.

She nodded tightly and gave the activity in the room a meaningful glance. "If I'd known what kind of gym you meant, I don't know that I would have."

His dark eyebrows drew together. "Why?"

Eyeing the muscle-bound giant battering a small punching bag beside her, she inched closer to Jonah. "I'm…rather out of place, wouldn't you say?"

A warm grin lifted a corner of his mouth. "Hey, I know these guys look pretty rough, but I assure you, you're perfectly safe here."

He rubbed his ribs and winced.

"Are you all right?" She knew more than she cared to about the sting of fist-imposed injuries.

He glanced down at his chest. "It's nothing. Just a reminder that when you're in the ring, you gotta stay focused on your opponent, not be distracted by what's happening outside the ring."

The older man who'd been coaching winked at her. "Even if the distraction is mighty pretty."

Jonah tossed a towel at the other man. "Down, boy."

Annie frowned. "I'm sorry if I—"

"No, no." He waved off her apology. "My fault. I'm just glad you came." To the silver-haired coach, he said, "Frank, I think I'm done for the day. Same time tomorrow?"

Frank nodded. "Sure." To the kid in the ring he called, "Okay, Billy. Hit the showers."

Jonah bit the lace on one glove and pulled it with his teeth, then moved on to the second.

Annie fidgeted with her purse strap. "I can't stay long. My kids—"

"Pull?" He lifted his hands toward her.

Annie blinked her surprise.

"Please," he added with a lopsided grin.

Unaccustomed to refusing any man's request, she awkwardly grasped one bulky glove and tugged. It didn't budge.

"Harder. You gotta really muscle 'em off."

Annie hesitated, jitters dancing in her gut. She slid her purse from her shoulder and set it on the concrete floor. Grabbing Jonah's boxing glove with both hands, she pulled. Hard. As he freed each hand, Jonah shook his arms and flexed his fingers.

"Thanks." He took the gloves from her and tossed them next to a duffel bag on the floor at the edge of the ring. Hitching his head toward the locker room, he said, "Give me five minutes to grab a shower, and we'll get started."

Annie sent another uncomfortable glance around the gym and bit her lip. "I should probably just get home. Maybe this was a mistake."

Furrowing his brow, he took her hand in his. His touch sent another flash of tingling heat over her skin.

He ducked his head to meet her gaze and squeezed her

fingers gently. "Don't go. Just five minutes. I need to talk to you, but right now I smell like a goat."

His farm-animal comparison earned a half grin from her. And her concession. She nodded. "Five minutes."

With another handsome smile, he snatched up the gym bag and headed toward the locker room.

"Jonah?"

He turned.

"Do you have a cell phone I can borrow? I need to call my babysitter and tell her I'll be late."

"Sure." He fished in his duffel and extracted a small flip phone. "Catch." He tossed the phone toward her, and, caught off guard, she barely snagged the cell before it hit the concrete.

While she waited for Jonah, Annie found a corner where she was out of the way and called her apartment. She filled Rani in on her delay, then talked to Haley, who bubbled with excitement over a new lost tooth.

"I saved it to show you, Mommy. And Rani says if I put it under my pillow, the tooth fairy will give me money!"

Annie smiled, loving the joy in her daughter's voice and trying to recall if she had any change in her wallet to hide under Haley's pillow.

"Hey, Mommy, maybe you could put *your* teeth under your pillow and get some money from the tooth fairy, too!"

Annie sputtered a laugh. "My teeth?"

"Yeah, then maybe you wouldn't have to go to work at the diner all the time and could stay home and play with me and Ben."

Remorse stabbed Annie, cutting her to the quick. "I don't know, sugar. I think the tooth fairy only wants kids' teeth."

"Oh."

The disappointment in her daughter's tone wrenched Annie's heart. "I'm supposed to have this Saturday off, though, and I promise we'll do something fun. Just you, me and Ben. Maybe go to the park? Okay?"

"Okay."

But Haley sounded skeptical. Too skeptical for a five-year-old. Knowing how many times she'd had to cancel plans with Haley when she had to work extra hours at the diner flooded Annie with fresh guilt.

Jonah emerged from the locker room, wearing a clean T-shirt and jeans, his wet hair combed back from his face. His gaze swept the room looking for her, and when he spotted her, a smile softened the hard planes of his face.

Annie's pulse missed a beat.

Jonah wasn't handsome in the classical sense. So why was he suddenly stirring this schoolgirl reaction in her?

She chastized herself. She was too busy making ends meet, fighting for her survival and reeling from her last devastating relationship to be in the market for a man. She had no business looking at Jonah as anything other than a regular customer at the diner. A mysterious man who'd rescued her from her attacker. The person who'd offered to show her techniques to protect herself and her family from further abuse.

"Haley, sugar, I have to go now. Be sweet for Rani and eat all of your dinner. Okay?" Annie watched Jonah cross the gym floor, his loose-limbed stride confident and relaxed. Her breath hung in her lungs.

Haley grumbled an unintelligible response as Jonah reached her.

"I'll be home soon, sugar. B'bye." She closed the phone and held it out to Jonah. "Thanks."

Taking the cell from her, he jerked his chin toward a nearby door. "Let's use the manager's office. It's quieter. More private."

More isolated. Her stomach flip-flopped as she fell in step behind Jonah.

"Hey, Frank," he called to the coach who was working with a boxer on a small punching bag. "Mind if we use your office for a while?"

The man eyed Annie, then sent Jonah a conspiratorial grin. "Be my guest."

After leading her into the windowless office with a sign

that read "Owner," Jonah closed the door behind him, muting the cacophony from the gym floor and spiking Annie's level of discomfort.

She was suddenly hyperaware that she was alone with a man she barely knew. The idea of being alone with Jonah both tantalized and frightened her. Drawing her purse against her chest, she glanced about the dim office. The decor was surprisingly upscale, with oil paintings and a leather couch. The large desk was covered with old photographs of a younger Frank posing with a pretty woman and a blond little girl.

"Why do I make you so nervous?" Jonah's question drew her gaze back to him. He angled his head and studied her with a lazy sweep of his eyes.

She forced a smile. "You don't."

Sitting on the edge of the wooden desk, Jonah waved a finger toward her purse. "Your body language says otherwise."

Annie glanced down at her white-knuckle grip on her purse and the defensive position of her arms crossed over her chest. Knowing he could read her so easily didn't help ease her tension.

She sighed. "I'm just...out of my element here. I don't know you well, and this whole business with Hardin and the money I lost has—"

"Stop." He said the word softly, but with enough cool command to freeze the words on her tongue.

Her gaze snapped up to his.

Jonah folded his arms over his chest and drilled her with his dark green eyes. "Let's get one thing straight. You didn't lose that money. You don't owe Hardin a thing. You were mugged, and the money was stolen. Period."

Annie opened her mouth to reply, but no sound came.

"As for your other points..." Jonah shrugged one shoulder. "Maybe you don't know me real well, but if you'd let me take you to a quiet dinner somewhere, we could talk and remedy that."

Her heart pounding in her ears, Annie gaped at him. "Like...a date?"

He nodded. "And if I'm right about you, you're not as out of place at this gym as you'd have me believe."

Already reeling from his invitation to dinner, Annie needed a moment before his last comment registered. "What do you mean I'm not out of place? Do I look like someone who enjoys punching a bag for thrills?"

His face sobered, and he pitched his voice low. "No. But I think you've been used as a punching bag by some bastard you once trusted."

Annie's head swam, and an odd buzzing rang in her ears. She staggered drunkenly to the nearest chair and dropped onto the seat.

Slowly, he moved toward her and crouched beside her. "Maybe a father. Maybe a husband or boyfriend. Am I right?"

Practiced denials sprang to her tongue but shattered under the weight of his piercing gaze. She struggled to draw a breath. "How... Why would you think—"

"Because I've been there."

Annie's breath backed up in her lungs. She shook her head, not sure she'd heard him right. Did he mean he'd been an abuser—or been abused?

Jonah nodded, his expression open and guileless. "I've seen what you've seen. I know the emotions you've known. I recognize the signs."

He reached for her left cheek and gently grazed her scar with his knuckle.

Mortified, she jerked away and scoffed. "That's from a car accident. I shattered my cheekbone and couldn't afford a fancy plastic surgeon after the emergency surgery."

The lie tumbled easily from her lips, while a hurricane of confused emotions twisted inside her. Guilt, relief, embarrassment, anger, frustration...

How did she begin to sort it all out?

"Part of that is probably true."

Clenching her teeth, she shot him a tight scowl. "Are you calling me a liar?"

He wrapped his hand around hers, and she flinched. Undaunted, he squeezed her hand. "I got good at lying about my injuries, too. To teachers, neighbors…even myself. It wasn't easy to tell anyone my dad had a nasty temper, and he'd beat us and our mom with little provocation."

Icy fingers clamped around her heart. Torn between empathy and wariness, she stared into his jade eyes, searching for some hint of insincerity. But his unflinching gaze shone with compassion and honesty.

Unsure what to do with his revelation, Annie gripped the edge of the chair and listened to the thundering of her pulse in her ears. "Why are you telling me this?"

"I wanted you to know I understood what you'd been through, and I know how—"

Annie stiffened, fury coursing through her blood. She shoved to her feet, balling her hands and glaring at Jonah. "Stop it! You can't begin to know what I've been through! And I don't know what your life was like growing up with a father who hurt you. Don't you dare try to tell me—"

"All right." He put a hand on each of her shoulders, and she tensed, realizing the mistake she'd made.

Her stomach knotted. Her mouth dried. Dear God, if she'd ever lost her temper and challenged Walt that way, she'd have paid dearly.

Inhaling sharply, she held her breath, bracing for Jonah's answering wrath.

Instead, he murmured softly, "I'm sorry. You're right. I only meant—"

When a tremble raced through her, he paused, his brow lowering in a concerned frown. Cupping her chin, he lifted her face toward his, his thumb stroking her jaw.

His tender gesture, so opposite the raw power she'd seen him display moments ago, caught her off guard. The warmth of his fingers, the crisp scent of soap that clung to him, the lulling calm in his voice had her senses reeling. Her head swam, and the heat of a blush prickled her skin.

"Relax, beautiful. You're safe with me. I swear it. I will

never hurt you." A husky growl of conviction emphasized his vow, a stark contrast to the tenderness of his touch.

Annie couldn't speak, couldn't move. Confused emotions tangled inside her. Part of her wanted to trust Jonah and believe the warm promise in his eyes. Another part of her remembered too clearly the brute violence he'd employed defending her in the alley last night and the power behind his punches in the boxing ring only moments ago. Despite his kindness and gentle touches, she'd witnessed Jonah's fierce strength and skill. Her body's reaction to him was only the natural response to being near so much virile magnetism. Wasn't it?

When she didn't respond, Jonah lowered his hand and stepped back. He sighed and glanced away, his expression pensive. "Annie, I asked you here because I have a bad feeling about what happened last night."

Sinking back onto the chair, she rubbed her throbbing temple and shoved aside distracting thoughts of Jonah's allure. "That makes two of us. Hardin isn't likely to forget the money I lost any time soon. He's going to make my life miserable until I repay him."

Jonah popped his knuckles restlessly and frowned. "I wasn't referring to Hardin."

She glanced up. "What do you mean?"

"I don't think your attack was random. I think the guy who stole the money was waiting for you, that he was expecting someone to be making that delivery for Hardin."

A chill shimmied through her. "Waiting for me?"

"I can't go into detail, but…I have reason to believe the money you were delivering was profits from a gambling ring that Hardin had laundered through the diner's accounts."

Her stomach seesawed. Annie's emotions had spun in every conceivable direction in the past few minutes, but Jonah's claim made her head reel. Hands shaking, she hugged herself and drew a ragged breath.

"The man who mugged you may have intended to kill you so that you couldn't make an ID. Or Hardin may have picked you to make the delivery because he thought you'd be least likely to talk, that he could keep you quiet through intimidation. Or...there are other scenarios possible, but they all boil down to this—you're involved now. You're in danger."

Chapter 5

This couldn't be happening. Not now. Not again!

Nausea flooded Annie's gut, and a bitter taste rose in her throat. She shook her head. "No. I can't... I didn't d-do anything. I don't know anything. I—I—"

Jonah dragged a hand over his mouth. "Like it or not, because of that delivery you made, because of the theft, you are involved now, and you're going to have to be careful. Watch your back. Take precautions."

Annie muffled a half gasp, half sob.

She'd just spent months escaping a possessive and vengeful husband, seen him brought up on charges of stalking and murder, feared for her life and her children's. She'd only recently started piecing her life back together, finding some sanity and calm.

As he wrapped a firm, warm hand around her wrist, Jonah's gaze drilled into her. "You need to be able to protect yourself. I want to show you a few basic techniques to deter an attacker."

She shook off his hand and narrowed her eyes, suspicion

tickling her neck. "How do you know all this? What proof do you have that Hardin's doing anything illegal?"

"I don't have anything solid enough to take to the authorities yet, but—"

"You didn't want me to call the cops last night. Why?" Her mind clicked, reviewing from a new perspective her attack, Jonah's rescue and his defense of her with Hardin that morning. "Are you involved in whatever's going on at the diner?" She rose and stumbled away from Jonah. "How do I know there really is a gambling ring or money laundering or...or—"

Her chest seized, and her stomach pitched at the idea of unwittingly becoming ensnared in unlawful dealings at the diner. The turkey sandwich she'd eaten at lunch roiled in her belly and threatened to come back up.

Jonah sighed. "I know because...I've spent the past six months on this investigation."

"This *investigation?* You're a cop?"

"I was. In Little Rock. But I left the force about a year ago, right before I moved here."

Mentally she reviewed everything she'd heard the other waitresses say about Jonah. "You told Susan you worked at the paper mill. That was a lie, wasn't it?"

He blew a deep breath out through pursed lips. "Yeah. That's my cover."

Annie's heart tapped a staccato rhythm, and she studied Jonah with new eyes, doubt and distrust nipping at her. "Your cover? Who are you? *What* are you? Why should I trust you? What do you want from me?" The questions tumbled from her in increasing volume as her fear mounted.

He quieted her by touching a finger to her lips. "I don't work for anyone. This investigation is personal for me. I've been looking into the gambling ring and money laundering because of a friend of mine. The men involved in the ring swindled Michael out of his entire retirement savings."

A sympathetic pang gripped her chest. Annie understood the gravity of such a loss. She lived paycheck to paycheck and couldn't imagine how she'd survive if her income disappeared.

Jonah stepped back and propped himself against the scarred desk again. "Last night, I asked you not to go to the cops because I was afraid police involvement in your mugging would scare some of the players into hiding. I'm getting close to nailing these bastards, and I didn't want any unnecessary outside law enforcement to rock the boat before I get the evidence I need."

Annie shook her head trying to wrap her mind around the scenario Jonah laid out. "Wh-what kind of evidence?"

"I need to see for myself exactly how the operation runs, who is involved up the chain. I'll need to videotape a transaction or record incriminating conversations. If I can get them, bank records, computer files, a log of wagers, any kind of paper trail to support my case." He wiped his palms on his jeans and shook his head. "But the deeper I get into their organization, the dicier it gets. These men have a lot of money at stake. If they get spooked, they'll protect themselves and their interests in the operation by any means possible. Even murder."

A numbing chill crept through Annie. She stared at Jonah, questions spinning through her brain, yet she couldn't make her tongue work. The weight of the situation settled on her lungs, squeezing the breath from her. By trying to save her job, had she embroiled herself in a scheme that could cost her her life?

The air in the tiny dark office vibrated with tension. Jonah held her gaze, his green eyes difficult to read in the dim light.

Swallowing the pressure in her throat, Annie voiced her doubts. "How do I know you're telling me the truth? Why should I trust you?"

"Your attack last night was real enough, wasn't it? Hardin's fury over the stolen money was no act. I've no doubt he's up a major creek right now with whoever that money was going to."

Joseph Nance. The name Hardin had given her flashed through her mind, but she kept silent, playing her cards close to her chest until she could figure out for herself who she should trust and where Jonah really fit in the dangerous scenario he described.

"I know I've dropped a bomb on you. I understand how scary this must be. But I need you to believe that I am the only person at that diner looking out for your interests. I want to protect you from any fallout, but you'll have to trust me."

Her trust had been shattered by the last man she gave it to and would be hard-earned for Jonah. Another biting chill nipped her skin. "What do you want me to do?"

"Nothing right now. But stay alert. Keep your eyes and ears open. And learn how to defend yourself." He pushed away from the desk and moved close enough for her to feel the body heat radiating from his skin. "That's where I come in."

Jonah reached for Annie, noting the wariness that shadowed her eyes. When he touched her arm, she stiffened and pulled away.

"What are you doing?" Alarm flashed in her mahogany eyes.

"Getting to the business at hand. Teaching you some defensive moves to protect yourself."

Her stance relaxed a fraction, but her expression remained cautious. He understood that caution better now. Her story about a car accident causing her facial scar aside, she hadn't denied his conjecture about her history of abuse. Her body language had told him all she didn't say. He had to proceed carefully. The last thing he wanted was to cause Annie any more pain.

But her protection was paramount, and he couldn't be with her twenty-four seven.

"Let's start with the basics." He squared his feet in front of her. "Your best strike points are your attacker's eyes, his groin and his throat. Concentrate your efforts there. Okay? Like this…"

Jonah lifted his arms to demonstrate the best hand position for a throat strike.

Annie rubbed a hand down her arm, her expression dubious. "I don't know. Fighting back will only make him mad, make him hurt me more."

Jonah lowered his hands and stepped back. He remembered how Annie had shut down last night, retreating into herself and giving her attacker no resistance. "Do you believe your life is worth fighting for?"

Her chin lifted, surprise flickering across her face. "Of course."

"Do you? Deep down, do you truly believe your life is worth defending at any cost? Because to save your life, you may have to do things that are difficult, or embarrassing, or impolite or disgusting. You have to believe you're worth it and be willing to do whatever it takes. Gouging eyeballs, biting until you draw blood…"

She winced and pulled her arms closer to her body.

Jonah scratched his jaw, reassessing his approach with Annie. His first task was helping her overcome her skittishness. Maybe showing her a few simple, less invasive moves would help build her confidence.

"Lower your arms to your sides," he said, doing so himself. When she complied, he gave her an encouraging smile. "Now I promise not to hurt you. I just want to show you a couple tricks you can use."

Her brow puckered skeptically.

"What would you do if someone grabbed your arm like this?" He wrapped his hand around her wrist with a secure grip.

She gasped and tried to jerk her arm back. He held tight.

"Instinct tells you to pull back, but unless you're stronger than your attacker, that won't work, will it?"

She raised a startled look from her wrist, meeting his gaze. "So…what do I do?"

Beneath his fingers, the flutter of her pulse beat harder, faster. He became acutely aware of the delicate softness of her skin, the poignant blend of hope and vulnerability in her expression and the answering thump of his own heart.

For weeks now, he'd been intrigued by Annie, attracted to her, and the protective instincts she brought out in him only deepened the connection he felt. Knowing how satiny smooth her skin felt stoked the fire that smoldered in his blood when he was around her and teased his imagination. *Steady, boy.*

"Step closer to me." When she hesitated, he added, "Come on. Keep your elbow down and close to your body."

Drawing a shaky breath, Annie edged nearer.

"Okay, look what that did to my grip, the angle of my wrist."

Her wary gaze still on him, she tipped her head like a curious puppy, then glanced down at the awkward cant of his hand.

"Now make a fist and twist it up toward my thumb and over my arm."

She followed his directions and broke free of his grasp. Instead of smiling at her success, Annie scowled. "I didn't do that. You let go on purpose."

He chuckled. "Yeah, because I didn't want a broken wrist. Here. Try it on me, and I'll show you."

Annie gripped the arm he extended at his wrist, and he worked through the steps he'd just shown her slowly, repeating, "Step in. Arm close to you. Fist. Twist toward their thumb and—"

"Ow!" Annie dropped his arm and shook her hand as he broke her hold. She blinked at him, her expression stunned.

He sent her a satisfied grin. "You okay?"

"Yeah, I—" She wet her lips and stood taller. A bit of the skepticism melted from her expression, replaced by intrigue. "It works."

"Of course it works." He chuckled. "I'm not gonna teach you stuff that doesn't work. What's the point in that?"

"Touché." The corner of her mouth twitched, and a pink flush stained her cheeks.

Even that sultry hint of a grin scrambled his concentration and filled his chest with a warmth that expanded until he couldn't catch his breath. But her delicate blush reminded him that despite her full lips and temptress hairstyle, Annie was off-limits. He had nothing to offer the young mother except heartache, and she'd seen enough pain in her life.

"Okay, next move." He stepped behind her, catching her shoulders when she tried to turn toward him. "No, this time let's suppose someone comes up from behind and grabs you like this…" He circled her with his arms, pinning her arms to her sides, and tugged her back against his chest. Again, she stiffened under his restrictive hold.

The light floral scent of her shampoo teased his senses. He gritted his teeth, steeling himself when her futile attempts to break from his hold caused her fanny to buck against his crotch.

After a moment of panicked wiggling, her breath coming in shallow gasps, she stilled. "Let go. Please. I—I don't want to do this."

"Struggling doesn't do anything but wear you out, Annie. You have to use your head. Stay calm."

She gave a small nod and drew a tremulous breath.

"You can break his grip by dropping to the ground. Just lift your feet. But shift all your weight onto his arms. Or if you throw your head back hard—although not now, 'cause I don't want a bloody nose—your skull is hard enough to bash your attacker's face."

She tipped her head back slowly until she lightly bumped his face. Her silky hair tickled his nose and stroked his cheek.

Another spike of arousal sucker punched him, and he wrestled down the urge to nuzzle her neck. He cleared his throat and stepped back, allowing her to face him. "That move, uh…will at least catch him off guard."

Mentally he regrouped, concentrating on the details Annie needed to know. He had only to think of the dangerous people who could be gunning for her after last night and the importance of her knowing how to protect herself to bring him back to the task at hand. "That's a key thing to remember. If you can pull a surprise move on him, it gives you back the upper hand for a few seconds. Use those seconds to strike a debilitating blow that will help you get away. Got it?"

"What debilitating blows? I'm not Bruce Lee."

"Remember those strike points I mentioned?"

She hesitated. "Eyes, throat and…groin."

"Good. We'll get to the Bruce Lee part later. But first you

have to break his hold. Once you're free, pull out your pepper spray and prepare to douse him."

Her forehead dented as she frowned. "I don't have pepper spray."

"Get some. Keep it with you." He waved her close again. "Let me show you something else."

When he stepped toward her, Annie visibly shivered, and Jonah's heart squeezed. He hated the fear that flickered in her watchful eyes. Some bastard had really done a number on her. The mugging last night hadn't helped.

He pressed his mouth in a taut line, realizing that, more than the physical scars on her cheek, Annie bore emotional scars on her heart thanks to the rough treatment she'd received from a man she'd loved. Just as his mom had.

But understanding the source of her ghosts made it all the more important to him that he not add to her pain. He had to be careful not to give her false expectations, not to follow through on the desire that pounded in his veins. He had to protect her from himself.

He paused and held his palms up. "You up for one more demonstration?"

She hugged herself and, closing her eyes, inhaled a deep breath. Blew it out slowly. "All right."

Pride washed through him. Given her history, he knew any reminders of violence and her vulnerability had to be frightening, yet she was here, giving his lessons a fair shake. She had the core strength and resilience that were essential to rebounding from the knocks life had given her.

From behind her, he held her waist with one hand and pressed his other forearm against her throat. "There are two things you can do if you're being choked like this. First, turn your head to the side, into the crook of his arm. That repositions your windpipe so that you can get air."

She moved her head accordingly.

"Good. Perfect."

As he splayed the hand at her waist wider, snuggling her

closer to his body, he heard the whisper of her breath catching. A tiny gasp. A feathery near sigh.

The sound shot fire through his blood. He could all too easily imagine her making sexy sighing sounds during sex. Her wispy breath caressed the arm he held to her throat.

Gritting his teeth, he stifled a moan. Jonah shifted his arm from her throat to complete the circle around her waist. Perhaps his idea of private lessons had been ill-advised. The intimate contact required to teach the defensive moves correctly would test even a monk's willpower. Especially when working with a woman as attractive and intriguing as Annie.

He took a moment to gather his composure, blocking out the mental images of stroking her pale skin and exploring the soft curves that were currently nestled against him like a custom-fit glove.

"If he's holding you—" Jonah stopped, hearing the rumbling, husky quality that darkened his tone and left no secret of his arousal. The subtle tensing of her muscles told him she hadn't missed the shift in the atmosphere, the crackle of sexual tension. He cleared his throat.

Without warning, Annie went limp in his arms. The sudden weight on his arms, the shift in his center of balance sent him sprawling forward. Just as he'd told her it would.

Using lightning reflexes, employed a half second too late to avoid falling, Jonah twisted, landing beside her rather than crushing her with his weight. His shoulder caught the brunt of the tumble, and he rolled to his back, his breath jarred from his lungs.

Annie scrambled away, climbing to her feet and edging to the far side of the room. With her head bowed to her hands, she stood with her back to him, shaking.

Jonah pinched the bridge of his nose. So much for protecting her from himself and reining in his attraction to her.

Private lessons were too intimate, too personal. Their proximity clearly intimidated her. But how was he supposed to help her learn defensive maneuvers without driving himself insane touching her, having her body close to his?

Perhaps more than self-defense lessons, Annie needed to exorcize personal demons. Fortunately, he knew where she could get help with both.

Chapter 6

Annie struggled for a breath and fought to calm the trembling that racked her muscles. She'd known she'd been wrong to come here tonight the minute she realized the kind of gym Jonah frequented. But her real mistake had been something she'd never expected.

She dragged in a cleansing breath and tried to ignore the weight of Jonah's stare. She knew he was waiting for an explanation of her sudden panic. But how did she explain what she didn't understand herself? Working one-on-one had been intimidating at first, but seeing how effective even simple moves could be had buoyed her confidence.

That self-assurance had shattered when he wrapped her in his restrictive hold. The binding hold of his arms had frightened and enticed her at the same time. How screwed up was that?

One minute his hold reminded her of being grabbed in the alley last night, spiking her anxiety. The next moment Jonah spoke his instructions in her ear and her tension dissolved, replaced by an odd thrum of desire.

Having his arms locked securely around her gave her a sense of safety she hadn't know in years. Feeling his body, a wall of strength and heat, pressed against hers made her head spin and her skin tingle. The scent of soap and man filled her nose and enticed her like forbidden fruit.

Then Jonah described an attack scenario for his demonstration that raised a cold sweat on her temple and stirred a fresh swell of panic in her chest.

She'd been fine, though, until she'd heard the change in his voice. His tone had dipped to a sexy rasp that told her she wasn't alone in her attraction. She'd sensed the jolt of awareness that rippled through him in the tensing of his muscles, the moist rasp of his breath on the back of her neck. And her body had responded with its own shudder of anticipation.

Squeezing her hands into fists, Annie tried to sort out the jumble of emotions churning her stomach and spinning her thoughts. Why did Jonah make her want to disregard all the painful lessons life had taught her about men?

"Annie, what's wrong?" The tender concern in Jonah's voice did little to calm the frenzy of activity inside her. The man confused her. Frightened her. Tempted her when she had no business ever giving another man a second glance.

Dear God, she'd just untangled her life and her children's from a controlling, abusive monster. The last thing she wanted was to become involved with another man. Especially one whose prowess in the boxing ring she'd witnessed herself. He could be lethal if he chose. So why did Jonah's gentle hands and warm eyes turn her insides to goo and scramble her sense of reason?

Turning, she forced a fleeting smile. "Nothing's wrong. I just…need to get home now. My kids…"

His steady probing gaze flustered her, and she snatched up her purse without finishing the excuse. Clearly, he knew she was lying.

"We've barely started. There's more you need to know. Important tactics—"

"No. I can't stay. I—"

"You need to protect yourself." He crossed the room, stopping her as she tried to sidle out the door. "Some other time then? I'll be here again tomorrow. Same time."

She shook her head, avoiding the unnerving intensity of his dark eyes. "I have to work."

"Then you pick the day. I'll be here."

"I don't think so. I—I'll get some pepper spray and...I'll be fine." She edged closer to the door, raising her head only long enough to slant him a quick smile. "Thanks, though."

He placed his hand on her arm, and her pulse jumped. His touch scorched her skin and weakened her knees.

"Annie, you're in the middle of a bad situation at the diner. I don't know what's going to happen now that Hardin's money was stolen, but you need to take precautions. I don't mean to frighten you, but—"

"But you are." She sighed and forced the starch back into her bones as she lifted her gaze to his. "I am frightened. But not just because of everything you've said tonight. I'm scared of a lot of things. I'm afraid I won't have enough paycheck to feed my kids through the end of the week. I'm scared I'll tick Hardin off and lose my job. I'm scared that while I'm working sixty-hour weeks at the diner, I'll miss seeing my kids grow up. Haley lost a tooth today, her first, and I missed it!" Tears thickened her voice, but she plowed on. Once her vent started, she couldn't stop the tide of frustration and pain. "And most of all, I'm terrified that some ignorant parole board will let my ex-husband out of prison, that I'll have to go into hiding again so he can't kill me!"

Jonah straightened his spine and firmed his mouth as if satisfied to have his suspicions confirmed. But the hard edge in his expression softened and compassion warmed his eyes.

In a quieter, more ragged voice, she whispered, "So yeah, I'm frightened, and your talk of money laundering and goons coming after me to shut me up doesn't help. All I want is to raise my children in peace. I never wanted—"

She choked on a sob, and Jonah tugged her into his arms, holding her against his wide chest.

Annie dug her fingers into his T-shirt and rested her forehead under his chin. She hadn't meant to spill so much of her personal life at his feet. But the damage was done now. He knew more than anyone else from the diner. More than anyone other than her women's center counselor, Ginny.

"I've seen what you've seen."

"It wasn't easy to tell anyone my dad was a mean drunk..."

Could Jonah actually understand something of the horror she'd been through? The possibility caused a hard tug in her chest. The comfort and protection of his embrace tempted her to lose herself for a few precious minutes. To lower her guard and let him into her heart.

But relying on Jonah for her safety meant falling back into the traps that had imprisoned her in a violent marriage. Depending on any man for anything, whether security or shelter or her identity, would be a step backward. Wouldn't it?

Her kids were counting on her to be strong, to be self-reliant.

She swiped at her runny nose with the back of her hand and shoved out of his arms. "I have to go. I've already stayed too long."

"Annie, if you'd—"

Before he could finish, she jerked open the door and fled.

"Annie, wait!" Jonah's voice boomed through the cavernous gym, chasing her out to the street. Without looking, she knew he was behind her, that he'd follow her home as he had the night before.

Just as she knew the feel of his embrace and warm breath in her ear were sweet sensations she wouldn't soon forget.

Chapter 7

The next morning as Annie left for work, she paused at the edge of the parking lot and turned to wave at Haley, who watched from the apartment window. Her goodbye ritual, which Haley insisted on, took an ominous turn when she glimpsed a man for a split second before he darted behind a tree.

Her heart fluttering erratically, Annie smiled and lifted a wave to her daughter, while keeping an eye on the large live oak tree where the man had disappeared.

Jonah? Probably.

For some reason she couldn't fathom, he'd appointed himself her guardian. As she'd expected, he'd walked her home last night, having caught up to her several blocks from the boxing gym. She'd refused his offer to drive her, not wanting to be alone with him in the narrow confines of his front seat. Yet even outside, an arm's-length away, walking the city streets back toward her apartment, he'd crowded her. His presence on her walk home had compounded the conflicting feelings her self-defense lesson had stirred. If Jonah was correct about the danger she was in, she appreciated his efforts to keep her safe. Yet the idea of needing a man's protection nettled her, especially now when she was supposed to be making an independent stand.

He had at least granted her wish for quiet, not bothering to make meaningless conversation. He'd only warned her to lock up when she got inside and bid her a good night at the foot of the stairs to her apartment.

So why, if he'd walked *with* her last night, was he being so furtive this morning? Sighing her irritation, Annie spun back around and marched toward the bus stop. She didn't see him get on her bus when it arrived, yet the sense of being watched, being followed, stayed with her all the way to the diner. Annoying, cloying, unsettling.

By the time she reached work, she'd grown edgy and waspish, and she planned to give him a piece of her mind. What was he doing tailing her like some pervert when his warnings of danger already had her jumpy and looking over her shoulder? The nerve of him!

Annie stormed through the diner's front door and slammed her purse under the front counter with a huff.

"Whoa," a familiar male voice said. "I was going to say good morning, but obviously yours hasn't been so far, if your mood is any indication."

She snapped her gaze up to the smiling man sitting at the lunch counter.

Jonah. With a half-eaten plate of eggs and grits in front of him.

Her pulse scampered as her pique morphed to dismay. "You're here."

The corner of his mouth hiked higher. "Aren't I every day?"

"But if you're here, then who—" A chill slid through her.

One dark eyebrow dipped over Jonah's incisive stare. "Who what?"

Annie pressed a hand to her swirling stomach and shook her head. "I... Nothing."

Had the man behind the tree been her imagination? Had she really been tailed to the diner, or had she conjured the sensation because she'd expected Jonah to escort her?

She twitched her lips, the closest thing to a grin she could manage at the moment. "Forget it. I…"

She cleared her throat and tried to shake the jitters that danced down her spine.

Jonah's concerned gaze lingered, reminding her that just hours ago she'd been in his arms, held close to his masculine heat and strength. Yesterday, when his hands had been splayed intimately against her ribs, his warm breath fanning her nape, how could she not have entertained sexual images of him? And how did she keep those same images from taunting her this morning?

She fumbled to unfold a clean apron, and though she studiously avoided Jonah's gaze, she felt his eyes tracking her movements behind the counter.

Susan, one of the other waitresses, stood by the order window, her long blond braid trailing down her back as she rolled silverware into napkins. "Mornin', Annie. Am I ever glad you're here! It's been a zoo."

Annie returned a smile, glad for the distraction. "Good morning."

No sooner had the words left her mouth than the morning took a decided turn toward *bad.* Two regulars, the rude and intimidating men Jonah had been sitting with the night she was mugged, sauntered into the restaurant. The men slid into their usual booth, and the larger man snapped his fingers to call her to the table.

As if she were a dog he could summon to grovel at his feet.

Annie's skin crawled, and she gritted her teeth.

Susan stepped over to top off Jonah's coffee. She gave the new arrivals a meaningful glance and rolled her eyes. "Want me to get their order for ya, hon?"

Jonah glanced over his shoulder toward the men in question. His shoulders tensed almost imperceptibly. If Annie hadn't been looking for his reaction, she'd have missed the subtle flinch. Why had Jonah been talking with the two men the other night? Were they involved in the gambling and money-laundering investigation he was conducting?

Hands shaking, she tied on her apron and shoved a fresh order pad in her pocket. She gave Susan a grateful smile and shook her head. "No. Let me go clock in, then I'll take care of them."

"Devereaux!" the shorter man called to Jonah.

Jonah sent Annie what she could only call a sharp, warning glance before he faced the men's table and nodded an acknowledgment.

The second man returned a nod, and Jonah carried his coffee over to sit at the men's booth.

Squelching the uneasy jangle inside her, Annie hurried into the kitchen to clock in.

"You're late!" Hardin shouted at her from his post beside the grill cook.

Without answering, Annie walked carefully on the slick floor and consulted the time clock as she punched her card. She was, in fact, ten minutes early.

He's trying to rattle you. As if she needed further rattling that morning.

Someone had followed her to the diner from her apartment. She was sure of it. If not Jonah, then who? And why?

And what was she supposed to make of that odd look Jonah had just sent her? Was he trying to tell her something? Serving the goons was unnerving enough without Jonah sending her unspoken signals.

Taking a deep breath for courage, Annie grabbed a coffeepot and headed to the goons' table.

Temporarily setting aside his concerns surrounding Annie's strange mood that morning, Jonah eased into the booth next to Pulliam and across from Farrout. "Morning, gentlemen."

Farrout arched one thick eyebrow. "You have something for me?"

So much for small talk.

Jonah fished in his back pocket, then slid a folded envelope across the Formica table. Farrout lifted the flap and verified the contents—a cashier's check for eight thousand dollars. The bookie sent him a dark look.

Jonah shrugged. "Like I said before, I'll have the rest at the end of the month, after I get paid."

Pulliam scoffed, and Farrout silenced him with a hooded gaze. "With interest."

His anger spiking, Jonah balled his hand, then sucked in a deep breath to cool his knee-jerk reaction. "You never mentioned interest the other night. We agreed that—"

"You want in or don't you?" Farrout interrupted, his tone flat.

Frustration gnawed at Jonah. He had to play by this scumbag's rules if he wanted firsthand knowledge of how the operation worked. He ground his teeth and finally gave a jerky nod. "How much interest?"

Farrout exchanged a look with his partner.

"Twenty-five percent," Pulliam said, angling his body to lean his back against the wall.

Jonah was ready to argue the point when Pulliam's gaze shifted.

The scents of fresh coffee and flowers alerted Jonah to Annie's arrival even before he turned. His libido snapped to attention. While she filled Farrout's and Pulliam's mugs with hot brew, Jonah inhaled deeply, and the floral aroma of her shampoo sparked memories of holding her body close at the gym. With effort, he shoved down his natural reaction to Annie.

For her sake, he couldn't give Farrout or Pulliam any indication there was any outside connection between him and Annie. He prayed she'd read his unspoken message warning her of the same before he'd joined the shysters at their table.

He hazarded a glance at her, but she kept her eyes on her pad as she took the other men's order. Before she left, her doelike eyes found his. "Anything else for you?"

Her gaze clung, asking more than just what food he wanted. Jonah schooled his face, wanting with every fiber of his being to reach up and stroke the worry lines creasing her brow.

He shook his head and tore his attention away before anything in his expression gave him away.

Once Annie left, Farrout got back to the business at hand. "Here's how it works. Your money goes into the pool with everyone else's. If your team wins, you split the pot with anyone else who had money on the winner. Minus our cut, of course."

Jonah frowned. "Your cut."

Farrout shrugged blithely. "Like your friendly office pool, but with higher stakes."

"And your rules."

"Exactly," Pulliam answered, a smug grin pulling his cheek. "We gotta make something for our services."

Jonah's gut churned. How could Michael have gotten mixed up with something so obviously crooked?

But Michael's perception had been altered. His gambling had become an addiction. Compulsive. An illness. The high stakes would have been as tempting to Jonah's mentor as a cold beer would be to an alcoholic.

"So how big is the pool? How many people have paid in?"

Farrout shook his head. "Proprietary information."

When Jonah scowled, Pulliam chortled. "What? You can trust us."

Trust them to fleece him like they'd fleeced Michael, perhaps.

Annie returned with the men's orders, and as she set Farrout's plate in front of him, he seized her wrist. "I didn't want toast. All I ordered was an omelette. Don't try to charge me for toast I didn't order, ya hear?"

Jonah bristled, remembering the thug's rough treatment of Annie a couple of nights earlier. He leaned forward, ready to rip the bastard's throat out.

But something in Annie's posture stopped him. Her mouth tightened, and color crept to her cheeks. Squaring her shoulders, she stared at Farrout's grip on her arm, then stepped closer to him. "The omelette comes with toast. There's no extra charge." She circled her wrist, twisting her hand toward his thumb. And freeing herself from his grip. *"Sir."*

She stepped back, her expression almost as stunned as Farrout's. Jonah bit the inside of his cheek to contain his proud grin and his chuckle of amusement at Farrout's expense. He wasn't in a position to gloat over Annie's victory while he had business of his own to conduct.

Farrout glared at Annie's back as she marched back to the kitchen. "She just lost her tip."

Jonah squelched his gnawing disgust for Farrout and focused on his goal. If his plan worked, he'd have the sweet satisfaction of ending Farrout's days of manhandling waitresses. Permanently.

He sat through the rest of his meeting with Farrout and Pulliam wishing he could scoop Annie into a bear hug and congratulate her for taking a stand, for her skilled use of the technique she'd only learned last night. He prayed that this demonstration of the technique's effectiveness would convince her to continue with the private lessons.

But did he want to teach Annie one-on-one for her sake—or for his? He couldn't deny his attraction to Annie. He wanted to spend more time with her, get to know her, explore the mysteries that surrounded her. But even without his nine years at the Little Rock Police Department, anyone could have figured out the intimate nature of the private lessons bothered Annie.

After Farrout and Pulliam left the diner, Jonah headed up to the lunch counter to pay for his breakfast. His encounter with the two bookies left him feeling contaminated, tainted by association. His gut told him these two lowlifes were responsible for conning Michael, sending him into the downward spiral that ultimately killed him.

Jonah itched to get into the ring and work off his frustration with the slow pace of his investigation. He needed to sweat off Farrout's invisible filth, which clung to his skin and infected his soul.

If you lie down with dogs...

Susan hustled over to the cash register to take his money, a wide grin at the ready. "Off to the mill, handsome?"

"You lied." Jonah mentally flinched remembering Annie's reaction to his cover of shift work at the paper mill.

"'Fraid so." He handed her his cash and managed a polite smile.

The blond waitress was attractive enough, and he usually enjoyed exchanging flirtatious banter with her. Today he only wanted to ruminate on where his investigation was going and how to crank it up to the next level without arousing suspicion.

"I think pot roast is on the menu for tonight." Susan handed him his change. "Tempt you to come back in for dinner?"

"Susan, you know it's not the food that brings me back every night." Jonah gave her a wink, then scanned the dining room.

He needed to speak to Annie in private before he left—and not just about her self-defense lessons. Something had spooked her this morning. When she'd arrived at the diner and seen him, the flush tinting her cheeks had waned to a ghostly pallor.

Jonah stalled, taking his time putting away his change and unwrapping a mint from the basket by the register. Finally, Annie bustled through the swinging door from the kitchen, casting a wary glance toward the table where he'd had his meeting with Farrout and Pulliam. Relief flashed over her face when she found the table empty.

Jonah moved behind the counter so he could speak to her without raising his voice. "Annie, do you have a minute?"

Spinning toward him with a startled gasp, Annie frowned. "You're not supposed to be back here."

He hitched his head toward the front door. "So follow me out, and we'll talk there."

She gave the dining room a meaningful glance. "I have customers."

"They'll wait. I just need a minute." He took her elbow and nudged her toward the front door.

With a sigh of exasperation, she accompanied him to the sidewalk in front of the diner.

The March sun warmed the air, and a spring breeze lifted her hair, revealing her scars. Annie quickly combed the tousled wisps back over her cheek with her fingers.

Tempted to thread his own fingers through the glossy strands, Jonah shoved his hands into his pockets. "They're not that noticeable, you know. I don't see why you cover them."

Annie shot a startled look toward him.

He angled his head. "Besides, sexy as that side part is, it hides your best feature. You have beautiful eyes, Annie."

She gaped at him for a moment as if she couldn't quite believe what she was hearing. "Is this what you brought me out here for? Patronizing flattery?"

He jerked his shoulders back. "Patronizing? I'm not trying to insult you."

She twisted her mouth into a dismissive frown. "What did you want to talk about? I have to get back to work."

"Why were you surprised to see me here when you got to work? What happened this morning on your way in?"

She crossed her arms over her chest and shrugged a shoulder. "Nothing."

But the nervous glint in her eyes betrayed her.

"The truth."

She cocked her chin up, but the protest on her lips died when he narrowed a hard gaze on her. With a resigned sigh, she turned to watch the traffic on the side street. "I thought you were following me. When I left my apartment this morning, I thought I saw…"

He waited for her to finish, but she only shook her head. "It was probably just my imagination." She slanted an irritated glance at him. "You've got me so paranoid about someone gunning for me because of that stolen money that I'm jumping at my own shadow."

An uneasy tremor rippled through him. Instinct told him that whatever she'd sensed, whatever she'd seen had been no trick of her imagination.

"Just the same, I think I should drive you home tonight, bring you to work when you—"

"No."

He reached for her arm, determined to make her understand the seriousness of the situation. "Annie, until I can be sure you're safe—"

"I said no." She wrenched free of his grip and took a big step back. "I'm not your responsibility, Jonah. I need to take care of myself."

"Then meet me tonight for another self-defense lesson."

Her shoulders drooped, and she shook her head. "I don't think so. I—"

"Annie, think about it—you've only had one lesson, and already you've put something you learned to use."

The corner of her mouth lifted, and she peeked up at him. "I surprised myself with that."

"Why are you surprised? You're a strong, capable woman. You can do anything you want if you apply yourself to it."

She rolled her eyes. "You sound like Ginny." Tipping her head, she met his eyes briefly. "She's my counselor at the women's center."

The simple statement told Jonah a great deal. The Lagniappe Women's Center counseled and aided women who'd been raped, abused or otherwise traumatized. This Ginny Annie referred to was likely responsible for helping Annie free herself from her abusive situation. A good ally to have in her corner. That Annie trusted him enough to confide having used the center's resources was progress.

Jonah grinned. "I like Ginny already."

Annie shifted her weight and sighed. "Look, I plan to buy a can of pepper spray on the way home tonight. I'll be fine."

"And what if someone really is following you? Pepper spray is a start, but to defend yourself from—"

"No!" She shuddered and raised both palms toward him. "Jonah, I appreciate your time yesterday and your concern for me, but... I just... I can't..."

When she hesitated, he asked, "Is it me? Is it working with me in private that bothers you?"

Her expression answered him even though she didn't. The awkward, apologetic look she gave him burrowed to his core. He'd suspected as much, should have known better.

"There's an alternative. The local police department offers ongoing self-defense classes for women at the training center on Wood Street. They meet four days a week at 5:00 p.m. The instructor is a woman. A police officer. The class is all women and teenaged girls."

She bit her bottom lip and furrowed her brow as if considering his suggestion.

"It's a good class. No charge. No commitment."

The knit over her eyebrows deepened. "And you know all this because…?"

Jonah balked. If he told her the truth, that he served as the training aggressor for the class, would his participation be a deterrent because of her discomfort around him? In the class, he wore a full-body, padded suit including a helmet with a face mask so the women could practice the defensive strikes without injuring him. Annie didn't have to ever learn he was involved in the class.

He opted for partial truth, hoping she'd forgive his sin of omission if she ever discovered his deception. "The lead instructor is a friend of mine. She told me about the class."

Before Annie could answer, Susan appeared at the diner door. "Annie, we need you. Orders are backing up."

"I have to go," Annie murmured, brushing past him.

He caught her arm, felt her tremble at his touch. "Please think about it. Even if this business with the stolen money comes to nothing, you need to be able to protect yourself."

She set her shoulders and gave him a tight nod. "I'll think about it."

Thinking was a start, but not really enough. He had to convince her to take the class. Her life could depend on it.

Chapter 8

Annie's thoughts drifted to Jonah time and again throughout the day. She had to admit, even the little bit of information he'd given her last night about defending herself had been valuable. After weeks of being manhandled by Mr. Farrout, breaking his grip on her wrist this morning had been surprising. Exhilarating. Encouraging.

The idea of learning more from Jonah was tempting. But so was Jonah. Being around him at the diner, remembering how his defense demonstrations made her body hum and her knees weak, was difficult enough. She'd be crazy to purposely put herself in his proximity. In his arms. Alone. Even to learn self-defense, she couldn't justify torturing herself with something so...

Annie wiped her hands on her apron and chewed her bottom lip. What was the right word?

Forbidden? She certainly had no business taunting herself with a physical relationship that could never be. She had no room in her life for a man, and she didn't do one-night stands.

Confusing? Jonah's fighting skills, his brute strength and size contradicted the compassionate concern he'd shown her and his gentleness when he'd touched her. So who was the real Jonah?

Intimidating? More than her ever-present fear of physical violence, Jonah's uncanny ability to read her, to guess her motivations, predict her responses and see through her excuses left Annie off balance.

"I wanted you to know I understood what you'd been through."

Even Ginny didn't claim to understand the turbulent emotions of Annie's abusive marriage, the terror, the self-doubt and self-recrimination. But Ginny had been raised in a healthy family, had a loving marriage to a wonderful man.

Jonah claimed he had experience with abuse, had grown up with a violent father. Was it possible he did understand her and the pain of her past?

"Yoo-hoo. Anybody home?" Susan asked, waving a hand in front of Annie and bringing her out of her deep reverie. "Table six is ready for his bill."

"Thanks." Annie pushed the distracting thoughts of Jonah aside as she flipped through her order pad and presented the businessman at table six with his check and an apologetic smile. "Sorry for the delay. Can I get you anything else?"

His gaze traveled slowly down her body and back up, lingering on her chest. "That's all today—" his focus shifted quickly to her name tag before he met her eyes "—Annie." He put peculiar emphasis on her name, and as he slid out of his booth, his grin could be better characterized as a smirk.

Annie returned to the counter, gritting her teeth. "Why do the smarmy guys always sit at my tables?"

"Luck of the draw. But you don't have a monopoly on scumbags." Susan took a couple of plates from the order window and sent Annie a commiserating look. "Just yesterday, I had a guy in here *with his wife,* and he grabbed my ass." She rolled her eyes and huffed in disgust as she carried the orders out to the dining room.

Annie did her best to shake off the heebie-jeebies the creepy businessman gave her and concentrate on her job the rest of the day. But thoughts of Jonah and his encouragement to take the self-defense class offered by the police department returned that afternoon when she left work.

On an impulse, Annie bypassed her bus stop and headed to the Lagniappe Women's Center. The staff at the center, in particular her counselor, Ginny Sinclair, had been instrumental in helping her leave Walt sixteen months ago. Ginny and her husband, Riley, had risked their lives to save her and her children and had become dear friends of Annie's. When Annie needed perspective, encouragement and straight answers, Ginny was always there for her.

Today, she needed a dose of Ginny's honesty and understanding.

Annie smiled to the receptionist as she made her way to Ginny's office door and knocked. Hearing Ginny call, "Come in," Annie cracked the door open and peeked in.

Her blond-haired counselor cradled her phone to her ear but smiled broadly when Annie stepped into the office. She waved Annie to a chair and rocked forward in her seat. "Gotta go, babe. Annie just arrived. I will. Love you, too."

Ginny sighed happily as she replaced the receiver, then lifted a glowing grin to Annie. "Riley says hi."

Annie returned a smile. Ginny's newlywed bliss was palpable, and Annie couldn't be happier for her friends, though she experienced a pinch of envy for the contentment that radiated from Ginny's eyes. Would she ever find that pure joy with a man or would Walt always cast a shadow over her?

Taking a chair opposite Ginny's desk, she took a deep breath. "I know I don't have an appointment, but I was hoping you had a couple minutes. Something's happened."

Ginny frowned. "What's wrong?"

Annie explained about the attack in the alley and the stolen money, the possibility that the diner was the hub of illegal gambling and money laundering. "Jonah thinks I could be in danger. He wants me to take a self-defense class, and he—"

"Whoa." Ginny held up her hand. "Back up a second. Jonah? Who is that?"

Annie glanced down at her lap where her hands fidgeted. "He's a customer at the diner. A regular. He…followed me the night I was supposed to make that delivery, and he…defended me from the mugger. Probably saved my life." She squeezed her eyes shut, picturing Jonah's rugged face, his warm green eyes. Her stomach twirled and pirouetted dizzily, but, surprisingly, the sensation was not an unpleasant one. Instead, thoughts of Jonah stirred her pulse with the exhilaration of a carnival ride.

Annie huffed and forcibly tamped down the tingling reaction. She had no business indulging in any frivolous schoolgirl distraction when her job, her life, her children's safety could well be in jeopardy. "Jonah…has made himself my guardian. He's taken it upon himself to teach me to protect myself or see that I take a self-defense class. He wants to drive me to and from work, and he…"

When she paused, Ginny said, "He sounds like a good guy to have on your side. So why do I get the impression you are less than thrilled?"

"I didn't ask for his help. Not that I don't appreciate his assistance the night I was mugged, but I…I don't want…"

Ginny leaned forward. "Spit it out. Don't edit your true feelings."

Annie took a deep breath. "I don't want to need him. I don't want to depend on him and get trapped in a relationship that's bad for me again."

Ginny picked up a pencil to doodle as she thought, a quirky habit Annie had grown familiar with in the past two years. "Is that where you think your association with him is headed? A romantic relationship?"

"I… No. I didn't mean… I just…" Annie sighed. "I don't know. I'm not looking for a relationship right now. Truly. But if I'm honest—"

Ginny raised a palm. "Honesty is the best policy…and all that jazz."

"I find myself thinking about him a lot. And I feel…safer somehow when he's around." Annie sighed, then hurried to add, "But that's the thing. I don't want to reach a point where I only feel safe with him around, where I depend on him for…well, for *anything*."

Ginny rubbed her chin, clearly weighing her response. "There's a difference between being emotionally secure and self-reliant, and isolating yourself out of fear. Don't be too quick to cut yourself off from people, Annie. We all need other people in our lives sometimes."

Ginny's gaze drifted to the wedding portrait on her desk, and the corner of her mouth lifted. "At its best, a loving relationship makes you a stronger, better person. The right man will complement you, not eclipse you. It's about give and take, sharing and supporting each other. Being a team where both partners contribute the best of themselves."

Annie stared at a knot in the hardwood floor of Ginny's office. Had her marriage to Walt ever been a partnership where they complemented each other? From the beginning, Walt had taken the lead and made decisions about their future, their lifestyle, their finances. Annie had been left to follow…or be forced into compliance.

"I only just got my freedom back, my independence. Getting into another relationship now seems…" She fumbled for the right word.

"So don't get into another relationship yet," Ginny said. "That's not what I'm telling you. Just don't be afraid of building something special with a man because you're afraid of losing yourself again. Because the right man will help you discover all your best qualities, will support you and let you shine. Just like you'll do for him." Ginny laced her fingers. "Stronger together. A team."

Annie nodded, stashing the advice away to ruminate on later. "And the other stuff I mentioned? The mugging, the money laundering, the self-defense classes…what am I supposed to do with all that?"

Ginny stabbed her desk with her finger. "Take the class. Knowing how to protect yourself is always a good thing. As for the money laundering...I can call Libby Walters in the D.A.'s office if you want an official investigation opened."

Annie shook her head. "No. Jonah doesn't want to involve the local police yet. He's afraid one of the players will get wise to his investigation and all his work will be lost."

"But if there is something illegal and dangerous going on—"

Annie sat up straight, her mind made up. "Jonah is an ex-cop. I believe he knows what he's doing."

Somehow saying the words reassured her. She felt no hesitation defending Jonah's handling of the investigation. What did that say about her deepest, truest feelings?

Ginny arched an eyebrow. "You're sure? Because if you ever change your mind about this, you can call me, and I'll have Libby look into—"

Annie gave a tight nod. "I'm sure."

"And the mugging. How are you handling that? Any nightmares? Trouble sleeping? Issues you want to talk out?"

"I've had...a few flashbacks of Walt's abuse." Annie fingered the hem of her uniform skirt. "Especially seeing Jonah using his fists so effectively." She paused and glanced up at Ginny. "Did I tell you Jonah spars as a hobby? He fights for fun. For exercise."

Ginny scowled. "Has he given you reason to think he'll turn that violence against you?"

"Not yet. In fact, like I mentioned, he's encouraged me to learn self-defense."

Relaxing in her chair again, Ginny absently scratched another doodle. "So...stay alert with him. Be watchful for signs he's dangerous, but...give him a chance to prove his worth, too." She glanced up, and her gaze invited a response. "What else has been happening?"

Gnawing her lip, Annie thought about the creepy sensation of being watched on her way to work. "Well, I get the feeling someone is following me when I come and go from the diner. But that could just be paranoia."

"Just the same, be extra careful. Take Jonah up on his offer of a ride. Better safe than sorry, huh?"

A knock on Ginny's door interrupted them, and the receptionist poked her head in. "Sally Hendridge is here when you're ready."

"Thanks, Helen." Ginny rose from her chair and circled her desk.

Annie took the cue that the meeting was over and stood as well, only to find herself drawn into Ginny's friendly embrace.

"Take care of yourself, Annie. And give those sweet kiddos of yours a hug from their aunt Ginny."

"I will." Annie backed out of the hug and picked up her purse. While Ginny made her feel more optimistic, in general, her friend had also given her a great deal to think about regarding Jonah.

Thinking in terms of a relationship with him was more than a little premature. Still, she reviewed everything Ginny had said as she left the women's center and headed to the bus stop.

Like that morning, the sensation of being watched dogged her on her trip home. She checked behind her numerous times, but never spotted any one person she considered a threat. But then her stalker, if there was one, wouldn't advertise his presence. Would he? Or was it, as she'd suggested to Ginny, merely her imagination and paranoia at work?

She tried to discount the odd feeling, but the next morning as she made her way through the predawn darkness to open the diner, the sensation returned in full force.

Finding the entrance to the diner unlit only heightened her jitters. Perhaps she should follow Ginny's advice and take Jonah up on his offer of a ride home. And she'd look into the Lagniappe PD's class, if for no other reason than to calm the jangling nerves that made her commute to the diner and back home so tense.

Annie fumbled to key the front door lock but discovered it was already open. Odd.

Grumbling under her breath about Mr. Hardin's multiple oversights in closing the restaurant the night before, Annie started a pot of coffee and headed to the kitchen to clock in and collect the cleaning supplies she'd need to prepare the restaurant for opening.

Instead, she found Hardin sprawled on the office floor in a puddle of blood.

When Jonah arrived for breakfast at Pop's, a swarm of cops milled around the entrance and crime scene tape barred the gathering of reporters and curious onlookers from entering the diner. His heart rose to his throat as a black body bag was wheeled out by the coroner and loaded in a hearse.

Panic squeezed his chest, and he struggled to recall the waitresses' work schedule he'd conned Susan into showing him, knowing Annie wouldn't share her schedule willingly.

Friday. Annie was slated to open the diner.

Dear God.

Adrenaline pumped through him, jangling his nerves. A cold sweat beaded on his lip as he searched the crowd for Annie's face.

Years of experience with crime scenes that should have allowed him some professional distance vanished. When someone you cared about was involved, objectivity flew out the window.

He spotted Lydia and shoved through the horde of reporters and cameramen. Seizing Lydia's arm, he spun her around. "What happened? Where's Annie?"

The gray-haired woman scowled at him and fought his grip until recognition dawned on her face. "Oh, Mr. Devereaux, it's you. I thought you were another vulture reporter trying to exploit this tragedy for ratings."

She huffed indignantly and sent a scathing look down the sidewalk to the aforementioned scavengers.

Jonah fought down the rising fear that coiled inside him, forced his voice to remain calm. "What tragedy, Miss Lydia? What happened?"

"It's Hardin. Poor Annie found him shot dead in his office when she got here this morning to open the place."

Relief that the body bag hadn't been for Annie, and a gnawing concern for her trauma, tangled inside him.

Lydia shuddered and wrinkled her nose in dismay. "I can't even imagine how grisly and horrifying that had to have been for her," she said, mirroring Jonah's thoughts.

"Where's Annie now?" He cast another searching glance over the rubbernecking bystanders. "What happened to her? Is she all right?"

"Shook-up real bad, but not hurt." The older woman's face crumpled in sympathy. "Poor dear. Last I saw her, one of the cops had put her in the back of a cruiser to take her statement, get her out of the diner and away from the pushy reporters." She aimed a finger down the block. "Over there."

Jonah squeezed Lydia's hand. "Thanks."

He jogged down the street in the direction Lydia had pointed, searching each of the numerous police cars for Annie. When he spotted her, a curtain of dark hair shielding her bowed face, her thin shoulders hunched forward, her body rocking rhythmically back and forth on the rear seat of a cruiser, his gut twisted. Her body language reflected abject misery and terror.

A suffocating urgency to reach her, comfort her, protect her, grabbed him by the throat. He darted around the cluster of uniformed officers holding court on the sidewalk and knocked on the car window. "Annie!"

Her head jerked up, eyes wide. A gray pallor leeched her complexion. In seconds, the officers on the sidewalk assessed Jonah as a threat and seized his arms.

"Back off, sir," one cop ordered as he hauled Jonah back from the police car.

Annie scrambled to find the door handle, beating it with her fists when she found herself trapped in the cruiser's escape-proof backseat.

"That's my girlfriend," he lied. "I just want to talk to her! Can't you see she's upset?"

"She's a material witness. Until the detectives question her—"

"I know the drill!" Jonah released his frustration on the uniform. "I was on the job in Little Rock for nine years! I just want to hold her, calm her down." He shook free of the man's grip and shoved past another cop blocking his path.

"Sir, you can't—"

Jonah stuck his nose in the second cop's face. "Look, pal, you can stand right next to us and monitor our conversation if you want. We won't discuss the case. But I *am* going to let her out of that car." He met the officer's narrowed gaze with a dark glare of his own, then grated through clenched teeth, "Now get the hell outta my way."

With a determined stride around the cop, Jonah snatched open the cruiser door.

Annie lunged from the backseat and fell into his arms. "Jonah!" she gasped, her body trembling. "They killed Hardin! They shot him! Oh, God, Jonah."

He crushed her slim body to his chest, only to find his arms were shaking as much as she was. Just holding her, knowing she was safe, released the knot of tension that strangled him. He clung to her, stroking her back and sucking in deep restorative breaths.

"Oh, Jonah, it was horrible. There was blood everywhere, and his eyes—"

"Shh," he murmured into her ear. "Don't say anything now. We can't talk about the case until you've answered all the police's questions. Okay?"

She raised frightened eyes to his and nodded. A near-convulsive tremor shook her, and she dug her fingers into his arms.

"Is this my fault?" she rasped under her breath.

Jonah's gut clenched. "No!"

"But I—"

His grip tightened, and his gaze drilled into hers. "No! You can't think that way."

"We both know why this happened."

Jonah cut a furtive glance to the cop standing a few feet

away, listening. He had to keep Annie from saying too much, incriminating herself or blowing his investigation.

She shivered, near hysterics. "A-and I'm the one who lost—"

He kissed her. Just a quick collision of mouths. Not the deep, intimate kiss she deserved and he hoped he could give her someday, but enough to shock her into silence.

Enough to tell him her lips were every bit as soft and sweet as they looked. Enough to fire both his libido and his primal protective instincts.

She blinked. Gaped. Lifted a trembling hand to her mouth.

Guilt kicked him. Perhaps now, when she was already vulnerable, shaken by Hardin's murder, wasn't the best time to complicate his tenuous relationship with Annie. Even if the kiss kept her from incriminating herself in front of the eavesdropping cop.

Blowing out a cleansing breath, he turned to the cop. "When will she be done here? I want to take her home."

The officer arched an eyebrow and flashed a suggestive I-just-bet-you-would grin. Jonah gritted his teeth, battling down the urge to wipe the smug look off the man's face. But getting arrested for assaulting an officer would do Annie and his investigation no good.

"We just have a few more questions to ask her. She was in shock earlier, and we were giving her time to calm down."

Jonah brushed the hair back from Annie's cheek and gently massaged the tense muscles in her shoulders. "You feel up to some questions?"

Annie turned a wide-eyed glance to the policeman. "Can h-he stay with me?"

"Sorry. No." When her face turned a shade whiter, the man hitched his head toward the sidewalk. "He can wait right there, though. This will only take a minute."

Jonah took Annie's icy hands in his and squeezed. "I'll wait for you." He brushed a soft kiss on her knuckles and backed away. "You're strong, Annie. You can do this."

Her expression, as she cut a glance toward the cop, said she didn't agree.

Jonah leaned his back against the brick wall of the building next door to the diner and kept a close watch as Annie gave her statement and answered questions. He only caught snatches of the conversation. But having conducted more of these interviews than he liked to remember when he'd been on the force in Little Rock, he could fill in the blanks. Crossing his arms over his chest, he scanned the gathered crowd, scrutinizing faces, taking mental note of who'd come to rubberneck.

Could Hardin's killer still be lurking in the area? Somehow he doubted it. The killing could have been a robbery gone bad, but he doubted that, too.

Annie's instinct that the killing was related to the cash delivery stolen from her was much more on the mark. But in this day and age, where money could be transferred from one account to another with the click of a mouse and the blink of a cursor, why deal with cash and messengered deliveries? The whole scenario reeked. He was certain the thief had been waiting for Annie, the delivery a setup to squeeze Hardin.

Was the head of the operation getting greedy, trying to eliminate the fringe players to keep more profit for himself? Had Hardin become a liabilty?

Jonah clenched his teeth. He needed more hard evidence soon so he could close his investigation, nail the bastards responsible. Before anyone else got hurt. Like Annie.

A cold ball of fear settled in his gut. Annie could easily be the thief's next target if he thought she knew too much.

Time to change tactics with Annie. She still needed to learn to protect herself, but Jonah wasn't about to leave her safety up to a few lessons in self-defense moves. Whether she liked it or not, he intended to stay at her side, watching her back until he knew the men responsible for Michael's death and Hardin's murder were behind bars—or dead.

Chapter 9

Cold permeated to her bones.

Annie rubbed her arms as she answered the cop's questions, but her hands did little to displace the chill that sank deep into her marrow. Hardin's lifeless stare haunted her whenever she closed her eyes. The metallic scent of blood overlaid by remnants of day-old grease lingered in her nose, churning her stomach with every inhaled breath.

"Do you own a gun, Ms. Compton?" the cop asked, jerking her attention back to the seemingly endless questions.

She blinked, stunned by the implication. Did they suspect *she* had killed her boss? That she had a motive to shoot Hardin?

And did it matter if she hadn't actually been the one to pull the trigger? Hardin was just as dead, and her careless loss of his money was why he'd been murdered. She knew that much with a horrifying clarity.

The icy numbness burrowed deeper. "N-no. I—I've never owned a gun."

"Do you have access to someone else's gun?"

She shook her head. "I didn't do this. I found him already...dead."

The cop was clearly unmoved by her denial of guilt. He fired a few more questions before finally flipping his notepad closed and eyeing her dispassionately. "All right. That's it. You can go for now, ma'am. But don't leave town. We may have more questions for you in the next couple days."

Annie nodded and wrapped her arms around her stomach, feeling she had to physically hold herself together or she'd shatter.

She glanced down the sidewalk to the spot where Jonah stood patiently waiting for her. Why turning to Jonah in this crisis felt right, she couldn't say, but when she'd seen him at the window of the police car, her relief had been immediate and immense. She'd held her breath as he fought to get past the officers blocking his path. She'd needed his calming comfort, his reassuring strength, and hadn't questioned why she'd instinctively known he'd come. As soon as the initial shock of finding Hardin dead had morphed into a bone-chilling fear for her own life, Jonah's had been the face she'd sought as the police gathered and morbidly curious crowds clogged the sidewalk.

Now he tucked her trembling body under his chin, his arms folded securely around her, and she let the tears she'd been holding at bay throughout the policeman's questioning wash down her cheeks.

His embrace was firm and reassuring without crushing her. The soothing strokes of his wide hand on her back eased the chaos and terror of the past hours. Nestled close to him again, she allowed her thoughts to drift back to the jolt that had shot through her when he'd surprised her with his kiss. More unexpected than the kiss itself was her body's electric reaction. If his intention had been to scramble her thoughts and distract her from the situation, he'd succeeded nobly for several breathless seconds. The tender caress of his lips had spun a soothing warmth through her terror-chilled blood.

"When you're ready, I'll take you home," he murmured, his warm breath stirring the hair at her neck.

Home. Her children.

A fresh wave of icy horror flashed through her. She stiffened and jerked back to stare at Jonah in dismay. "My kids! What if the people who did this go after my kids?"

Nausea swamped her gut. If anything happened to Haley or Ben...

Jonah's grip tightened slightly, and he took her chin between his fingers and thumb. "That's not going to happen."

Frowning, she pulled her chin from his grip. "You don't know that. They could be at my apartment now!" She glanced to the cluster of policemen half a block away and lowered her voice to a harsh whisper. "I'm the one who lost that money. If they did this to Hardin, then why wouldn't I be next on their list?"

"I'm not denying that you could be in danger. But I promise you, I won't let them hurt you or your kids on my watch." The rough edge to his voice, the penetrating heat of his dark eyes rippled through her with concentric waves. Another tiny piece of her trust surrendered to his firm persuasion.

Jonah had bulldozed his way into her life and appointed himself her counsel and guardian. She knew so little about him, and what she did know was conflicting and confusing. By all rights, she should be running in the other direction. She'd had enough of bossy, controlling men.

Yet Jonah's concern for her and her family seemed genuine. That alone was novel in her experience. Walt had been selfish, cared little for what his drinking and cruelty were doing to her and the children.

And Jonah had encouraged her to become self-reliant, empowered, confident. Walt had preyed upon her through fear and intimidation.

He nodded his head toward the parking lot. "My truck is over here."

She followed him to his pickup and climbed inside. As they drove to her apartment in silence, Annie's head pounded with questions, terrifying images of death and a numbing fear that she'd once more lost control of her life.

Jonah parked in a visitor's spot on the far side of the parking lot, and she climbed out of his truck. Relief poured through her when she spotted Rani and her children playing on the grassy quadrant between apartment buildings.

Jonah placed a proprietary hand at the small of Annie's back as they started across the crumbling asphalt.

Haley noticed her first, and her daughter's face brightened. "Mommy!"

She ran across the parking lot to intercept her mother, and Annie stooped, catching her little girl in a fierce, protective bear hug. Holding Haley, knowing her kids were safe, melted a layer of the chill in her bones.

"How come you're home, Mommy?"

"I…just got the day off." Clinging to her daughter, Annie inhaled the sweet scent of the baby shampoo Haley still used, and a rush of tender emotion washed through her. Her children were everything to her, and if she had to go into hiding again to protect them, so be it.

Haley pushed back from the hug. "Does that mean you can play with us? Can we play with my Barbies?"

Excitement and hope laced Haley's voice, and joy lit her eyes.

"In a little while. I need to…take care of a few things first." Annie stroked her daughter's hair and kissed her forehead. "But later, I promise to play Barbies with you."

Her daughter grinned her satisfaction, then turned a curious look to Jonah, who'd stayed back as she greeted her daughter.

"Who are you?" Haley asked, wrinkling her nose.

Annie sent Jonah an apologetic glance. "Haley, if you want to meet someone, you introduce yourself politely. Remember?"

"Oh, yeah." Haley scratched her nose and gave Jonah a measuring look.

Annie watched Haley's reaction to him closely. Jonah was the first new man she'd brought around the kids since the ordeal with Walt came to a head more than a year ago.

He stepped forward and held his hand out for Haley to

shake. "I'm Jonah Devereaux, a friend of your mom's. Nice to meet you, Haley."

Jonah's hand swallowed her daughter's smaller one, and an uneasy tremor fluttered through Annie, a reminder of how vulnerable her children were.

Rani had reached them with Ben in her arms, and she gave Annie a worried look. "Ms. Annie, is everything all right?"

"Well, yes and no. The diner had to close today unexpectedly. I can watch the kids today."

Rani gave her a brief update on what the kids had eaten and when Ben had woken up that morning as she passed the toddler over to his mother.

"I'll call you when I know what's going to happen tomorrow. My plans are kinda up in the air right now," Annie said. She sighed as Rani told the kids goodbye and headed toward her apartment.

If fearing for her life and her children's weren't enough, Annie hated the uncertainty this turn of events cast over her future. Would she have a job tomorrow? Would the diner close indefinitely? Would she have to leave Lagniappe to protect herself from the person who murdered Mr. Hardin?

As she herded Ben and Haley back toward their apartment, Haley stopped to play with the neighbors' cat. Eager to get the children inside, out of view of any eyes that could be watching her, stalking her, she opened her mouth to chastise Haley for dawdling.

But Jonah crouched beside Haley and joined her in stroking the cat's back. Annie paused, watching her daughter give the cat solid thumping pats.

"Gently," Jonah murmured. "See how he put his ears back? That means he's unhappy. You don't want to hurt him, right? Kitties like soft pats."

Haley gentled her touch and tipped her head. "Like this?"

"Yeah, good."

The lesson in kindness to animals caught Annie off guard. His concern that Haley not hurt the cat contributed to her confused feelings toward Jonah. She tried to reconcile Jonah's fighting skills with this protective and loving attitude toward animals.

A shiver raced over her skin remembering how safe she'd felt in his arms when he'd gotten her out of the police cruiser. How could someone who sparred as a hobby, who didn't hesitate to take on another man in a dark alley in hand-to-hand combat have such a gentle soul? The contradiction flew in the face of everything her personal experience taught her. She was risking a lot bringing Jonah home, exposing her children to him.

She prayed she didn't regret taking the chance later. But she needed answers from Jonah, and the diner wasn't safe for this particular discussion.

"Do you have a cat?" Haley asked. Her wide-eyed innocence twisted in Annie's chest.

Jonah blinked his surprise, then chuckled. "Well, no. Do you?"

"No, sir. Me and Mommy want one, but she says we can't. She says maybe we can someday."

Jonah arched an eyebrow and divided a smile between Haley and Annie. "And when is someday?"

"Haley, take Ben and go on inside. I'll fix you a snack when I get upstairs." Annie waited until Haley had led her toddling brother up the steps and closed the door before turning back to Jonah. "I don't know when someday will be. It can't get here soon enough for me." She gripped the railing to steady herself, recalling the darkest days of her life. "Someday is when I don't have to worry that my husband will hurt an innocent animal to scare or control me. I couldn't justify exposing a pet to Walt's volatile temper and cruelty."

Jonah's expression inexplicably tensed and softened at the same time, anger and empathy clearly battling for dominance.

"Someday," she continued, struggling to keep her voice steady, "is when I'm not on the run, living in hiding to escape the murderous intentions of my husband. I didn't know from day to day where we'd sleep at night, if Walt would find us and make good his threat to kill me. A cat would have been impractical."

Jonah nodded, his dark eyes boring into her. Rather than rattle her as his intense gaze usually did, his focused attention encouraged confidence and soothed her frayed nerves.

She cleared the knot of emotion clogging her throat and added, "Someday is when I don't have to stretch my paycheck so thin you can see light through it. I can barely keep a roof over our heads and food in my kids' stomachs with what I earn."

The neighbors' cat wound through her legs, rubbing, and Annie bent to pick it up. Cuddling the feline close to her chest, Annie buried her face in the cat's soft fur. "I would love to let my baby have a pet, but cat food and vet bills aren't in the budget."

Jonah reached for her, but instead of patting the cat, he stroked Annie's cheek with his wide palm. "Someday may be closer than you think."

She scoffed and set the cat back on the ground when it squirmed. "How can you say that after this morning? Even if the diner reopens and I still have a job, Hardin was *murdered* because of that stolen money. How do I know I won't be next?"

Conviction and determination blazed in Jonah's eyes. "Because I won't let that happen. Hardin's isn't the first life lost because of these bastards, and if it is the last thing I do, I'm going to find the people responsible and see that they pay."

As Annie fixed her kids an early lunch, the bone-deep chill returned when Jonah's remark replayed in her head. Who else had been killed? How had Jonah become involved in investigating the gambling and money laundering?

Her children's restless squabbling drifted in from the living room where she'd left them watching TV with Jonah. She hurriedly finished draining the boiling water from the macaroni, eager to get back to the children and quiet their bickering. Jonah had to be uncomfortable around her fussy kids. Even the most stalwart soul could grow edgy around cranky children. Lord knew, the kids crying had been enough to set Walt off.

She shuddered remembering how often she'd had to run

interference, bend over backward to keep the kids quiet when Walt was in one of his moods. And the backlash when her efforts hadn't been enough.

With those dark memories haunting her, Annie set the macaroni aside and rushed to the living room to break up her children's latest squabble.

"That's the way! Punch it again. Harder," Jonah said as she stepped around the corner from the hall. He held a sofa pillow in front of him, egging Ben to jab the cushion with his tiny fists.

Outraged, Annie snatched the pillow away, her temper spiking. "Stop it!"

Both Ben and Jonah lifted startled looks.

"Annie?"

"How dare you teach my son to fight! I risked my life getting away from my husband so that my kids wouldn't learn his abusive ways. I will *not* allow you or anyone to teach my son it is okay to hit!" Anger and hurt raised the level and pitch of her voice. Her body shook, and tears bloomed in her eyes as she glared at Jonah.

He raised a placating hand and rose from the floor to face her. "Your son already knows how to hit. I was trying to teach him to punch something *other than* his sister. I told him hitting a girl was never okay. I wanted him to redirect his frustration on an inanimate object."

Annie stared at Jonah, dragging in air and needing a moment for his explanation to pierce the skin of her anger. With her heart thundering, she recalled seeing Ben punch Haley in a fit of anger more than once. She'd asked Rani to do all she could to squelch the behavior when she saw it.

Her gaze darted to Haley, who blinked at her, wide-eyed and pale. Compunction plucked at Annie. She'd assessed the situation at face value and unfairly jumped to a biased conclusion. Now she choked down the bitter fear and resentment that strangled her and worked to calm her runaway pulse before addressing her daughter. "Ben was punching you?"

Her daughter bobbed her head.

"Why?"

Haley poked out her bottom lip and looked away. "I took his truck."

Annie inhaled a slow, deep breath. Counted to ten. "Go to the time-out chair. You know not to grab your brother's toys from him."

Her expression contrite, Haley sidled over to the chair in the corner of the room. Feeling Jonah's gaze on her, Annie steeled her nerves and schooled her face before facing him. Rather than accusation, his expression was patient, forgiving. Her awkward guilt grew. "I'm sorry. When I saw you—"

"I understand."

She tipped her head, studying him. "Do you? Do you have any idea how much it scares me to think of my son following his father's example? He was a baby when I left Walt, but not a day passes that I don't worry that Walt's abusiveness could be genetic."

A muscle in Jonah's cheek twitched. "Behavior is learned, not inherited."

"I wish I could be sure," she murmured, shifting her gaze to Ben, who'd toddled over to cling to her leg. He whined and raised his arms to be picked up. Annie lifted Ben to her chest and bear-hugged him. "Oh, Ben, what am I going to do with you?"

Slanting her a lopsided smile, Jonah stepped closer and stroked a hand down Ben's wavy baby hair. "You're gonna be all right. Aren't you, little man?"

The loving gesture stole Annie's breath. Walt had claimed to love their kids, but she'd never seen him show his affection with a tender touch, a softly spoken encouragement or a warm smile.

Ben lifted his head from her shoulder and, grinning impishly, wagged a finger at Jonah. "No hit."

Chuckling, Jonah caught Ben's finger in his hand and gently squeezed. "That's right, pal. No hitting Haley."

Annie's throat tightened, and she struggled to assimilate her new impressions of Jonah in the wake of the horror and gore she'd witnessed this morning at the diner. How did this caring, conscientious man fit in the landscape of violence and illegal activity she'd become embroiled in at Pop's? How did she reconcile this gentle side of Jonah with the violent skill she'd seen him employ firsthand?

Her mind spinning, Annie nodded toward Haley. "Once she's been in the chair two more minutes, will you bring her into the kitchen to eat?"

He tweaked Ben's chin. "Sure."

She backed out of the living room, knowing something fundamental had shifted in her relationship with Jonah, but too overwhelmed by the events of the morning to examine the change closely.

Their relationship? The word clanged in her head and made her stomach whirl. She didn't have a relationship with Jonah. He was a customer at the diner, nothing more.

But you don't kiss a man who is nothing more than a customer.

No, *he* kissed *her.* Annie's lips tingled from the mere memory of that brief kiss. Warm, sweet, breath-stealing.

And totally off-limits. She had enough upheaval in her life at the moment without complicating matters with a new relationship. When she was ready to become involved with a man again, assuming she ever was, she'd want someone stable, safe, considerate.

Not a man who'd elbowed his way into her life, for whom hand-to-hand combat was a sport, and who turned her emotions topsy-turvy with his soul-piercing eyes.

After settling Ben in his high chair, Annie finished mixing the cheese sauce into the pasta. She was just about to check on Haley when Jonah carried her into the kitchen on his hip.

Her daughter gazed at him with such implicit trust and admiration, Annie's heart hammered. She'd expected Haley to be much more circumspect around men following Walt's frightening behavior both before and after Annie had left the marriage.

Not that Haley hadn't been exposed to positive male role models, too. Riley Sinclair, her counselor Ginny's husband, for one.

Jonah situated Haley at the table and took a bowl from the counter. "Can I help serve?"

"I—" Before she could answer, Jonah had scooped a spoonful of mac and cheese in the dish and carried it over to Haley.

"It's too hot," her daughter complained without tasting her lunch.

"Can't have that." Jonah stepped up behind Haley and bent low over the table. "Help me blow out the fire."

Together they both blew on the bowl with their cheeks puffed, and Ben giggled.

"Me, too!" Ben's attempt to cool his food resembled a raspberry more than a puff of breath. Now both children giggled, and Annie's heart swelled. Her children's mirth sang through her blood, a lyrical, magical melody that she treasured more than gold.

When Jonah peeked up and winked at her, Annie's joy over her children's laughter and Jonah's rapport with the kids morphed into a knee-weakening skip in her pulse. Her children had trusted and bonded with Jonah quickly and easily. Did they sense something about him that she'd overlooked, or was he preying on their innocence and naivete to get to her?

Before he left today, she intended to find out.

Chapter 10

Jonah was examining Haley's baby picture on a side table in the living room when Annie finished settling the kids in for their naps. Her heart ached, knowing she'd not had a professional picture made of Ben as an infant. The early months of his life had been the tumultuous prelude to her leaving Walt, and the months since her divorce had been too financially tight, too busy with her hours at the diner to have her son's picture made.

But she needed to capture her son's early years on film soon, someday....

"Someday may be closer than you think."

Though she said nothing, Jonah turned as if he sensed her standing behind him. "Your children are precious. You've a right to be proud of them."

"Thank you." She managed a small smile of appreciation, then grew serious. Time for answers. "Tell me about your childhood."

Jonah raised his head, stood straighter, arched an eyebrow in surprise.

"You said you were abused. How bad was it? What did your mother do? How did it change who you were?"

Jonah inhaled deeply and dragged a hand along his jaw. His callused palm rasped against the shadow of beard on his chin as he released his breath slowly through pursed lips. "Wow. You know how to cut to the chase."

He jerked his head toward the sofa she'd gotten from the secondhand store. "Sit?" He settled on one end of the couch and patted the cushion next to him.

Instead she took the rocking chair across the room from him and squeezed the knobby armrests. "I'm listening."

Jonah leaned forward, propping his forearms on his thighs and bridging his fingers. "I grew up in a white-collar neighborhood, went to a good school, had a circle of friends I hung out with. Most of the normal stuff."

He shrugged. "But every once in a while my dad would lose his temper and take out his frustrations on Mom. If I tried to defend her, I'd catch as bad as she got. He generally left my older sister alone, but even she took a backhand across the mouth for a sassy remark or an ear-ringing slap if she was in the wrong place at the wrong time. As I got older, when I sensed he was in one of his moods, I'd provoke him so that he'd come after me to start with instead of Mom.

"I lied to my teachers or whoever would ask about where my bruises came from. By the time I was thirteen, I'd started picking fights with kids in the neighborhood. Part of that was me venting my internal rage, and part of it was to cover the constant parade of injuries my dad gave me. I got the reputation of being a bully on purpose, so no one questioned the black eyes and split lips as much."

A bully. Annie shuddered.

"And your mother? How could she let this happen to you? I left Walt when I realized he could turn his violence against our kids next."

"She tried to protect me and got hurt for it. But she also lived in denial. Dad would apologize and beg her forgiveness, promise to change, tell her he'd get counseling and she'd stay. She loved the bastard for some reason, and I couldn't convince her to leave him. She died of cancer when I was fifteen. My sister was away at college by then, and I had no desire to live alone with my dad, so I left home."

Annie frowned. "And went where?"

"The streets for a while. Then I went to this gym one day, looking for work."

"As in a *boxing* gym like the one where we met the other day?" She couldn't hide the disdain in her tone.

He nodded. "Yeah, but in my hometown in Arkansas. For a while I did odd jobs, real menial stuff, in exchange for a cot in the locker room. Then I found out you could earn money working as a sparring partner with the guys who were training for competitions. I asked for that job and got it."

When she sent him a dubious look, he shrugged and flashed her a self-deprecating grin. "I had plenty of experience getting beat up, so why not get paid for taking a few hits?"

Annie stared down at her lap, her hands fidgeting restlessly. While her heart ached for the teenager Jonah had been, relying on the violence that was his father's legacy to survive, her new insights about his past only confirmed what she'd feared. Violence was a part of who he was. His casual attitude about hopping into a boxing ring to pound another man chafed against her memories of being Walt's punching bag.

"So you turned the abuse your father taught you into a profession?" She surged from her chair and paced across the living room, uneasy with the truths she was learning. How could she be attracted to another man with a tendency toward violence? What was wrong with her?

"A profession?" He snorted. "Hardly. I just made a few bucks exchanging jabs with guys in the evening. And sparring was nothing like the abuse I took from my old man. For one thing, I wore pads and headgear."

She spun to face him with a sigh. "My point is, when you got away from your father, rather than leave the abuse in the past, you continued fighting. It was a lifestyle for you. You *chose* to fight."

He met her gaze evenly. "I chose to heal. I chose to turn my life around and use what I knew to help other people in the same situation."

She blinked, gave him a humorless laugh. "Excuse me? How does sparring help other people?"

A muscle in his jaw twitched, and he took a slow, measured breath. "It doesn't necessarily. But being a policeman does, if you do your job right."

She sat straighter, remembering his telling her he'd once been a cop. She listened attentively as he explained.

"The thing is, the kid who went to that gym looking for work, the teenager who got into the ring to earn a few bucks isn't the same guy sitting here today. Back then I was full of rage, full of hatred for what my father did. I was confused, alone, just…mad at the world. But the owner of the gym saw something worthwhile in me and took me under his wing. He talked to me, listened to me when I was ready to spill my guts and helped me work through that anger I had pent up inside. He showed me how that fury was destroying me, how holding on to that anger hurt *me,* not my dad."

His words reverberated through Annie, and she hugged herself. She'd heard much of the same admonitions and advice from Ginny. Ginny had been her rock when she'd felt overwhelmed by the turmoil and danger of leaving Walt. Annie understood without his explaining further how important the owner of that gym had been for Jonah.

Jonah rubbed his palms on his jeans and continued. "He taught me to channel those bottled-up emotions and release them through my boxing. I sweated out the grief and worked off the tension and hatred. Took it out on a punching bag so that I *didn't* blow a gasket one day and let it out on some shmuck who ticked me off. I poured all the fear and frustration and rage I had for my father and what he'd done to us into my workout and learned to fight a clean, fair fight in the ring. No cheap shots. Keeping control and perspective.

"I'd been in a downward spiral, and he pulled me back from the brink and set me on a better path."

"How so?" Annie leaned forward, enthralled by what she was learning about Jonah's past.

He rolled a palm up. "I went back to school, joined the police academy and was on the job for nine years before I left the force."

Annie drew her eyebrows together and shook her head. "Why did you quit?"

Jonah flopped back on the sofa and rubbed his hands over his face. Grunted. "I guess I...answered one too many domestic disturbance calls and had had enough."

He clenched his teeth, and the distant look in his eyes told her his thoughts were miles away from her living room, deep in troublesome memories from his years as a cop. Annie's heart thundered as color crept up his neck and flooded his cheeks, his nostrils flared and his jaw tightened.

"Every time I'd leave a home where I knew abuse was happening, regardless of whether I'd been able to do anything to help the people involved, I'd feel that frustration knotted up inside me again, and I'd go to the gym to work through it, work it off." He inhaled deeply and expelled it in a whoosh. "But in all the years I was a cop," he said, meeting her eyes with a hard, level gaze, "I *never* lost my cool with an abuser—much as I wanted to knock the snot out of 'em. Never." He paused, letting that fact sink in.

A shiver chased up Annie's spine as all her conceptions about Jonah shattered and reassembled in new patterns. Her spinning thoughts made her restless, and she shoved to her feet, paced across the floor and back.

"So...boxing, sparring saved my life. The things I learned from Michael kept me on track, kept me sane."

Her pulse tripped, and she jerked her head up. "Michael. You've mentioned him before. He's the one you said lost his savings to the gambling ring that operates out of the diner."

Jonah nodded. "He was my mentor, my guardian angel

when I needed him. He moved down here to Lagniappe a couple years ago to manage Frank's gym, the one we were at the other day." He paused and drew his eyebrows into a frown. "Michael was a good man at heart, but…he was no saint. Gambling became an addiction. When he lost his savings, he…lost hope. He was ashamed and thought he was out of options."

Annie heard the grief that vibrated in Jonah's tone. He sucked in a deep breath and pushed it out through pursed lips. "He…killed himself just over a year ago."

She gasped and pressed a hand to her mouth. "Oh, no. Jonah, I'm so sorry."

His jaw tightened. "I blame the thugs who stole his money for his death. That's how I got involved with this investigation. I wanted retribution for Michael. I wanted to shut down the bastards' operation and bring them to justice."

"Alone?"

He sighed and glanced away. "For the most part. Right now I'm just getting information, trying to figure out who's involved, how the operation is run. When I have all my facts laid out, enough proof to hang these guys, I'll take it to the authorities. But I don't want anyone, even someone on the fringes of this thing, to get away. I want solid information, hard evidence that no judge can toss out, no lawyer can explain away."

The passion in his voice fueled the fire inside Annie, the determination she had to free herself from the danger she'd unwittingly landed in. If she wanted to keep her kids safe, if she wanted to protect herself and still scrabble out a living, the criminals at the diner had to be stopped.

But she wouldn't sit back and leave it to Jonah to bring the men involved to justice. She would not be a victim again, would not passively let someone ruin her life again as Walt had done.

Screwing up her courage, Annie balled her fists and pulled her shoulders back. "I want to help. I can search Hardin's office for files or financial records, or—"

"No." Jonah shook his head.

Irritation tickled her gut. "But I have access to his office and can—"

"No! I can't let you get in this mess any deeper. It's too dangerous."

She crossed her arms over her chest. "It's not your decision whether I'm involved or not. And I'm already in danger. You said so yourself."

"Think of your kids, Annie. You can't put yourself in harm's—"

"I am thinking of my kids! The sooner we build a case against these creeps, the sooner I can get my life back."

"Not *we*. Let me handle this. The only reason I told you what was going on is because you needed to be aware, be alert. So you could protect yourself. But now, with Hardin's murder, the stakes are higher. I have to be careful how I proceed. Changing anything now about the cover I've set up might tip someone off."

She pictured Hardin's bullet-riddled body and almost changed her mind. The idea of being so vulnerable, with an unknown enemy lurking, lying in wait, scared her senseless. She swallowed the bitter taste of fear in her throat and raised her chin. "All the more reason to let me search Hardin's office. You don't have the opportunity and the access I have. I can do this. I *have* to do this. I can't let fear or danger dictate my life again."

Jonah surged off the couch and strode over to her. "Look, I know how much you want this all to be over, and I respect your courage and willingness to help, but—"

"Courage?" She gave him a humorless laugh. "It's not courage, Jonah. It's desperation. Panic. I'm scared to death, but I have to do something before the whole situation explodes in my face. If there's even a chance I could be on their hit list because of that stolen money, I have to act. I won't sit by and risk my children getting hurt by this. It's necessity, not courage."

He cupped her cheek in his massive hand and stroked her jaw with his thumb. The comforting gesture sent ribbons of sweet sensation coursing through her, muddling her thoughts.

"Don't sell yourself short," he murmured, his low voice stroking her, adding to the pleasant hum vibrating from deep inside her. "Leaving your husband, starting over, standing up for what's right…you had to have a lot of courage to do all you've done. Being brave isn't the absence of fear—"

"It's doing what you must despite the fear. I know, I know." With a disgruntled sigh and a nod, she lifted her hand to his wrist and pulled away from his deliciously distracting touch. She needed to stay focused on the problem at hand. "Ginny practically tattooed that saying on my forehead. So, fine, call it what you want, but I need to help. Don't shut me out of this, Jonah."

He shook his head again. "If you want to do something to protect yourself, then go to the self-defense class at the police station we talked about. But stay out of this."

She raised her chin. "Fine. I'll go to the class. But I'm tired of sitting back while the world stomps all over me. I have to *do* something—with or without your help."

"Annie—" His dark brow lowered, and his eyes narrowed to slits. "If I agree to let you help, do you promise you'll follow my instructions? No going it alone or taking unnecessary risks. Understood?"

Her pulse fluttered with anticipation and dread. "I promise."

"Remember, these people have a lot of money at stake, and if they suspect you of meddling in the operation or feeding information to the police, they'll kill you without asking questions."

Her stomach pitched, but she steeled her nerves. She had no choice but to help Jonah. She couldn't live under this cloud of fear, couldn't bear the idea of her children living under a threat of danger. Wishing she weren't in this predicament didn't make it so.

"You promise you'll go to the class?" he asked, his eyes drilling hers.

She raised a hand. "Promise."

Sighing his resignation, Jonah drew her to the sofa and pulled her down onto the cushions beside him. "All right. Let's make some plans. I don't want to leave anything to chance. We have too much at stake."

Jonah angled the seat in his truck to a more comfortable position, settling in for the long night ahead. Annie would balk at the idea of him camping out on the street to watch her apartment, but the stakes in this case kept getting higher. He remembered her saying she'd thought someone followed her to work the day before. Coupled with Hardin's murder, he wasn't about to leave her home unguarded.

Acid flooded his gut when he thought of Annie becoming involved in his investigation. He should never have agreed to let her help him, but what choice did he have? He'd seen the determination and passion that fired her eyes. She'd have acted on her own if he hadn't let her help him. At least this way, he could keep closer tabs on her involvement.

He scanned the parking lot and the oak-tree-lined yard. Everything was quiet, dark, still. A stark contrast to the turmoil writhing inside him.

Telling her about his abuse, his history with Michael and his mentor's suicide had been wrenching. Painful. He never relived those memories if he could help it. But Annie had asked him point-blank, and she wouldn't have been satisfied with evasion or half-truths. He needed her to trust him.

The question he was left with, however, was where did they go from here? He couldn't deny his attraction to her. His feelings went deeper than the protective instincts she aroused in him. But given her history, knowing the hardships she'd already survived, he was the last person she needed in her life.

Even after he'd explained to her how he'd gotten involved with sparring, explained how the physical outlet for his emotions kept him sane, he'd seen the doubts and disapproval in her body language. She wanted nothing to do with any form of violence, even the controlled, therapeutic version he practiced at the gym.

Not to mention the fact that any future with Annie had to include being a father figure to her kids. And his only example of fatherhood was the horrid one his father had set. What kind of father would he be?

The notion of having a family, sharing his life with a wife and being a role model for children left him in a cold sweat. He wanted those things, deeply, but only if he was sure he could give his family what his father hadn't. Love. Security. Happiness.

He didn't have a clue where to begin creating a healthy family life. It wasn't that he feared he'd physically hurt Annie or her kids—he'd cut his hand off before he'd raise it against them—but there were so many other ways to fail a family. He'd be damned if he'd repeat his father's mistakes, but he didn't have any other point of reference. On the job, he'd faced down armed gangbangers without a second thought. But being a husband or father, being in a position to screw up the lives of those you love, scared the hell out of him.

Which left him with only one option. Never marry. Never have children. Never recreate the hellish existence that passed for his childhood home.

Jonah dragged in a lungful of oxygen, his chest knotting with regret. As much as he wanted his own family, as much as he wanted Annie, he was destined to be alone.

Chapter 11

Two days later, the police released the murder scene, and the diner reopened. Annie arrived early for the breakfast shift, hoping to look around in Hardin's office before the diner filled with the morning rush.

She pressed a hand to her stomach, trying to calm the battalion of butterflies swooping in her gut as she stepped through the swinging door into the kitchen. The images and smells of the last time she'd walked through this door were all too fresh in her mind.

Enough dawdling. She had limited time before the rest of the kitchen help and waitstaff arrived. And the interim manager. Who would take Hardin's place and was he connected to the money laundering the way Hardin was?

She had no doubt whoever was in charge of the illegal operation would handpick Hardin's replacement.

Sucking in a calming breath, Annie pushed through the door and surveyed the kitchen as she crept cautiously back to the manager's office. Would the police have removed the financial records and computer drive for their investigation of Hardin's murder? What were the odds that, had there been any proof of money laundering before Hardin's death, the men responsible for his murder would have left any evidence behind to incriminate themselves?

Annie reached the door of the office and, knees shaking, turned the corner into the cramped office. No trace of blood or death remained, other than the faint chemical smell of the cleaner used to erase the evidence a man had been shot and bled to death on this floor.

An uneasy jitter crawled through Annie, but she shoved down her discomfort and set to work. She started with the file cabinet in the corner. The disarray of the papers and the haphazard order of the contents told her that someone had already rifled through the papers. But had it been the police...or Hardin's murderer?

Order forms and delivery slips from various grocery vendors were jumbled together with personnel applications and insurance documents. Records of health inspector visits had been jammed to the back of the top drawer, but she saw nothing resembling a financial ledger or a computer spreadsheet of expenses and profits.

Of course not.

Did she really think it would be that easy? That she'd flip through a few files until she found a neat and organized record of all past criminal activity along with a typed and signed confession of those involved?

She scoffed. Anything she found would be far more subtle. Just a piece of a bigger picture.

She moved on from the file cabinet to Hardin's desk. She rummaged through the center drawer but found nothing beyond basic office supplies and an opened pack of cigarettes. Next she searched the deep side drawer where it appeared the most recent paperwork was kept. As she fingered through the files, she realized the kind of evidence she was interested in wouldn't be kept in the obvious places. Evidence of wrongdoing would be hidden. Protected.

Was there a safe? A bank lockbox?

She pulled the drawer all the way out and felt behind the hanging files. Nothing. Same with the next drawer she searched. Then, on an impulse, she pulled the center drawer all the way out, off its tracks, and emptied the contents onto the desk. As she flipped the drawer, her heart sank when she found nothing stuck to the underside other than a wad of very old gum.

"Looking for something?" a deep voice growled behind her.

Gasping, she whirled around, her heart hammering at the dark glower she met.

Martin Farrout.

A chill washed through Annie as she faced Farrout's intimidating glare. "Uh, sir, the kitchen is for employees only."

His black eyebrows beaded. "I'm well aware of that. And from now on this office is off-limits to anyone but the new manager." He paused a moment, his head cocked at a haughty angle.

A staggering heartbeat later, understanding dawned through the muddle of her spinning thoughts. "You're—"

"The new boss. Yes. So what are you doing snooping in my office?"

Annie's breath backed up in her lungs. "I—I was looking for—" She glanced at the mess she'd dumped from the center drawer. Grabbing the first item she saw, she held the opened pack of cigarettes out. "These. I...needed a smoke. Hardin let me have his when—"

"So you got 'em. Now beat it."

She jerked a nod, praying she'd returned the other drawers to enough order that he couldn't tell the full extent of her searching.

Scrunching the cigarette pack in her hand, she hustled out past the large man. He refused to step aside, so she was forced to turn sideways and sidle out of the office. Heart thundering, she rushed out to the dining room, where Lydia was chatting with the first breakfast customers. The older woman glanced at the cigarettes Annie squeezed and propped a hand on her hip. "I didn't know you smoked."

Annie pressed her free hand to her chest, struggling to calm her ragged breathing. "I don't."

Lydia gave a meaningful nod toward Annie's fist. "What are those for, then?"

Annie glanced down at her hand and sighed. "Nothing. I...was just—" She stopped herself, realizing something hard and distinctly uncigarette-like poked her hand through the paper packaging.

"The first step to quitting is admitting you have a problem," Lydia said with a teasing grin and a bump from her hip as she headed out to the tables.

Annie turned her back to the customers sitting at the counter and upended the crushed pack. Several bent cigarettes slid out—along with a small silver key that pinged as it clattered onto the counter. Why did Hardin have a key in his cigarettes? What did the key go to? She studied it, turning it over in her hand, her pulse picking up. Folding the key into her palm, she peeked into the packaging to be sure she hadn't missed anything else. Empty.

She brushed the cigarettes and empty package into the trash and jammed the key into her apron pocket.

Would Farrout be looking for that key? Would he suspect her when he found it missing? Did the key unlock something here at the diner or was it part of Hardin's personal property?

She wondered if Jonah would stop by the diner today and what he'd make of the key she'd found. The key she'd *stolen*.

Her heartbeat thundered in her ears.

Stolen. If Farrout or the other men involved in this money-laundering scheme found out—

"You have any grape jelly? I'm allergic to strawberries," a woman at the counter asked, jarring Annie from her disturbing thoughts.

"Oh, uh, sure." She wiped her sweaty palms on her apron and took a moment to redirect her thoughts. As she turned to the tray where they kept the condiments, another man at the counter caught her eye, and her stomach dipped. The businessman who'd ogled her earlier in the week was back, his weighty gaze following her every move.

Her skin crawling from his discomfiting scrutiny, Annie found the grape jelly and handed it to the woman with the strawberry allergy.

She cast a surreptitious glance to the businessman as she moved the pot of decaf coffee that had finished brewing to a warming burner. He caught her eye and lifted his eyebrow and his mug. "I'll take some of that, doll."

Squelching the uneasy jitter that he elicited, Annie crossed to him with the coffee just as a handsome, familiar face arrived at the counter. Relief and pleasure spun through her as Jonah took his seat at the counter.

When had she decided his face, with his broken nose bump, the scar over his black eyebrow and his perpetual five-o'clock shadow, was handsome rather than rough-hewn? Comforting instead of daunting?

She'd have been the first to deny she'd formed any attachments to Jonah, yet the leap in her pulse and the lift in her spirits when she spotted him were undeniable. He held a central role in her thoughts lately, too, whether she was at home or at work, thoughts that had her lying awake at night with a restlessness stirring inside her.

He shook his head slightly, a subtle reminder of the warning he'd given her last night not to greet him with more than normal, businesslike attention. He wanted to keep their association as low-key as possible when at the diner.

"Morning," she greeted him casually. "Can I get you coffee?"

She wanted desperately to tell him about the key she'd found but knew now was not the time or place.

"Sure. And I'll have the sunrise platter." He lifted a corner of his mouth in a polite grin, but as she filled his mug, his attention shifted and his countenance clouded. She turned, curious to see what had darkened his mood.

Martin Farrout stood just outside the kitchen door, casting an imperious glance over the dining room like a ruler surveying his land. Her new boss's gaze lingered on Jonah, then skipped briefly to the businessman beside him before moving on.

"Our new manager," she told Jonah under her breath.

She could almost see the wheels in Jonah's head clicking, figuring how Farrout's appointment as manager fit into the money-laundering scheme and Hardin's murder.

Lydia returned from the tables, brushing past Farrout, and clipped new orders up for the cooks. "I could use some help out there if you can, Annie. Notoriety over Hardin's murder has brought out the morbidly curious this morning, and tables are filling up fast."

"Of course." Annie surrendered to the frenzy of the breakfast rush but kept tabs on Jonah's progress through his meal. She needed an opportunity to talk to him before he left.

He'd cleaned his plate and had nodded to her for his bill before inspiration struck. In tiny printing at the bottom of his order ticket she wrote *Meet me at restroom.* Jonah gave no visible sign he'd noticed her message as he checked his total and handed her his cash. She held her breath as he left his seat, glanced at the morning paper on the rack beside the cash register and took a toothpick from the dispenser on the counter. She tried to hand him his change, but he waved it away.

After pocketing his tip, she picked up a rag to wipe the counter and watched him make his way to the back hall that led to the bathrooms.

Relief unfurled in her chest, and she wiped her hands on her apron as she made her way toward the back hall, using the employee entrance from the kitchen.

Jonah stood by the pay phone at the end of the hall thumbing through a well-worn phone book. Glancing about to be sure they were alone, she hurried over to him and pulled the key from her pocket. "I found this in a cigarette pack in Hardin's desk." She kept her voice low, kept an eye on the door to the dining room. "Guess it's Farrout's desk now."

Wrinkling his brow, Jonah took the key from her palm and examined it. "Any idea what it goes to?"

"None. I didn't find it until after I left the office. Farrout caught me in the office earlier and asked what I was looking for. I had to make up a quick excuse and get out of there. I told him I was there for the cigarette pack, so I grabbed it and left. But I could try to get back in there later when he's not around and see—"

"No! If Farrout is already suspicious, it's all the more dangerous for you." Jonah bounced the key in his hand. "Besides, this looks more like a locker key. Like the ones at my gym or the kind at the bus depot."

She nodded her agreement. "So how do we find the locker it goes to?"

He shrugged. "I'll look into that today." He held the key toward the light and narrowed his gaze, studying it closer. "There's a number on it—223. That should help narrow the search."

"I want to go with you when you open the locker."

As soon as Jonah started shaking his head, Annie snatched the key from his hand and shoved it down the front of her waitressing dress and inside her bra. "You promised not to shut me out. I found the key. I want to go with you when you open the locker or whatever the key goes to."

Agitation shaping his expression, Jonah clenched his teeth and sighed.

She saw the businessman from the counter before Jonah did and cut off his protest, saying, "Yeah, that phone book is way out of date. You'd do better to just call information. Sorry."

Jonah's gaze flicked to the man in the pressed suit who strolled past them into the men's room. "Okay, thanks anyway."

As soon as the men's restroom door swished closed, Jonah whispered, "Annie, give me the key. I never promised you could be involved in every aspect of my investigation."

She backed toward the kitchen, whispering back, "I can get off at two, if Susan will cover my last hour. You can meet me at the bus stop on Third Street, and we'll go together from there to start looking for the locker this goes to."

"Annie." His tone dipped in warning. "Give me the key."

"I will." She backed to the kitchen door, mouthing, "At two."

At five minutes until two, Jonah sat in his car waiting for Annie at the Third Street bus stop stewing over her stubbornness and the cheap tactic she'd used to keep the key from him. If it had been anyone besides Annie, he'd probably have gone after the key without blinking. But he figured Annie was the last person who needed to be manhandled and groped—even if she'd all but dared him to with her ploy. He chuckled despite himself. Her moxie had caught him off guard, but he wouldn't be so easily outmaneuvered again.

The show of gumption also encouraged him. Beneath the layers of shame and intimidation her ex had heaped on her with his abuse lurked a strong, vibrant woman waiting to be freed. She just needed a safe environment, the right timing and the encouragement of people she trusted to revive the side of herself she'd forced into hibernation.

A few minutes later, Annie opened his passenger-side door and slid onto the seat. "So where do you want to start?"

He cranked the engine. "Not the gym. I checked, and those lockers are numbered one to one hundred. We'll try the bus depot first."

When they reached the bus station, Jonah took a gym bag inside with him. He placed a proprietary hand at the small of her back as he ushered her into the dingy brick building. They located locker 223 easily, and she handed him the key.

"Bingo," he said when the metal door opened.

Annie huddled in close as he examined the locker's contents. The light, feminine scent that clung to her was distracting. With effort, he focused his attention on the locker and not the thrum of his blood and the pounding desire to pull Annie into his arms.

Gritting his teeth and shoving down the hum of desire, Jonah pulled out computer CDs that lay on a top shelf and shoved them into his gym bag. Next he rifled through printed files stacked below. He handed Annie one of the files stuffed with pages of data. "Read through some of this and see what it is."

Jonah pulled out a file for himself and began flipping pages. His folder held financial records, long lists of deposits with names and—*hold the phone*—sports results listed by each entry.

His pulse roared in his ears as he scanned the list for a particular name. Michael's. The deposits were listed chronologically, and he skimmed quickly through the past several months until he found the sheet for the last month Michael was alive.

Beside him, Annie gasped. "Jonah, look at this."

She pointed to a page where a name and phone number had been scribbled at the top of the sheet.

"Joseph Nance?" he said, reading the name. "You know him?"

"Not exactly. But I know the name. That's who I was supposed to deliver the package of money to the night I was attacked. Hardin was very adamant that I only give the money to him."

Jonah's heart thundered in his chest. A name. He had a name.

He closed his file folder and pulled out his cell phone. "Read me that number."

As she did, he dialed. His breath hung in his throat as the phone rang once, twice.

"Lagniappe PD. Detective Nance speaking," a gruff voice answered.

Jonah pulled his eyebrows together, stunned speechless. Nance was a cop?

"I'm sorry. I have the wrong number." As he thumbed the disconnect button, Jonah lifted a confused gaze to Annie.

She frowned, gripped his wrist. "What? Who answered?"

"Apparently Nance is a detective with the Lagniappe police."

"The police? So…Hardin was working with the cops to bust the gambling ring?"

"Or we have a crooked cop on the force taking payoffs." Jonah stroked the stubble on his cheek and mulled the turn of events.

"Or someone ratted Hardin out, and he was being set up for arrest," Annie countered.

"Anything's possible, I suppose." He nodded toward the file in her hand. "What else you got in there?"

"It's an accounting of receipts and expenses for the diner, but…I don't see how it can possibly be right. According to this, the diner consistently brought in more than five thousand dollars a day. Maybe a large restaurant can do that kind of business, but Pop's Diner doesn't do that kind of volume." She lifted a knowing gaze. "Methinks these are the cooked books you were looking for."

He grinned at her antiquated language. "Methinks so, too."

Annie's smile morphed to a frown, and she scowled as she turned her gaze to the locker. "I don't know, Jonah. This all seems…too easy. You've been working this case for months, making only baby steps of progress—"

"Well, that was intentional. Hard as it was to sit back while the investigation inched along, I didn't want to send up any red flags, either. I took baby steps in order to gain Farrout's trust. I wanted to fit in at the diner before I approached him. Impatience can blow an investigation."

Jonah studied the way the harsh fluorescent lights of the bus depot danced over the soft curves of Annie's face. He needed the same kind of patience with her. He had to take baby steps until he'd earned her trust. Annie was worth waiting for.

On the heels of that thought, a chill unrelated to the hyper-cold air-conditioning skimmed up his back. What business did he have harboring any ideas of a future with Annie? And if he didn't intend to hang around and be part of her ready-made family, he had no right to give her any misleading cues, either. The absolute last thing he wanted to do was hurt Annie.

Annie propped a hand on her hip and shook her head. "What I mean by too easy is, it's as if Hardin had packaged all this information together, building a case against the people involved. It's all here, laid out with everything except the bow on top."

Jonah refocused his thoughts, considering Annie's point.

"True. So maybe he was about to turn it all over to the cops. Maybe that's why he was killed."

"Or maybe this is all a setup. Maybe none of this information is real, and if we take this to the authorities, we expose ourselves to the higher-ups in the operation without having anything that will actually stick."

Jonah clenched his teeth and made two decisions. "Regardless of what all this means, I know two things. First and most important, you're out. I don't want you connected to any of this if it should blow up in my face."

"But—"

He held up a hand, cutting her off. "Second, we won't decide anything here and now. I need time to study these files and put all the pieces together."

She closed the file in her hands and handed it back. "I can still be of help to you. Let me go over these records with you."

Jonah started shoving the contents of the locker into the gym bag and shook his head. "I've already involved you more than I should have."

She put a hand on his, and his heart fisted when he met her pleading gaze.

"I need to do this, Jonah. I need to feel I'm doing something to make my life better, safer. For too long, I've drifted along letting life happen to me and suffering because I gave others too much control over my life. Please don't ask me to sit on my hands now. I am involved whether I like it or not."

He drew a slow breath, his respect for Annie blossoming inside him. He grazed his fingers along her chin. "I appreciate what you're saying. I understand and applaud you for wanting to change your life. But if I allowed you to get mired deeper in this muck…"

"I'd still be in danger, through no fault of yours." Turmoil swirled in the depths of her dark eyes, landing a sucker punch to his gut.

Before he could counter her argument, she glanced at her watch and bit her bottom lip. "Which reminds me…I want to go to that self-defense class at the police station that you mentioned. It starts in thirty minutes. Can you drop me off?"

Jonah nodded, relieved to hear she was taking her personal safety seriously. "Of course."

Studying the rest of the locker's contents would keep until that evening. Making sure Annie stayed safe was his top priority, and the class was, for the time being, the best means to that end.

Besides, he was headed to that class himself—though he decided it was best that Annie not know of his role.

Chapter 12

Jonah let Annie out at the door to the gymnasium housed at the back of the Lagniappe Police Department. A hollow ache filled her as she waved goodbye to him and watched him drive down the block and out of sight. She'd see him again soon enough. At the diner tomorrow, if nothing else. So why did parting from him cause this bittersweet emptiness inside her?

She wasn't falling for him. She couldn't be growing attached to a man at this delicate crossroad in her life. She'd only been free of Walt a little more than a year. Too soon to give her heart again. But since when did love follow any prescribed schedule?

She barked a harsh laugh as she turned from the street. Love? Now she was really rushing things. Jonah was a friend. Nothing more.

With a cleansing breath, she faced the large brick building that housed the city police department. The name they'd found on Hardin's file flashed in her mind. Joseph Nance. *Detective* Nance.

If she marched inside the station now and found Detective

Nance, told him everything she knew, could this whole frightening scenario finally be over?

Or would she create an even bigger nightmare for Jonah?

"Impatience can blow an investigation."

She owed it to Jonah to do things his way. She trusted him to figure out the whos and whats of the criminal activity at the diner in his own time.

Warmth flooded her veins as she turned that truth over in her head again. She trusted Jonah. No small feat.

The class had already gathered around a set of floor mats in the center of the gym. She hesitated, remembering how intimidating the private lessons with Jonah had been. Even knowing he wouldn't truly hurt her, his strength and sheer masculinity had resurrected so many vivid memories of Walt's power over her.

Annie was having second thoughts about joining the class when the instructor spotted her lurking by the door and waved her in. "Hi! You're not late. We're waiting for our practice aggressor to arrive. Please have a seat."

Taking a deep breath for courage, Annie walked toward the mats.

"I'm Jan, the instructor, and you are...?"

"Annie."

"Welcome, Annie." Jan flashed a warm smile. "Feel free to join in or just watch today. Whatever you feel comfortable with."

Annie sat cross-legged on the floor next to the other women and pressed a hand to her jittery stomach. As much as she wanted to leave, wanted to crawl into a safe cave somewhere and pretend Hardin hadn't been murdered, she hadn't been mugged and she hadn't divorced or ever been married to Walt in the first place, wishing didn't make those things true. *"Do it for your kids."*

She only had to think of the years she'd let Walt intimidate and hurt her, think of any man doing the same to Haley, to know she had to do something now to turn her life around. She wanted to pass on strength and courage to her daughter, not a legacy of fear and doubt. Putting Haley's innocent face front and center in her mind's eye, Annie raised her gaze to the instructor and squared her shoulders.

"Remember, you *can* protect yourself, and you have a right to protect yourself. Your job is to convey those ideas to your attacker. Frankly, most aggressors are looking for an easy target. If you send him the message that you won't go down easily, that you know how to defend yourself and are willing to hurt him to protect yourself, there's a good chance he'll back off and look for an easier target." The instructor paused when the locker-room door creaked open. "Ah, here's Joe now." To Annie, Jan said, "That's what we call the volunteer in the suit. Generic Joe. Mr. Any Man."

A man, decked from head to foot in a heavily padded suit, lumbered into gymnasium. With a slow, stiff gait, impeded by the bulky pads, he approached the mats where the class had gathered.

None of the other women seemed daunted by his hulking appearance, but Annie couldn't help shifting uneasily. The man's face was completely hidden, the bulky suit and shielded helmet conjuring images of masked horror movie monsters. She had the prickly sense that the man's attention was focused on her as he took his place in the center of the mats. Digging deep in her floundering willpower, she fought the urge to flee from the room.

The woman beside Annie offered to be the first to practice the defensive moves the instructor demonstrated. Annie watched in fascination as the petite woman shouted at the padded man, commanding him with a forceful tone, "Stop! Get back!"

The demonstration continued with the diminutive woman striking the pretend attacker's face mask with an upward arc of her palm, then following with a knee to the groin and a sharp kick to his kneecap. The women applauded as the man lifted a hand and hobbled back. The class continued in this way for the remainder of the hour.

As the instructor gave final instructions and dismissed them, Annie glanced around the circle again, her outlook buoyed by the positive mood of the other women. The support and encouragement they gave each other fed the constructive energy of the class.

Other than Ginny, Annie hadn't had a network of friends or support for a long time. The idea of these women becoming a base of encouragement and help appealed to her. Maybe they could understand the struggle she faced, the seemingly insurmountable odds. Jan touched Annie on the arm as the group scattered and "Joe" clomped back toward the locker room. "Thanks for coming, Annie. I hope you learned something and that you'll come back."

She nodded. Though the class had seemed intimidating at first, she'd gained a new perspective as she watched the other women.

Annie grabbed her purse and headed outside. What a day! Her thoughts drifted to the cooked financial records they'd found in Hardin's locker, and her heart pattered with a combination of hope and trepidation. Having that proof of illegal activity put her and Jonah in an even more dangerous position. But Jonah's investigation took a huge step forward. The sooner he resolved the case and the people responsible for Hardin's murder were caught, the sooner she'd be safe and could move on with her life.

Finding that evidence, taking the self-defense class… Annie inhaled deeply and let a warm tingle of satisfaction and accomplishment flow through her. They were baby steps perhaps, but any forward progress was better than wallowing in the mire her life had become. Taking back control in her life rather than drifting along at the mercy of the pervading winds felt good.

Hadn't there been a time in her life when she'd met daily challenges with a zest for life, when she'd felt confident and capable and ready to leave her mark in the world?

Yes—before her world had narrowed to the handsome Special Forces soldier who'd married her as he left for overseas duty—and returned a different man.

The hiss of hydraulics and squeak of brakes called her attention to the bus arriving at the stop across the street. Her bus. Shaking off memories of Walt, she clutched her purse to her chest and jogged to the corner. With a quick glance left and right, she checked for oncoming traffic and stepped out into the street.

Suddenly, tires squealed.

A man shouted, "Annie!"

From the edge of her vision, a blur of steel and dark glass streaked toward her.

A wall of muscle plowed into her from behind.

Asphalt bit her hands, her knees.

A crushing weight landed on her, knocking the breath from her lungs.

The same weight wrapped around her, rolling her aside as a car raced past her head, missing her by inches.

Adrenaline spiked through her blood, and a violent tremor shook her. Trapped by the dearth of oxygen in her lungs, a scream lodged in her throat.

"Annie! Are you all right?" Large hands roamed over her face and arms.

She blinked, struggled to draw in air. Jonah?

Her heartbeat staggered as his rough-hewn features swam into focus above her.

"Honey, answer me! Are you hurt?"

Her joints ached. Her palms and knees stung. Her head buzzed numbly.

"No," she rasped.

Jonah examined her bloodied hands and swore under his breath.

"Wh-what are y-you doing here?"

He steadied her with a hand under her arm as he helped her to her feet. "I intended to give you a ride home from the class. I had a hunch they might try something like this." He sighed and glanced around at the people who gawked at them from the sidewalk. "Although I didn't think they'd make their move in such a public place."

She stumbled numbly beside him out of the path of traffic. Slowly the buzz of terror that filled her ears faded, allowing his words to sink in. She jerked her head toward him and drilled him with a dubious stare. "You think that was deliberate? That that car was trying to run me over?"

His mouth pressed in a taut line, his jaw stiff. "They pulled out from the curb the second you stepped into the street, gunned the engine and drove straight at you. Seems pretty conclusive."

A chill washed through Annie as she felt the tingle of blood draining from her face. She looked down the street, not certain what she was searching for. "Well, maybe they just didn't see me…or maybe…"

"Annie, they didn't stop." He put one hand on each of her shoulders and met her eyes evenly.

A fierce quaking started deep inside her, working outward in concentric waves of terror. She knew what he would say before he said it, but hearing the words, acknowledging the truth, made the event all the more frightening.

"Honey, this was no accident. They tried to kill you."

Chapter 13

Jonah kept a close eye on Annie as he drove her back to her apartment. For someone who'd almost been killed, she seemed too calm. He worried that her reserve meant she was in shock, though when asked direct questions, she gave coherent answers.

Her hand trembled when she raised it to brush her hair from her eyes, and her pale complexion told him she wasn't totally unaffected by the near-miss with the speeding car.

But when he thought about her past, all the tragedy and trauma she'd survived, a new concern presented itself to him. After Hardin had been murdered, she'd shown surprising composure and detachment also. Maybe Annie was suppressing her reaction, bottling up her emotions as she'd learned to do in her marriage. If so, she was a ticking bomb. How much trauma could she handle before she broke?

She gave her children a brave smile when they rushed to greet her in her kitchen. Haley held a fat cat in her arms, though Annie seemed to barely notice. She hugged both of the kids at the same time and held on to them even when they wiggled for release.

Finally Haley and the cat fought free of Annie's embrace. "Mommy, can Fuzzy sleep with me tonight?"

Annie blinked at her daughter and stared at the cat as if just seeing it for the first time. "What's that cat doing in here?"

"I let him come in to play. I named him Fuzzy. Can he stay in my room tonight?"

Annie drew a slow careful breath. She seemed so tired and disoriented, Jonah stepped closer, in case she toppled.

Smoothing a hand over her forehead and into her hair, Annie shook her head. "Baby, that's the Smiths' cat. You can't keep him. The Smiths would miss him too much."

"But, Mo-om—"

Jonah intervened when the whining started. He took the cat from Annie's daughter and carried it to the door. "Maybe you can play with Fuzzy again tomorrow. Right now he has to go home for dinner. Okay?"

The cat scooted out the opened door and trotted away.

Haley glared at him, her lower lip poked out in full pout mode. "When can I have a cat, Mommy?"

The tortured, world-weary look in Annie's eyes when she glanced at her daughter shredded Jonah's heart. She rubbed her temple with her fingertips. "Someday, sweetie."

Rani strolled in from the next room, her arms full of toys. "Sorry about the cat. I didn't think it would hurt for her to play with him inside for a little while. Then she started talking about keeping him and—" The babysitter winced. "My bad."

Annie shook her head. "It's okay." She hesitated, still looking dazed. "Have the kids eaten dinner?"

"Yes, ma'am. And Ben's had his bath. I was just putting the toys away when you arrived."

Thanking the babysitter, Annie showed her out before sending Haley off to get ready for bed. Her worried eyes met his then, and she tipped her head. "Will the couch be all right for you?"

Jonah lifted an eyebrow. "Pardon?"

"You were going to sleep in your truck and watch my apartment again like the other night, weren't you?"

"You saw me?"

She nodded. "Rather than try to dissuade you from your guard duty, I figured I'd offer you a more comfortable post. I'm not sure I want to be alone tonight."

A tender ache swelled in Jonah's chest. Annie looked so fragile, so near breaking, and the powerful urge to pull her into his arms, kiss away any fear or doubt that weighed her down nearly suffocated him. "The sofa is fine."

She gave a quiet, stoic nod. "I'll get you a pillow and blanket."

She disappeared down the hall, and Jonah sighed his frustration. He hated the resignation that shadowed her gaze. She needed to tap the fiery, fighting spirit he'd seen before, the determination that blazed in her eyes when she talked of protecting her children. Annie needed to approach her own safety and happiness with the same moxie. Through the screened helmet of his "generic Joe" suit, he'd noted her withdrawn and dubious body language at the self-defense class.

Not that he expected her to overcome years of intimidation from her marriage in one session, but so much of her healing and her progress in the class would depend on her attitude. The attempt on her life had clearly rattled her, shaken what confidence she had. She was teetering on the edge of giving up. He couldn't let her retreat into that cave of defeat. His gut told him Annie had a vibrant, core strength. He needed to find a way to revive her hope, fan the fire inside her and give her the courage to fight back.

The desire that Michael had lost. The hope that had been snuffed out in him by the bastards who swindled him.

The hot burn of acid bit his stomach, and he gritted his teeth. He wouldn't let Farrout and his men, or whoever the hell was involved with the attempt on Annie's life, rob Annie of her will to rebuild her life.

Focus, Annie scolded herself for the umpteenth time that day as she let her thoughts drift to the dark car that had hurtled toward her yesterday. She'd already mixed up three special orders thanks to her drifting attention. But every time a car horn blasted on the street outside, or the distant whine of a siren sounded over the murmur of the lunch crowd, her mind jumped back to the instant terror, the jolting realization that someone had tried to run her over.

And the heady rush of warmth and security when Jonah had scooped her into his protective arms.

Stop it. She gave her head a brisk shake to clear the images of Jonah's long legs and broad shoulders curled uncomfortably on her sofa this morning.

"I need two cheeseburgers, well done, hold the onions please." She slapped the order slip under a clip on the order wheel and started scooping ice into glasses for tea. Had they said sweet or unsweet tea?

Damn it. She had to get her mind back on work. She couldn't give Farrout any reason to fire her now. She filled the glasses with sweet tea, going with the odds. Most Southerners took their iced tea sweet. As she carried the drinks out to the customers, she glanced to the front door, waiting to see Jonah arrive.

He'd left her apartment before sunrise, making himself scarce before her kids got up, then waited in his truck to drive her to work. He'd dropped her off just before the breakfast rush, and after promising he'd stop by for lunch, he'd kissed her scarred cheek.

The memory made her pulse stumble. What would it be like to kiss him? Not a chaste, sweet kiss like he'd startled her with after Hardin's murder, but the kind of long, deep, soul-shaking kisses lovers shared. What would it have been like to lie down beside him on her narrow couch, nestle herself in the crook of his body and let him hold her in his arms?

She huffed, irritated by the track of her thoughts. She had no business considering such intimacies with Jonah. Wasn't it bad enough that she'd grown so dependent on him that she didn't feel safe in her apartment without him sleeping on her couch? She couldn't add a physical relationship to the mix, couldn't complicate a relationship that already confused her.

Annie wiped her damp palms on her apron and sent another glance to the front door as a new customer strolled in.

Not Jonah. She squashed the pluck of disappointment and took the bill slip and cash the man at the next table handed her as she walked past.

"Keep the change."

"Thank you, sir." She mustered a smile for her customer and headed back to the counter to ring up the sale. The mundane task was not enough to keep her head from straying back to the question, What was happening between her and Jonah?

The shared attraction was obvious. The common goal of rooting out and stopping the people threatening her life and running the money laundering at the diner was a given. But what about after that threat had been eliminated? Assuming they could find the people involved and stop them before—

"How was your class yesterday?" Susan asked, hustling in from the dining room with a tray full of dirty dishes.

Annie took a moment to focus her train of thought. "My class?"

"Yeah. When you asked me to cover your afternoon hours, you said you had some kind of class."

"Oh, right. It was…fine."

Susan tipped her head and grinned. "Fine? That's all you can say? You sound like my kid. How was school? *Fine.* How'd you do on your math test? *Fine.*"

Annie dropped the change from the man's ticket into the community tip jar. "Okay, it was…intimidating at first since it was my first time going. But I guess I learned a little bit."

Susan grunted. "Better. So…what the heck kind of class are you taking down at the police station anyway?"

Annie shrugged, hoping to minimize the truth. "Self-defense. So, was the dinner hour busy last night?"

She prayed her change of topic would steer Susan away from questions about why Annie felt the need to defend herself or other queries of a personal nature. The less her coworkers knew about her private life, the better, as far as she was concerned. Especially when it came to her relationship with Jonah. If someone connected the two of them—

"Howdy, ladies."

Annie's head snapped up at the sound of the familiar baritone voice. As if her thoughts had conjured him, Jonah took a seat at the counter, dividing a smile between her and Susan. A thrill of pleasure spun through Annie, though she worked to hide her reaction. Curling her fingers into her apron, Annie bunched the material in her hand and gave Jonah a quick nod of acknowledgment.

"Order up!"

Annie rushed to the kitchen window and took down the plates waiting for her. Balancing the plates, two in her hands and two on her arms, she cast a furtive glance toward Jonah as she headed out to the dining room.

The heat and intimacy in the hooded glance he returned almost made her trip.

Oh, Lord, she was in trouble. How did she fight the powerful magnetic pull she felt toward him?

Jonah hadn't had an opportunity to speak privately with Annie before he left the diner after lunch. He'd spent the better part of the morning going over the files they'd retrieved from Hardin's locker at the bus depot. Based on the organization of the files, the specificity of the incriminating information in the documents and the detective's name at the top of one of the most recent printouts, Jonah was convinced Hardin was working with Detective Nance to expose the money laundering. Whether as part of a plea arrangement, as revenge against the other parties in the criminal operation or out of some civic-minded sense of duty, Jonah had yet to determine. Hardin could have had any number of motivations for helping the Lagniappe police detective gather evidence, and dead men couldn't explain themselves.

Which gave a new light to Hardin's murder. Perhaps the manager's death was less about the stolen package and missing money than it was about silencing an informant.

Had the higher-ups in the gambling and money-laundering ring suspected Hardin's betrayal?

Jonah rubbed his temple, pondering all the new angles, as he parked behind the police station and headed in the back entrance to the gymnasium. In the men's locker room, he began dressing in the bulky gear he wore for the self-defense class and wondered if Annie would show up.

Given twenty-four hours to assess her situation, had the attempt on her life yesterday fired her resolve to take back control of her life or had it scared her into retreat?

She'd all but ignored him at the diner today. Probably a smart idea. They were already risking a lot spending as much time together away from the diner as they did. Anyone could see them together on the street or outside her apartment.

Jonah bit the inside of his cheek as he mulled that point. While he didn't want Annie and her kids alone in her apartment until he'd neutralized the threat against her, he couldn't risk jeopardizing the investigation, either.

He'd have to devise a way to be more discreet about his arrival and departure from Annie's home. Just in case her apartment was being watched.

After donning his protective gear, Jonah lumbered out to the padded mats where the women waited. He was relieved to see Annie sitting with the other ladies. Soon he needed to tell her the role he played in the class. Somehow keeping his identity secret felt like lying to her. But he hadn't wanted to scare her away from the classes.

Jan acknowledged him and turned to the women. "Who wants to go first?"

Jonah glanced at Annie. She stared at the floor, but her body was stiff, her hands balled. Suddenly, she surged to her feet.

"I will." Her voice was strong, yet Jonah heard the warble of nerves.

Pride swelled in his chest for her courage, her willingness to defeat the doubts and move forward.

Annie stepped forward, squared her shoulders and lifted her chin, but Jonah saw the shadows of trepidation darkening her eyes.

Come on, honey. You can do this.

"All right, Annie. Joe is going to be a kidnapper in a parking lot. It's night, and he approaches you as you are walking to your car. What do you do first?"

Annie took a deep breath. "Warn him away."

Jan nodded. "Right. Do that."

Jonah moved toward Annie, taking an aggressive stance.

He saw the panic flare in her eyes. "No. Stop. Get back," she said in a raised voice but without any real command.

Jonah kept coming.

"Louder, Annie. Say it like you mean it," Jan coached.

Raising her hand, Annie stumbled back. "Stop!"

Nervous energy quivered in her voice.

Jan glanced at Jonah and waved him away. "Let's try it again. Annie, put more force behind your words. Your tone has to tell him you will *not* be his victim. Stop!" Jan barked the word and several ladies, including Annie, flinched, startled by her shout. "Get back!" Jan tipped her head. "See the difference?"

Annie nodded, and Jan waved Jonah forward again.

He moved faster this time, growling as he lunged forward.

Annie gasped and threw her hand up. "Stop! Get back!"

Jan smiled and clapped. "Much better!"

Jonah lumbered back, keeping an eye on Annie's reaction.

She opened and closed her hands, then wiped her palms on her uniform skirt.

"Okay, now suppose he doesn't stop. I want you to fight him off with anything and everything you've learned here. Don't hold back." Jan gave a nod to him, and Jonah sucked in a deep breath before closing in on Annie again. Bracing. Hoping.

Come on, Annie. Let me have it.

Raising wide, apprehensive eyes, Annie backpedaled. When he grabbed her arm, hauling her into a restrictive hold, she gasped, tensed.

"Fight back, Annie. Joe won't hurt you, but a real attacker would. You can't be afraid to inflict some damage yourself."

Annie struggled some, tried a puny jab or two with her elbows. Jonah tightened his grip and stumbled back a step with her, simulating a kidnapping. "Get in the car," he grated in a low voice.

Annie's breathing grew ragged, fast. She was hyperventilating.

Without waiting for Jan's directive, Jonah released Annie.

After giving Jonah a quizzical look, Jan noticed Annie's irregular breathing.

"Annie, are you okay? Calm down. You're safe here. This is just practice, remember. Do you want to sit down and rest a minute while someone else tries?"

Clutching a hand to her chest, Annie shook her head and fought to slow her breathing. "No. I—I have to try again."

A mix of concern and admiration swirled in Jonah's gut. He understood her motivation, knew the need that drove her. But the fear that brightened her eyes made her seem fragile, ready to break.

"You're sure?" Jan asked.

Lifting her chin and inhaling deeply, she nodded. "Just…give me a second. I…" She shook out her hands and closed her eyes, clearly drawing on her inner strength.

A few members of the class clapped and shouted encouragement. "You can do it."

"Go get 'em, girl."

"Hang in there."

When she opened her eyes and faced him, Jonah saw the same doubts and hesitation. The fear.

And he knew he had to do something. He had to make her dig deep into the well of her buried emotions, had to remind her of what was at stake, had to help her past the hurdle of intimidation her husband had heaped on her.

His heart hurt, even as he did what he knew would galvanize her.

"What's the matter, bitch? Didn't your old man ever teach you your place?" he growled from behind the protective mask.

Annie's head snapped up, alarm blanching her face.

"Your kids are gonna grow up without a mommy, 'cause I'm gonna kill you," he taunted in a dark growl, hating the pain he knew his barbs caused while praying his tactic worked.

From the periphery of his vision, he caught the stunned, querying glance Jan sent him. He was out of line, breaking protocol.

But he didn't care. Only Annie mattered. She needed to get past her anxiety, and anger was the best way he knew to trump fear. He tapped into her protective rage. The fury of the injustice done to her. The hostility toward her husband that she'd suppressed for years.

The women watching murmured to one another with expressions of dismay and disgust. Annie gaped at him, quivering, her cheeks flushing, her eyes full of confusion, hurt and horror.

Pain squeezed his chest as he stepped closer and stuck his helmeted face close to hers, grating, "Are you going to let your husband win? Are you going to let fear win? As long as you listen to the doubts he put in your head, you give him power. If you want a better life for yourself and your kids, then prove it."

Tears sparkled in her dark eyes. But he'd reached her. He saw the instant his message penetrated her fear. Like a light switch flipping on the power to her private reserve of energy and guts, Annie's gaze lit with passion and determination. Her posture shifted. Her muscles tensed. Her expression filled with raw emotion and fire.

"Now hit me, Annie. Fight for your life, damn it. You deserve to live, and you deserve a good life. Now show me you care. Show me you want to be free of your past."

Jonah grabbed her around the waist, and she reacted instantly, landing a swift knee to his groin. The blow had power behind it, strength and anger.

Thank God for the protective pads.

"That's it, Annie. Fight back. Don't give him an inch," Jan coached.

Jonah made another move to subdue Annie, and she swung

her hand up toward the face mask, demonstrating a nose strike. Jonah's head snapped back from the unexpected force of the blow. The class cheered.

"Great job," Jan said. "Who wants to be next?"

He shook off the hit and turned toward Annie. Despite Jan's dismissal, Annie clearly wasn't finished with him. She had a lethal glare narrowed on him, and she charged. Again she lashed out with a nose strike, then a strike to his throat.

"Annie?" Jan called to her, concern lacing her tone.

Annie didn't seem to hear. Jonah recognized the intent, the emotion blazing in her eyes. She'd tapped a wellspring of poisonous memories, and the flow of bitter emotion had rushed to the surface.

He held a hand up, stopping Jan when she tried to approach Annie and calm her. Self-defense techniques dissolved into a flurry of unbridled frustration and hurt and anger. Tears streamed down her cheeks as she swung at him, pounding him with tightly clenched fists. Annie's grunts of exertion and emotion as she pummeled his protective suit ripped through Jonah's gut. This catharsis was good for her, he told himself, even as his heart broke seeing her unleash her temper, her suppressed bitterness and sense of helplessness.

After several minutes, when Annie's rage hadn't cooled, the first whispers of doubt crept in. What had worked for him when Michael had goaded him to release his bottled-up anger in the gym might not have been the best approach for Annie. Who was he to tell her how to heal?

His heart thundered, and worry wrenched his chest as her meltdown continued. She seemed to have blocked out all but the target of her flailing fists and feet. Teeth gritted, Annie sobbed and snarled and lashed at his chest. Even through the protective suit the force of her blows reverberated through him.

"Jonah, stop her. She's going to hurt herself," Jan called to him over the buzz of the stunned women who watched.

"Annie, that's enough." He tried to catch her swinging hands, but the protective suit made him awkward.

"You animal! How could you do this to me?" she screamed, her eyes unfocused. He hated to think what horrible beating, what demeaning taunts she was reliving. Seeing her anguish clogged Jonah's throat with regret and sympathy. Shared pain.

His hand came away with a smear of red on his palm. Blood. Annie's blood.

She'd opened wounds on her knuckles from the force and frequency of her strikes to the padded suit, but she seemed oblivious to the condition of her hands.

Guilt swelled in Jonah. He'd provoked her, he'd goaded her into this rage. He had to do something to stop her, had to talk her down somehow and be there for the aftershock.

Chapter 14

"Annie, stop! It's over!" Jonah yanked the face mask off, so he could see more clearly. So she could see his face and know who was with her. So he could claim responsibility for his part in her breakdown.

He wouldn't hide from his part in this.

Her lashes kept coming, though she seemed to be running out of steam.

Around them, he was aware that Jan had dismissed the class and ushered the other ladies out of the gym.

Following her violent outburst, her uncontrolled sobs, Annie gasped for breath. Her final swings were devoid of energy.

"Annie! Annie, listen to me. I'm here. You're safe. It's over." He gently swiped a tear from her cheek. "It's over, honey."

Stiffening, she jerked her gaze up, blinked at him. Confusion muddied her expression.

He peeled open the top Velcro fastenings of the padded armor and shucked his arms out so that the pads hung from his waist.

Sweat plastered his T-shirt to his chest, but, free of the suit, he could at least breathe easier, move without so much bulk.

"Annie? Are you with me? Are you okay?"

Her breathing was still ragged, and her eyes flashed with turbulent emotions.

Jan crossed from the gym door where she'd seen the class out. She brought an ice pack and a clean rag with her, both of which she handed to Jonah. "Want me to stay, to talk to her?"

He shook his head. "No. I'll take her home when she's ready. Go on."

"You're gonna be okay, friend." Jan squeezed Annie's shoulder, and Annie flinched.

Jonah extended a hand, unsure how he'd be received. "Come 'ere, honey. You're safe now. Take a deep breath."

Slowly Annie's surroundings sharpened into focus through her tears.

The gymnasium at the police station. The self-defense class. But everyone else was gone. She was alone with "Generic Joe."

She gave her head a clearing shake. The memories had seemed so fresh, so real.

But Walt wasn't there.

Jonah was.

She narrowed her gaze on him, wondering if he was another illusion.

Jonah was Joe? He'd been the one taunting her, egging her on to vent her rage?

She rubbed her arms. The air-conditioning blowing on her perspiration-damp body left a chill on her skin. Or maybe the iciness came from the remnants of her flashback, the wake of her tantrum.

She'd really lost it. Snapped. The anger, once she'd allowed it to sneak to the surface, had almost consumed her.

Annie shivered, stunned by the power of the fury and loathing that had washed through her. Fresh tears puddled in her eyes. Would she ever feel normal again? Would Walt always taint her life, even from behind bars? Could she ever heal the deep emotional scars he'd gouged in her soul?

"Annie?"

She raised her gaze to Jonah, who studied her with a dark veil of concern shading his expression. A prick of embarrassment jabbed her. What must he think of her after witnessing her meltdown?

She sniffed and wiped the wet tracks from her face. "Sorry, I—"

"Don't you dare apologize." His voice trembled, and she'd have sworn he had tears in his eyes. He stretched his hand toward hers, then gently wrapped his hand around her aching fingers. "Gimme…"

He placed an ice pack on her knuckles, and she winced when she saw the raw scrapes. She felt equally chafed and bleeding inside. Shaken.

Her legs buckled, and she no longer had the strength to stay on her feet. With a weary sigh, she crumpled to her knees. Her shoulders sagged, and she stared at the reddened knuckles in disbelief. The hot well of tears, nudged by shame and frustration, tainted with the bitterness of her marriage to Walt, flowed down her cheeks as she quietly sobbed. She'd gotten good in days past at crying without making any noise. So her children didn't hear her. So Walt wouldn't know, wouldn't make an issue of it.

Jonah sank down on the mats beside her. When he tugged her closer, she didn't have the energy, the willpower to refuse.

Besides, collapsing against the solid strength of his chest, resting in the embrace of his arms held great appeal. He scooted awkwardly closer, the protective Joe suit impeding him somewhat.

Laying her head against his chest, she listened to the drumming of his heart, steady and soothing. Her fingers curled into his damp T-shirt, while his hands rubbed her back the way she calmed Haley after a bad dream.

Annie closed her eyes, inhaling the musky, masculine scent of his overheated skin, tinged with sandalwood and spice. His fingers combed through her hair and stroked her cheek. Every gentle touch and comforting caress lulled her deeper into a time and place where only the two of them existed.

Her tears slowed as she slowly gained her composure. But as the adrenaline and tension that had fueled her tantrum waned, she found a different source for the rapid beating of her heart, the heady swirl of desire that hummed inside her.

After losing herself to her emotions, scaring herself with how easily she'd lost control, Jonah's embrace was a safe haven. Had she really found this gentle man intimidating before?

His fingers worked their magic, massaging the tension and tightness from her neck muscles, and she relaxed against him. Wrapping her arms around his chest, she clung to his solid strength like a life raft in a turbulent sea.

The last thing she wanted was to fall back into a position of need, dependency and defeatism that had trapped her in her unhappy marriage. Yet in Jonah's arms, though she leaned on him now for physical and emotional support, she didn't feel needy or weak. Jonah gave her peace of mind, encouragement, the affection of friendship.

Or was it more than friendship with Jonah?

She pushed aside the ugly dregs of her flashbacks of Walt's abuse, of Hardin's murder, of the attempt on her life, and she concentrated on more pleasant memories. The soft kiss Jonah had surprised her with the day Hardin had been killed. The warmth in his eyes when he'd met her children. The sweet quiver of expectation that rippled through her when he'd lock his penetrating green eyes on her. His gaze said he could see straight through her, knew her darkest secrets and blackest fears...but accepted all her flaws without reservation.

"Better?" he murmured.

She nodded. *Much. Thanks to you.*

He shifted slightly, and she realized how long she'd subjected him to a rather awkward position, huddled on the dusty floor mats.

Though her anguish had faded, she wasn't ready to leave the comfort and sweet refuge of Jonah's arms, his warm touch.

Unwise though it might be to get involved with another man when her life was in such disarray, she wanted to cherish these few moments alone with him. She wanted to block out the reality of cars trying to mow her down. She needed to forget for a moment the vortex sucking her into the shadow of illegal activity at the diner, and the specter of finding her boss murdered.

"Annie," Jonah said, breaking the still silence. "Forgive me. I shouldn't have pushed so hard, sweetheart. I'm sorry."

His voice cracked, and she tipped her chin back to meet his gaze. The sorrow and compassion she found staring back at her arrowed deep, warming her from the inside out.

"The things you said—"

"Were awful," he interrupted, regret darkening his eyes. "Hurtful. I'm so sorry. I was just trying to get you mad enough to get past your fear and hesitation."

She lifted a corner of her mouth in a melancholy grin. "It worked."

"Too well. I shouldn't have—"

"I'm glad you did. Maybe this was what I needed. You said boxing, working out on the punching bags was cathartic for you."

"But we're all different. Maybe you just needed to leave the baggage in the past and move on. Maybe I did more harm than good. Annie, I never want to hurt you or cause you more pain."

How could the words *hurt* and *pain* ever be associated with Jonah? She'd never met a man so kind and gentle, so understanding and generous. But his comment made her think, made her dig deep for her own understanding of what it would take for her to feel safe again. When would she feel her life was her own again?

Haley and Ben sprang immediately to mind. Everything she did was for her children, their happiness, their future.

"When I know my children are safe, when I can know they're provided for and will grow up healthy and happy—" She peered up at Jonah. "That's all I want."

A deep crease puckered his forehead. "And what about you? What about your happiness?"

She lifted a shoulder in a tired shrug. "Maybe someday…"

Jonah gripped her chin, and his fierce gaze drilled into hers. "Annie, listen to me. You deserve to be happy every bit as much as your children do. You deserve to seize happiness with both hands and hold on to it. It is your right."

The passion in his tone and intensity of his magnetic gaze burrowed deep inside her, shook her to her core. "I—I know."

"Do you?"

The air in her lungs stilled. Could she really find the joy for life she'd had when she was younger? She wanted desperately to reclaim the hope and promise, the simple pleasure life offered.

"Promise me you will go after whatever it is you truly want, whatever it is that will make you happy again, Annie." Jonah stroked his fingers through her hair until his palm cradled the back of her head. "Promise me you will fight for your happiness."

Staring into his fathomless eyes, how could she refuse? A fist of bittersweet emotion squeezed her throat. "I promise."

Jonah dipped his head and touched his lips to hers. The warm caress of his lips spun a sweet pleasure through her blood, and she savored a taste of what that happiness might be. She leaned into the kiss, enticed by the tender persuasion of his mouth.

Jonah angled his head and captured her lips more fully, yet his kiss remained infinitely patient, his touch light and careful.

Annie raised a hand to his shoulder to steady herself and curled her fingers into his damp shirt. The tip of his tongue teased the seam of her mouth, and she opened to him. She was shocked to realize the breathy sigh that whispered through the quiet gym was hers. After a moment, she grew impatient with his caution, his restraint.

Hadn't he just made her promise to go after whatever made her happy? For a few precious moments, she wanted to lose herself in Jonah's kiss, in the mind-numbing sensations he stirred and the gentle comfort of his caress. Drawing on the boldness he'd encouraged in her and the assurance that she was safe with this caring man, Annie slid her hand to Jonah's nape and pulled him closer, drawing hard, more deeply on his lips.

A satisfied moan rumbled from his chest, filling Annie with a heady sense of empowerment. She'd taken the initiative, and she had elicited that husky growl of pleasure from him.

Though Jonah matched her intensity, he never pushed her past the limits she set. The quiver of restraint in his muscles told her he'd surrendered the pace to her. That evidence of his control gave her the confidence to sink against him and explore the hard ridges of his muscled back with her fingers while her tongue darted into his mouth, testing, seeking more.

Finally, Jonah laid her back on the floor, covering her with his wide body and pressing her into the mats with his weight, his heat. Annie's heart thrashed against her chest like a trapped animal, her blood rushing past her ears with a deafening whoosh.

He paused long enough to gauge her reaction, his eyes dark with desire, his breath lashing her cheeks with hot, ragged puffs. She answered his unspoken query by raising her mouth to his again and tunneling her fingers into his short, cropped hair.

Jonah raked his palm along her thigh, under the skirt of her waitress uniform. His touch skimmed tantalizingly close to the spot where her body wept for his touch, but his fingers skittered away, raising a delicious shiver on her skin. He moved his hand up along her hip to the dent of her waist, then cupped her breast through the ugly fabric of her uniform. Even with the barrier between them, her nerve endings fired, and her nipple beaded, aching for his touch.

She mewled her approval without breaking their kiss. Jonah had offered her a glimpse of the kind of passion and freedom she'd never had before, and she didn't want to squander any part of it. The press of his body and the heat of his mouth on hers thrilled her, terrified her, tempted her.

Somehow through the dizzying bliss, a tiny voice whispered to her.

What was she doing? How could she give herself to Jonah and not lose her heart, not set herself up for heartache?

Her head spun, and the thrum of pleasure shouted down the voice of caution and doubt in the back of her brain. Here with Jonah, no one was trying to kill her. She didn't have to face her mountain of unpaid bills, and she could escape the memories of the man who'd started her life on this downward spiral.

When Jonah moved his kiss to the fluttering pulse at her throat, Annie drew a shuddering breath.

"Annie," he murmured against her skin. His voice rasped with unspent desire. Jonah raised his head and gulped oxygen. "We have to stop. This is…the wrong time. Wrong place."

His words slashed through the lusty fog she'd lost herself in, and she blinked her surroundings into focus. A ripple of shock shot through her.

Dear God, had she been ready to make love to Jonah in the middle of the police station gymnasium?

Mortified by the total loss of her senses, she bolted upright. The sweet hum of passion fled, doused by the cold wash of reality.

"Annie?" Jonah placed a soothing hand on her arm as she dragged in the stale air of the gym.

Her pulse pounded at her temples. "Yeah…wrong."

With his fingers, he angled her chin toward him. "No, I said wrong time and place." He brushed his thumb along her bottom lip, still swollen from his crushing kiss. "Everything else about kissing you was…nirvana."

The sound of a door closing down the hall echoed through the empty gym. Glancing in the direction of the noise, Jonah shoved to his feet and extended a hand to help her up. "Let me take you home."

She inhaled, searching for the shreds of her composure, then clasped his hand.

Once he'd hauled her to her feet, she hugged herself and rubbed her arms self-consciously.

"Will you be all right for a couple minutes while I put this thing away?" He indicated the padded suit that hung from his waist.

She nodded, and Jonah lumbered off toward the locker room, already ripping open the Velcro enclosures on the protective pants.

While she waited for Jonah, Annie's thoughts traveled a windy, troubled path. Jonah was Joe. That's how he knew of the class. Why he'd recommended it.

And why he'd been close by yesterday when she'd gotten out of class. When the car had tried to run her down. When he'd saved her life.

Are you going to let your husband win? Are you going to let fear win?

She experienced the same bone-chilling dread that had kick-started her breakdown in class. Sometimes fear could be a stronger motivation to act than anger. For her, the idea that Walt could still be controlling her from his prison cell because of his legacy of intimidation frightened her more than anything else. She would do whatever it took to be free of Walt's lingering effect.

"What the heck kind of class do you take at the police station anyway?"

The kind that helped you climb out of the morass of anxiety and self-doubt your ex-husband left you in.

Annie purposefully moved her musings around that mental quicksand. Dwelling on Walt now would only depress her, and she wanted to hold on to the last wisps of cloud nine where she'd drifted briefly with Jonah.

Nirvana, he'd called it. She closed her eyes and tried to recapture the sweetness of those moments, but her mind snagged on another memory instead.

"What the heck kind of class do you take at the police station anyway?"

She frowned as Susan's question replayed in her head.

"Ready to go?" Jonah's voice jarred her from her introspection. "Hey, what's wrong? Why so serious?"

"I never told Susan where my class was. So how did she know?"

Chapter 15

"Are you sure you didn't mention the police station when you asked her to cover your shift?" Jonah asked later in his truck as they drove toward her apartment.

Annie leaned her head back on the seat and closed her eyes. "I don't think so. But maybe. I— No. No, I'm sure I didn't."

Annie's revelation didn't worry him much. Susan struck him as an astute listener, a curious sort of busybody, but not a killer. Still, he wasn't comfortable leaving the loose end unexplained. "Did you tell anyone else where you'd be? Someone else could have told her."

She cut a sharp glance toward him. "Only you."

He arched his dark eyebrow. "I didn't say anything, if that's what you're thinking."

"You asked who I'd told." Sighing her fatigue, Annie raked her fingers through her hair. Jonah's gut tightened remembering the silky feel of her hair twined around his fingers. The soft crush of her lips against his had packed a more powerful punch than he'd have imagined. One small taste of Annie wasn't nearly enough. Her eager response at the gym had rocked him to his core.

Wrong time, wrong place. But someday...

His body thrummed with the expectation, anticipation. He wanted to make slow, sweet love to Annie as much as he'd ever wanted anything in his life.

But she had to make the first move. No way would he push her, pressure her. He'd wait until she was ready if it killed him. Which, judging by the pressure in his jeans, the pounding at his temples and the fine sheen of sweat on his back, might be sooner than later.

Jonah cleared his throat, bringing his attention back to the discussion at hand. "We'll keep an eye on Susan. If you see or hear anything suspicious, let me know. Meantime, be on your toes around her. Okay?"

She nodded, wet her lips. "Will you stay for dinner?"

"If you want me to." He parked on the street a couple of blocks from her apartment, in case her parking lot was being watched. When she didn't answer, he angled his body toward her on the seat, waiting.

Finally she peered up at him through a fringe of dark eyelashes. "I do."

Her gaze clung to his for a breathless moment before her focus shifted to his mouth. Drawing her own lip between her teeth, she inhaled a choppy breath.

"I can't promise much more than cold-cut sandwiches and canned peaches. I need to get groceries, but I have to wait for payday."

When he stroked her chin with a bent finger, he felt the tremble that chased through her, heard the catch in her breath. He knew better than to offer to buy her groceries. A woman searching so fiercely for her independence would see the offer as charity and flatly decline. "A sandwich sounds fine. But if you'd rather, I could take you and the kids out for a burger somewhere. Or I know an Italian place where the kids could get spaghetti and the manicotti is out of this world."

The expression in her eyes softened. "You sure you want to start dating a mother with two kids? I thought the idea of kids gave most single men cold sweats."

He grinned. "I like your kids."

She climbed out of his truck, and he escorted her through the maze of other buildings in her complex and across the yard behind her apartment.

Getting involved with Annie's family did unnerve him a little, but not for the reasons she might assume. Family was just a concept that carried too much history for him, not enough useful experience to feel confident in that realm.

"If calling it a date bothers you—" He shrugged. "Call it 'I know you're tired, and I thought I'd offer an easy out from cooking.'"

She cocked her head as they made their way to the back entrance to her building.

"Making a sandwich is hardly cooking. And if Ben throws one of his two-year-old tantrums at the restaurant, I doubt you'll still be calling it an easy out."

She had him on that point. He hadn't the faintest idea how to deal with any aspect of parenting young kids. His father was the last model of discipline he'd ever use, and his mother had been withdrawn and all but absent in his life.

Turning up a palm, he said, "Your choice."

She squeezed his hand. "Thank you, but not today. I'm beat, and the kids need to be in bed in an hour or so."

"Another time?"

She poked her door key into the lock and flashed a half grin. "Yeah. Maybe. Someday."

Someday. She'd said the same about when she'd get the cat she wanted. A pluck of disappointment tugged at him. She deserved more than to keep her dreams, her desires on ice while she dealt with life's hard knocks. He hated to think of Annie putting her life on hold, suspending all her happiness until *someday.*

While Annie paid the babysitter and started the sandwiches,

Jonah listened as Haley jabbered excitedly about the DVD Rani had checked out of the library for them to watch. The best he could figure, the movie started as animation, then switched to live action, and involved a prince and a talking chipmunk. Beyond that, he lost track of the girl's convoluted explanation.

"Come on," she begged, tugging his hand. "We can watch it now!"

"Dinner first, Haley," Annie said without missing a beat as she set four places at the table. "Wash your hands. Time to eat."

Haley whined her protest, and Annie visibly tensed. The past few hours, to say nothing of her shift at the diner, had taken their toll on her. A fussy child was the last thing she needed.

He had no notion how a parent normally dealt with cranky complaints, but his instincts told him distraction was a promising option. "Haley, have I shown you my magic trick?"

Forget that he had no real trick. Haley was hooked. Eyes wide, she gaped at him as if he'd hung the moon. "You know magic?"

Annie tipped her head, giving him a curious look.

Jonah scrambled for a plan, making things up as he went. "Sure, but…you need clean hands for this trick. Let's wash up, okay?"

Hands clean, Haley sat down at the table with him, watching expectantly.

Um…

"I can…make this sandwich disappear!" Jonah picked up his sandwich and waved a hand over it.

"Do it! Make it disappear!" Haley squealed, and Ben clapped his hands.

Annie's cheek twitched in amusement.

Jonah ate the sandwich in three large bites.

"Ta-da!" he mumbled around his mouthful of food. He waited for the inevitable look of disgruntled disappointment from Annie's daughter. Instead, she giggled and rolled her eyes.

"That's not magic!"

He chewed some more so he could speak. "It's not?"

"No!" The girl laughed, but she picked up her sandwich and eyed it. "I can make my sandwich disappear, too!"

And she did.

"Thank you," Annie mouthed from across the table.

After dinner, he helped clear the table, then followed Haley to the living room with Ben while Annie finished cleaning the kitchen.

The Disney movie held Haley's rapt attention as Jonah took a seat on the couch. Ben glanced at the television occasionally but was more absorbed in stacking his wooden blocks and knocking the towers down.

After watching the process for a while, Jonah moved to the floor with Ben. Rolling a wooden block in his fingers, Jonah replayed the afternoon's events in his mind.

He prayed Annie's meltdown today had been her needed catharsis. But now she needed a healthy outlet for the future, a safe environment where she could continue the healing process. Ginny would provide some of that counseling and support.

But would that be enough?

Annie was strong, but even the bravest woman needed a soft place to land when the world crashed around her. A soul-deep yearning tugged inside Jonah, twisting, aching. He wanted to be Annie's safe harbor, her confidant, her life partner so much his teeth hurt. But that damn niggling voice that had been whispering to him for weeks now wouldn't be quieted. The uneasy feeling that committing himself to her and her family would be a disaster.

Ben's tiny hand grabbed the block Jonah held, and the brush of those tiny fingers reverberated to his marrow. How could he ask Annie or her children to tie themselves to him when even he had doubts about his ability to be part of their family?

A movement at the edge of his vision told him Annie had come to the living-room door. He glanced up at her and curled up one corner of his mouth. She returned a twitch of a grin, her gaze flicking from one child to the next. A mother hen assuring herself that her chicks were safe.

Haley crawled forward and punched the volume up on the Disney DVD. The cartoon princess who'd landed in real-life New York City had just arrived at a costume ball.

"Bok."

Jonah glanced down at Ben, who held a block out to him. "Yeah. Block. That's good, buddy." He took the offering from the boy's chubby hand and slanted a look toward Annie.

Her attention, like Haley's, was riveted on the television screen as the princess and the handsome New Yorker who'd befriended her swirled around the dance floor. A melancholy ballad played and glittery confetti surrounded the starry-eyed, star-crossed couple.

Jonah sat back, leaning against the sofa, and watched Annie stare at the fairy-tale movie. Tears sparkled in her eyes and wistful longing transformed her expression. His heart slowed, stuttered at the sadness on her face and his new insight.

The woman who'd raged and pummeled her imaginary attacker today until her knuckles bled was a died-in-the-wool romantic at heart. An optimist who'd had her dreams of happily ever after brutally ripped from her.

The desire to put a smile on Annie's face, whatever the cost, slammed into Jonah with a force that stole his breath. If anyone in the world deserved a happily ever after, Annie did. She'd survived so much, been so brave and strong for her children.

He shoved to his feet, his muscles protesting, and pulled the coffee table out of the way. Stepping over to her, he held out his hand. "May I have this dance, pretty lady?"

Annie blinked at him, stunned, then shook her head, swiping jerkily at her damp eyes. "No…Jonah, I can't—"

"Sure you can." He took her hand and tugged her close, despite her startled gasp.

"What are you doing?" She stiffened and gaped at him with wide, dubious eyes.

"Trying to dance, but you're not following my lead." He tugged harder, until she stumbled into his arms. He was a clumsy dancer at best, but he shuffled his feet in a sidestep, and

Annie staggered along with him, still staring at him like he'd lost his mind.

He anchored her slim body closer, so she wouldn't fall as he swept her around in small circles, careful not to trip on Ben's blocks. He wiggled his eyebrows at her. "And I've never darkened the door at an Arthur Murray Dance Studio."

A small awkward laugh snuck from her, and she turned up the corner of her mouth. "I can tell."

He sent her an expression of mock affront. "Hey! I'm not that bad!"

The movie music swelled, and he swooped her around in grander twirls. Annie clung to him to keep her balance, her eyes brightening.

Haley noticed them dancing and jumped up from the floor. She giggled and clapped her hands. "Me, too. I want to dance!"

As her daughter twirled and pirouetted around the floor, Annie's smile grew, and her cheeks flushed. A genuine smile blossomed on her lips, and her face glowed—all the encouragement Jonah needed to continue swirling around the confines of her living room, colliding with Haley. When the little girl tumbled onto her bottom, he broke his hold on Annie long enough to scoop the girl onto his hip.

Haley squealed her delight as the three of them continued to dance and spin. Annie's laughter joined her daughter's giggles, and Jonah's chest filled with a bittersweet pleasure and satisfaction. Annie's smile and lyrical laugh were intoxicating. He'd give anything to know he could make Annie this happy for longer than a few moments of silliness. As he'd suspected, her smile transformed her face from attractive and intriguing to knockout beautiful.

Haley wiggled to be put down again, and he let her slide to the floor without breaking his hold around Annie's waist. Once Haley scampered down the hall, calling something about her princess crown, Annie lifted a grateful smile and a teary gaze to his.

Jonah's heart clenched, and he tucked Annie under his chin as they made another circuit around her small apartment. Like that afternoon, the crush of her petite body against his made his nerve endings crackle and spark. Holding Annie, the sweet scent of her shampoo filling his senses, taunted his libido. He craved her kiss, the touch of her skin against his.

But as they danced, her smile warming him to his core, the hum of his body took a dangerous turn. His heart was involved. Her laughter bubbled inside him like a disinfectant cleansing the poison and pain from his soul.

The music from the DVD slowed, and Annie lifted a heart-breaking gaze that punched Jonah in the gut.

He was in trouble. The mix of emotion filling Annie's damp eyes was much like that of the Disney princess as the dance with her true love ended. Longing and reluctance, gratitude and regret, and—probably the hardest for Jonah to bear—hope.

The last thing he'd wanted to do was build false hopes for Annie. He was no one's prince. He couldn't give her a story-book ending. Dancing with her had been a mistake. Encouraging her romantic notions only set her up for more heartache when he couldn't fulfill her happily ever after.

But, damn it, seeing her smile, knowing he'd made her laugh, giving her even a few moments of happiness after the gut-wrenching day she'd had had been worth it. Hadn't it? Or was it just his own selfish need to feel he'd slayed a dragon for her, given her a few minutes of lighthearted joy when the rest of her world seemed so difficult?

Even after the ballad stopped, Annie stood close to him, her eyes searching his as if they held all the answers to her problems.

His pulse hammered. Big trouble.

When he brushed a hand along her cheek, she trembled and raised her lips. Need slammed him, knocking the breath from him. As much as he wanted to kiss her, he couldn't, *wouldn't* mislead her about his ability to give her a fairy-tale ending. Instead he pressed a kiss to her forehead and stepped back.

A shadow of disappointment, colored with embarrassment, dimmed the spark in her eyes as she stepped out of his arms. Guilt kicked him in the shin.

"Look, Jonah!" Haley pranced back into the living room wearing a plastic tiara. "I have a crown like Giselle's."

Her daughter's arrival provided a welcome distraction, and an excuse to tear himself from the temptation Annie served. He cleared the thickness from his throat. "Hey, princess. Don't you look pretty?"

"Can you dance with me again?" Haley lifted her arms to him.

Annie hugged herself, clearly still fighting an onslaught of emotions. "Haley, I…I think it's your bedtime."

Jonah gritted his teeth, struggling to sort out for himself the shift in his feeling toward Annie. So much had changed today. He'd be wise to leave, to get some distance to clear his head.

Haley pouted, and her shoulders slumped. "But, Mommy—"

"No whining, please."

Jonah tweaked the girl's chin. "Hey, another time. I promise."

Annie avoided his eyes as she stooped to collect Ben's blocks and pile them in a basket. "You, too, Ben. Go get your jammies for me. Haley, brush your teeth."

The kids, with mixed degrees of protest, toddled toward their bedrooms, leaving him alone with Annie. He crouched beside her and helped collect blocks.

"You have a beautiful smile. You should use it more often."

His comment stopped her. Her hand hovered over a block, shaking. Finally, she looked up, and confusion and pain clouded the dark eyes that moments ago had held such joy and hope. "What do you want from me?"

He rocked back on his heels. "Only for you to be happy. And safe."

"Do you see yourself as part of that happiness? Is that why you're here?"

His gut pitched. Why was he here? What was he doing inserting himself in her family dynamic if he had no intention of staying?

"I'm here because you had a rough day, and I wanted to be sure you were all right. I thought you could use a hand with the kids tonight."

And because he knew Farrout and his cohorts still saw her as a threat to be dealt with. She was still in danger.

His answer clearly didn't satisfy her. She frowned as she moved the basket of blocks to a corner of the room, then dropped onto the sofa. "Why do you feel that's your job? I'm not your responsibility. You don't owe me anything. It's not your fault my life is in the pitiful shape it's in."

"Maybe not, but I want to help." He took the seat beside her on the couch and resisted the urge to brush her cheek again. The wary distance that had returned in her eyes told him his touch would be unwelcome.

She picked at a loose thread on the sofa cushion for a moment, then raised a level gaze. "I'm not looking for someone to rescue me. I refuse to depend on anyone ever again." Steely determination colored her tone.

"Especially not a man."

She squared her shoulders and scowled. "I didn't say that."

"You didn't have to." He raised a hand to interrupt when she opened her mouth to protest. "I don't blame you. The men in your life so far gave you reason to be cautious. But I'm not your husband. I'm not Hardin. If you don't want me in your life, I'll leave. But I'm worried about what's going on at the diner and how it could all play out. I want you to be safe, and I want you to know you can trust me."

She stared at him for several long, tense seconds, gnawing her bottom lip. Every one of her conflicting emotions played across her doelike eyes as if he were watching her thoughts on a monitor.

"I'm so scared, Jonah. Not just because of the mess at the diner. I'm scared of the future. When I think about raising those two babies by myself, supporting them with my pathetic paycheck, trying to teach them right from wrong…I feel overwhelmed. Alone. But…" She shivered and rubbed a hand along her arm. "But when I think about getting involved with someone again…oh, God, that scares me the most. I don't want to spend my life alone, but how can I risk…?" She closed her eyes and swallowed hard. "What if they turn out to be like Walt?"

Her honesty grabbed him by the throat, simultaneously spreading warmth through him and chilling him to the bone. While he was flattered that she trusted him enough to reveal her fears, her worries echoed the doubts that had dogged him, haunted him with increasing frequency as his feelings for Annie deepened.

While he'd cut off his own hand before he'd ever raise it against a woman or a child, his memories of family life, the legacy of his own painful youth warned him away whenever he considered marriage. Family. Children.

Despite the drumbeat of caution pounding in his brain, Jonah dragged a hand down his jaw and looked for a way to reassure Annie. He wouldn't lie to her. But he wanted so badly to give her even a morsel of the hope she deserved.

"When the right man comes along, you will have the wisdom and discernment that your experience gives you to know, in your heart, whether he's like Walt or not." The notion of Annie with another man scraped him raw. But if he couldn't give her what she needed, didn't she deserve to be happy with someone else?

Of course. But that didn't make it any easier for him to think of another man touching her, holding her, making love to her.

His gut knotted, and his mouth dried, but he forced the words she needed to hear from his tongue. "When the time is right, you'll know you're ready to commit yourself to a relationship."

Her expression softened. "I want to believe that."

"Then do. I believe it. One hundred percent."

The tender longing that lit her eyes made it difficult to stay on his side of the couch. As much as he wanted his next breath, he wanted to press her back in the cushions and convince her with his kiss that he was the one who could make her happy, that he was the one she was looking for.

But Haley ran into the room, providing the diversion he needed to regain his focus and control.

"Done brushing. See?" She flashed her teeth.

Annie seemed equally relieved for the distraction. She lifted a corner of her mouth in a grin of approval. "Very good. Now scoot to bed. I'll be back in a second to read you a book."

"Can Jonah read to me tonight?" her daughter asked, trotting over to flop against Jonah's legs.

Annie shook her head, clearly ready to protest.

Though his gut tightened at the notion of helping with something as domestic and familial as tucking Haley into bed, Annie was exhausted, and if reading Haley a book would help her, he'd read a whole library.

"If it's okay with your mom." Jonah sent Annie an inquisitive glance. "I don't mind. Really. You tend to Ben."

Her stunned look told him what words didn't. He ex-husband had never volunteered to help put the children to bed. When it came to raising her kids, she'd been as alone in her marriage as she was now.

Haley tugged his hand, and Jonah rose to follow the girl to her bedroom. She scampered under the covers and grabbed a book from the foot of the bed. "This one. It's my favorite."

Jonah glanced down at the title. *Skippyjon Jones.*

"And you have to do the Spanish accent like Mommy does," Haley added as she scrunched down under her sheet.

"A Spanish accent, huh?" Jonah scratched his chin, already having second thoughts about the task he'd volunteered for. He cracked the book open and began reading the humorous tale of a Siamese cat who thought he was a Chihuahua. Hearing a noise in the hallway, he glanced up and saw Annie's shadow on the wall outside Haley's door. Annie hovered by the door, out of sight, no doubt listening—whether protectively monitoring his interaction with her daughter or simply curious to hear his attempted Spanish accent, he couldn't say. It didn't matter. In her place, he'd do the same.

He turned the page and continued reading.

"Jonah?" Haley interrupted.

"Yeah?"

Haley angled her head on her pillow to peer up at him with

brown eyes, much like her mother's. "Do you think my mommy's pretty?"

He grinned and nodded. "I do. I think she's beautiful."

"She has a scar on her face." Haley wrinkled her brow as if deep in thought.

"I know. So do I. See?" He pointed to the scar over his eyebrow. "I've had that since I was just a kid."

She winced. "Does it hurt?"

"Not anymore."

"My daddy broke Mommy's cheek. She had to have surg'ry. That's why she's got a scar."

He heard a soft gasp from the hall, and his chest tightened imagining Annie's concern for her daughter.

Please, God, give me the right words for this little girl.

"You know your daddy can't hurt you or your mom anymore. You're safe."

She nodded matter-of-factly. "Daddy's in jail."

"Right." He looked down at the book again, half expecting Haley to ask another question, but the girl stared silently at the stuffed cat clutched in her hands. He could let the subject drop, finish reading the book and escape the topic relatively unscathed. But avoidance never solved anything. More important, he needed Haley—and Annie—to know his true feelings. "You know what? I think your mom's scar is part of what makes her so beautiful to me."

Haley glanced up, giving him a funny, wrinkle-nosed grin. "Really?"

"Really. To me, it's like a badge of courage. A sign of her love for you and of her incredible inner strength. Even though your daddy's in jail, she's made a new life for you and Ben. Sometimes it's hard to be a mommy, but she's one of the best mommies I've ever met."

Haley smiled and bobbed her head.

"Her scar tells me she's willing to do whatever it takes to protect the people she loves." Jonah tapped the girl's nose with his finger. "That's pretty brave, huh? Pretty awesome."

"Yeah." Haley hugged her stuffed cat tighter. "And that's why you think she's pretty?"

Jonah shrugged. "That and her beautiful eyes, and her smile—"

"And her hair?" Haley volunteered, grinning.

"Yep."

"And her mouth?" She giggled.

She'd digressed to silliness now, and Jonah groaned internally. He scrambled mentally for the best way to nip the laundry list in the bud. "Head to toe. I think all of your mom is beautiful. Okay?"

"Like a princess?"

"Sure. Like a princess."

"Are you her prince?"

"I, uh—" His mouth opened like that of a fish out of water. He should have seen that one coming. Conscious of Annie still listening at the door, he chose his response carefully. "Aren't princes supposed to be handsome and charming?"

"You're handsome and charming," Haley said guilelessly.

Jonah chuckled and scratched his jaw. "Well…thanks, sweetie. But I think your mom gets the deciding vote on that."

"Mr. Jonah?"

Fearing another side trip into territory he didn't want to cover, Jonah waggled the book in front of her. "Shouldn't we finish the story now?"

Haley ignored his question and sat up in her bed. Leaning in to hug him, she whispered, "I hope Mommy votes for you."

His heart lurched, and a tangled mix of emotions squeezed his chest. For someone who didn't want to be part of a family again, he'd sure gotten himself in deep with Annie's. So how did he get out without hurting her or her kids?

And why did the idea of future bedtime stories stir such a bittersweet longing in his soul?

Chapter 16

Annie dabbed at the tears tickling her cheeks as Jonah stepped out of Haley's room and pulled the door shut. Her heart gave a heavy throb, so full of affection and gratitude, she thought it might burst.

Clearing his throat quietly, he studied her face. With the pad of his thumb, he dried one of her tears and twitched the corner of his mouth into an awkward smile. "I see you heard my attempt at a Spanish accent. Maybe if we're lucky, the child won't have nightmares of monsters who roll their *R*s."

She grinned through her tears. "Joke all you want. But what you did for her…for me…just now…"

A knot choked her throat, but she forced it down, determined to tell Jonah what was in her heart. "Just so you know—" She rose on her toes and wrapped her arms around his neck, leaning into his large, taut body. "I think you are both handsome and charming." She kissed his cheek. "Gentle and kind." She brushed her lips over his. "A fierce protector and an honorable man."

He heaved a weary sigh and stepped back, his gaze troubled. "Annie, I'm no prince."

She studied the deep lines of worry and fatigue in his craggy face. "I…I'm not looking for a prince."

A muscle in his jaw twitched, and he met her gaze evenly. "Aren't you?"

Annie squared her shoulders, shoving down the knot of disappointment that rose in her chest. "I know better than to believe in fairy tales."

He shook his head. "You can't lie to me. I saw the look in your eyes tonight, the longing and hope."

She scowled, disturbed by the notion he saw through her so easily. "What do you mean? When? What look?"

Jonah edged close again. He tucked her hair behind her ear, leaving the jagged scar on her face exposed, much as her soul felt bared when he drilled her with his dark eyes. "You deserve more than I have in me to give. I will do everything in my power to make sure you and your kids are safe, to stop the people responsible for scamming Michael. But I don't know how to be what you need after that."

A bitter pain slashed through Annie, and she jerked away from his gentle caress. Her spine stiff, she glared at him through hot tears. "I don't need anything from you. I've been alone for most of my life and survived just fine! I'm not your charity case, Jonah. If that's what you think, then you can just…go. Leave now."

"Annie, I didn't mean—"

"No, it's better this way. I don't want my kids growing attached to you if you plan to leave us when this is over. They've been hurt enough."

"I would never intentionally harm you or your kids, Annie. Never. If you want me to leave, then I will." His stubbled jaw firmed, and he set his mouth in a taut line, though his gaze stayed soft and warm.

Jonah's eyes really did reflect his soul. Her heart did a tap dance inside her. Her emotions played a vicious tug-of-war. She felt safer with Jonah nearby, but how did she justify depending on him, allowing him to become any more deeply rooted in her children's affection. Or hers.

She answered with a jerky nod, and he sighed his resignation. Pain clawed her chest, knowing she'd put that defeated expression on his face.

He patted his hip where his phone was clipped. "I have my cell with me if you need anything. I'll be watching your place from my truck and can be back up here in seconds."

"Jonah…" An invitation to sleep on her couch again was on the tip of her tongue, but she swallowed it. She'd given him an opening to deny his intention to walk away at the close of his investigation at the diner, but he'd kept silent. Better that she begin untangling him from her life now.

Nothing had changed, despite the tantalizing glimpses of a better, happier life she might have with Jonah. Depending on a man for her safety, her happiness, her strength, only led to heartache and disaster. Experience had taught her that in the harshest way. She'd be a fool to forget that lesson.

Jonah was still in his truck, parked just down the street from her apartment, when Annie left for work the next morning. When she spotted him, her pulse leaped like a schoolgirl's. She'd missed sharing a cup of coffee with Jonah this morning, his hair sleep-tousled, his cheek bearing the impression of her couch upholstery like a tattoo. Being around his easygoing companionship in the early morning hours had started recent days with an optimism she'd not had in years.

Knowing how cramped and uncomfortable his truck had to have been overnight stabbed her with a sharp edge of regret. She acknowledged him with a raised hand but ignored his signal when he waved her over. Turning, Annie hurried to the bus stop on the corner, hearing him call to her, then crank his engine.

Accepting a ride from him to the diner as she had done in recent mornings would be the easy way out. With his investigation winding down, she had to return to doing things for herself, looking out for her own interests, breaking the fragile bonds they'd formed.

"Annie, come on. What are you doing?" he called from his truck as he double-parked on the side street.

Thankfully, her bus chugged toward the stop just as Jonah climbed from his front seat. She couldn't bear a confrontation.

"I don't know how to be what you need...."

His rejection last night had gnawed at her all night, kept her tossing and turning through the dark, lonely hours. A heavy ache pinched her chest as she hustled onto the city bus without a backward glance.

What did Jonah think she needed? What demand had she made of him that he thought he lacked? She'd tried so hard not to ask anything of him, not to assume anything about their relationship. And despite her best intentions, she *had* developed a relationship with Jonah, though she was at a loss as to how to define it.

Her skin prickled at the memory of the sweet pressure of his lips on hers, the pleasure of his kiss. He'd wanted her as much as she'd wanted him, hadn't he? Had she misjudged what happened at the police gymnasium? After all, she had just suffered an emotional meltdown. Maybe he'd just been offering pity sex. Had she thrown herself at him in some desperate moment of weakness like a cheap tramp?

Her face heated with mortification. Jonah, being a gentleman, had not taken advantage of her and had stopped her from making the next great mistake of her life.

Her heart squeezed, and she blinked back the moisture that puddled in her eyes. If making love to Jonah would have been such a mistake, why did she still long with every fiber of her body and soul to sink into his arms and lose herself in his kiss, his touch? Deep inside her, she knew Jonah would be infinitely gentle, generous and attentive as a lover. That was the nature of the man she'd gotten to know these past weeks, the man she'd learned to trust, the man who'd stolen her heart when she wasn't looking.

But Jonah had made it clear last night the affection was one-sided.

"I don't know how to be what you need...."

Stifling the self-pity that nipped at her, Annie dug deep inside her for the shreds of determination and hope that she'd clung to like a tattered blanket since she walked out on Walt almost two years ago.

She'd survived just fine before she'd let Jonah into her life, and she had to do the same again. Though she couldn't stop him from playing guardian, she didn't have to indulge the fantasy that he would ever be more than a transient part of her life. As she always had, she'd focus her energy and her life on giving her kids the best childhood she could as a single, working mother.

The bus slowed with a hiss of its brakes, and Annie made her way to the door, giving the driver a polite smile as she stepped down to the sidewalk. Before she'd even walked a block, Jonah's truck was beside her on the street.

"Annie, I know you're mad. You have every right to be. But your safety has to come before your pride. Please, get in the truck."

She waved a hand down the street. "It's only another block."

The car behind Jonah honked, but he ignored it. "We need to talk. About us."

She lifted her chin but kept her gaze forward as she strode toward the diner. "There is no us, Jonah. You made that perfectly clear last night."

"Annie—"

She flicked a hand to cut him off. "No, it's fine. You're right. I guess I just let the emotions of the day get to me. It's better this way."

"It's not that I don't want to be with you, Annie. But I don't—" He bit out a curse word. "I can't have this conversation through the window of a moving truck. Annie, please get in."

"I'll be late for work." Sighing, she stopped walking and

faced his truck. "We can talk tonight, if you want. But you don't need to make any apologies or excuses. There is no us. I get that. I'm okay with that. I just forgot that in a moment of weak—" To her dismay, her voice cracked, and scalding tears clouded her eyes. She pressed her lips in a tight line and swung back toward the diner, her steps brisk and clipped.

"Damn it, Annie. You're not weak. Just give me five minutes to—"

The rest of his plea was silenced as she breezed through the diner's front door and it closed behind her.

Jonah appeared at his usual seat at the counter within minutes, but Annie left it to Susan to wait on him. By mutual agreement, their interaction at the diner was to remain casual and all-business. The true nature of their relationship might not be a secret if someone was, in fact, following her, watching her apartment, but she decided discretion was still in order.

Annie did her best to pretend the weight of Jonah's gaze didn't follow her as she served breakfast to the other customers, but the prickle of awareness told her without looking that he was monitoring her every move. Her hands shook as she poured coffee for her customers, and her stomach stayed in knots. Ignoring Jonah was tantamount to pretending there wasn't a bull loose in the china shop. She felt his commanding presence in every cell of her body.

"Annie." His voice thrummed through her as she searched behind the counter for more sugar packets. Cautiously raising her gaze, she met the dark intensity of his eyes, and a shudder rippled through her.

"May I...have some more coffee?"

She glanced at his full mug and sent him a skeptical look. "Aren't you going to be late for your shift at the mill, Mr. Devereaux?"

He returned a chagrined smile, but the unspoken plea in his eyes raked her heart with razor-sharp talons. He hesitated, then his shoulders sagged. "Touché. Then just my bill."

What had put that hint of pain in his gaze? Was it guilt? Regret? Or something deeper and more personal?

Her throat tightened, and she had to swallow twice before she could speak. "I'll get your waitress."

After Jonah paid for his breakfast and left the diner, Annie tried to bury herself in waiting tables, refilling saltshakers and making idle chatter with customers. But her head and her heart were filled with questions about Jonah and the poignant look he'd given her as he walked out the front door.

At lunchtime, Annie glanced toward the door as new customers came in. Ginny and her husband gave Annie a smile and a wave as they chose a table and sat down. Her spirits lifted, seeing her friends, and she hurried over to their table.

"Wow, y'all are a sight for sore eyes." She gave them a weary smile as she handed them each a menu.

Ginny cocked a blond eyebrow. "Oh? Something wrong?"

Annie gave Riley a side glance and shrugged. "Just, um…"

Ginny's husband cleared his throat and slid back to the end of the booth seat. "If you'll excuse me, ladies. I think I'll…grab a newspaper from the machine by the door."

Annie sent the handsome fireman an appreciative grin. "Thanks, Riley."

He gave her cheek a friendly kiss as he left her alone to talk to Ginny.

Ginny's gaze followed her husband to the front door, her happiness glowing in her cheeks. "For a guy, he's pretty perceptive."

Turning her attention to Annie, Ginny captured Annie's hands and pulled her onto the seat beside her. "So, what's up? Would your glum mood have anything to do with the guy you mentioned last time we talked?" She knitted her forehead and waved a finger as she thought. "Jonah? Was that his name?"

Annie tugged up a corner of her mouth in a wry grin. "Riley's not the only perceptive one."

"Well, don't forget, I was in a quandary over what to do about Riley not that long ago. I recognize the look."

Annie toyed with the string of her apron. "What look?"

"The one that says you are crazy about this guy, but you're scared to death to take a shot at being happy with him."

Annie leaned back against the booth seat and frowned. "Who says I would be happy with him? What if what I really need is to forget about having any man in my life and concentrate on raising my kids?"

"Is that really something you want to do alone?"

"No. But Walt didn't leave me much choice in that matter."

"Sure he did. He divorced you. You can give the kids a new father. Question is, is that what will make you happy? Is Jonah who will make you happy?"

Annie idly traced a crack in the tabletop. "Ginny, we're getting way ahead of ourselves here. Jonah hasn't even said he wants to be more than my guardian until this mess with—" She caught herself and glanced toward the counter where Susan was ringing up a customer. She lowered her voice. "This other mess I told you about. I still have that hanging over my head."

Ginny leaned closer, matching Annie's quiet tone. "Maybe it's time you went to the police with your suspicions and the information you've found."

Annie shook her head. "Not yet. Jonah has a plan and I trust him. When he's got everything he needs for the police to make their arrests, then he'll turn it over to the authorities. But he's afraid if we involve the cops too soon, the people involved higher up will close shop and go into hiding. Or cut their losses some other way to protect themselves. Jonah already suspects that is why Hardin was murdered."

A frown dented the bridge of Ginny's nose. "Annie, I don't like you being involved in this. Get out. I'll help you get another job. You don't have to stay here if—"

"I can't quit now. We're too close to catching the people behind this thing." She cast another surreptitious glance toward Susan. "Besides, leaving the diner won't end the threat to me. I have reason to believe these people know I have information about their operation. That threat doesn't go away just because I quit. You know the saying, keep your friends close—"

"And your enemies closer," Ginny finished for her. "Oh, Annie. Please be careful."

She nodded. "I will."

Ginny's worried gaze clung to hers for a few more seconds before she shifted in her seat. "And what about Jonah?"

"What about him?"

"Do you love him?"

Annie sputtered, and her face grew hot. "I—I—"

Ginny grinned. "You're blushing. I think I have my answer."

Annie averted her face. "Ginny, I don't know how to feel about him. And after last night, it may all be a moot point anyway."

Ginny tipped her head. "Why? What happened?"

A rock lodged in Annie's gut. "He all but told me he's not interested in a future with me."

Ginny squeezed Annie's hand. "What exactly did he say?"

"That he can't be what I need him to be."

Ginny arched an eyebrow. "Ah. He's afraid."

"Afraid?" Annie jerked her eyebrows into a frown. Fear was the last thing she'd ever associate with Jonah. And yet...

She thought of the haunted look in his eyes this morning, the uncertainty in his voice when he begged for a chance to talk.

"Afraid of what?"

Ginny leaned back and shook her head. "Could be almost anything. You know him better than I do. Maybe he's afraid of hurting you. Didn't you say his size and his fighting skills scared you? Do you think he's worried about—"

"Oh, no." Annie vehemently shook her head. "He would never hurt me or the kids."

As soon as the words left her mouth, Annie heard them echoing through her head, heard the certainty in her voice and waited for the niggling of doubt that never came. When had she come to this conclusion? When had Jonah convinced her of his trustworthiness and honor? How did she know in her heart of hearts that she was truly safe with Jonah in every way?

She didn't know how or when she'd known. But she was sure of it.

Ginny's bright blue eyes lasered into her. "Maybe it's not physical pain he's afraid of causing you. Maybe he's afraid of commitment or failure or letting you down. He could be worried about breaking your heart—or you breaking his."

Annie inhaled sharply. Had she let Jonah's brawn and rough-around-the-edges appearance blind her to his Achilles' heel? Jonah had told her about his history with his father, his grim childhood, the pain of losing his mentor last year. Could her tough-on-the-outside protector be hiding a vulnerable heart?

When Annie didn't respond, Ginny said, "Either way, my question to you remains the same. Do you love him?"

Ginny's query flustered Annie, made her feel trapped and panicky. "I think…I could. I'm happier when I'm with him. He makes me feel braver, stronger, more hopeful."

Turning up a palm as if to say the answer was obvious, Ginny flashed her a satisfied grin. "Then fight for him. You stood up to Walt, saved yourself and your kids from his abuse and started a new life. After everything you've struggled to achieve, don't give up on the one person who can give you the love you deserve. These past few weeks, you've learned you're safe with him. Now show him he can be safe with you, that you won't let him be hurt, either. Show him he doesn't have to be afraid of a future with you. Just don't let him go without a fight."

Annie's heartbeat thundered in her ears. After years of withdrawing to protect herself, of shutting down and pulling in to avoid conflict, could she throw herself into the fray, to put her heart in the line of fire for the chance at a future with Jonah?

As she weighed the risks of such a bold leap of faith, Annie noticed Susan staring at her from behind the front counter. The other waitress gave her a stern glare and then a meaningful hitch of her head to the rest of the dining room. Customers were waiting.

Annie shoved to her feet. "I…need to get back to work. I have tables waiting."

As she turned away, Ginny grabbed her hand and sent her a penetrating look. "Trust your heart, Annie. Allow yourself to be happy. You deserve a man who will cherish you and fill your life with joy. Don't let what happened with Walt skew your vision with Jonah. I almost made that mistake with Riley and would have blown the best thing that ever happened to me."

Annie pulled in a deep breath. "Okay."

"And…can we get two cheeseburgers with sweet iced tea? I'm famished." Ginny gave her a wide, cheerful grin.

"Of course." She hustled to the order window, scribbling Ginny's request on her pad. If she'd thought talking with Ginny would help calm her whirling thoughts and confusion, she'd sadly miscalculated.

Trust her heart? Fight for Jonah? She didn't know where to begin. The realization that she felt truly safe with Jonah eliminated what Annie had believed was her main reason for not getting involved with him. Yesterday she'd almost made love to Jonah at the police station gymnasium. Clearly, physical chemistry wasn't her problem.

His instincts and interactions with her kids warmed her heart, so she couldn't blame parental protectiveness for her reluctance. Having experienced his gentleness, his compassion, his loyalty, his honor, how could she question what kind of husband he'd be?

But Ginny had challenged her to do more than admit her feelings for Jonah. Ginny wanted her to act on those feelings, drop her defenses and muster a courage she wasn't sure she had inside her. What would happen if she let herself love Jonah, gave him her body, heart and soul, and he still walked away when his case here at the diner was solved? That was the issue that scared her spitless. She'd already lost so much.

But wasn't Jonah worth the risk?

A niggling unrest stirred in her gut, a desperation that lit a fire in her soul. The same inner voice had roused her from the nightmare of her dysfunctional marriage and given her the courage to save herself and her children from Walt.

She'd faced down her demons before when her life was on the line. Tonight, she would put her love on the line for a chance to be happy, a chance to share the kind of love she'd always dreamed of. She'd risk her heart—for Jonah.

* * *

Jonah spent a frustrating day going over the files from Hardin's bus-station locker but found himself distracted by thoughts of Annie's sweet kiss. That afternoon, he rhythmically lashed the speed bag at the boxing gym. He'd hoped that exhausting himself with an intense workout would expel the thrum of desire that wound him tight.

Hammering the punching bag should have given his mind something else to focus on besides the wistful longing in Annie's eyes last night, the musical sound of her laughter as they danced and the poignant ache in his heart as he'd put Haley to bed. Instead, giving his body over to the repetitive motion of his workout gave his brain free rein to review the same images over and over again.

He'd done the one thing that scared him most, the one thing he'd sworn not to do with Annie. He'd become involved with her family, grown attached to her kids, developed deep, complicated feelings for her. How did he extricate himself from the relationship without hurting her and her family? Without losing a piece of his own heart and soul?

Bad enough Haley had begun thinking in terms of him marrying Annie, but if Annie interpreted his recent actions as a promise of a future, an expression of feelings deeper than friendship, he was bound to let her down. Considering the cold shoulder she'd given him this morning, he guessed his withdrawal last night had already hurt her.

He gave the bag an especially forceful punch. Damn it! Hurting Annie was the last thing he'd wanted.

But had that stopped him from kissing her senseless at the Lagniappe PD gym? Had he considered the repercussions when he'd engaged her daughter in a cozy, fatherly chat at bedtime? Watching her home from his truck would have been safer for his own sanity and not created the intimate connection he now felt for Annie and her kids.

But had he weighed the risks when he'd slept on her couch?

Apparently not. Because in unguarded moments, even he

conjured fanciful ideas of what it would be like to help Annie raise her children, or wake in the morning beside Annie rather than on her lumpy sofa.

Heat coursed through his veins as he imagined himself wrapped around Annie's naked body, making love to her night after night. Perhaps creating a child of their own. His heart fisted. He couldn't deny how much he wanted Annie, how sweet the promise of joining her family was.

But too many unknowns cast a specter over that homey ideal. How did he build a loving family with Annie when his own family had been so screwed up? Sure, he could try to make Annie happy, try to give her kids the kind of fatherly role model they needed, but trying wasn't good enough. A wife and family wasn't something he could attempt and risk failure. Annie had already had one husband fail her. She deserved more than his bumbling attempt to fill a role he knew nothing about.

He refused to add to her pain. He simply couldn't commit to Annie without assurances that he could make family life a success. But with a lack of experience to draw from and with innumerable cases of marital hell etched in his memory thanks to domestic disturbance calls while on the job in Little Rock, he knew far more about what not to do than how to get family relationships right.

Gritting his teeth, he pounded the speed bag until sweat blinded him and his arms ached.

"Hell, man! What's gotten into you?"

Catching the swinging bag with one hand, Jonah turned to Frank and swiped stinging perspiration from his eyes with his forearm. "I'm sorry. What'd you say?"

"I asked what got into you. You were beating that poor bag like a man possessed. What gives?"

After shucking his gloves, Jonah picked up his towel and wiped his face and arms. "Just have a lot on my mind. I needed to let off a little stress, clear my head."

Frank chuckled. "Did it work?"

Jonah scowled. "Not as much as I'd hoped. I'm still not sure what I'm going to do."

"A woman or money?"

"Excuse me?"

"Well, a man's problems usually boil down to either his lady or his finances. So which one's got you all in a twist?"

Jonah hesitated. Did he really want relationship advice from the stodgy owner of the gym? He scoffed as he tossed his towel back on his gym bag. The advice and guidance Michael had given him had saved his life, and Michael had run the gym in Little Rock. He glanced up at Frank. "A woman."

"Marry her."

Jonah arched an eyebrow and cocked his head. "What?"

"Between my wife and daughter, I've lived with women for more than thirty years. I know how they think. If your woman's got you this tied up in knots, she's gotta mean more to you than a casual roll in the sack. I say, man up. Marry her and quit waffling."

"But I'm not—"

"On the other hand, if you're already married, and she's giving you this much grief—"

Jonah folded his arms over his chest, curious where the older man's generalities about female relationships would go.

"—chances are she's probably at least partly right about whatever she's steamed over, so suck it up, buy her some flowers and tell her you're sorry. You may have to eat some crow, but at least it will get you off the couch and back in the bedroom."

Frank hadn't missed the mark by much. Jonah had to admit thoughts of moving off Annie's couch and holding her in her bed had been part of what wound him so tight. He could have made love to Annie last night, if his conscience hadn't been gnawing at him. Her kiss outside Haley's bedroom had been full of unspoken promises. The air around them had crackled with desire and expectation.

A sultry fantasy of Annie peering up at him through her sexy curtain of hair while she reclined on starched white sheets taunted him. Jonah's libido kicked him where it counted, and he muffled a groan.

Frank shrugged. "I'm just telling you what I've learned— both in marriage and as a business owner. Sometimes you have to sacrifice to get what ya really want."

The gym owner gave a satisfied nod as if he'd just solved world hunger and the energy crisis. "Right now, what I really want is a cold beer and a wide-screen TV to watch the basketball championship. Wanna join me?"

Jonah perked up. He'd almost forgotten the final round of the college tournament he'd bet on with Farrout. He should watch the game, so he'd be able to talk about it with some authority when he met up with Farrout later.

Frank stared at him, waiting for an answer.

If he could get the television away from Haley, perhaps he could watch the game at Annie's. He didn't want her unprotected tonight, and she'd promised to listen tonight to his explanation of why he'd balked last night. Anticipating *that* conversation raised a sweat on Jonah's forehead unrelated to his workout.

He shook his head. "Thanks, Frank, but I'll watch it at home."

"With your lady friend? Ha. Good luck with that." Frank waved a dismissive hand, then jerked his chin. "Who ya pulling for?"

"UNC."

Frank scoffed. "They don't have a chance."

Shrugging, Jonah tossed his towel on his gym bag. "My gut tells me they'll pull it out, no matter what the oddsmakers are saying."

With a tip of his head, Frank gave him a measuring glance. "You sound pretty sure of your team. Wanna put a little money on that?"

Jonah sighed and scooped up the straps of his gym bag. "Already did."

Frank's eyes widened, and he folded his arms over his chest. "Ya know…if you're interested in making some serious coin on the game, I might know someone who could hook you up."

A chill skimmed down Jonah's back. Was Frank the one who'd sent Michael to Farrout? Could Frank have information about the gambling ring Jonah needed?

The gym owner smoothed a hand over his silver hair and lifted a shoulder. "Think about it and let me know. Stanley Cup is coming up, the Masters Tournament, NBA finals. Plenty of opportunities to make a little on the side if you're interested."

Frank strolled into his office, waving goodnight to another boxer.

As Jonah headed into the locker room to shower, he made a mental note to quiz Frank further on his connections to sports betting. For now, he had more immediate concerns—like ten thousand dollars riding on a college basketball game and a single mother of two who made him want things that were out of his reach.

Chapter 17

When Jonah rapped on her door that evening, Annie's heart gave an answering knock. She smoothed her hands down the slim skirt she'd changed into after work, denying to herself that she'd dressed to impress Jonah. But in truth, she felt frumpy in her waitress uniform. If she wanted to convince him to take a chance on a relationship with her, she needed every scrap of confidence and all the positive vibes she could scrounge.

"Hi," she said, standing back to let him in. Her voice sounded breathy and seductive even to her own ears. But just the sight of him, his hair damp from a recent shower, the evening sun casting shadows across his face that highlighted the masculine cut of his jaw and cheekbones, sucked all the oxygen from her lungs.

The lopsided grin he gave her coiled around her heart and filled her with a longing so powerful she ached.

"Trust your heart," Ginny had said.

Right now her heart was telling her to grab hold of Jonah with both hands and never let go. This man, with his dark gaze that could see through to her soul and a tender touch that never failed to turn her bones to mush, had snuck past her defenses and stolen her heart.

His gaze slid over her, drinking in the narrow blue jean skirt that emphasized her hips and the white cotton T-shirt that made the most of her unimpressive cleavage. His pupils rounded as his perusal lingered at her lips before drifting to her scarred cheek.

On an impulse, she had pinned her hair back from her face with a cloisonne clip, leaving the harsh jagged marks exposed. Her scars were a part of who she was now, and tonight she wanted no secrets or barriers between her and Jonah.

She held her breath, anxiously waiting for his reaction to the prominence of her scars, until his mouth curled in a warm grin. "Hi yourself. You look…beautiful."

Her pulse pattered, and her cheeks heated with pleasure. The way he looked at her, like a cat ready to pounce, made her feel pretty for the first time in years.

She cleared the nervous tightening from her throat. "Have you eaten?"

"I—"

"Jonah!" Haley squealed as she bounded in from the living room wearing her plastic tiara. Ben toddled in behind his sister, and a drooly grin lit his face when he saw their guest. Her daughter hugged Jonah's legs, and he stooped to lift her into a bear hug.

"Hi, princess. How are things at the castle?" he said, tweaking her nose, then tousling Ben's curls. "Hey, slick. How's the block business?"

Haley giggled, and Annie's heart somersaulted. Jonah had a natural rapport with her kids and showed none of the stiff reluctance she'd seen when other men got around children. His ease with her kids went a long way toward assuring her she'd made the right decision, allowing him into their lives.

For dinner, they shared a delivered pizza, Jonah's treat and an indulgence the kids reveled in. With their stomachs full of pepperoni pizza, Haley and Ben were in a better mood when time came for their baths and bedtime. Jonah read *Skippyjon*

Jones to Haley again, then disappeared to the living room to watch a basketball game while Annie settled Ben into his crib for the night.

Once both children were soundly sleeping, Annie sat next to Jonah on the couch and tucked her feet under her. "Who's playing?"

"UNC and Kansas." He sent her a side glance, then turned back to the television. "This is the final round of the NCAA championship."

"Mmm." An uneasy prickle nipped her spine. Walt had been especially grouchy and sensitive to interruption when he'd been watching sports. She'd quickly learned to make herself scarce on nights when her ex watched a game.

Disappointment knotted her stomach. She'd hoped to have time tonight to talk openly with Jonah about her feelings. The game on TV didn't bode well for a discussion or any intimacies.

When a commercial came on, Jonah turned to face her and swiped a hand down his face. "So...kids asleep?"

She nodded. "Will this be on much longer? I'd hoped we could talk."

His eyes softened, and he stroked her chin. "I'd like that, too." He hitched his head toward the TV screen. "This is the tournament I bet on with Farrout. I need to see how it shakes out, but I want to talk once it's over. There's only about ten minutes left in the game."

His explanation both lifted her spirits and twisted new strands of dread inside her. Even if she settled things with Jonah, nothing was settled with the gambling and money-laundering operation.

Working to tamp the apprehension the problems at the diner knotted inside her, she covered his hand with hers and nodded. "I can wait ten minutes."

He winced. "It could go into overtime."

His boyishly apologetic expression was so far from the irritated glower Walt used to give her, she had to smile. "Okay, but no shouting at the TV. You'll wake the kids." Pulling her lips in a flirtatious grin, she snuggled closer to him and threaded her fingers through his hair. "And I'd really like them to stay asleep."

The lift of his eyebrow and darkening of his gaze spoke of his intrigue with her intimation. "I'll keep that in mind." Jonah slid an arm around her waist and pulled her closer. "Help me pull for my team. I've got ten grand riding on this game."

Annie jerked away from him. "Ten grand? Where did you get that kind of money?" Immediately, she shook her head and held up a hand. "I'm sorry. That's not my business. It's just…that much money is—"

Jonah laced his fingers with hers and kissed her palm. The soft brush of his lips on her sensitive skin sent a delicious thrill spiraling through her.

"You have a right to know. The money is from an insurance settlement. My dad was killed in a car accident a couple years ago."

She caught her breath, sympathy plucking at her. She knew the mixed feelings he had toward his father and the confused emotions he'd have experienced because of the loss.

"A guy ran a red light and T-boned him," he continued. "The other guy's insurance company offered a healthy settlement if my sister and I signed papers saying we wouldn't sue. Dad also had a good bit of life insurance listing my sister and me as beneficiaries." He gave a cursory glance to the television, where the game had resumed. "I hadn't wanted anything to do with my dad when he was alive, and I sure as hell didn't want to profit from his death. I took the money and put it in the bank. Left it there. Didn't want anything to do with it, until—"

When he paused, ducking his head, Annie slid a hand along his cheek, then lifted his chin to meet his gaze. "Until?"

"When Michael died and I decided to investigate who was behind the gambling operation, I resigned my position on the police force in Little Rock and moved down here. I've been living off the money from my dad's death for the past year. Michael was more of a father figure to me than my dad ever was. It seems like poetic justice somehow that the money I inherited be used to catch the people behind Michael's death."

"Poetic justice, indeed."

After a drawn-out moment where the world seemed to still around them, his gaze dipped to her mouth.

Her lips gravitated to his, and a low moan rumbled from his chest. The vibration reverberated through Annie, licking her veins and encouraging her to be bolder, to take what she craved without fear or regret. She sealed her mouth over his and teased the seam of his lips with her tongue.

Jonah's arm tightened around her, and he tugged her onto his lap. His fingers burrowed into her hair, and he met her questing tongue with his own. Every velvet stroke spun her senses reeling faster. She clung to Jonah for support and could feel the rapid-fire beat of his heart against her chest. A bulge at his fly ground intimately against her hip. Knowing that she'd roused his body to that state emboldened her, filled her with a sense of power she hadn't know in years. In Jonah's arms, she felt feminine. Respected. Cherished.

Her restless hands skimmed over his wide shoulders, along the muscle and sinew of his arms, then settled on his hard chest. Her fingers curled into his shirt, and she raised her eyes to his, breathless from his kiss. The heat and hunger blazing in his gaze sent shock waves rippling through her, firing every nerve. Her whole body quaked with need and strained closer to him. "Jonah, I want…"

Her breath hung in her lungs. She should stop now, retreat. Protect herself from inevitable pain. She might not fear physical abuse from Jonah, but the risk to her heart was too great. If she gave her body to Jonah, she'd lose a piece of her soul to him, too.

Trepidation dried her throat, and she nervously wet her lips. His gaze tracked the quick swipe of her tongue. His grip tightened, and smoky desire darkened his eyes.

"What do you want, Annie?" His husky growl stroked her like a physical caress. "Name it, honey. Anything."

His warm hands framed her face, and he brushed butterfly

kisses to her nose, her cheeks, her closed eyes. His tenderness touched a raw, aching place deep inside her, soothing, calming. His warmth thawed the chill of fear that had frozen her, paralyzed her for too long.

"Trust your heart."

Even if it cost her a piece of her soul, she wanted the respite his arms offered from the turmoil of her life. She ached for the sweet joy and heady bliss of his kiss.

After years of running, bone-deep pain and endless nights of loneliness, she desperately wanted a few stolen moments of happiness, of escape, of...*Jonah.*

"This," she whispered, her voice catching. "I want this. I...want you."

A heartbreaking expression molded his face. Moisture clung to his eyelashes, and a shocking vulnerability shaded the bright yearning in his eyes. "Are you sure?"

The tremor of wistful longing in his tone shook Annie to the core.

He could be worried about breaking your heart—or you breaking his.

Her chest clenched, realizing that Jonah's need and doubts echoed her own. Her pulse tripped over the idea her warrior protector bore scars from his own past. Was it possible Jonah needed her as much as she needed him? Did her kiss offer him the same balm to old hurts as his did to her? Could two broken spirits, two wounded birds find solace and hope with each other?

"It's about give and take, sharing and supporting each other."

Ginny was right. More than anything, Annie wanted to give Jonah the hope and happiness, the healing that his patience and gentleness had given her.

Annie dragged in a shaky breath and stroked her fingers down his cheek to cup his jaw. She touched her lips to his, felt his shudder. "Make love to me, Jonah."

After checking on her children, Annie joined Jonah in her bedroom, her heart tapping an anxious tattoo. She walked in just as he pulled a small foil packet from his wallet and tossed it on the bedside stand.

Her heart turned over. *Always the protector.*

Hearing her enter, he glanced up, and a muscle in his jaw bunched. "Just so you know, you're safe with me."

Annie bit her lip, a flutter of anticipation dancing in her belly. "I know."

His mouth pressed in a hard line, and his gaze narrowed on her. "What I mean is...I don't sleep around. I don't take sex light—"

She pressed a finger to his lips to stop him. "I trust you."

His throat convulsed as he swallowed, and his pupils rounded. He tugged her close and sighed into her mouth. "Annie, sweet Annie..."

She sank into his kiss, ribbons of pleasure unfurling inside her. When he skimmed his lips over her chin and down to the pulse point at her throat, shimmering sparks danced over her skin. His hands worked under her T-shirt and massaged her back, strumming the bumps of her spine and lulling her with tender strokes.

Weeks of tension and anxiety melted by degrees at his touch, and she gave herself over to the magic of his hands.

Bracing her hips securely against his, he leaned her back and ducked his head to nuzzle the valley between her breasts. The arch of her body pushed her hips more intimately against the ridge of his arousal, and with a sway of her body, she rocked against him. A low moan rasped from his throat. The effect she had on him thrilled her, heightened her own pleasure, made her bolder.

Grasping his shoulders, Annie straightened and stepped back. Holding his hot gaze with hers, she whisked her shirt off and let it drop on the floor. Her bra followed, and Jonah released a stuttering breath as he palmed her bared breasts. He molded and shaped her gently before shifting his hands so he could roll her nipples under her thumbs.

Staggering sensation pulsed through Annie's blood, a hot rush that melted her bones and made her legs buckle. She curled her fingers into his shirt, gasping for a steadying breath. Jonah pivoted with her in his embrace and lowered her carefully to the bed.

He stood beside the bed only long enough to yank his own shirt off and shove his jeans down his legs. He kicked free of the pants, then braced himself on his arms above her.

Annie drank in the sight of his toned muscles and broad chest dusted with black hair. Rather than frighten her, his brawn and powerful potential made her feel safe, protected. She brushed her hand across the taut skin, savoring the warmth and texture, lightly scraping his nipples with her fingernails and smiling when she felt his answering shudder. Her gaze followed the path she blazed with her fingers, until a wide jagged patch of pale skin stopped her cold.

A long scar stretched across his lower abdomen. She sucked in a sharp breath. "Jonah, what…?"

He glanced at her with heavy-lidded, passion-drunk eyes and shrugged. "A punk with a knife resisted arrest."

She pulled back to appraise him with fresh eyes and renewed concern, and she noticed a small puckered circle on his shoulder. She touched it. "And this?"

He groaned. "Do we really need to catalog all my scars *now?* We could be here a while."

A poignant ache squeezed her chest, and she tipped her head, her gaze scanning him. "Oh, Jonah."

How many more scars did he have? More important, how did she help him heal the internal wounds that stitches and bandages couldn't help?

Jonah had been surrounded by violence all his life, been its victim, learned to use it as his tool for catharsis. A hot stab of pain lanced her heart, understanding all too well the kind of pain he'd endured.

But Jonah, despite his inauspicious start in life, despite the odds against him, had turned his life around, joined the police force, become a defender, a protector rather than succumbing to the violence that had marred his life. With Jonah on her side, how could she not overcome the obstacles her own life had thrown at her. A burning determination fired in her gut, a conviction that a better life was within her grasp if she had the courage to seize it, to fight for it. And Jonah was a huge part of the life she wanted for herself and her children.

Tears clogged her throat as she gazed up at him. She captured his lips with hers and poured everything that was in her heart into her kiss. Drawing her closer, he pressed her into the mattress with his weight, and she wrapped her legs around him. Jonah explored her body with tender roaming caresses and sultry kisses until she quaked with longing and burned with need. She reveled in the freedom to enjoy his taut muscles and masculine angles with equal leisure and passion. When he settled between her legs, she arched toward him, her body aching to feel the heat and weight of him inside her.

In short order, Jonah sheathed himself with a condom and rolled her on top of him. "You're in control, Annie. You set the pace."

A blissful contentment and trust, a sense of rightness and fulfillment swelled inside her until she couldn't breathe. She held Jonah's gaze, savoring the moment as he entered her. Somehow she sensed her whole life had been leading to this moment, this man. Everything she'd suffered, all she'd sacrificed and lost only made this moment that much sweeter. She belonged with Jonah. They bore the same scars, yet together they were stronger, better. Whole.

Tears of joy stung her eyes as her body stroked his, and the heat and need pounding through her blood coiled tighter, burned brighter—until she shattered in his arms.

She clung to him as he sighed her name and shuddered with his release. Then, in the still darkness of her bedroom, they held each other. Silent. Still. Complete.

Safe in Jonah's embrace, Annie drifted into the first truly peaceful sleep she'd had in years.

Jonah folded an arm behind his head and stared into the inky blackness of Annie's bedroom. With his free hand, he stroked Annie's silky hair and listened to her deep, even breathing as she slept.

He'd been unprepared for the way making love to Annie would rock him to his marrow. Beyond powerfully satisfying sex, joining his body with hers had felt so fundamentally right, like a homecoming, that something had shifted in his soul and grabbed him by the heart. He'd known sleeping with her was a mistake, that it would make giving her up harder and would hurt her more deeply when he had to leave. But when she'd looked at him with her heart in her eyes and asked him to make love to her, denying her request, when every fiber of his body ached for her, had been impossible. He'd thought he could give her the pleasure and comfort she deserved and keep his heart out of the mix, keep the emotional distance that would allow him to walk away when it was over.

He'd been wrong. So wrong.

He blinked hard when the sting of tears burned his eyes and brutally shoved down the bout of self-pity. He had to think of Annie, not his own bleeding heart.

Because if he'd learned nothing else tonight, he'd seen the truth of his feelings for her. He'd fallen in love.

His chest throbbed as bitter regret and frustration raked his chest with sharp talons. No matter how it hurt him, he had to do the right thing for Annie. He couldn't give her the family, the future, the happiness she deserved, and he had to stand aside so that another man could.

Jonah gritted his teeth until his jaw throbbed. Thinking of Annie in another man's arms, building a life with her, burned in his gut like acid.

But she needed better than the patchwork attempt at a real family that was all he had to offer. For him, failure was unthinkable, inexcusable. Annie had survived one bitter marriage, one damaged attempt at family without burdening her with his tarnished history. He couldn't risk her happiness should he bomb as a husband and father.

But in the short hours until morning, he could soak up as

many precious memories as possible. Then, when daylight came, he had to do what was best for Annie.

He had to let her go.

Chapter 18

Jonah was gone.

Annie blinked and groped sleepily on the bed beside her when her alarm clock beeped the next morning. His pillow still bore the dent from his head, and his scent clung to the sheets, but he'd already risen and disappeared from her room.

Disappointment stabbed her. She'd wanted his face to be the first thing she saw that morning, had hoped for a few stolen kisses before she stumbled to the shower.

But perhaps his discretion was for the best. Maybe it was better that Haley and Ben didn't find a man in their mother's bed when they tiptoed in for their morning snuggles.

Even though she didn't have to be at work until that afternoon for the late shift, Annie dragged herself out of bed and into the kitchen to start a pot of coffee. She checked the living-room couch for Jonah, then glanced out her window toward his truck. Not only was Jonah in neither place, but his truck was gone as well.

The first niggling doubts squirmed restlessly inside her as

she returned to pour a cup of the fresh coffee. Where could he have gone? And why hadn't he told her he was leaving?

A tousle-headed Haley staggered into the kitchen and dropped into a chair with her stuffed cat tucked under her arm.

"Morning, sunshine." Annie pushed aside her nagging questions and disappointment over Jonah's absence to concentrate on her daughter. Mornings like this, when they could share breakfast together and have time to play before she left for work, were rare, and she didn't want to waste a minute.

Haley yawned and scratched her ear. "Can we make pancakes, Mommy?"

Annie took out a frying pan and smiled at her daughter. "Absolutely."

Tar Heels Win Nailbiter, the front page of the sports section read. Jonah sat in his truck and sipped the convenience-store coffee he'd bought when he got the newspaper and scanned the game summary. While he'd been making love to Annie, his team had pulled out a narrow victory. He should be happy. Instead, he felt rotten. After the most amazing night of his life, he'd woken to the reality that Annie could never be his and the day had gone downhill from there.

Well…except that his team had won. Unable to muster the appropriate satisfaction for his winning bet, he tossed the newspaper aside and took another throat-scorching gulp of his coffee. Pulling out his cell phone, he dialed Farrout's number. When the bookie answered, Jonah forced a note of satisfaction to his tone and gloated, "UNC by three. I believe you owe me some winnings, Farrout."

A moment of silence followed during which Jonah pictured Farrout's narrow-eyed glare and glowering countenance. Then, "Tonight at Pop's. At eleven. I don't like a crowd around for transactions."

Jonah inhaled deeply. Annie worked the late shift.

He really didn't want Annie anywhere around when he did

his business with Farrout, but he didn't feel he had the luxury of contradicting the bookie. "I'll be there."

Farrout disconnected without comment, and Jonah returned his phone to the clip on his belt.

Things were beginning to fall into place. He had Hardin's files, and if he wore a wire tonight, maybe a camera in a lapel pin, he could get proof of the gambling transactions Farrout ran. Perhaps it was time to bring his investigation to a head. He wanted the business finished, wanted the people involved behind bars so Annie would be safe, so Michael could rest in peace and so he could move on with his own life.

His gut roiled.

A life without Annie.

He imagined her disappointment upon waking alone, and he clenched his teeth. When he'd dressed in the predawn hours, she'd looked so peaceful, he hadn't had the heart to tell her he was leaving. Acid bubbled and seared inside him, and he groaned. In truth, he hadn't had the guts to look into her wide, vulnerable eyes and break her heart.

He needed to go by her apartment before she left for work, explain himself. Or maybe he could drive her to the diner that afternoon, and he could use the time alone to tell her the decisions he'd made. Jonah sighed miserably and pinched the bridge of his nose where a headache was starting. How did he look the woman he loved in the eye and…rip her heart to shreds?

His cell phone trilled, and he checked the caller ID. It was the call he'd been waiting for. "Devereaux."

"I got your message," his caller said.

Jonah cranked the engine of his truck. "We need to meet."

Annie waited all day for Jonah to show up at her apartment. Or call. Something. Anything. But she heard nothing.

The dinner hour came and went at the diner without any sign of him as well, and Annie's dread, the certainty that something had gone horribly wrong last night that she hadn't realized, continued to grow. Was Jonah gone for good? Had he been conning her all along, looking for a vulnerable woman to get in the sack? Had she fallen for pretty lies and smooth talk, and now that he'd slept with her, he'd moved on?

She swallowed hard, forcing down the knot of hurt and disappointment that choked her. Around ten o'clock, she cleared a table for an elderly couple who'd come in for a late-night dessert.

"Two apple pies, one à la mode, one plain," the old man said.

"I'm lactose intolerant," his wife volunteered as the elderly gentleman patted her wrinkled hand.

The loving gesture brought a fresh sting of tears to Annie's eyes. Was it so wrong to want the kind of love this couple shared? A lover, a partner, a companion for her retirement years? The kind of happiness that Riley and Ginny had? She'd thought Jonah might be the one she could spend her life with, grow old with. But the later it got without word from Jonah, the dimmer that hope looked. As badly as Walt had hurt her physically, the pain of losing Jonah when she'd just begun believing she could be happy with him stung far worse.

Clearing her throat and forcing a smile for the elderly couple, Annie said, "One plain, one à la mode pie coming up."

As she shuffled behind the counter to begin serving the pie, Susan moved up beside Annie. "Aren't they sweet? Look at him holding her hand." Susan sighed. "So romantic."

"Mm-hmm," she hummed, and gave a jerky nod, not trusting her voice.

"Hey, are you all right?" Susan asked. "You look…upset."

Annie shook her head. "I'll be fine. I just—" The rest of her sentence hung in her throat as Jonah strolled in the front door and took a seat at a booth instead of his usual place at the counter.

His eyes met hers and held for a moment before he glanced away. Annie's heart thrashed in her chest and rocks settled in her gut.

"Oh. I see." Susan's voice pulled Annie's attention back from Jonah. The other waitress gave her a smug grin and hitched her head toward Jonah's booth. "Man trouble. Am I right?"

Annie released a shuddering breath. "No. I... Don't be silly. Jonah's just...a friend."

"Riiight." Susan sauntered away, tossing a knowing grin over her shoulder.

Annie finished scooping up two slices of apple pie for the elderly couple and carried their desserts out to them before approaching Jonah. She squared her shoulders and pasted a smile on her face, determined not to let him see how his disappearing act and silence had hurt her. "Hi, you. I missed you today."

He flattened his hands on the table and gave her a brief grin. "Sorry about ducking out this morning without saying anything. You were sleeping so peacefully, I hated to wake you."

She shrugged. "I wouldn't have minded."

He looked away guiltily. "And I had some things to take care of today. I got busy—"

"Jonah, it's okay. You don't...owe me any explanations." Hating the wobble in her voice, she squeezed the pen in her hand until her fingers blanched.

"No, it's not okay." Jonah grabbed her hand and pulled her down on the seat beside him. "I should have called or stopped by or something. I'm sorry, Annie. Truly. You deserve so much better than to be treated like a one-night stand." His tone rang with passion, conviction...and regret.

Her spirits lifted a little, dared to hope.

"The thing is," he said, his voice more hollow-sounding now, "I messed up last night, Annie. I shouldn't have slept with you, shouldn't have misled you, and I'm sorry."

Her heart plummeted to her toes. "Misled me? What do you mean?"

He sighed heavily and scraped a hand over the bristles of his unshaven jaw. "I never wanted to hurt you, honey. Please believe that."

"Jonah?" Her throat closed, and the dread she'd been feeling all day settled on her chest like a lead weight. "What are you saying?"

He stared down at the table, wouldn't meet her eyes, and his evasion told her what he couldn't.

"You're dumping me."

"Annie…"

"No, *dumping* isn't the right word. That implies we had something to start with, something you were ending." Anger and hurt sharpened her tone as she struggled to keep her tears at bay. She would not cry over him, would not show him her pain. "But I guess we never really had any kind of relationship for you to dump me from…other than the pity sex, of course." She shoved out of the booth, and he seized her arm.

"Annie, wait! You've got it all wrong. I care about you. I…I love you, but…"

Her pulse jumped. Freezing, she gaped at him as he fumbled, clearly as shocked by his confession as she was.

After a moment to catch her breath, she shook her head. "You can't say 'but' after 'I love you.' Love has to be unconditional, or it's not really love."

He raised his eyes to hers, and the anguish and pleading in his green gaze wrenched her heart. "I'm sorry, Annie. I want to be with you, to give you everything you deserve. But I don't know how."

She sank slowly down on the booth seat again, feeling numb, confused, cold. "I don't understand. If you really love me, then…" She caught her bottom lip with her teeth, her chest tightening until she couldn't breathe.

A muscle worked in his jaw, and he chafed her frozen fingers with his thumb. "I tried to warn you the other night not to fall for me, not to put your hope and faith in me. I could tell your deepest desire and dream was to have someone who could promise you a happily ever after. But that someone isn't me."

She glanced toward the table where the elderly couple fed each other apple pie, and she couldn't deny Jonah's assertion. She did want happily ever after. But didn't everyone? Was that wrong?

"Why do you think we wouldn't be happy?"

"Maybe we would be…for a while. But I don't know how to be a husband, how to be a father, how to be a family. When I think about my dad, the awkward, painful way our family operated, the lies and deceit, the distance, the anger, the isolation…" His voice cracked, and he swiped a hand down his face. "I don't ever want to go through that again. I don't want you to have to deal with my ghosts, and I can't promise you a future when I can't be sure if I'll get it right. I want you to be happy—for always—but I don't know if I can be what you need."

"So you won't even try?"

"You deserve better than just an attempt—"

She jerked her hand away from his and lurched to her feet. "Why don't you let me decide what I deserve?" She drew a shaky breath and blinked back the burn of tears. "I have work to do." She took two steps toward the kitchen before turning back. "Do you want to order anything?"

He met her glare with a sad, apologetic gaze that burrowed deep into her breaking heart. "Your forgiveness?"

His image blurred, and she swiped angrily at the moisture clouding her eyes. "I'm sorry, sir, but we're fresh out of forgiveness tonight."

With that, she hurried to the ladies' room for the privacy to fall apart.

As the hour grew later, the diner emptied of customers, and as Jonah watched Annie studiously avoid him, he felt increasingly empty inside as well. He couldn't leave things so raw and unsettled between them. He needed to talk with her again, make her understand his decision.

"I'm sorry, sir, but we're fresh out of forgiveness tonight."

Annie's parting shot replayed in his head, and as always, her words kicked him in the gut. She had reason to be angry, to hate him. Despite his best intentions, he'd hurt her. Deeply. He wasn't sure he could forgive himself for that.

A few minutes before eleven o'clock, Farrout and Pulliam

came in the front door of the diner, and Jonah braced himself. Farrout said a few words to Susan and swept an encompassing gaze around the empty diner before joining Jonah at his booth.

Annie stopped what she was doing and watched the men with wide, frightened eyes. Jonah longed to wrap her in his arms, keep her safe.

When Pulliam flipped the lock on the front door and headed into the kitchen, a chill of suspicion washed down Jonah's neck. He met Farrout's narrowed gaze with one of his own. "You have my payout?"

Farrout lifted a shoulder. "We'll get to that. First, you have something I want."

Jonah didn't show the other man any reaction, but a cold spike of apprehension drilled his chest. If something was about to happen, if Farrout had caught on to his investigation, Jonah wanted Annie safe, wanted her out of the diner.

He took a moment to appraise Farrout, then answered coolly, "I don't know what you mean."

"I thought you'd say that." Farrout leaned forward and pitched his voice to a low growl. "I want Hardin's files. I want whatever you took out of the locker at the bus depot, and I want whatever your girlfriend stole from my office."

Inside, Jonah's nerves were jumping, but he kept his gaze steady, his body still. "For starters, I don't have anything of Hardin's. All I got at the bus depot was a bag of my gym clothes I'd stashed there before a trip."

Jonah leaned across the table now, matching Farrout's aggressive cant. "But clearly you've been following me, which I resent and which begs the question, *why?* What do you have to hide?" He paused, but Farrout only glared. "And I don't have a girlfriend, so I have no idea what is missing from your office. Maybe you should be asking your lackeys these questions, 'cause I sure as hell have no answers for you."

Farrout sent a dark glance and a nod toward the counter where Pulliam propped, chewing a toothpick. In a heartbeat, Pulliam circled the counter and grabbed Annie's arm. Snaking an arm around her waist, he hauled her close, and Jonah tensed, alarm streaking through him.

"Perhaps we should ask your girlfriend the same questions. What do you suppose she'd have to say?" Farrout asked, his tone gloating.

Jonah squeezed his fingers into a fist and growled, "Leave her out of this."

"Oh, but she is a part of it, isn't she? She was Hardin's courier the night a small fortune went missing, and she was with you at the bus depot and later at the police department. I caught her snooping in my office the other day, too. Start talking, Devereaux. What's your game? What are you after?"

"I just want the money I won on the basketball tourney. I put ten grand on UNC."

Farrout frowned and tipped his head. "I don't recall any wager like that on UNC. Pulliam, you remember Devereaux placing any bets?"

"Nope."

Jonah struggled to cool the fury rising in him. He glanced over to Pulliam, who had pulled Annie's arms behind her back. A chill washed through Jonah.

Dear God, don't let them hurt Annie.

Jonah weighed his options and made his decision. "You let Annie walk out of here, and we'll talk." He leaned forward, nailing Farrout with his glare. "We'll talk about how you killed Michael Hamrick."

"Word I heard was Hamrick offed himself." Farrout's negligent shrug, as if Michael's death meant nothing, fanned Jonah's rage. "Anyway, I had nothing to do with his death."

"You had everything to do with it. You cheated him out of his retirement savings just like you're trying to cheat me now. You destroyed his life."

"I didn't make him place his bets. He was an addict. He lost his money all on his own. I'm just a businessman, all too happy to make a profit wherever I can."

Jonah forcibly swallowed the bitter reply on his tongue,

fought the urge trembling in his arms to smash Farrout's face. He couldn't, wouldn't give Farrout the power to make him lose control. He wasn't his father, and he would never let his life go down the violent path his father took.

He glanced again to Annie, whose dark eyes were wide with fear. "Tell your goon to take his grubby hands off Annie," he grated. "Now."

"Give me Hardin's files and whatever else your girlfriend stole from my office," Farrout countered. The man's eyes were flinty, emotionless.

Jonah didn't like the imbalance in this standoff. Farrout held all the cards, and Jonah had everything at stake. Because Pulliam had Annie. The woman he loved.

And that gave his enemy the upper hand.

Annie's heart knocked wildly in her chest. She was a liability to Jonah.

Every time Jonah glanced her way, she became more certain. As long as he was distracted by what Pulliam might do to her, Jonah was working from a disadvantage. She had to do something to even the odds. Stall for time.

When Pulliam grabbed her, she'd watched from the corner of her eye as Susan sidled into the kitchen. Surely Susan or the fry cook, Daniel, had called the police by now.

Annie clung to the hope that the cavalry was on the way. Her breath hung in her throat, knowing instinctively that her life was at a pivotal point, a defining moment. What direction fate took her depended largely on her response to the crisis, the choices she would make. She refused to wait helplessly for rescue, refused to be the victim of another man's abuse. In order to help Jonah, she had to help herself.

Mentally, she reviewed what she'd learned at the self-defense class, the things Jonah had coached her on. While a plan of attack coalesced in her mind, she followed the tense confrontation between Farrout and Jonah.

"What makes you think I have anything of Hardin's?" Jonah

said. His body language said he'd gladly leap over the table and rip Farrout's larynx out at the slightest provocation. That he hadn't throttled Farrout at his first chance spoke volumes to Annie about Jonah's control over his emotions, his restraint with the sparring skills he knew so well. Admiration swelled in her chest.

"Because I don't believe in coincidence. You showed up in the Fourth Street alley just after Hardin's delivery got nabbed. Your girlfriend was Hardin's courier, and she was snooping in my office the day the diner reopened." Farrout's glare narrowed on Jonah. "And my man saw you take a gym bag into the bus depot to a locker we saw Hardin use a week earlier. Given all that, what would you think?"

Annie swallowed hard. Farrout had them cornered. She'd seen enough nature shows to know what even the weakest animals did when cornered. They fought.

Annie took a deep breath, sent up a silent prayer...and fought back.

With all the force she could muster, she slammed her head into Pulliam's nose.

The thin man wailed in pain and released her wrist to cradle his face.

Hand freed, Annie grabbed a metal water pitcher from the counter. Twisted. Swung it in a powerful arc toward Pulliam's head.

"Damn bitch! You broke my—"

The pitcher smashed into the man's head with a resounding thunk. He wobbled, eyes rolling back, then crumpled onto the floor.

The scuffle of feet behind her yanked her attention to Farrout. The rotund man lurched to his feet. With his black gaze locked on her, he reached inside his jacket.

Jonah sprang a millisecond behind Farrout, tackling the giant man as he drew his weapon. He kicked Farrout's feet out from under him with a sweep of his leg and pinned him to the floor.

Farrout's gun fired, the blast deafening.

Annie gasped and stumbled back.

In a seamless move, Jonah reached for his ankle and came up with a small gun of his own. He jammed the gun against Farrout's head and grated, "Drop your weapon!"

Farrout struggled, cursing and bucking. Jonah jerked Farrout's arm into a painful-looking, unnatural angle. "Drop it, or I'll break your arm."

Growling an obscenity, Farrout let his gun clatter to the floor. Quickly, Jonah stuck his own gun into the waist of his jeans and palmed Farrout's larger gun.

Annie froze, stunned at what she'd just witnessed. But Jonah had served for many years with the police. Of course he knew how to subdue a man twice his size.

Jonah dug plastic bindings from his pocket and secured Farrout's hands behind his back. Bound his feet. Then shackled him to the leg of the nearest table with handcuffs.

Farrout continued to spout filth, and Jonah grabbed his throat in a hard pinch at his carotid artery. In a moment, Farrout passed out.

Jonah looked up at her. "Don't worry, he's not dead. He'll revive in a few minutes."

Annie released the breath she hadn't realized she was holding. Could it really be over? Relief swept through her, welling tears in her eyes and making her knees tremble.

Swiping perspiration from his forehead, Jonah asked, "Are you okay?"

She nodded, a smile blossoming on her lips. But Jonah's gaze shifted to something behind her and hardened.

Spinning around, Annie found Susan behind her. The waitress's mouth was pressed in a grim line. Her glare was icy.

And she aimed a gun at Annie's heart. "Not so fast, sweet cakes. We have unsettled business, and the boss is on his way."

Chapter 19

When he saw the revolver pointed at Annie, Jonah's gut roiled. He shoved away from Farrout's inert form and, rising to his knees, he swung Farrout's 9 mm toward Susan.

Annie had mentioned her concern that Susan had known things Annie hadn't told her. He'd downplayed the significance, discounted the importance of Susan's comments.

He'd screwed up. Failed Annie.

Acid guilt gnawed inside him, rebuking him.

"Lower your gun, Susan," he commanded, his tone firm but calm. "No one else has to get hurt. Just put it on the floor and step back."

Susan's answering laugh had a bitter edge. She stepped closer to Annie. "You wish."

Jonah's hands sweated, but he kept a firm grip on the 9 mm he had aimed at Susan.

Annie backed away from Susan until her back came up against the wall. "Daniel!" she yelled. "Call 911!"

Susan lurched forward, grabbed Annie's arm. "Sorry, honey.

Daniel left twenty minutes ago. Pulliam sent him home when he and Farrout arrived."

While Susan's attention was shifted to Annie, Jonah pushed smoothly to his feet.

Susan jerked her head back toward Jonah and poked her revolver behind Annie's ear. She tightened her grip on Annie's arm, and Annie winced. "Stop right there, Jonah. I don't want to hurt her, but I will."

Annie grew still, her eyes pleading with him. *Now what do I do?* her gaze asked.

Jonah dug deep for the professional detachment he needed. He had to treat this situation like any other he'd encountered on the force. Let training take over. Keep his emotions out of it.

But he'd never been in a standoff with the woman he loved caught in the crosshairs. How could he live with himself if anything happened to Annie? What would he do without her in his life?

A ball of cold realization settled in his gut. By ending their relationship and walking away, he'd already cut her out of his life. Because he feared the unknown. Because he couldn't bear to revive memories of his childhood. Because he was a coward.

Yet Annie had found enough courage to face her past, her demons, her fears. Enough to leave her abusive husband. Enough to give a future with him a chance. Enough to help him stop Farrout and his men.

Because she loved her children. Because she loved him.

Jonah's heart constricted. Annie had trumped fear...with love. If he loved Annie, how could he do any less?

He ground his teeth together, battled down the doubts and questions jabbing him. He had to focus on freeing Annie. If he could keep Susan occupied, distracted, he had a chance. If his plan was falling in place as arranged, backup was coming. He just had to buy a little time.

"What are you doing, Susan? Why are you involved in this?" Jonah asked.

Annie chewed her bottom lip, tried not to think about the

muzzle jabbing her skull. Her children needed her. She couldn't die here. Wouldn't leave her babies without a mother. She might not know how to get out of this macabre turn of events, but she had faith in Jonah. She trusted him with her life. And if she found an opportunity to help the situation, she'd act.

Susan snorted in answer to Jonah's query. "I'm not stupid. I know easy money when I see it. Why wouldn't I want my cut? Besides, you could say it's my family legacy."

Jonah furrowed his brow. "What do you mean?"

Susan shrugged, and the gun poked Annie harder. "My father runs the operation. He let me in on the action. Working at his diner is just my cover, so I can keep an eye on the people who work for him."

"Your father is the Pop of Pop's Diner?" Jonah's tone was calm, conversational. But Annie saw the cunning and purpose that blazed in his eyes.

"That's right. Pop himself. I'm the one who found out what Hardin was up to." Susan gave a smug-sounding chuckle. "I knew Hardin had been in trouble with the cops recently for some drug violation. When those charges went away a little too easily, I got curious. And Hardin started acting funny."

"Define funny," Jonah said, his weapon never wavering.

Annie watched him, amazed by his cool confidence, waiting for some clue from him as to what he needed her to do.

Susan grunted. "Hardin started acting nervous and looking crappier every day. Like he wasn't sleeping. Like the stress was eating his lunch.

"I warned Pop something could be up, and Pop had someone follow him. Pop's guys saw Hardin take a bunch of files from the diner to the bus depot. Then a little eavesdropping gave me enough information to help arrange someone to intercept the transfer of cash and gambling records to his police contact. We had all the proof we needed to justify eliminating Hardin. He'd become a liability."

Annie tensed. "Y-you killed Hardin?"

Susan scoffed. "Hell, no. Not me. Pop has men on his payroll to do that."

"Farrout and Pulliam." Jonah nodded to the men unconscious on the floor.

"Maybe. Or the guy who jumped Annie in the alley. Maybe someone else. I don't know who. Don't care."

Annie felt Susan shift her weight, draw her body up and press the gun harder against her head. She blew out a frustrated huff.

"Damn it, enough talking. I didn't mean to say that much. Now…put your gun down, Jonah, or I'll…I'll hurt Annie."

Jonah's eyes narrowed almost imperceptibly when Susan hesitated. Annie could swear she saw the wheels in Jonah's brain turning.

Rather than lower his gun, Jonah curled his finger around the trigger. "You don't want to hurt Annie, Susan. She's your friend. She's a mother. She's not involved in my investigation." He paused, narrowing his eyes again. "On the other hand, I have no qualms about shooting a woman."

His penetrating gaze met Annie's eyes then and held. Drilled her with their bright intensity. A chill crawled down Annie's spine, certain he was trying to tell her something.

Still holding her gaze, Jonah said calmly, "If you hurt Annie, I won't hesitate to *drop* you in the *blink* of an eye."

His gaze clung to hers another heartbeat, before he shifted his lethal stare back to Susan. His unflinching green eyes blazed with intent.

Then he blinked.

Annie dropped like a rag doll.

A single blast shook the room, and Susan screamed.

From the floor, Annie glanced back to see Susan clutch her shoulder, drop her gun and slide down the counter to the floor.

"You bastard!" a male voice growled. "What have you done to my daughter?"

A familiar-looking, silver-haired man stood in the door to the kitchen.

Pop had arrived.

* * *

Jonah reaimed the gun toward the new arrival.

And his pulse kicked when recognition dawned. "Frank?"

The gym owner snatched up the gun Susan had dropped and swung it toward Jonah. "I can't tell you how disappointed I am to see you here, Devereaux. You're one of my best sparring partners. I hate having to kill you. You're gonna be missed at the gym."

"*You* own the diner? *You're* behind the gambling and money laundering?" Jonah heard the disbelief in his voice and shook off the lingering shock to focus on the problem at hand. Namely, the gun in Frank's grip.

Jonah cut a quick glance to Annie. She'd grabbed a clean towel and pressed it to the wound on Susan's shoulder. Ever the caregiver. Even though her patient had just held a gun to her head.

Frank strolled closer to Jonah. "Folks were all the time wagering on sports at my gym. I saw a way to make a profit and took it. I'd bought the diner years back, and it proved the simplest way to clean the money, filter it into special accounts. But as an operation like mine grows, problems come up. People you thought you could trust turn on you to save their own skin."

"Hardin?"

Frank jerked a nod. "Good riddance. The man had proved unreliable at best. He got greedy. Got careless. I should have taken him out years ago."

Jonah drew a slow breath for composure. "And Michael Hamrick? You fleeced him. Before he died, he told me the operation he'd gotten tangled up with had welched on paying him what he was owed on winning bets. That you duped him into investing his life savings on high-stakes games."

"No one held a gun to his head, if that's what you mean." Frank smirked. "He took care of that himself."

White-hot rage exploded in Jonah. Ducking his head, he charged at Frank. "You son of a bitch!"

"Jonah, no!" Annie launched from the floor, threw herself at Frank.

Grabbed for Frank's gun.

A flash. An earsplitting blast. A gut-wrenching cry.

With a gasp, Annie collapsed against Jonah, the front of her apron marred by a bright red stain.

"Annie!" Jonah sank with her to the floor, horror ripping through his chest.

Frank reangled his weapon.

Glass shattered. Men in uniform breached the front door. Guns at the ready, Lagniappe's finest swarmed the diner.

"Freeze! Police! Lower your weapon and lie facedown with your hands out!"

As the police filed in, Frank sighed defeat, set his gun on the floor and lay down spread-eagle as ordered.

Jonah shot an angry look at the man leading the charge. *Joseph Nance.* "About damn time! Annie's been shot! Get an ambulance *now!*"

Chapter 20

"Mommy?" The sweet tiny voice cut through Annie's drug-induced haze. A small hand touched her cheek, and she blinked Haley into focus. On some level she knew she was in the hospital. The beeping monitors and medicinal smells told her that much. But her daughter held her attention, made her heart swell.

"Hey, darlin'. How's my girl?" she rasped, her throat raw and aching.

"I'm okay." Her daughter snuggled closer, bumping her ribs. Annie gasped as a sharp pain ripped through her chest.

"Say, princess, why don't you sit here with me? Remember I told you your mommy didn't feel good?"

Annie angled her head, searching for the man who'd spoken.

Jonah sat in a chair beside the hospital bed. Unshaven, clothes wrinkled, hair mussed, he'd never looked better to Annie. His eyes met hers, and she read the questions there. The doubts.

"I don't know if I can be what you need."

Fresh pain, unrelated to the bullet that had ripped through

her, slashed her heart. Despite the dramatic events at the diner, nothing had been resolved between her and Jonah.

Haley climbed onto Jonah's lap, and he gave her daughter's head a loving stroke and cuddled her close. "Don't be scared," he murmured to Haley. "Remember I told you how strong your mom is? She's going to be fine."

Haley nodded and glanced back at her mother. "Mr. Jonah says you're a hero, Mommy. You saved his life and helped catch a bad guy."

"He said that?" Annie raised her eyebrows and shot Jonah a querying look.

"Don't worry. I gave her the Saturday-morning cartoon version. I figured a well-filtered version of the truth was better than a lie." He looked unsure of himself, and Annie tugged up a corner of her mouth.

"You were right. Thank you for your discretion."

Jonah sighed, relief replacing a fraction of the tension lining his face.

"Where's Ben?" Annie croaked.

Jonah whispered something to Haley, and her daughter slid from his lap to hand Annie a cup of ice chips.

"Thanks, sweetie."

"Ben is with your friend Ginny. She offered to keep Haley, too, but nothing would do for Haley until she saw her mommy at the hospital."

A scuffle of feet drew Annie's attention to her door. Ginny's husband came in with two large cups of coffee. When Riley noticed Annie was awake, he paused and grinned. "Hey, welcome back, Sleeping Beauty. I don't know what kind of drugs they gave you, but they sure knocked you out."

Annie wrinkled her brow. "How long was I asleep?"

Jonah checked his watch. "About thirteen and a half hours." He grinned sheepishly and added, "Thirteen hours and thirty-six minutes to be exact. Longest thirteen hours and thirty-six minutes of my life."

Riley handed one of the coffees to Jonah and tousled

Haley's hair. "So now that you've seen for yourself your mom's okay, what say we let her rest and go give Ms. Ginny a hand with your brother?"

Haley gave her mother a dubious frown, but with a few more reassurances, she allowed Riley to lead her from the room.

Then Annie turned to Jonah, nailing him with an expression that was all-business. "You stayed with my children overnight?"

He nodded. "I wanted to here with you, more than anything. But I knew your priority would be your kids, so I stayed with them. Burned up the phone line calling the hospital every five minutes to check on you, but..."

Annie grinned. "My hero."

He pulled his eyebrows into a skeptical V. "I don't know how you can say that. I let you down. You wouldn't be here if—"

"I'm here because I was dumb enough to try to get Frank's gun away from him."

"No, you were brave enough to act when my life was at risk. I owe you one."

She shrugged carefully, but even the small movement caused her ribs to burn. "You've saved me more than once. Call us even."

Jonah's cheek twitched in a weak grin, and he lowered his gaze to his hands.

Annie broke the awkward silence. "What did my doctors say? Last thing I really remember is the EMT giving me something for pain. Then I passed out."

"The bullet's angle was shallow, but it hit and broke a rib. You'll be in some pain for a few weeks, and they want you to take it easy to allow yourself to heal."

Annie gave a soft laugh. "Did you tell them there's no such thing as rest for the mother of two young kids?"

Jonah shot her a warning look. "Annie...do as your doctor says. Ginny, Rani and I will help with Haley and Ben."

A seed of hope lodged deep inside her. "You?"

He met her eyes warily, a heartbreaking sadness dimming

his eyes. "If you'll let me. I know I hurt you, Annie. Everything I said the other night... I..." His eyes closed, and he dragged a hand over his face, the picture of misery.

"Jonah, before you tell me you don't know how to be a husband and father, think about what we've already done together."

His gaze found hers again, and he cocked his head. "Go on."

"Every time I thought the worst had passed the other night, that the nightmare was over, something else would happen. Susan showed up with a gun. Then her father did. I didn't know what to do, how to get us out of the pickle we were in, but I had faith. Between us, we got through it. We survived by working together, and the bad guys were caught." She paused, frowning. "They were all caught, right? The whole mess at the diner is over. We don't have to worry about anyone else popping out of the shadows?"

Jonah nodded. "The four at the diner were arrested and taken in for questioning. Farrout and Pulliam, hoping to buy lighter sentences, started singing like birds. Names, addresses, the works. As we speak, the rest of Frank's cronies are being rounded up." He nodded. "It's really over."

Relief washed through her, and she closed her eyes, replaying the moment the police had swarmed the diner. One face in particular stood out. "The smarmy businessman," she mumbled. She jerked her gaze back to Jonah. "Joseph Nance? He'd been in the diner before. I recognized him, because he'd watched me so close every time he came in, it gave me the creeps."

"Hardin had contacted him but had been really vague about what he wanted with the police. So Nance got suspicious when Hardin was murdered. He'd started his own investigation by the time I called him."

She arched an eyebrow. "So that's how the cops knew what was happening last night? Somehow I didn't think that was coincidence."

"Naw. After going through Hardin's files, I decided it was time to bring in the authorities. I called Joseph Nance, showed him what we had, and we made a plan. I was wearing a mic

last night. They heard everything and knew when to step in."
He paused. "Detective Nance has offered me a job with the
Lagniappe PD."

Annie caught her breath. "Will you take it?"

He nodded. "I plan to."

Annie sank back in her pillows, digesting it all. "I guess all
this means I'm out of a job, though." She chewed her lip, wondering how she'd make ends meet now.

"Think of this as opportunity knocking. You can do whatever
you want with your life, Annie."

She curled her fingers into the sheet, letting her deepest desires
filter to the light. "Ginny told me once the women's center offers
scholarships for women who want to finish their education.
Maybe I'll go back to college. The local university has a student
worker program and family housing I can look into."

Jonah smiled. "I like that plan."

One problem had been resolved, but the greater threat to her
happiness remained.

"Jonah," she started again carefully, her heart rising to her
throat. She had to convince him their love was worth taking a
risk. "Considering all we've been through already, how can you
doubt our ability to make a marriage work? And I say *our*
ability for a reason. Because you won't be alone anymore.
We'll be a team."

Jonah caught his breath, and she saw warmth flash in his
eyes, chasing away some of the shadows darkening his expression. The seed of hope in her chest planted roots.

He rose from the chair and sat on the edge of her bed. He
stroked her face gently and held her gaze. "We do make a
good team."

She covered his hand with hers. "I know the idea of family
brings back painful memories, but I want to be there to help
you face down those ghosts from your past…if you'll let me."

He answered her by kissing her palm.

Encouraged, she forged on, "I know that our life together
will have bumps and potholes along the way, problems to

overcome. Every marriage does. But last night—for the past several weeks, in fact—we've met every challenge we faced *together* and seen it through. We can do the same as a family, no matter what life throws at us."

He leaned close and pressed a kiss to her forehead. "Last night when Susan had that gun on you, I was terrified she'd hurt you and I'd lose you. Then I realized I'd already lost you, because I'd let fear rule my heart instead of my love for you, and I was ashamed of myself." He placed a soft kiss on her lips. "You deserve so much more."

She tensed. "Jonah, don't let fear keep you from being part of our family. I've seen how you are with my children. You're kind and gentle and protective, but you're also appropriately firm and instructive when you need to be. You have good instincts with them. You know what they need to hear to ease their fears without misleading them. The fact that you knew they needed you last night more than I did speaks volumes to me. You put them first. Trust those instincts, and you'll be a wonderful father."

He dragged a crooked finger along her jaw. "I know you're probably right, I...just have to sort some things out."

Annie stroked his face. "Jonah, what...what more do you need to know?"

He squeezed her hand, and the vulnerability that flickered in his gaze stole her breath.

"Only that you trust me."

She knitted her brow, concerned where Jonah was leading. "You know I do."

"Good. Then rest now." He kissed her lightly and backed away from the bed. "And know that I love you."

A few weeks later, Annie was putting the final touches on her hair, clipping the strands away from her face the way Jonah liked it, when she heard the doorbell.

"It's Jonah!" Haley squealed as she sped past the bathroom door.

Down the hall, Annie heard Jonah greet her daughter and son, and her heart gave a little kick. Quickly she snapped her hair clip in place and smoothed her hands down slacks before hurrying to join her kids and Jonah.

When she rounded the corner to her living room, Jonah swept an appreciative gaze over her and smiled brightly. "Hello, gorgeous."

"You're early," she said with a teasing scowl.

"I couldn't wait any longer to see you again. And I had a surprise for you that wouldn't keep."

"A surprise?" She noticed for the first time that he held one hand behind his back. Visions of boxed chocolate or cut flowers tickled her imagination. She lifted the corner of her mouth. "Do tell."

"I hope you like it." Jonah drew a deep breath and produced from behind him…a kitten.

Haley cheered. Ben giggled. "Kitty!"

Annie gaped, and Jonah flashed her a devilish grin. "Way I see it, every *new family* should have a pet."

Ignoring the children's outstretched and eager hands, he stepped closer to Annie and settled the tiny black and white tabby in her arms. Pinlike claws dug into her blouse, and a sweet fuzzy face peered up at her. Annie's heart melted. "She's precious, but—"

"No buts. You said you wanted a cat *someday.* When you were safe from Walt, and your life calmed down, and your future looked bright." He brushed his fingers along her cheek and lowered his voice. "I know you were hoping for a ring, but…for now, will April do?"

"April?"

"That's what I've been calling the cat…to mark the month we started our new life with our new family." Jonah's eyes glowed with warmth and love. "A token of my promise to be the best husband and father I can."

She wrapped an arm around Jonah's neck and kissed him soundly on the lips. When Haley reached for the kitten, Annie surrendered the fuzz ball to her daughter's hands. "Gently, Hal. She's just a baby."

"I'm gonna call her Pookie," Haley cooed as she rocked the kitten in her arms.

"Pookie?" Jonah pulled a face.

Annie laughed as tears of joy sprang to her eyes. "Pookie, April, whatever... I love my surprise. And I love you, Jonah. You helped me find myself when I was lost."

Jonah drew her into the circle of his arms, smiling warmly. "And you gave me the courage to claim a new family when I was drifting and alone."

"So are we partners? Can we tackle the future as a team?"

"You've got a deal." Joy lit Jonah's eyes, and he rested his forehead on Annie's. "Welcome to someday."

* * * * *

UNDERCOVER WIFE

MERLINE LOVELACE

An Air Force brat, **Merline Lovelace** grew up on military bases all around the world. She spent twenty-three years in the United States Air Force herself, pulling tours in Taiwan, Vietnam and the Pentagon before she hung up her uniform for good and decided to try her hand at writing. She now has more than eighty-five published novels under her belt, with more than twelve million copies of her works in print.

Merline and her own handsome hero live in Oklahoma. When she's not glued to her keyboard, she loves travelling to exotic locations, chasing little white balls around the golf course and enjoying long, lazy dinners with family and friends. Be sure to check www.merlinelovelace. com for release dates of future books.

To my darling, who loves to ramble and explore as much as I do. Thanks for the castles of the Loire Valley, picnicking under the arches of the Pont du Gard, lunch at the Ritz Carlton in Cannes and most of all—for Mont St. Michel.

Prologue

"**W**hat do you think it is?"

His voice muffled by his surgical mask, the patholo-gist at the U.S. Fish and Wildlife Service Forensics Lab yielded his place at the electron microscope to his partner.

"Damned if I know," the second scientist answered as he peered at the sample taken from the carcass. "It doesn't match any known viral strains."

He straightened, and both men's glances went to the glass enclosure separating them from the creature stretched out on the autopsy table. It was a *nomascus concolor,* or Western black-crested gibbon, very rare and native to the jungles of Asia. The two pathologists had no idea how it had made its way to the ditch beside California's Highway 101 where it had been found dead, its carcass pecked almost to pieces by crows. The fact that those same crows lay in lifeless heaps beside the gibbon raised an immediate red flag with the road worker who stumbled across them. Within hours, local authorities, worried about a possible outbreak of avian flu, had sealed and shipped the remains to the U.S. Fish and Wildlife Service Forensics Lab in Oregon.

The pathologists performing the autopsy could confirm that bird flu had killed neither the monkey nor the crows. The mounting evidence of what *had* killed them scared the crap out of both scientists.

"Looks like we've got us a mutant virus," the senior member of the team acknowledged reluctantly. "Very contagious and very deadly. We need to issue an immediate alert."

The alert went out to all government agencies. The Centers for Disease Control reissued it to the civilian sector, where everyone not directly involved in health care or simian research pretty much ignored it.

Except for one individual halfway around the world. When the alert painted across the screen of a computer configured to search for such items, it was read with fierce, almost primal satisfaction.

"Soon." Exultation shattered the stillness of the darkened room. "Soon my revenge will be complete."

Chapter 1

The town house halfway down a side street just off Massachusetts Avenue, in the heart of Washington, D.C.'s embassy district, looked much like its neighbors. It boasted an elegant, federal-style facade and tall windows framed by black shutters. A short flight of steps led to an oak door painted in gleaming vermilion.

A bronze plaque beside the door identified the town house as home to the offices of the president's Special Envoy. The position was one of those jobs created to reward rich campaign contributors with a yen for a Washington office and a taste of power politics. Only a handful of insiders knew the Special Envoy also served as Director of OMEGA, a supersecret government agency with an elite cadre of operatives activated only in extreme emergencies.

It wasn't an emergency that had brought a small legion of agents in from the various ventures that provided cover in their civilian lives, however. They were gathered in the director's office to welcome back one of their own.

Elizabeth Wells had served as executive assistant to OMEGA's director for almost two decades. The silver-haired grandmother had fallen while doing a foxtrot on a big-band cruise of the Potomac with her latest beau. After hip-replacement surgery and months of rehab, Elizabeth was ready to resume her duties.

Three of her bosses were present for the homecoming. Adam Ridgeway, code name Thunder, had hired Elizabeth all those years ago. Tall and broad-shouldered, Thunder stood with one hand in the pocket of his hand-tailored slacks and a pained expression on his face while his wife—also a former operative and one-time OMEGA director—related the latest exploits of their youngest.

"Tank insists it wasn't his idea." With a rueful grin, Maggie Sinclair, code name Chameleon, continued her description of her son's assault on the hallowed halls of Harvard. "He also insists he did *not* position Terence atop the bust of John Adams, at the perfect angle to spit into the face of the dean of the Business School."

Terence, as the assembled operatives all knew, was the orange-and-purple-striped iguana Maggie had brought back from a mission in Central America years ago. The evil-tempered creature was the bane of Adam's existence. He'd been looking forward to its demise for as long as anyone could remember, but his wife and three children adored the damned thing. So much so that

Adam Jr.—known to his family and friends as Tank—
had carted off the lizard with him to enjoy the delights
of his freshman year at Harvard.

Tank's sister took up the tale at that point. "You
should have seen Dad's face when the dean called."

Laughter sparkled in Gillian Ridgeway's vivid blue
eyes. She had her father's gleaming black hair and aristocratic features. From her mother, she'd inherited a flair
for languages and an irrepressible sense of humor. On
extended leave from her job with the State Department,
Gillian had filled in as executive assistant to OMEGA's
director during Elizabeth Wells's convalescence.

"Dad won't say what it cost to keep both Tank and
Terence on the student rolls, but I suspect Harvard got
a hefty endowment out of it."

"I suspect they'll get *several* endowments before
Tank graduates."

That came from Nick Jensen, code name Lightning,
OMEGA's current director. Lightning had headed the
agency through three successive presidential adminis-
trations. Although he hadn't made a formal announcement, the betting was he'd resign the directorship after
the upcoming election. When his wife, Mackenzie, surprised herself and everyone else by turning up pregnant
with their first child, the bet had become a sure thing.

"There she is!"

Alerted by a glimpse through the window of a sleek
limo gliding to a halt at the curb, Lightning strode out
to greet his executive assistant. A few moments later
he escorted the slender, gray-haired grandmother into
his office.

Agents with code names such as Slash, Rogue, Cowboy, Diamond and Cyrene welcomed her with warm hugs. Elizabeth had tears in her eyes when Maggie gave her shoulders a gentle squeeze and Adam dropped an affectionate kiss on her cheek. While the champagne corks popped, Elizabeth dabbed her eyes with a lace-trimmed handkerchief before proceeding to stun the entire gathering.

"I have an announcement. I'm afraid my return is only temporary."

Instant concern replaced the smiles and good wishes. Lightning's voice went taut. "What's happened? Did you experience complications you didn't tell me about during my last visit?"

"As a matter of fact, I did." Her pale blue eyes filled with a combination of chagrin and delight. "I'm getting married next month. Next week, if Daniel has his way."

After a few seconds of stunned silence, Lightning recovered. "Daniel? Who the hell is this character, and why didn't you let us check him out?"

"You did. Very thoroughly, as I recall. It's Daniel Foster. *Dr.* Daniel Foster."

"Your surgeon?"

"One and the same." A hint of red crept into Elizabeth's cheeks. "Apparently he thinks I have rather elegant hips, before and after the surgery. *I* think he just wants to admire his handiwork."

Whoops erupted throughout the room. When they subsided and champagne flutes made their way into everyone's hands, Lightning lifted his glass.

"To you and Dr. Dan. He'd better make you *very*

happy or some extremely lethal undercover agents will show up on his doorstep."

Several similar toasts later, Elizabeth brought up the subject of her successor. Her expression was as warm as her voice when she turned to Gillian.

"Lightning says you did a magnificent job covering for me, Jilly. Will you stay on, dear, until you decide whether you want to go back to the State Department?"

"Well..."

Lowering her lashes, Gillian twirled the stem of her champagne flute between her fingers. She'd planned to wait to make her own announcement. Since Elizabeth had set the stage, however...

"Actually, I *am* staying on. As an agent."

"The hell you are!"

The explosive remark surprised everyone, including the operative it burst from. Red surged above the collar of Mike Callahan's shirt collar as all heads turned in his direction, but the frown he directed at Gillian was fierce and unapologetic.

She answered the thunderous scowl with one of her quick smiles. "It's a done deal. Uncle Nick gave his stamp of approval yesterday."

"Not without considerable arm twisting," her honorary uncle muttered under his breath.

Mike Callahan, code name Hawkeye, tightened his jaw. "You're not trained for this kind of work, Jilly."

"I'll get the training."

Gillian's smile took on an edge that either of her siblings would have recognized in a heartbeat. "I held my own in Scotland. Didn't I, Rogue?"

The tall, slender blonde she addressed nodded. "That you did, girlfriend."

Yeah, Callahan thought savagely. And he hadn't drawn a full breath until he'd put her on a plane for home.

A former military cop, he was a dead shot with every weapon in the government's arsenal and a good number that weren't. Hence his code name, Hawkeye, which most of his fellow agents shortened to Hawk. In his civilian life he was a marksmanship instructor at the Federal Law Enforcement Academy at Quantico, Virginia. He'd also taught all three of the Ridgeway off-spring to shoot.

Gillian-with-a-J had been the first. The *J* was a standing joke that went back to their initial meeting. All arms and long, long legs, the teenager had grinned up at him and introduced herself as Gillian, pronounced with a soft *G,* like in Jillian.

Hawk had lost part of his heart to the gangly teen right then and there. In the years since, he'd come damned close to losing the rest of it. Like most of the male agents at OMEGA, he was seriously in lust with the stunning, sensual creature Gillian Ridgeway had become. The woman could set off a firestorm in his belly with a single glance from those electric blue eyes.

He'd kept the fire in check, however. Despite the hints she'd been throwing his way recently, he knew damned well he was too old for her, too rough around the edges. He also knew that undercover work could be dangerous not only for him but for anyone who went into the field with him.

He looked at her now, his insides twisting as another

face superimposed itself on Gillian's classic features. He could hear the splat of bullets tearing through the vines. Feel the vicious downwash of the chopper hovering above the canopy. See the sprawled, lifeless body of the woman he'd gone into the jungle with.

Slamming the door on the searing memory, he swung toward Gillian's parents. "You've both been field agents. You know what it's like. You're good with this?"

"Yes," Maggie said instantly, then flashed an annoyed look when her husband gave a less enthusiastic response.

"I'll admit I'm not particularly thrilled with the idea," Adam said coolly, "but I trust Gillian's instincts."

Christ! Hawk's gut kinked again. Couldn't they see she lacked the killer instinct? She was too refined, too educated, too damned beautiful to...

The sudden buzz of the phone on Lightning's desk sliced into Hawk's chaotic thoughts. The blinking red light that accompanied the buzz stiffened his shoulders.

He and everyone else in the room knew that blinking light was the direct line to the White House...and that they should clear out of the director's office, fast. Depositing their champagne glasses, they made for the door.

Maggie and Adam could have stayed. They'd both taken direct calls from past presidents and were still cleared at the highest levels. But Lightning now shouldered responsibility for OMEGA. Unwilling to intrude on his turf, they joined the general exodus.

The operatives headed for the elevator that would whisk them to the ultra-high-tech Operations Center on the third floor of the town house. Hawk hesitated several seconds before he, too, strode toward the elevator.

Adam's eyes were narrowed as he followed the man's progress. Maggie's were thoughtful. Hooking her chin, she signaled for Jilly to accompany her to the ladies' room just off the first-floor foyer.

"Okay, daughter of mine." Leaning her hips against the marble counter, Maggie crossed her arms. "Tell me again, no frills, no fuss. How much of your decision to join OMEGA's ranks stems from a real desire to work undercover and how much from a determination to prove to Mike Callahan that you're all grown up?"

Jilly didn't blink. "I'm one hundred percent...on both counts."

Maggie eyed her daughter for long moments. She knew Hawk's paternalistic and overly protective attitude irritated Jilly no end. The irritation had increased exponentially since their trip to Scotland. Maggie thought of all the advice she could offer and reduced it to one caution.

"Don't push him too hard, Jilly. You might not like it when he pushes back."

Her daughter's jet-black brows snapped together. She looked so much like her father when he was annoyed that Maggie's heart kicked over.

"You and Dad have known Hawk for years. This is the first time you've ever hinted that you have a problem with him."

"We don't. We would trust him with our lives."

"But not with your daughter. What do you know about him that I don't?"

Maggie hooked a strand of golden-brown hair behind one ear, considering her answer. She'd cheerfully rip out the heart of anyone who threatened her husband or children. But she had to weigh that fierce, primal love against her loyalty to the men and women she'd lived, worked and sweated blood with for so many years.

"I don't know the details," she said slowly. "No one does. Hawk has never talked about why he left the military, but…"

"But?"

"Your father ran into his former commanding officer at some function or another. The general didn't go into specifics, but he did say Hawk hung up his uniform after a botched mission in Central America. Hawk went in with two other operatives. One of them didn't make it out. The general didn't say so but the implication was he buried his heart with her there in that steamy jungle."

"Her?" Jilly echoed softly. "That explains a lot."

"I thought it might. Tread carefully, sweetheart."

Maggie couldn't resist giving her daughter's silky black hair a gentle yank. Where was the wide-eyed toddler who'd pulled up the just-planted pansies to decorate her mudpies? What happened to the mischievous little girl who loved to dress an ungainly iguana in doll clothes, deposit him in her baby sister's buggy and stroll nonchalantly around the block? When had the giggling teen with braces grown into this smart, self-assured woman?

With a silent sigh, Maggie gave her daughter's hair another tug and shooed her out of the ladies' room. "You'd better go see what that call was about, Special Agent-in-Training Ridgeway."

She tried to contain her emotion as she watched Jilly make for the elevator, but her husband knew her too well.

"She'll be okay."

Adam forced a smile as he looked down into his wife's face, but acid rolled around in his stomach at the thought of what lay ahead of his darling, his little princess. He'd been out there. So had Maggie. Her exploits in the field had aged Adam well beyond his years. Remembering those turbulent times, his smile relaxed into a rueful grin.

"She'll be okay," he repeated. "She's her mother's daughter."

The atmosphere inside OMEGA's third-floor Control Center left no doubt in Jilly's mind. Something was up. Something big.

She'd been up to the busy Control Center any number of times while filling in for Elizabeth. But the realization that one of those amber lights on the digitized world map that took up an entire wall would soon represent her sent a shiver of excitement down her spine.

Most of the agents had already dispersed, some to milk OMEGA's computers, some to work the phones. Lightning stood at the main console with Hawk, their eyes glued to the data scrolling across a monitor.

They couldn't be more different, Jilly thought as she approached the two men. With his tawny hair, deep tan and sartorial elegance, Lightning looked very much like the sophisticated jet-setter he now was.

Mike Callahan, on the other hand, looked very much like the man *he* was. Tough, uncompromising, no nonsense. He was more rugged than handsome, with a square chin and a mouth that rarely smiled. He wore his dark brown hair cut military short. His gold-flecked hazel eyes missed little. So little that Jilly had always believed that's how he'd come by his code name of Hawkeye.

Until she'd seen him shoot, that is. The first time had been at an International Law Enforcement Tri-Gun Competition. Her parents had taken her to watch the final round, where Hawk scored top honors in the handgun and heavy metal categories. To his disgust, he'd come in second in the shotgun class. He rose to hero status in her eyes that day. She'd been trying to bring him down to the level of mere mortal ever since.

Soon, she vowed as both men acknowledged her arrival with a quick glance. Soon.

"What have we got?" she asked.

Her deliberate use of the plural produced a scowl from Hawk, but Lightning accepted her into the fold.

"Some sort of mutant virus," he replied in a grim voice. "Scientists at the U.S. Fish and Wildlife Service Forensics Lab found it a week ago when they autopsied the carcass of a…" He glanced at the computer monitor in front of him. "A *nomascus concolor.*"

Jilly didn't even try to pretend she knew what that was.

"It's a monkey," Lightning informed her. "Or rather, a gibbon. A species of small ape native to southern China and Southeast Asia."

He swiveled the monitor around to display a black, furry creature with tufts of white on his cheeks and impossibly long arms.

"It's the most critically endangered ape species in the world. Supposedly, its very scarcity makes it highly prized as a sacrificial offering in certain far-out religious cults."

The tiny ape on the screen stared back at Jilly with an inquisitive expression in his caramel-colored eyes. The thought of this cuddly little creature being carved up by religious fanatics raised goose bumps on her skin.

"Someone tossed the carcass of one of these gibbons into a ditch in California," Lightning continued. "Both the road worker who discovered it and the animal-control officer who responded to his call are now in intensive care. Their docs are still trying to find the right combination of drugs to combat the virus infecting them."

That was scary. Gillian knew all kinds of nasty diseases like HIV, SARS and Ebola were linked to primates. Now, apparently, a new one had appeared on the scene.

"How did this gibbon get into the States?"

"We don't know. But the bug that killed it has proved so virulent that Homeland Security tasked one of their top agents to track down the person or persons who brought it in." Lightning's voice went flat and hard. "That agent was found this morning in a back alley in San Francisco, with a bone-handled knife through his throat."

His glance cut to the operative standing stone-faced and rigid on the other side of the communications console.

"Hawk was just about to tell us why his name was the last word the agent uttered."

The clatter of keyboards and hum of voices in the Control Center stilled. A tense silence descended until Hawk broke it with slow deliberation.

"Charlie Duncan and I served together. A long time ago. In Special Ops. He saved my life. My guess is he was hoping I'd repay the favor by hunting down whoever put that shiv through his throat."

His rigidly controlled tone belied the feral light in his hazel eyes. For the first time in her life, Jilly was just a little afraid of him.

Her mother's warning rang in her ears. But as quickly as the goosey feeling came, she shoved it aside. This was Mike Callahan. The man who'd cradled her against his chest, corrected her aim and taught her to put nine out of ten rounds dead center. He was big, certainly. Gruff, sometimes. Hot as hell, always. She refused to be afraid of a man she fully intended to bring to his knees.

Unaware of his fate, Hawk zeroed in on Lightning. "I want this mission."

"You've got it."

"I'll fly out to California tomorrow, see what leads the locals have on Charlie's death."

"You might want to talk to the folks at the Centers for Disease Control here in D.C. first."

"Will do."

"I can help," Jilly said. "I spent three years in Asia. I could…"

"No."

Hawk rounded on her.

"Listen to me, Gillian-with-a-J. We're talking a potentially lethal virus. Possibly radical religious nuts. A cold-blooded killer or killers. That's enough for me to handle without worrying about you running around playing amateur secret agent."

Heat rushed into Jilly's cheeks and fire into her eyes. Before she could let fly, Hawk raked a hand through his short-cropped hair and offered a grudging compromise.

"I don't like the idea of you getting into this game.

You know that. But... Well, it looks like you've made up your mind. I'll mentor you, Jilly. Teach you some of the tricks of the trade I've picked up over the years. After I get back from this mission. In the meantime, I need you to stay out of my way."

Mentoring was the last thing she wanted from Mike Callahan. This was hardly the time to tell him so, however.

"I'll stay out of your way," she promised, masking her anger with icy politeness, "but at least let me work my contacts at the State Department. They have a special desk tracking religious splinter groups. One of the analysts might have something we can use."

"All right, but let me know immediately if you find anything."

His tone implied that he was highly doubtful, and Jilly had to subdue a thoroughly unprofessional impulse to flip him the bird. The gesture would have been wasted in any case. He'd already turned his attention back to Lightning.

Chapter 2

Jilly steamed all the way to Foggy Bottom.

None of the other passengers on the Metro would have guessed she was pissed. She smiled her thanks to the tattooed kid who moved aside to give her room. She apologized to the Navy lieutenant she bumped into when the train took off. And she had herself well in hand when she exited the Metro and took the soaring escalator at the Foggy Bottom–George Washington University stop.

Foggy Bottom got its name from the mist that swirled through the low-lying area between the Potomac River and Rock Creek. The Bottom was home to a host of well-known institutions, including George Washington University, the Kennedy Center and the infamous Watergate Hotel. Most Washington pundits, however, believed the "fog" emanated from the government agency that took up an entire block on C Street.

The headquarters of the U.S. Department of State was a monolithic square of concrete and glass. Jilly could still remember the thrill that had danced through her when she mounted the front steps for the first time as a very new and very junior Foreign Service Officer. She suspected her father's considerable pull had something to do with her acceptance into the highly competitive Foreign Service. That, and acing the Foreign Service Officers' exam. The fact that she'd inherited her mother's flair for languages and had snagged a graduate Fulbright scholarship to study Mandarin at Peking University hadn't hurt, either.

Her linguistic skills had led to her first assignment as a cultural affairs officer in Beijing. Those three years had been exciting as hell but convinced Jilly she wasn't the stuff bureaucrats are made of. She'd loved the people she worked with and fully appreciated the positive effects of cultural exchanges but *hated* the paperwork.

She'd returned from Beijing undecided about a career with the State Department. The months she'd spent filling in for Elizabeth Wells had settled the matter. As an OMEGA operative, she could still travel to exotic locations, still engage with people of all nationalities and political persuasions. But she wouldn't have to write a twenty-page report after every contact.

Since she'd handed in her State Department ID along with her resignation, she had to wait at the visitors' entrance for an escort. He emerged from the inner sanctum moments later and greeted her in fluent Mandarin.

"*Nee hao,* Gillian. *Ching shou, nee huey lai dao State!*"

Laughing, she shook her head and answered in kind. "Sorry, Don. I'm not returning to the fold. I'm here as a civilian. And a supplicant."

Don Ackerman huffed in disappointment. He was one of several senior Foreign Service Officers who staffed the China desk. He'd tried every stratagem in his considerable repertoire to keep Jilly in his sector, including outright bribes and her choice of assignments.

"What can I do for you?" he asked after he'd signed her in and she'd processed through security screening.

"Point me to whoever's handling radical religious cults these days."

"You're kidding, right? You know very well two thirds of our antiterrorist division is working that threat."

"This one doesn't sound jihadist, unless they've gotten into animal sacrifice."

"Animal sacrifice?" Don scratched his chin and led the way down a long corridor. "We've got several of those. The most visible is the Santeria sect in south Florida. But the Supreme Court decided their ritual sacrifice of chickens during ceremonies is an expression of religious freedom, so we don't classify them as radical anymore."

"How about monkeys? Or small apes?"

Ackerman's lips pursed. He was a big man, going soft around the middle these days, but still possessed the encyclopedic knowledge of world cultures that had made him a legend at State.

"That sounds more like the Vhrana Sect." He came to a full stop in the hallway. "They're bad news, Gillian. What's your interest in them?"

Although she suspected State had received the same urgent missive Lightning had, Jilly hadn't been cleared to discuss it with anyone outside OMEGA. All she could tell Don was a basic version of the truth.

"I'm doing some research for the agency I now work for."

His penetrating gray eyes drilled into her. "You'd better talk to Sandra Hathaway. She's our Vhrana expert."

Sandra Hathaway was a dark-haired, intense analyst. The kind, Jilly guessed, who doled out information sparingly to folks in the field. She hunched over her computer and made no effort to disguise her annoyance at the interruption. Her irritation morphed instantly into a closed, guarded expression when Don mentioned the Vhrana.

He overrode her bureaucratic caution with a blunt order. "Gillian was one of our own until she bailed. Despite that serious lapse of judgment, I'll vouch for her. Give her whatever information you can about the sect."

"Whatever" turned out to be scary as hell. The Vhrana, Jilly soon learned, were an even more dangerous splinter group of the religious fanatics who set off chemical bombs in a Tokyo subway some years back.

"The Vhrana believe the only true path to enlightenment is to cleanse the world of evil, as they see it," Hathaway related. "They practice rites that derive from Buddhism and ancient forms of Hinduism, with a dash of Turkish Sufi thrown in. The more 'advanced' in the sect go into trances and spin around for hours."

"Like whirling dervishes?"

"Precisely."

"And they also practice animal sacrifice?"

"In ancient times, they sacrificed humans. Usually enemies captured after a battle. The Vhrana drank blood from the vanquished warriors' skulls to imbibe their valor before devouring their hearts and livers."

"Nice guys."

"Don't delude yourself. The women in the sect were—and still are—every bit as bloodthirsty. You don't want to get crosswise of a Vhrana priestess. Nowadays, of course, human sacrifice has been outlawed. So has animal sacrifice, for that matter, but the Vhrana still practice it on holy days. They're rumored to offer up a variety of animals, but their sacrifice of choice is a monkey or ape."

The picture of the little gibbon flashed into Jilly's mind.

"I thought most Hindus revere monkeys. In fact, I remember reading about the hordes of monkeys that now overrun New Delhi because the devout feed them peanuts and bananas."

"The Vhrana have perverted that reverence. Or elevated it, I guess you could say. Since primates are the closest things to humans, they believe they're honoring the animal by sacrificing them to their gods."

"Do you have a fix on the Vhrana sects in the U.S.?"

"We're tracking seven different branches. The largest is in California."

Where the dead gibbon was found. A frisson of excitement jumped along Jilly's nerves. She didn't have the training or field experience of a seasoned agent, but every scrap of intuition she possessed told her she was on the right trail.

"The second-largest sect is right across the state line,"

Hathaway continued, "in Baltimore. It draws most of its followers from the D.C. area." Swinging around, she clicked a few keys on her computer. "Here's a shot of the exterior of their temple."

Jilly studied the windowless brick building. "It looks like a warehouse."

"It is. We've ascertained that the owner has no idea what goes on in his building between the hours of midnight and dawn. His night manager takes over then."

Another click brought up a shot of a handsome man in the turban of a Sikh. Next to him was a smiling, doe-eyed female in a turquoise sari and veil.

"That's the night manager's wife, the current high priestess. We've been told she wields the knife at the altar. We hope to verify that tonight."

"Tonight?"

"It's the first night of the second full moon since harvest. One of their holiest days."

"Who's going in?"

"Special Agent Nareesh. He was one of us until he transferred to the FBI."

"Benjamin Nareesh?"

"Yes. You know him?"

"I do! We trained together as junior FSOs."

Her pulse tripping, Jilly got Nareesh's number from Sandra Hathaway.

The afternoon sun had warmed the air when she emerged from State. She stood for some moments on the wide front steps, debating her next step. She really, really wanted to follow this lead on her own. If it produced results, Hawk would have to eat his objections to her lack of training and experience. Common sense and the awareness that she was part of a team had her reaching for her cell phone.

Since she hadn't yet been equipped with one of OMEGA's handy-dandy, supersecure communications devices, she couldn't directly access the Control Center or any of the operatives. Instead, she dialed the number for Lightning's executive assistant.

"Offices of the Special Envoy. How may I help you?"

"Elizabeth, it's Jilly. I need to speak to Uncle Nick."

"He's still in conference, dear."

In conference was code for upstairs, doing duty as OMEGA's director.

"I thought he might be. Ask him to call me on my cell when he's free."

Her cell phone pinged moments later.

"Where are you, Jilly?"

"Just leaving State. I may have something."

Or not. The lead was pretty tenuous at this point.

"I want your okay to accompany a friend on a visit to a temple tonight." She couldn't go into more detail over an open line. "I'll brief you after the visit."

The silence on the other end was deafening.

"Are you sure you know what you're doing?" Lightning finally asked.

"No, but my friend does. He's with the Bureau. His boss might call you for confirmation that it's okay for me to ride along. Will you give it?"

Another silence, longer this time.

"Uncle Nick? Am I good to go?"

"You're good."

She restrained her exultant whoop but couldn't resist punching the air with her fist.

Hours later, she huddled beside a turbaned Ben Nareesh in his darkened car. Their intent gazes were fixed on the small screen in his handheld unit. It was fed by cameras the FBI had positioned to cover the brick warehouse. Figures had been slipping through the cloudy night and into the warehouse for the past half hour.

"I still can't believe I let you talk me into this," Nareesh muttered. "Or that my boss gave the green light. You must have some powerful contacts."

Jilly merely smiled as Ben's gaze swept over her, looking for a chink in her disguise.

He didn't find one. She was draped in a silk sari she'd purchased in a downtown D.C. shop that catered to the city's large Indian and Pakistani population. Tinted contacts darkened her eyes. Thankfully, her jet-black hair had needed no touching up. She'd parted it in the middle and fashioned an intricate series of braids that now tugged at her scalp.

"Just follow my lead," he instructed. "And if we do find any sacrificial animals, we both stay the hell away from them."

Ben hadn't taken her warning about a potentially lethal virus lightly. In addition to his team of backups, he now had a crew encased in biohazard protective gear standing ready. All were prepared to move at his signal.

Jilly's nerves were strung tight when Ben stowed his unit and shifted to face her.

"Ready?"

She hooked the silk veil across the lower half of her face, dragged in a deep breath and nodded.

"Ready."

Hawk was huddled with a team of scientists at the Centers for Disease Control's Washington office when a cell phone chimed.

"That's mine." Annoyed at the interruption, the woman opposite Hawk flipped open her phone. "Dr. Cook."

He could tell the news was electrifying. The doc jolted upright in her chair and whipped a startled gaze his way before snapping the phone shut.

"The FBI just raided some kind of underground temple. One of the folks on the raid wanted to know if you're still here."

Hawk's insides turned to ice. Jilly. That had to be Jilly.

"They found several animals being prepared for sacrifice. One of them is an extremely rare *nomascus concolor*. The team has the animals in isolation units. They're delivering them to the containment lab as we speak."

All three scientists were already out of their chairs. Hawk stayed right on their heels as they raced through a maze of darkened corridors, down three flights of stairs and through an underground tunnel to a brightly lit lab.

He'd had to accept that Lightning had given her the go-ahead to accompany this friend of hers. A thorough check of Special Agent Nareesh's background and credentials had resolved some of Hawk's misgivings. That, and the fact that she would just ride along. As an observer. Not a direct participant.

He was still nursing that mistaken notion when he picked up the wail of a siren.

"Stay in the observation booth," Dr. Cook instructed as she zipped herself into biohazard protective gear. "It's sealed off and safe."

The booth's glass wall gave Hawk a clear view of the team that entered the lab some moments later. Looking like space travelers in their hooded suits, the team carried plastic cages with controlled breathing units. One of the cages contained what looked like a small rhesus monkey, the other a slightly larger primate with white tufts of fur on its cheeks. The gibbon's eyes were huge and frightened and seemed to lock on Hawk through the glass window.

"Poor babies."

He recognized Jilly's voice instantly but had to look twice to ID the woman who rushed into the booth, followed by a tall, slender man in a white turban.

Black mascara rimmed her eyes, which looked decidedly not blue from where he stood. A red caste mark decorated her forehead. To go with the pistachio green sari draped across one shoulder, he surmised, and sweet, cloying scent of incense that surrounded her like a cloud.

"Hawk! They told me you were still here. This is Special Agent Ben Nareesh. Ben, this is Mike Callahan."

She paused, smiled and looked Hawk square in the eye and said, "Mike and I work together."

Hawk got the message. In her own, inimitable way, Gillian-with-a-J had just thrown down the gauntlet. If he didn't accept her as an equal, right here, right now, it would be war between them.

He knew he would come out the victor. He fought too dirty to be vanquished by a pampered, privileged country-club type. Except Gillian Ridgeway, for all her pampering and privilege, possessed some real smarts under that sleek, silky mane. And she had the guts to match. She'd proven that tonight.

With a wrench that took him back to a place he never wanted to go again, Hawk yielded the field and extended a hand to Nareesh. "Good to meet you."

He couldn't miss Jilly's flash of triumph. It stayed on her face until she turned back to the observation window.

"They won't hurt them, will they?"

After his session with the folks at the Center, Hawk had a pretty good idea what might happen to the primates. It wasn't pretty.

"Depends on whether they show signs of infection."

"If they don't?"

"I don't know. They might be used for testing or research. Or turned over to a zoo," he added as Jilly's brows snapped together.

"Poor babies," she muttered again. "I wonder..."

Her lips pursed, and her expression turned thoughtful. Hawk had a sudden vision of Jilly showing up at the Ridgeway place with two hairy primates in tow. Maggie wouldn't mind. He could only imagine Adam's reaction.

"Ben, promise you'll keep me posted on what happens to these little guys."

Her request took the FBI agent by surprise. Obviously, he'd assumed his responsibility for the animals ended with the raid.

"I...uh...sure."

The man was putty in Jilly's hands.

Join the club, Hawk thought sardonically.

"Or," Nareesh countered in an attempt to wiggle out of the charge, "you could probably get the folks here at the Center to advise you directly."

"I could, if my partner and I weren't leaving for Hong Kong as soon as we throw a few things in a bag."

Enough was enough. Goaded, Hawk hooked her arm and swung her around. "Damn it, Gillian. How many surprises are you planning to pull tonight?"

"Sorry."

Her contrite look didn't fool him for a minute.

"I should have mentioned it right away. One of the worshippers arrested in the raid told us how the sacrificial animals were smuggled into the States."

She paused, playing the info for all it was worth. Hawk had to concede she'd earned her moment of glory.

"They were hidden inside a shipping container packed with antiques exported from Hong Kong. The shipping agency is Wang and Company."

Behind her tinted contacts, her eyes held only limpid innocence.

"Unless your Chinese is better than mine, Hawk, you might want to reconsider whether or not I'll be in the way when you call on Mr. Wang."

Chapter 3

Early the next morning, Hawk contacted the San Francisco detectives investigating Charlie Duncan's murder. They had no witnesses, no suspects and no leads. Frustrated, he used the remaining hours before he and Jilly departed for Hong Kong to supervise her transition from one-time Foreign Service Officer and temporary executive assistant to full-fledged undercover operative.

Jilly discovered a new Mike Callahan during those hours. This one was impatient, demanding and absolutely relentless. He began in OMEGA's training center with a crash course in down-and-dirty offensive and defensive maneuvers. Jilly was drenched with sweat and sporting several nasty bruises before she finally managed a takedown.

Hawk didn't allow her time for so much as a smirk to celebrate. Rolling to his feet, he hustled her into the weapons facility. He'd taught her to shoot, knew she could handle the polymer-based Beretta Sub-Compact she'd carry on this mission. Still, he made her snap in a clip and shred several paper targets before he turned her over to OMEGA's communications team.

Despite her grungy gray sweats and sweat-flattened hair, Jilly paid close attention while the team drilled her on communications procedures. Her only break came when Mackenzie Blair, Lightning's wife and the guru of all things electronic for OMEGA and several other government agencies, marched in.

"Well, my sweet, you certainly didn't waste any time snagging your first field op."

"What can I say? Duty calls."

Raking back her limp hair, Jilly grinned at the brunette she considered more of a big sister than an honorary aunt.

"How's the baby?"

Mac rounded a hand over her prominent belly and made a face. "The little stinker sleeps all day and kicks all night. Want to see what I have for you?"

Both women instantly switched gears. Mac's high-tech devices had made her a legend with the agencies she supplied. Jilly couldn't wait to see what supercool, James Bondish gadget she'd come up with this time.

It didn't look all that high-tech at first. The gold charm was pretty, though. It was in the shape of a Chinese character and embedded in a bezel of what looked like rare blue jade.

"Do you know this character?" Mac asked.

"Fu. It means good luck." Jilly had to laugh. "Appropriate."

"I thought so, too. This particular Fu, my sweet, just happens to conceal the world's smallest and most sophisticated encrypted satellite communications system."

With her belly nudging the table, Mac laid the charm in the palm of one hand and poked at it with the other.

"If you press on this little squiggle…"

"That squiggle is the character's radical, or root symbol."

After four years of Mandarin in college, two more in grad school and a three-year tour of duty in Beijing, Jilly spoke several Chinese dialects with a fluency rarely acquired by "foreign devils."

Reading and writing were entirely different matters. By various counts, there were somewhere between forty and fifty thousand Chinese characters. Thankfully, each character contained one of only two hundred and fourteen roots. If you could figure out the root, you could count the character's remaining strokes and—most of the time!—look up the word in a dictionary.

"The roots came down from ancient times," she told Mac. "Originally they were pictographs representing basic elements like man, woman, fire, water, and so on."

"If you say so. Press the root…radical…whatever…once to transmit, twice to receive. Go ahead, try a voice transmission."

Jilly pressed once. "Mary had a little… Whoa!"

She jumped as the nursery rhyme boomed through the Control Center's speakers.

"You'll be in silent mode most of the time," Mac advised, "but you'll know when someone's trying to contact you. Put it on, and I'll give you a demo."

The chain was long enough to loop easily over her head. The jade felt cool and smooth against her throat—until Mac signaled to one of her assistants. The next moment, the semiprecious stone warmed like toast.

"Nice," Jilly murmured, palming the charm. "Very nice."

"It's also equipped with GPS, an electronic jammer and a direct link to Hawk's comm unit."

"Don't tell me you decked him out in a gold chain and charm, too?"

"I wish! No, his comm is in his watch." A wicked gleam lit Mac's brown eyes. "But I did spiffy that up to go with your cover. You should have seen his face when I presented him with a solid gold Rolex."

Also appropriate, Jilly thought. She and Hawk would hit Hong Kong in the guise of a wealthy couple on a Far East buying junket.

A *married* couple.

Sharing a hotel suite.

So Hawk could keep an eye on her.

She'd bristled at that last bit. Not for long, however, since adjoining bedrooms in a luxurious hotel suite dovetailed nicely with her non-mission-related objectives.

Assuming she didn't pull out her Beretta and pump a round into Hawk before they left for Hong Kong, which she seriously contemplated doing an hour later.

Not content with her firm grasp of OMEGA's internal communications codes, Hawk insisted she memorize the NATO phonetic alphabet used by police officers and medical response agencies worldwide. That Jilly could rattle the letters off with some assurance wasn't enough. He wanted every one burned into her subconscious.

"Give them to me again."

She gritted her teeth. "How many times do I have to…?"

"Again, damn it." The gold flecks in his eyes burned with intensity. "I'm not going into the field with someone who can't call for backup if we run into an ambush."

Was that what happened all those years ago in the jungle? Had Hawk and his partner and this woman he once loved been ambushed? The thought of what he'd lost in that murky green darkness put a lid on Jilly's irritation.

"Alpha-Bravo-Charlie-Delta-Echo-Foxtrot-Golf-Hotel-India-Juliet-Kilo-Lima-Mike."

She pulled in a breath.

"November-Oscar-Papa-Quebec-Romeo-Sierra-Tango-Uniform-Victor-Whiskey-Xray-Yankee-Zulu."

She finished on a whoosh of air and gave him a nasty glare.

"Satisfied?"

"Yeah."

He didn't look satisfied. With his two-day's worth of stubble and red-rimmed eyes, he looked almost as ragged as she now felt.

"We've got less than an hour before we have to head for the airport," he informed her after checking his gleaming Rolex. "We'd better get up to Field Dress."

Finally! A shower, a shampoo and a quick blow-dry.

She couldn't wait to shed her rank sweats and change into whatever the wizards in OMEGA's Field Dress Unit had waiting for her.

Gillian emerged from FDU's dressing room a different woman. Nothing like a French silk demibra and panties, an Emanuel Ungaro pantsuit in cobalt-blue and Bruno Magli ankle boots to make a gal feel like she could take on the world again. She'd have to wait until Hong Kong to see the other delights packed in the Gucci suitcases waiting beside the dressing room door.

Hawk was waiting, as well. His gaze raked her from head to toe. A small grunt was her only indication that her duty uniform passed inspection. She, on the other hand, could barely keep her jaw from dropping.

She'd known him for so long, had seen him rigged out in everything from camouflage gear to a hand-tailored tux. But this was the first time she'd *ever* seen him with his brown hair slicked back and his nails manicured. Or in an Armani sport coat that molded his wide shoulders. Or Italian leather loafers. Or…

"If you're through conducting your inventory," he said impatiently, "we need to hit the road."

She popped a salute. "Yes, sir! It's just that… You look so different."

The Field Dress tech who'd outfitted them both frowned. "Not too different, I hope."

After discussing the matter with Lightning, Hawk had decided he should stick to his civilian persona. He was too well-known in the international marksmanship circuit to do otherwise. But his recent marriage to a wealthy heiress had plucked him from the shooting range and plunged him into the world of manicures and priceless artifacts. Or so he and Jilly would pretend.

With a spurt of real glee, she contemplated the crash course in Oriental antiques she would subject *him* to during the long flight to Hong Kong.

"I'm ready if you are," she told him.

"Not quite. We have one more piece of business to take care of."

She couldn't hold back a groan. "Not more codes!"

"Just one. You haven't picked your code name."

"We've been going nonstop since dawn. Who had time to think names?"

"So think now. What, or who, are you?"

"I don't know."

"We need a name, Jilly."

Fiddling with the pendant that nestled just above the swell of her breasts, she searched her mind.

"I can't come up with... Wait!" She stroked her thumb over the smooth round bezel. "Jade. I'll go by Jade."

Hawk's expression softened. For a moment, just a moment, she was sure she caught the ghost of a grin on his rugged face.

"Is that with a *G* or a *J?*"

"*J.*" She smiled back.

"I'll let Griff know."

Dan Griffin, code name Ace, would act as their controller during this op. Only a few years older than Jilly, the former Navy pilot with the killer grin had already made a name for himself at OMEGA...and with the women who couldn't seem to get enough of him.

Hawk made a half turn and swung back to Jilly. "One more thing. You'd better put this on."

He dug in the pocket of his Armani jacket and withdrew a jeweler's box. When he popped the lid, Jilly gasped. Nested in velvet was a circlet of marquise-cut diamonds banded by sapphire-studded ring guards.

"It's gorgeous."

"Yeah. Field Dress doesn't miss a trick."

Her heart stuttered and almost stopped when he slid the wide band onto her ring finger. Cover, she reminded herself with a gulp. This was strictly for cover.

Which didn't explain why Hawk kept her hand in his for several seconds longer.

"I told them I wanted the ring guards in sapphire. To match your eyes."

She pondered that gruff comment all the way across the Pacific.

Hong Kong was everything she remembered from shopping excursions during her assignment to Beijing. And more. So much more.

As their plane swooped in for a landing, Jilly saw dozens of new skyscrapers crowding the harbor on both Hong Kong Island and the Kowloon Peninsula on the mainland. Contrary to the dire predictions when the British relinquished their hold on the territories known collectively as Hong Kong, their teeming economy hadn't collapsed. Instead, it was exploding.

Gillian soon discovered that the traffic she recalled from previous visits had exploded, as well. Their limo driver added frequent blasts of his horn to the cacophony rising from taxis, trucks and Japanese-made vehicles of every sort. Masses of humanity, most with cell phones jammed against their ears, thronged streets with signs in both English and Chinese. Narrow alleys radiated from avenues with names left over from the British occupation. Sheng Tung Street bisected Waterloo Road. Kam Lam ran into Argyle. Tak Shing, Kan Su and Nanking all converged on the shopaholic's mecca, Nathan Road.

Jilly almost salivated as the Rolls-Royce limo glided past shop after shop. She would have loved to put herself into the eager hands of tailors who could take her measurements and deliver an entire collection of suits and shoes and ball gowns to her hotel the next day. Or the jewelers who could craft an exquisite pair of diamond earrings or a ruby slide to her specifications within hours.

Then there were the designers. Prada, Chanel, Versace and Kate Spade all had boutiques on Nathan Road, as well as in the high-end malls scattered throughout the city. Too bad the Gucci suitcases stowed in the trunk of the Rolls-Royce made those boutiques and jewelry stores superfluous. Not to mention the ring on her left hand.

She snuck a glance at the sparkling stones. She hadn't gotten used to their weight yet. Or the odd sensation that came with even a pretend marriage to a man like Hawk.

Women always sat up and took notice when he entered a room. Their admiring glances had never bothered Jilly before. So she couldn't explain her annoyance with the redhead who'd almost tripped over her own feet while ogling Hawk at the airport. Or her irritation when a certain flight attendant became a little *too* attentive.

"That's the Peninsula ahead, sir."

The uniformed chauffeur pulled up at a red light and tipped his head toward the venerable hotel dominating the next block.

"Unfortunately, construction of the new subway line has temporarily blocked vehicle access to our main entrance. I'll have to let you out at the side entrance."

Well, darn! The Peninsula was one of Hong Kong's most revered institutions. Jilly had wanted Hawk to see the front portico with its massive white pillars, liveried doormen and fleet of Rolls-Royces at the ready. On impulse, she grabbed the door handle.

"Let's walk from here. The driver can drop off our bags at the side entrance. I want you to get the Peninsula's full effect."

The noise of a large and vibrant city hit them the moment they emerged from the Rolls. Car horns honked. Street vendors hawked their wares. Jackhammers and cranes added their signature sounds to the solid mass of humanity that thronged the streets. And above the din, Jilly caught the whistle of an arriving Star Ferry.

"You have to see this."

With a quick change in direction, she joined the crowd crossing the street. A short flight of steps led to the wide promenade that circled the Kowloon side of the Victoria Harbor.

Across the gray-green waters were the towering skyscrapers of Hong Kong Island. Victoria Peak rose above the columns of glass and steel, her summit wreathed in hazy mist. And there, just pulling into the terminal, was one of the distinctive green-and-white ferries that still served as a primary means of transportation.

Smiling at the sight, Jilly leaned her arms on the promenade's rail and breathed in the mingled scent of salt water and diesel fumes.

"They built a high-speed tunnel to connect Kowloon and Hong Kong some years ago," she told Hawk, "but I always take the ferries when I'm here. They're crowded, noisy and swarming with pickpockets, but they're quintessential China."

"I'll remember that."

Hawk obviously had more important matters on his mind as he shot back his cuff and checked his Rolex. "We'd better get settled in at the hotel, then call on Mr. Wang."

Jilly gave the magnificent skyline across the bay a last look and pushed away from the rail. Hawk put a hand to the small of her back to turn her toward the stairs. She shouldn't have felt his touch through layers of Hermès and Emanuel Ungaro. Shouldn't have but did. The skin under those layers tingled even as she issued another stern reminder.

Cover, girl! It's just cover!

Preoccupied with both the thought and the touch, she didn't see the pint-size street vendor in pink sneakers and T-shirt who'd approached them. Neither did Hawk until his abrupt turn brought them into direct contact.

"Ai-ah!"

The girl—she couldn't have been more than four or five—landed on her bottom. The wooden cage she was carrying also hit the concrete. The cage door flew open, and the canary inside made its escape.

With another cry, the girl scrambled to her feet and tried to catch the bird, but it was already soaring on the stiff breeze off the bay. Jilly would have bet the thing would soon be gull bait if she hadn't witnessed a similar performance during a previous visit to Hong Kong. That one had involved caged crickets, but the theatrics were the same.

Sure enough, the little girl's shoulders slumped pathetically. When she turned back to face them, tears rolled down her cheeks.

"I'm sorry, kid." Hawk reached into his pocket and pulled out the wad of Hong Kong dollars he'd purchased at the airport. "I'm really sorry."

"You might want to wait on that," Jilly advised.

"I bowled her over. How much should I give her for the bird? Five? Ten?"

"What you do to Mei Lin?"

The indignant query came from the boy who charged up the promenade stairs two at a time. He was older than the girl. Nine, maybe ten. Like her, he wore jeans and a faded T-shirt of indeterminate origin. But his AirMax Nikes, Jilly noted, looked brand-new.

"What you do?" he demanded again, but didn't wait for an answer. Waving his skinny arms, he launched into a tirade of broken English. "You hurt little sister. You break cage. She lose bird, lose money. Lose face with Grandfather."

The girl's tears continued to flow, and the boy's accusations were starting to attract attention.

"Here, kid. Will this save your sister's face?"

No fool, the boy took the twenty and held it up to the sunlight. Counterfeit money was as pandemic in China as bootlegged DVDs and Prada knockoffs.

The boy didn't lose his angry scowl, but his message to the girl held smug triumph. "We plucked a fat goose," he said in swift Cantonese. "Come, we'll buy hot dumplings to take to Grandfather."

Jilly said nothing while he scooped up the empty wooden cage. The two took off without another word and disappeared behind the oleanders separating the section of the promenade from the next.

Obviously relieved that the fracas was over, Hawk pocketed the rest of his money. "Let's go."

"Hang on a sec."

"Why?"

"Just listen. Yep, there it is."

The chirpy trill carried clearly over the hubbub of the harbor. A moment later, a flash of yellow nose-dived into the oleanders.

The man beside her was silent for several moments. "I knew it was a scam."

"Uh-huh." Grinning, Jilly hooked her arm through his. "You're on my turf now, fella. You might want to consult me before forking over any more twenty-dollar bills."

Hawk was a whole lot more concerned with his body's instant, instinctive reaction to the press of her breasts against his bicep than the fact that he'd been gulled by a couple of con artists.

What was with him, for God's sake? He'd held her in his arms before. And not just at the firing range. A few months ago, he'd escorted her to a black-tie reception and used her as cover while scoping out a congressman suspected of selling government secrets. He'd nailed his target, but sweat still gathered at the base of his spine when he remembered how Gillian-with-a-J had moved in a strapless, flame-colored column of silk that bared more of her than it covered.

Damn it all to hell! He had to get his head straight. Too much rode on this op to let his fantasies about this blue-eyed siren override his common sense.

"Let's go," he repeated with a distinct edge to his voice. "We have business to take care of."

Chapter 4

The first item on the agenda was to check into the hotel. Hawk was too preoccupied to appreciate the British colonial ambiance of the Peninsula's pillared entrance or the soaring lobby with its brass fixtures, rattan chairs and potted palms. Jilly, however, drank in the elegance as they walked to the reception desk.

"Welcome to the Peninsula, Mrs. Callahan."

With a small jolt, she realized the clerk at the reception desk had addressed her. "Thank you."

"I hope your flight in wasn't too exhausting."

"Not at all."

Once Hawk had stopped drilling her on operating procedures and let her get some sleep that is. She'd retaliated during the final leg of their journey with a lecture covering four thousand years of Chinese dynastic history.

"Is this your first trip to Hong Kong?"

"I've visited several times before but my…er…husband hasn't."

Hawk covered the near stumble by sliding an arm around her waist. "Still takes some getting used to, doesn't it, darling?"

His slow smile ignited sparks just under Jilly's skin and darned near melted the receptionist where she stood. Like hopeless romantics everywhere, the young woman got all googly-eyed. "Are you on your honeymoon?"

"We are."

"Congratulations." Her fingers tapped the keyboard. "Perhaps we might be able to switch you to the… Oh, I see you're already booked into one of our finest suites. I'll send up some champagne and fresh strawberries, compliments of the house."

"Sounds wonderful. We'll put them to good use."

There was that smile again. Tender, intimate, so full of sensual promise that heat raced through her like a California wildfire.

"Your luggage has already been taken up to your suite. If you'll just sign the registration form, Mr. Callahan, I'll scan your passports and credit card."

She didn't question the fact that Jilly's passport was in her maiden name. The blushing new bride wouldn't have had time to change it.

"You're in the Tower, sir. Edward will show you the way. And once again, my congratulations."

"Thanks."

As they followed the uniformed attendant to the elevators, Hawk kept the pretense up—and the wildfires raging—with a casually possessive hand to the small of Jilly's back.

The heat didn't cool until they reached the twenty-second floor and their escort slid a key card into a lock.

"There are two entrances to your suite," he informed them. "This one accesses the foyer. The other, just there, takes you into the walk-in closet and storage area."

Jilly thought that was pretty handy until she saw Hawk eyeing the second door with a crease between his brows. Two entrances, she realized belatedly, meant twice the necessary security precautions.

Damn! She'd better start thinking more like a field agent.

"Here you are."

Handing Hawk the key card, the attendant stood aside to let them precede him into the foyer. All marble and cream, with an artistic arrangement of snowy-white chrysanthemums on a side table, the entryway led into living and dining rooms that blended Asian and European with flawless symmetry.

Rich, jewel-toned Oriental rugs softened the parquet floors. Jilly's heels sank into the plush thickness as she admired the twin black lacquer chests inlaid with mother-of-pearl that framed the fireplace. The mantel held an artistic display of porcelain ginger jars in a delicate blue-and-white pattern that complimented the wingback chairs and sofas.

But it was the terrace with its floor-to-ceiling sliding-glass doors that knocked the breath back down her throat. Shedding her jacket, she aimed straight for the doors. Once outside she felt as though she was standing at the top of the world.

A stiff breeze whipped her hair while she watched gulls circling above a fishing junk that chugged through the gray-green waters of the bay. Across the harbor, late-afternoon sunlight glinted on the glass towers of Hong Kong. Twenty stories below, a cruise ship was just pulling into a berth alongside the Ocean Terminal.

"Hawk! Come see this view!"

When he didn't answer, she turned and found him with a phone already held to his ear.

"Guess the honeymoon is over," she murmured to the squawking gulls.

"That's right," Hawk was saying when she slid the terrace doors shut behind her. "Mr. and Mrs. Michael Callahan. We e-mailed Mr. Wang about arranging shipment of the furniture and antiques we intend to purchase in Hong Kong."

With one ear tuned to the phone conversation, Jilly went to explore the other rooms. Both sumptuous bedrooms boasted spectacular views of the skyline. So did the two bathrooms. Even the marble hot tub was set in a window enclosure with tall, angled windows that gave a sweeping, two-hundred-and-seventy-degree vista.

Their bags, she noted, had been laid on side-by-side racks in the walk-in luggage storage area that adjoined the master bath and dressing room. Hawk's raisin-colored leather suit bag hung next to her designer bag. The sight sent a sizzle of anticipation along Jilly's nerve endings.

She'd nursed a teenage crush on Mike Callahan for

years and had flirted with him all through college. He'd been so much a part of her life—the cool older guy with a string of international marksmanship awards she would brag about to her friends.

Her three years in Beijing had put some distance between them. Conversely, it had also compressed the years that separated them. Hawk was still the cool older guy in her mind, but she was long past girlish crushes and playful flirtations.

She ran her fingertips over the soft leather, thinking, planning, plotting her next move in this...

"Wang's not available."

Hastily, Jilly dropped her hand.

"We're meeting with his partner," Hawk said, striding in from the living room. "Her name's Hall. Adriana Hall. British, from the little I could glean. I've got OMEGA control checking her out."

"What time is the meeting?"

"Forty-five minutes from now. I've ordered a car. We'll have to leave in fifteen."

"Fifteen!"

She swallowed a groan as he retrieved her tote and his overnighter from the luggage room. So much for all her plotting and planning. The hot tub would have to wait. So would any "accidental" glimpses Hawk might snare of the sexy underwear Field Dress had procured for her.

"Which bedroom do you want?" he asked, bags in hand.

Separate bedrooms hadn't factored into her plotting, either. She mulled the matter over for a few seconds before responding.

"Word is going to spread among the hotel staff that we're on our honeymoon. Especially when they send up that champagne." She gave him her best secret-agent shrug. "It'll be tough to maintain our cover if we occupy separate bedrooms."

His eyes narrowed at the comment. Or maybe it was the shrug. Jilly wasn't sure she'd pulled that off.

"You think the black marketeers we're hunting have bribed the staff to spy on us?"

"Maybe not yet," she conceded. "But they might if they hear we're sniffing around, asking questions about them."

She didn't elaborate. Hawk had been in the business a whole lot longer than her day and a half. He had to know that a fistful of Hong Kong dollars could buy any interested party all kinds of information about the couple sharing this opulent suite. Like what they ordered from room service. Whether they preferred the foam pillows to feather. How many foil wrappers ended up in the wastebasket each night.

Heat jolted through her, fast and hot. With some effort, Jilly suppressed the image of Mike Callahan, tall and lean and naked except for a condom.

"You decide how we should play it while I'm in the bathroom."

Hawk didn't move for several moments after the door whisked shut behind her. He'd been so wrapped up in prepping Jilly for this mission—and so intent on getting to Wang and Company once they arrived in Hong Kong—that he'd shoved everything else into a separate compartment in his mind.

Jilly had just sprung that compartment wide-open. The mere thought of her slender body stretched next to his got Hawk hard. So hard that he had to clamp his jaw against the sudden urge to follow her into the bathroom and give the hotel staff some fuel for the fire.

Oh, for God's sake! What fire?

Smothering an oath, he forced himself to think rationally. They didn't need such deep cover. Not yet. The nameless, faceless smugglers they were hunting had to know another agent would pick up the investigation interrupted by Charlie Duncan's murder. But unless Hawk got sloppy and tipped his hand, the smugglers didn't know *he* was that agent. Or that he had a neophyte in tow.

The oath was more vicious this time. Stalking into the living room, Hawk threw his carryall atop the ornately carved rosewood desk. If Jilly got hurt, if she took a bullet and went down…

She wouldn't, he vowed savagely. Whatever it took, whatever lies he had to tell or protective walls he had to erect, he'd keep her out of the line of fire. He wasn't going to leave another piece of his heart lying in some back alley or dark, smothering jungle.

His jaw set, he unzipped his carryall and extracted a folded kit. The intrusion detection discs inside the kit were smaller than a dime, wafer thin and completely transparent. The recorder that went with them looked and acted like an iPod. With eighty gigs of memory, it could hold ten thousand songs, hundreds of JPEGs, downloaded movies and recent TV shows, as well as a whole address book full of contact information and a busy executive's calendar. After MacKenzie Blair and her magicians went to work on it, the device also contained a security system that would have made the folks at Fort Knox sit up and take notice.

Hawk attached one of the transparent discs above the transom of the door to the foyer, another above the luggage room door. He didn't like this double entry. He would have to plan for a worst-case scenario involving simultaneous assaults. On the other hand, the back door could provide an escape route for Jilly, if necessary.

Not particularly reassured by the thought, he attached additional discs to the terrace doors. Long habit had him opening a desk drawer a mere sliver. He also shifted one of the ginger jars gracing the tall Chinese chests a few inches to the left. A single glance would tell if someone had gone through the desk or lifted the lid to the chest.

The toiletries and wardrobe Field Dress had provided got the same careful attention. Hawk snagged his leather suit bag from the luggage area, intending to hang the items in his bedroom closet in precise order…and found himself right back where he'd started ten minutes ago.

Together, or separate? Honeymooners, or not?

"Hell!"

Stalking into the master bedroom, he yanked open the closet doors. He returned a few moments later for Jilly's hang-up and suitcase.

If she noted the side-by-side garment bags when she emerged from the bathroom and joined Hawk in the living room, she had the good sense not to comment on them.

"I'm all set." Her glance snagged on a silver ice bucket and domed tray. "Oh, good! The strawberries and champagne."

Not just strawberries, she saw when she lifted the lid. The sumptuous arrangement also included crystallized brown sugar and a creamy sauce for dipping.

"We need to go," Hawk insisted. "I'll put the tray in the fridge. You can feast tonight."

Jilly managed to snag one plump berry and a quick dip. Her taste buds gave a collective gasp of joy at the first bite. The sauce was white chocolate flavored with Grand Marnier. She polished off the berry in three bites.

"Did Control get back to you on Wang's partner?" she asked when Hawk returned.

"They did. You've got white stuff on your lower lip."

She swiped her tongue along her lip. "All gone?"

"Not quite. Here, let me."

His thumb brushed her mouth. Once. Twice. Jilly looked up, saw herself reflected in his eyes. She saw something else, something that made her breath catch. It came and went so fast that Hawk didn't give her time to feast on it.

"Let's go. I'll brief you on Adriana Hall during the drive."

"She's English," he confirmed as a gleaming Rolls-Royce whisked them through the tunnel connecting the Kowloon and Hong Kong Island. "According to Control, she's Wang's silent partner. Has been for several years."

A glass partition separated them from the chauffeur. The Rolls' incredible engineering blocked all tunnel noise and fumes. Traffic was light for Hong Kong and moved fast.

"She was married to Sir Reginald Hall. Control is still working him, but initial indications are he's descended from Singapore's last colonial governor. There were no children from the marriage. Sir Reginald's wife got into the antiquities trade in Singapore, then shifted her base of operations to Hong Kong after his death."

He drummed his fingers on his knee. Jilly waited, sensing he had more.

"There's a gap," Hawk confirmed. "Almost eight months between the time Hall died and his widow bought in as Wang's silent partner."

"Maybe she needed to adjust to losing her husband?"

"Maybe. The silent partner bit bothers me, though. Although Hong Kong reverted to China more than twenty years ago, old mystiques die hard. You'd think a savvy businesswoman would cash in on her connection to a peer of the British Empire."

Jilly fiddled with the jade pendant. Hawk's point was valid. Parts of Hong Kong still had something of a colonial air about them. Street names such as Argyle and Hamilton and Nathan Road were one example. This gleaming Rolls-Royce was another. But she could understand why a grieving widow might want to maintain a low profile.

She'd met a good number of British matrons over the years, first through her parents' international connections, then through her work as a cultural exchange officer at the U.S. Embassy in Beijing. The women she'd encountered exemplified the stiff upper lip the Brits were so famous for.

This one, this Adriana Hall, was probably cut from

the same cloth. She would carry on through adversity, all the while wrapping her grief in a cloak of privacy.

The woman whose twelfth-story office they entered a little later blew Jilly's ideas of British matrons all to hell.

This one looked as rare and exotic as the priceless antiques displayed in lighted niches around her office. Blond and slender, she was at least five-eight or -nine, although her three-inch stiletto heels accounted for some of that willowy height. Her features might have been sculpted by a master's hand. High cheekbones, aristocratic nose, green eyes framed by thick lashes, a wide mouth glistening with gloss in a dark shade of red that matched her nails.

She wore her hair up and anchored atop her head with ebony sticks in the Chinese style. Her dress was Chinese, too, a tightly fitting *cheongsam* in emerald silk, with a high mandarin collar, intricately knotted fasteners and side slits for ease of movement.

Tradition ended there, however. Where most *cheongsams* were slit to the knee, this one hiked high enough to display a length of smooth white thigh when she rose to greet her visitors.

"Mr. and Mrs. Callahan?"

Her voice was low and throaty, with only a trace of England left in it after so many years in the East.

"Welcome to Wang and Company."

She came forward, her hand outstretched. Jilly took it first and had to contain a start of surprise at the tight, almost knuckle-crunching grip.

The widow loosened her hold and turned to Hawk,

but he made no move to take her hand. Instead, he stared down at the woman with an expression Jilly couldn't interpret.

Neither could the widow, evidently. Chin tilting, she regarded him with a question in those forest-green eyes.

"Mr. Callahan?"

"I'm sorry." He gave his head a little shake and folded her hand in his. "It's just… Your perfume… It reminded me of someone I used to know."

Jilly took a surreptitious sniff and caught the barest hint of some exotic blend. Jasmine, she thought, and rose, mixed with dark, erotic musk.

Hall slipped her hand free of his and put it to the collar of her dress. Her eyes held Hawk's as she treated him to a cool smile.

"It's called Pandora. I have it imported from the south of France." Her long, red-tipped fingers fluttered at her throat. "You'll excuse me, I hope, if I say your friend has exquisite taste."

When Hawk gave a noncommittal nod, she gestured toward the sofa and chairs grouped near a glass wall with a panoramic view of the Kowloon side of the harbor.

"Would you care for a spot of tea? Or coffee? Or perhaps something stronger?"

"I would love a cup of tea," Jilly answered. "My husband prefers coffee."

She got it out this time without a stutter or stumble. Proud of herself, Gillian settled into a chair angled for maximum view. Hawk took the chair next to her.

After pressing the intercom to place the order with her assistant, Hall seated herself comfortably and crossed her legs with a whisper of silky nylon. "I read the e-mail you sent Mr. Wang. Although I tend to shy away from a direct role in our joint venture, I do occasionally work with clients."

She steepled her fingers and rested her chin on the bloodred tips.

"Now that I've met you, I think… Yes, I know I would enjoy helping you locate the treasures you hope to buy in Hong Kong. For a fee, of course."

"Which is?" Hawk inquired.

"Our standard finder's fee is fifteen percent. That could increase depending on the rarity of the items you're looking for and the time we spend finding them. What do you have in mind?"

Hawk deflected the question. "Before we get into specifics, I want to be sure your people can handle the packing and crating necessary to protect our purchases. We've had some problems in that area in the past."

"I assure you, we've shipped the most fragile items imaginable all over the world."

"Nevertheless, I'd need to see that side of your operation."

"Very well. Our warehouse is in Sheung Wan, the old part of the city." She glanced at her thin gold watch. "We could go this afternoon, but most of our workers will have left by the time we fight the traffic. It would be better if we went tomorrow morning."

"That works for us."

"Shall we say ten o'clock? I'll have a driver pick you up at your hotel. I believe you said you're putting up at the Peninsula?"

"We are," Hawk confirmed. "No need to send a car. We'll use one of the hotel's fleet."

"Very well. I'll have my secretary write out the address for you. Ah, here's our tea."

As Adriana poured hot water onto the fragrant tea leaves, excitement pulsed through her in fierce, feral waves. Her hand didn't shake, but only because she exercised every ounce of the unbreakable will that had kept her alive despite all odds.

She'd waited so long for this moment. Had planned it with such meticulous detail. Now he was here. The man she'd once loved and now hated with every thread of her being.

He didn't recognize her. How could he after so many fists to the face, so many broken bones? When she'd finally escaped, the surgeon who patched her together had botched the job so badly she hadn't recognized herself.

It had taken three bouts of cosmetic surgery to create the creature she now was. Different face. Different figure after all those months of near starvation. Very different voice, thanks to the bullet that had pierced her larynx.

Through all the years, all the pain, she'd survived the darkest, most horrific nights by retreating deep into herself. And by repeating a silent vow, over and over again.

They'd pay. Charlie Duncan. Mike Callahan. They'd pay for abandoning her to the bastard who'd raped and tortured her. They'd pay dearly.

She could still see Charlie's astonished face when she'd revealed her true identity. Still feel the hot blood that gushed down her arm when she'd slit his throat.

Now Mike had walked into her web.

The thrill of it, the savage delight of it, was an incandescent fire in her belly. She reveled in the scorching heat as she lifted her head and gave the woman playing his wife a cool smile.

"Milk or lemon, Mrs. Callahan?"

Chapter 5

"Hawk?"

The clink of silverware and crystal almost drowned the murmured query. Jilly crossed her elbows on the snowy linen tablecloth and leaned forward. Across the flickering candle, Hawk's face was a study in light and shadow.

The sight of him there, so strong, so solid—and so remote—started a strange ache in her chest. She felt left out. Or rather, left behind. Wherever he'd gone, she couldn't follow.

"Hawk?" she said again, louder this time.

His gaze shifted from a spot just over her shoulder. "What?"

"You've barely touched your dinner, and I finished mine ten minutes ago. Shall we skip dessert and have coffee up in the room? That way you can tell me whatever it is that's bugging you."

He nodded and signaled for the waiter. They'd opted for an early dinner in one of the Peninsula's restaurants, as Jilly was starting to feel the cumulative effects of the long flight and busy day. Hawk had seemed to take both in stride...until that odd moment in Adriana Hall's office.

She thought about that as the elevator glided upward and about the woman herself. Hall was so gorgeous, so perfect.

Too perfect. She'd had some work done. Jilly took that as a given. The woman seemed young yet for nips and tucks, but then appointments with a cosmetic surgeon were now as common as visits to the hair salon.

"Here we are."

Hawk keyed the entry to their suite. When they entered, he reached into his suit coat pocket for the handheld scanner disguised as an iPod. A click of the wheel chirped out a report from the sensors he'd placed earlier.

"Key card entry, door one, nineteen hundred hours, six minutes. Key card entry, door one, twenty hundred hours, nine minutes."

Jilly made the mental calculation. "That's us. 8:09 p.m. The earlier entry was probably housekeeping. I see the bed is turned down."

One bed. Only one.

Housekeeping had jumped to the logical conclusion, given that their clothes hung side by side and their toiletries cluttered a single bedroom with its private bath.

The sight of that turned-down bed vaporized Jilly's weariness on the spot. A tingling sense of anticipation

replaced it. The sensation sizzled along her nerves as
Hawk pocketed the scanner.

"All clear?"

"Not yet."

Refusing to rely solely on technology, Hawk insisted
on a physical sweep. Jilly watched and learned as he
checked both bedroom suites and the luggage storage
room before returning to the living area.

The dining room passed scrutiny, but he came to a
sudden stop in the middle of the living room. His shoulders went taut, his eyes narrow.

"What is it?" Jilly asked, tensing.

"The ginger jar. It's been moved."

She followed his intent stare to one of the Chinese
chests flanking the fireplace. A tall, lidded jar sat atop
it. With its delicate, blue-and-white willow pattern, it
matched the jar on the other side of the fireplace. Both
jars sat dead center on their respective chests.

"It doesn't look to me like it's been moved."

"I pushed it a few inches to the left before we left this
afternoon. Someone's moved it back."

The tension she'd picked up from him eased. "It must
have been housekeeping. You can't mess with *feng shui.*"

She could tell from his impatient look that he wasn't
into New Age decorating. Only the concept wasn't new
in China. It went back thousands of years.

"*Feng shui,*" she repeated. "The phrase translates lit-
erally to wind and water. It has to do with striving for
harmony with the forces of nature. That urge once
governed everything from how a peasant plowed his
field to the direction a woman faced while crouched on

the birthing stool. Since *feng shui* also involved magic, sorcery and geomancy, it's been banned in modern China. The concepts of spatial and visual harmony are imbued in the culture, however."

Hawk still wasn't convinced. Jilly thought about reminding him that he was on her turf now. He should trust her on this. Instead, she shrugged out of her jacket and kicked off her shoes. Sinking into the plush sofa, she curled her feet under her.

"The idea of achieving a balance with nature isn't unique to China. The Greeks and Romans sacrificed to the gods of earth and sky. Ancient pagans believed spirits inhabited trees and boulders. They conducted all sorts of rituals designed to let them live in concert with their surroundings. Our so-called experts on global warming are dealing with exactly the same issue today."

"We're talking ginger jars here, not melting ice caps."

"Same problem, different scale. And speaking of global warming, I see the ice has melted in the champagne bucket. Why don't we pop the cork and finish off the strawberries for dessert?"

"Sounds good. You get the strawberries, I'll do the honors with the champagne."

The silver tray was dewy and cold to the touch. Jilly swiped the bottom with a napkin before positioning it within easy reach on the black lacquer coffee table. She snuck a berry and curled up on the sofa again while Hawk worked the foil cap off the cork.

He'd shed his Armani sport coat and rolled up the cuffs of his blue shirt. Jilly couldn't imagine how it had come through the long flight wrinkleless. The wizards

in Field Dress, she mused as her appreciative gaze
roamed the muscled chest and shoulders covered by the
blue cotton blend.

When he untwisted the wire on the cap, the glint of
gold on his wrist reminded her of unfinished business.

"We haven't called Control to give them an update
on the mysterious Mrs. Hall."

Hawk was already busy with the champagne. "Go
ahead and call in."

"Me?"

He frowned at her over the silver bucket. "Mac said
she checked you out on your comm device."

"She did, she did! It's just… This is my first transmission from the field."

His mouth relaxed into a grin that said clearly every
secret agent had to pop her cherry sometime.

"Go for it."

She lifted the pendant, held it out as far as the chain
would allow and pressed Fu's root symbol. "This is
Jade. Come in, Control."

She waited a few beats, straining to hear whatever
came through the device's microdot speaker, before she
remembered she had to press twice to receive.

"…and clear, Jade." Griff's laid-back Texas drawl
came through with right-next-door clarity. "Ace here.
What can I do for you?"

"Hawk and I wanted to know if you've dug up any
more on Adriana Hall."

"Not yet. The lady's real savvy 'bout guarding her
privacy. If we get her to squeak, I'll let you know."

"Okay. Or should I say 'roger'?"

"Most of us tend toward 'roger that,' sweet thing."

She could hear the laughter in his voice. Grinning, Jilly pressed the root again. "Roger that, stud. Now how do I terminate this transmission?"

"The usual phrase is over and..."

He broke off at the sound of a loud pop and came back with a sharp, "Jade?"

"It's okay. Hawk just opened a bottle of champagne."

"Did you say Hawk opened a bottle of bubbly? *Our* Hawk? Ole Deadeye himself? Well, well."

She lifted her gaze and caught ole Deadeye smiling and shaking his head.

"Y'all be sure to down a glass for us poor slobs in the trenches."

"We will," Hawk retorted. "Now clear the airways and get the hell back to work."

"Aye, aye, skipper. Over and out."

The pendant dropped back to the swell of Jilly's breasts. The jade bezel had warmed in her hand. She felt its heat through the silk of her blouse.

She could feel Hawk's warmth, as well, when he passed her a crystal flute and joined her on the sofa. His thigh nudging hers, he lifted his glass.

"To your first transmission."

"My first transmission, with many more to come."

His noncommittal grunt took some of the fizz from her sip of champagne.

"Still not happy about me going pro?"

"No."

"Hey, don't sugarcoat it on my account. I'm a big girl. I can take it straight."

His eyes locked with hers. "That's the only way I give it."

"Then tell me this. You went into the field with Diamond when she was a rookie. You trained Rogue from day one. Why are you so opposed to doing the same with me?"

"Diamond may look like a supermodel, but she's as tough as her code name. Same with Rogue. You…"

Jilly scrunched around and balanced her glass on the back of the sofa. "Me, what?"

"You're different."

"Not good enough, Hawk. You taught me to handle everything from a snub-nosed .38 to a 12 bore, double-barreled Thomas Turner. You've seen what I can do. You know I don't rattle or lose my cool when things go boom."

"You don't rattle or lose your cool on the firing range or at a trap shoot. They're a world away from the streets and sewers that spawn the kind of garbage we run up against."

He tipped his glass and downed a swallow, his eyes never leaving hers.

"The same streets and sewers spawned me, Gillian-with-a-J. When I fight, I fight dirty. In ways a girl with a lifetime membership to the Rock Springs Golf and Country Club could never stomach."

His reverse snobbery raised her hackles, but it was that "girl" that made her see red.

"So that's it."

Uncurling, she snapped her champagne glass down on the black lacquer coffee table. She didn't unleash her temper often, but when she did, her younger sister and

brother knew to clear out. It was time—past time!—
Hawk opened his eyes and saw her as she was, not as
he wanted to see her.

"First, I stopped being a girl some years ago. Second,
the fact that I play an occasional round of golf or tennis
at my folks' club doesn't mean I can't handle whatever
crawls out of a sewer. And that…" she stabbed her fore-
finger into his chest "…includes you, Michael
Callahan."

"Jesus, Jilly."

"That's the problem in a nutshell. I'm still sweet
little Jilly in your eyes."

In her own, too, she realized. Well, that would end,
here and now.

"No more Jilly, Hawk. I'm Gillian. Or Jade. Got
that? Jade."

She pushed up onto her knees. The abrupt movement
tumbled her hair forward, onto her forehead. She tossed
it back impatiently.

"Say it, Hawk. Jade."

"For God's sake."

"Say it!" She gave his chest another hard poke. "Jade!"

Cursing, he caught her hand and forced it down.
Anger overrode her common sense at that point.

"All right." She twisted free of his hold. "Maybe this
will convince you."

Bunching her fists in his shirtfront, she swooped in.
The heat, the anger, fused her lips to his for the first
second or two. When he remained rigid and unrespon-
sive, sheer stubbornness took over. She altered her angle
of attack and moved her mouth over his.

"How do you like it, Hawk? With teeth?"

She nipped at his lip, scraping the warm flesh.

"With tongue?"

Her hands slid over his shoulders, locked behind his neck. Her tongue taunted his.

His low growl triggered a memory of her mother's warning not to push him too hard or too far. A distant corner of her mind screeched at her to stop. Now. She'd made her point. In spades.

But she was beyond caution, beyond caring. What had begun in anger had stirred a fury of a different sort. The taste of him, the feel of him consumed her. Hunger stormed through her. Like a tsunami, it roared in her ears and swept everything away in its path except the violent need to feel his naked flesh. With her mouth locked on his, she dropped a hand again and tore at his shirt buttons.

A heartbeat later, she was flat on her back.

He straddled her, pinning her to the cushions. His fists banded her wrists and yanked her arms up. Those hazel eyes were merciless.

"You play with fire, *Jade,* you're apt to get burned."

She should have felt a flicker of fear. A few days ago she would have. Yesterday even, she might have cried uncle at this point and shied away from the ferocity in his eyes.

Now, everything in her exulted in the fact that she'd finally crashed through the wall. Her reply was low and throaty, her smile an invitation.

"So burn me, Hawk."

His grip tightened. His eyes darkened. He hovered

over her for two seconds. Three. Then his weight came down and he took what she was offering.

She strained upward, matching his fury. This was what she'd wanted from him. This was what she'd demanded from him. Raw hunger. Unthinking response.

Lost in the storm, she didn't realize he'd released her wrists until he raked a hand through her hair to anchor her head. His other hand thrust under her hip.

One tug, and he had her repositioned on the cushions. His knee pushed between hers, forcing them apart. A hard thigh pressed against the juncture of her thighs. Liquid heat shot from her belly to her breasts.

"Hawk," she gasped, trying to wedge her hands between them. She was desperate to get at his shirt again, in a frenzy to rip it open and plane *her* palms over his naked chest.

"You're crushing me," she panted. "Shift to the side. A little. Please."

He went still. Absolutely still. Then he muttered a vicious curse and shoved upright.

"I'm sorry. Jilly. Sweetheart. I'm sorry."

Oh, God! He'd completely misinterpreted her breathless plea. Groaning, she scrambled up and reached for him again.

"I'm not little Jilly anymore, Hawk. I'm Gillian, remember? Or Jade."

He frustrated her attempt to reconnect by simple expedient of getting to his feet.

"Okay. All right. Message received. I've had my head up my ass the past few years. I missed the transformation. Or maybe I just didn't want to see it."

The fury had died, but enough of the fire still burned for her to press him. "Now that your eyes are open, what do you see?"

His gaze dropped to her mouth, lifted again.

"I see trouble."

"Huh! Give me a minute to decide whether to feel flattered or insulted."

"What you should feel is relieved."

He raked a hand through his hair. It had lost its sophisticated, slicked-back look. So had Hawk. That almost made up for the wall he erected once again.

"The blinders are off, Jill...Gillian. I won't make the mistake of underestimating you again. But this isn't the time for either of us to open Pandora's box."

Pandora. The name conjured up a subtle blend of floral and musk. It also brought forcefully to mind the woman who ordered the scent from the south of France. As Hawk had known damned well it would.

"Okay," she conceded, blowing out a long breath. "*Your* message has been received. We need to shelve whatever this is between us and refocus on the mission."

"Yeah, we do. Starting now."

Was that regret in his eyes? It came and went so fast she couldn't be sure. But when he turned and went to the desk, he was all brisk business.

"I'm going to boot up the laptop. I want to pinpoint the location of Wang and Company's warehouse. I like to know before I go in how to get out."

"Need some help?"

"No."

Message received. Again. He wanted time and space

to let the last of the embers die. Her lips still throbbing from their tussle on the sofa, Gillian surrendered the field.

"I'm exhausted. I'll hit the shower and then go to bed."

An hour later the champagne bottle tilted in its bucket of lukewarm water. Hawk's flute sat untouched beside his laptop.

The shower had cut on about the time he'd pulled up a map of Sheung Wan district. It cut off while he was studying the maze of narrow, winding streets and alleys that climbed from the harbor to halfway up Victoria Peak's steep slopes.

He'd kept his eyes glued to the screen and forced himself to work possible escape routes. Despite his attempt at total concentration, he'd picked up the unmistakable swish of the duvet being pulled back. That was followed by the thump of a fist pummeling a pillow into shape.

Hawk was still at the computer when the bedroom light clicked off. Even then, he didn't relax. Jilly—Gillian—*Jade!*—had wound him so tight it would be next April or May before he worked out the kinks.

Utter silence blanketed the suite when Hawk finally rose and shoved aside the drapes. Any other time, Hong Kong's incredible nightscape would have drawn an admiring whistle. Tonight, he barely noticed the long wavy ribbon of lighted skyscrapers reflected in the waters of the bay.

He couldn't get Jilly—Jade, damn it!—out of his head. The taste of her. The feel of her. The jump she'd made from girl to woman to sensual, seductive female.

He hadn't been totally truthful with her earlier. He
hadn't had his head *all* the way up his ass. He'd noticed
the changes. Hell, he'd have to have been blind not to.
He'd simply refused to acknowledge them.

Just as he'd refused to admit she had the smarts and the
skills to survive in this dirty business. His every instinct
made him want to protect her, shield her. Keep her from
being gunned down and choking on her own blood.

He gripped both hands on the terrace railing. Eyes
unseeing, he stared at the lights across the harbor.

That's how Diane had died. Choking. Gurgling.
Sobbing for him, for Charlie, for *someone* to help her.

Hawk had heard her. Despite the roar of the chopper
hovering above the canopy. Despite Charlie's frantic
shouts that they had to get out of there. Despite the
bullets splatting through the vines and the searing agony
of Hawk's shattered leg.

He'd heard her and staggered to his feet.

Blood from a head wound poured into his eyes,
blinding him. He tripped over a root. He went down
again, his injured leg ablaze with pain.

The breeze carried harbor scents. Fish. Diesel. But all
Hawk could smell was damp earth and rotting vegetation.

Diane! Hold on!

He'd rolled onto his good side.

Dug his fingers into the spongy ground.

I'm coming! I'm coming!

The cries stopped before he'd crawled five yards.
The choking continued for another second, maybe two.
Then Charlie was shouting and dragging on his arm.

She's dead, Mike. She's dead.

The hell she is!
She's dead! We gotta get on the chopper.
No!

Snarling, Mike threw off his grip and tried to get his good leg under him.

That's when Charlie clipped him. A swift, bruising fist to the jaw. With his vision a blurred curtain of red, Mike didn't see it coming. He went down, landing on his shattered leg once more, and the world exploded into darkness.

He woke two days later to the mingled scents of starched sheets and antiseptic. But even now, even after all these years, he carried the stink of that damp, decaying vegetation inside him.

That, and the distant memory of the perfume Diane always wore.

Chapter 6

Gillian woke to a haze of diffused sunlight and the tantalizing scent of fresh brewed coffee. Knuckling the sleep from her eyes, she rolled over and propped herself up on an elbow.

Hawk had slept beside her last night. The pillow on the far side of bed was indented, the covers rumpled. By contrast, the space between them yawned wide and undisturbed.

Some honeymoon.

Huffing, she flopped back down on the Peninsula's luxurious sheets. She couldn't help imagining how different last night might have been. She'd certainly stirred the proverbial sleeping tiger. Even now, her skin flushed at the memory of his mouth rough and hard on hers, his hand mounding the tender flesh of her breast.

If only she'd kept her mouth shut! So Hawk's weight had crushed her in the sofa cushions? Telling him so had produced exactly the wrong result. He hadn't just shifted his weight, he'd removed it entirely. Then he'd gone all guilty and remorseful on her.

Not her. Jilly.

With a grimace, she threw off the covers and padded into the bathroom. The black lace negligee Field Dress had procured whispered against her skin as she planted both hands on the marble vanity.

"Do *not* forget," she instructed the tangle-haired female in the mirror. "You declared your independence from little Jilly last night. There will be no regressing."

She looked her alter ego square in the eye.

"You're Jade. Hard-nosed undercover operative. Cool. Confident. Totally and completely focused on the mission. Now get your butt in gear."

Twenty minutes later, she strolled into the living room. She'd dressed casually but elegantly in the Bruno Magli ankle boots, black wool slacks and a cashmere sweater set in cobalt. The sweaters complimented the sapphires in her ring and gave the stones a deeper hue. Her jade charm dangled from its gold chain.

Hawk was at the dining table, a silver tea and coffee service at his elbow. He, too, had opted for casual. Gray slacks, a fawn-colored turtleneck and a navy blazer. The blazer's breast pocket sported the embroidered patch of the American Marksmanship Association.

Despite her stern lecture in the bathroom, the mere sight of the man triggered all sorts of inappropriate thoughts. Most of them centered around what it would be like to face him across a breakfast table if they'd finished what they'd started last night.

She pinned on her best cool, confident secret-agent smile. "Good morning."

His eyes met hers over the coffeepot. "'Morning."

Well, thank goodness! She wasn't the only one dogged by thoughts of what did—and didn't—happen on that sofa. The wariness was evident in his carefully neutral greeting.

"I wasn't sure what you usually have for breakfast, so I waited to order from room service. Or would you prefer to go down to one of the restaurants?"

So polite. So deliberate.

"Room service works for me. Just toast," she said when he lifted one of the cordless phones conveniently scattered throughout the suite. "Wheat, not white, with plum preserves."

He added a full English breakfast to her order while she looked over the assortment of teas on the silver tray. White Willow, she decided, anticipating its delicate kick. While the tea steeped, she settled into the chair beside Hawk.

"Is that the map you pulled up last night?"

Nodding, he angled the printed sheet in her direction. "I don't think we'll have much problem with an escape route if we need one. Not in this maze."

Maze understated the case by exponential degrees. The map detailed the wharves edging the waterfront of Hong Kong Island, directly across Victoria Harbour from Kowloon. Wide boulevards and the skyscrapers of the business district fronted the wharves. Jammed in behind the skyscrapers was the area known as the Mid-levels, so named because it climbed and twisted and clung halfway up the steep slopes of mountains dominating the island.

Streets, such as they were, tripped all over themselves. Some doubled back to where they started. Others wound in seemingly endless circles. Gillian had heard varying estimates of how many million people lived and worked, loved and played, were born and died, in the teeming Mid-levels. The correct number was probably lost in the mists that rolled down from the Peak on rainy days.

"I take it this is Wang and Company's warehouse?"

Hawk had marked the building with a red *X*. It was in the heart of Sheung Wan, close to the wharves.

"Good location," she commented. "Very handy for moving containers of antiques to the dock for transport to the main container facility."

The Ching Mai Container Facility was a huge, sprawling complex. Gillian had caught a glimpse of it when they'd landed yesterday. Thousands upon thousands of containers the size of railroad cars had been lined up in rows, waiting to be loaded onto ships.

"Do you think the infected monkeys could have been stuffed into a shipping container at the main port facility?"

"It's possible," Hawk replied. "Smugglers working the black-market animal trade could easily have cohorts among the dockworkers."

"What's security like at those complexes?"

"Tight, given the terrorist threat these days. Very

tight. But where there's a will—and enough money changing hands—there will always be a way. Case in point, the eleven Nigerian refugees who were found dead at the Port of Miami last year. Immigration officials estimate the temperatures inside the container they were locked in topped a hundred and thirty degrees."

Gillian couldn't have worked for the State Department without hearing reports of the flourishing human smuggling trade. Young Thai girls, especially, had been victimized in recent years. The thought of any living creature being locked into a dark, unventilated container and shipped halfway around the world made her really, really want to nail some of the bastards engaged in the despicable trade.

"Based on what you learned from the raid on the Vhrana temple," Hawk said, frowning down at the map, "we know at least one endangered gibbon arrived in the States in a container leased by Wang and Company. We start there. See how they package the items they ship. Talk to their warehouse manager. Go through the facade of purchasing several items for shipment. If nothing pops there, we'll track the items to the container facility."

Gulping, Gillian flashed again on those thousands of metal containers lined up at the Ching Mai facility. She was still dealing with the possibility of having to trudge through endless rows when their breakfast arrived.

Gillian noticed the odd tingle while spreading plum jam over a slice of toast. A second later, she gasped and dropped her knife.

"Oh!"

Hawk's head whipped around. With a shamefaced grin, she set the toast on her plate and reached for her Fu.

"Sorry. I wasn't expecting... The warmth... Er, incoming."

He didn't actually roll his eyes, but he wanted to. She could see it in his face as she fumbled with the charm.

"This is Jade. Come in, Control."

"Mornin', sweet thing."

Griff's lazy drawl drifted through the microdot speaker.

"Morning, Ace."

"You and ole Deadeye nursin' sore heads from too much champagne?"

"Nope."

"That's 'negative' in spook talk, darlin'."

"Okay, negative. What's up?"

His teasing tone faded. "Hawk there with you?"

"Right here," he answered.

"I finally turned over some info on Wang and Company. Turns out, there is no Wang. Or any company, for that matter. It's a dummy holding account, a front for a corporation called Pan-Dor, Associated."

Gillian's gaze flew to Hawk's. "Did you say Pan-Dor?" she asked.

"Roger that. The corporation is owned by a shadowy entity I haven't been able to pin down. The attorneys who set it up must have received their legal training from the mafioso. I've hit so many blinds and double-blinds, they're making me dizzy. But I'll press until I put a face or faces to the name."

"I think we already have one," Hawk said. "Adriana Hall. She let drop yesterday that she orders a special perfume from the south of France. It's called Pandora."

"Coincidence?"

"Could be. Then again…"

"Yeah, I know. Coincidences can get you real dead, real fast, in this business. If Adriana Hall *is* Pan-Dor, Associated, the lady has a thing for keeping her business dealings private."

"So it seems. We're meeting with her again this morning. We'll let you know how it goes."

"Roger that."

Hawk reset his iPod-like intrusion-detection system before they left the suite. Gillian waited in the foyer with her purse slung over her shoulder, while he physically rechecked the alignment of the items in the dresser drawer and positioned his laptop and the desk notepad at precise angles. That done, he eyed the blue-and-white ginger jars atop their black lacquer chests.

Common sense said Gillian was right. If he moved one of the things, housekeeping would probably do the *feng shui* thing and recenter it. He started for the foyer, took three steps, and stopped.

With all those little drawers and top-lifting lids, the lacquer chests provided too tempting a target. Anyone conducting a search of the room wouldn't pass them by. Neither could Hawk. He strode back and nudged one of the ginger jars to the right.

"I know," he said to a plainly amused Gillian. "Some habits just go too deep to jettison."

* * *

Some memories, too.

Hawk's vectored in with savage velocity when Adriana Hall came forward to greet them at the entrance to her storage and shipping facility.

It was the perfume. That damned perfume. The scent crawled all over his nerves.

"Good morning, Mr. and Mrs. Callahan."

She was wearing a Chinese dress again this morning. Scarlet silk, this time, embroidered with gold. The male in Hawk couldn't fail to notice how the high-collared outfit clung to her slender curves. Or how the side slits swished open when she walked.

"I trust you slept well after your long flight?"

"Very well, thank you."

He didn't contradict Gillian's polite reply, but sleep had been the last thing on his mind last night. He'd finally made it to the bedroom just before dawn. Even then he'd dozed only in snatches.

Some of his sleeplessness he could blame on the raw memories of his last mission with Special Ops. Most of it, however, was the direct result of the hunger Gillian had unleashed. He still couldn't believe how close he'd come to taking what she'd offered. Her angry attempt to make him see her as woman had short-circuited every one of the systems he'd put in place to keep from doing just that.

He knew now he'd *wanted* to think of her as Jilly. *Wanted* to nourish an avuncular relationship between them. In fact, he'd worked damned hard to maintain his role as an old family friend. He'd been comfortable with that role. Most of the time.

He'd felt himself slipping on occasion. Like when she would grin and invite him to share some private joke. Or when those melting blue eyes would widen with assumed innocence, a sure sign she was about to say or do something outrageous. Or that time she'd swung around in her chair and her skirt had hiked up. Hawk couldn't walk straight afterward. Adriana Hall gave Gillian Ridgeway zero competition in the leg department.

Or any other. Remembering how she'd moved under him last night made sweat pool at the base of Hawk's spine.

"Are you a sharpshooter, Mr. Callahan?"

He wrenched his mind from the vision of Gillian stretched out and panting on the sofa and found Adriana Hall studying the patch on his blazer pocket. With its rifles crossed over a bullseye, the embroidered insignia held her intent gaze.

"He's one of the world's best," Gillian bragged with wifely pride. "My husband has won medals at every international competition on the books."

"Is that so?" Those green eyes lifted to Hawk's face. "Do you shoot trap? Skeet? Paper targets?"

"Whatever is in my sights."

"Indeed? How interesting. Would you care for tea before I show you around?"

Gillian answered for them again. "We're fine, thanks." Playing to her role, she tucked her arm in Hawk's. The diamonds and sapphires on her left hand winked in the sunlight. "We slept in and had a late breakfast this morning."

"Very well," Hall said coolly. "You mentioned that

you wanted to see our packing and crating operation. Please, come with me."

She led the way up a short flight of steps to a concrete loading dock. Two metal shipping containers sat on the dock. One was closed. The other was open and half-filled with wooden crates. Hawk made a mental note of the address stenciled on the crates before dropping a casual inquiry.

"Any chance Mr. Wang will join us?"

Hall halted and turned to face them. Chin tipped, she regarded Hawk through the screen of her lashes.

"There is no Mr. Wang…as I suspect you may have already discovered."

"I did some digging after our meeting yesterday," he acknowledged. "Care to tell me why my wife and I should do business with someone who hides her true identity?"

"Ah, yes. My true identity."

There was no mistaking the expression in her cat's eyes now. The amusement had an edge to it, though, as did her retort.

"Which identity would you prefer, Mr. Callahan? I have several. Bubble-headed blonde. Helpless female. Bereaved widow, still struggling to cope with the death of her lord and master. None of those personas inspire confidence in buyers intending to outlay rather large sums on money on the treasures I acquire for them. Hence the fictitious Mr. Wang."

"What skin are you wearing today?" Gillian inquired politely. "Or did you slither into a new one for us?"

That drew a swift, narrow-eyed stare from Hall and a warning squeeze of her arm from Hawk.

"I'm sorry," she said with a bland smile that implied the opposite. "I didn't mean to sound rude. But as you indicate, we intend to spend a large amount of cash. We want to know who, exactly, we're dealing with."

"You're dealing with the real me, Mrs. Callahan." Her gaze shifted to Hawk. "Complete and unadorned."

Unadorned, hell!

Gillian managed to swallow her response to that ridiculous statement. The effort almost choked her. She did *not* like this woman. She liked even less the way Adriana Hall ate Hawk with her eyes.

Bitch.

"Please tell me, Mr. Callahan. Do we proceed now that you know I am Wang and Company?"

The woman was determined to cut Gillian out of the conversation. *Double bitch.*

Hawk didn't let her get away with it. "What do you think, sweetheart? Do we proceed?"

"Well…" Sweetheart pretended to ponder the question. "Since we're here, I guess we should let Ms. Hall show us her operation."

"Why don't you call me Adriana?"

Why don't you kiss my ass?

"Certainly. And I'm Gillian."

That produced a regal nod and another glance in Hawk's direction.

"Mike," he said.

"Mike," she echoed, her eyes all over him again.

Gillian identified the emotion that slashed into her without the least difficulty. Jealousy, pure and simple. Yielding to it, she kept Hawk's arm tucked tight against her side throughout their tour of Wang and Company's packaging and crating operation.

It resembled many similar operations she'd observed in Beijing and its environs. The facilities were basic at best. Concrete floors. No heat or air-conditioning. Long, wooden workbenches positioned under strings of naked lightbulbs.

A crew of six women sat at one bench, wielding bubble wrap and padded brown paper with careful efficiency. Gillian's appreciative eye roamed the objects they were preparing for shipment. The treasures included cloisonné vases, Tang dynasty bronzes and exquisite terracotta statues that might have come from an emperor's tomb.

One piece in particular snagged her attention. The small ceramic altar sat by itself at the end of the workbench. It was about a foot long and six inches high. Several small drinking vessels and plates in different shapes sat atop the altar. To be used for offering food and libations to departed ancestors, Gillian knew.

Her breath catching, she dragged Hawk toward the end of the bench. "This looks like a Ming dynasty altar table!"

Looked like, but wasn't.

She recognized it for a fake the moment she bent for a closer inspection. The chop incised in one leg of the table used present-day rather than twelfth-century symbols. Before she could voice her disappointment, Adriana Hall stroked a hand over the ceramic glaze.

"I procured this altar for an Australian buyer, but he balked at the price. If it interests you, I might be willing to come down a bit."

Recalled to her role as a determined buyer, Gillian feigned a collector's greed. "To what?"

"Shall we say five thousand?"

"Dollars or pounds?"

"Pounds."

Triple bitch.

"We'll take it."

"Whoa!" Hawk's protest held a ring of genuine hus-bandly alarm. "Shouldn't we discuss this first?"

"Oh, dear. I keep forgetting."

The pouty smile Gillian turned on Hall was as phony as the one the woman had turned on her earlier.

"I now have to answer to a lord and master. That *is* how you phrased it, isn't it?"

Adriana had to work at masking her feelings as she moved away to give the couple privacy for their "dis-cussion." Mike's pseudo wife was adding unexpected kick to the vengeance she'd waited so long to exact.

Callahan wasn't the only one who'd done some digging. Adriana had spent a good part of last night milking her sources. She knew all about Gillian Ridgeway. Her queries had yielded a wealth of information about the pampered daughter of one of Washington's power couples.

The woman would have to be eliminated. That was a given. Obviously, she was working with Callahan. Why else would she pretend a marriage Adriana could find no record of? Or disguise the knowledge she must have gained during her years at the American Embassy in Beijing? Ridgeway had recognized the altar table as a fake the moment she'd bent to examine the chop. Yet she'd played the eager collector to perfection, followed hard by the chagrined wife.

With a swift change of plans, Adriana decided to fleece the rich Mrs. Ridgeway out of every dollar she could before she had her body dumped into Victoria Harbour.

Chapter 7

"I don't like that woman."

Gillian plunked the bubble-wrapped altar onto the limo's seat and snapped on her seat belt.

"Aside from the fact she deals in reproductions instead of the genuine article, she…"

"What?" Hawk's startled glance dropped to the package nestled between them. "Are you saying you just wrote a four-figure check for a fake?"

She dismissed the money with an impatient wave. "Don't worry. I'll e-mail my bank and have them sit on the check until we determine whether Ms. Hall is as bogus as her merchandise. Although…"

Honesty compelled her to make a grudging concession.

"She didn't actually *say* it was genuine. Nor did she

offer to provide a certificate of authenticity. She just let her latest fish swim onto her hook."

And swim she had. Gillian had stuck to her role but had *not* enjoyed playing the fool for Adriana Hall.

"So what's your take?" she asked Hawk. "Did you pick up anything to indicate Hall is into the black-market animal trade as well as counterfeit antiques?"

She certainly hadn't, and God knew she'd looked into every corner and listened closely to the workers' chatter. She would love to pin a smuggling rap on the condescending blonde. To her intense disappointment, Hawk shook his head.

"Nothing popped for me, either. But I'm not taking Hall out of the picture yet. There's something about the woman... I can't quite get a fix on her."

Gillian could, and the fix wasn't pretty.

"Why don't we just ask her outright about the gibbons?"

"It may come to that," he replied, "but I'm not ready to tip our hand yet. We'll keep up the facade for a little while longer. Let her take us around to some of her sources, as she offered to do."

The prospect didn't particularly thrill Gillian. Adriana Hall had made it abundantly clear she considered Hawk's wife a minor player.

"Did you notice how she directed most of her comments to you? You'd think someone who disguised her true role in the company because of prejudices against women would be a little more sensitive in how she dealt with other women."

"You'd think," he agreed, his gaze fixed on something he'd spotted through the side window. "What the hell is that?"

She leaned around him and gave a yelp of delight.

"That, my friend, is the next best way to experience Hong Kong after a ride on the Star Ferry." A flick of a switch slid back the Plexiglas partition. "Stop the car," she told the driver. "We're getting out here."

"We've got work to do," Hawk protested. "We need to nail down the truck company that transports Hall's containers to the deep water port and…"

"We will, we will." She already had the door open. "After we take a ride on the Mid-levels Escalator."

Hawk got out beside her and craned his neck to look up. And up. And up.

"Jesus. How long is this thing?"

"Loooong. A half mile or more."

The covered, outdoor escalator looked like a metal caterpillar zigzagging from the central business district to the residential neighborhoods of the Mid-levels. Its twenty separate segments and moving sidewalks traveled downward during morning rush hour, then changed direction around ten-thirty. A quick glance at her watch confirmed Hong Kong's high-tech people-mover had made the switch.

"C'mon. We need to buy an Octopus card."

She hauled Hawk to a booth in the ultramodern base station to purchase the ticket that served as an instant credit card. Depending on how much the purchaser shelled out, the chip embedded in the card allowed him or her to purchase everything from public transportation to cell phones.

"And we think we're so advanced," Hawk muttered as he flashed his card at an optical scanner. Moments later, they joined the stream aiming for the first set of moving stairs.

"Walkers to the left, standers to the right," Gillian warned. "You'd better scoot over if you don't want to get mowed down."

He edged to the right on the step behind her and kept one hand on the rail. When she angled around to act as tour guide, she was nestled in the crook of his arm.

Hawk's mind had still been on shipping containers and trucking companies, but their closeness produced an instant reaction. He could feel his body harden as a sparkle lit her eyes.

"We've missed rush hour. That's when the ride is really fun. It's elbow-to-elbow, everyone in lockstep then. Right now, the crowd is mostly tourists and shoppers and school kids."

She loves this, Hawk realized. The hustle and bustle of humanity, the pulsing vitality and ageless mystery of the East. Most Westerners would feel out of place or nervous about trying to find their way through the jumble of streets. Gillian just dived right in.

"The trip up only takes about twenty minutes," she told him as they got off the first escalator and walked the few yards to the next. "But we'll travel a thousand years or more in terms of culture and tradition. From modern day Hong Kong…" Her sweeping gesture encompassed the skyscrapers and multistory condos of the lower district. "…to the shops and houses and temples of the old city."

When they traveled upward, Hawk began to see the transition she'd described. At the lower levels, down near the business district, the department stores' windows lining the moving stairs displayed designer labels and the eating and drinking establishments sported names like Starbucks and Josephine's.

Gradually these trendy department stores gave way to small shops displaying local produce, clothing and the inevitable electronics. Interspersed among the shops were noodle parlors and temples where worshippers could pause on their way to or from work to buy a stick of incense and say a quick prayer.

Apartment buildings crowded the shops. Mostly utilitarian buildings constructed of gray concrete. The higher up Gillian and Hawk went, the narrower the apartments got, until they appeared little more than one room wide. Satellite dishes were attached to a number of balconies. Others sported bamboo poles with washing speared through them to dry.

As the escalator carried them upward, Hawk caught glimpses of life inside those narrow apartments. TVs flickered in some. Family altars and red banners displaying Chinese characters in gold decorated the entrances to others.

"We're coming into the really old section now," Gillian advised when they reached the fifteenth section. "It's gradually being squeezed out by new construction above and below, but you can still get a feel for what life was like before electricity and satellite dishes."

Wooden shanties clung to the steep hills on either side of the escalator. They were piled one on top of the other in seemingly endless, tip-tilted layers. Dirt tracks cut between the layers. These narrow streets were alive with activity. Chickens, goats and the occasional pig rooted amid baskets of refuse waiting for collection. Women in straw hats and traditional Chinese dress squatted in the dirt, cooking or washing clothes in kettles. Children tossed balls or climbed hills. Old men in long coats shambled along.

Commerce was alive and well in this section of Hong Kong, too. Vendors waited at each of the escalator stops, selling cheap hats, postcards, pomegranates and tea steeped in brass kettles suspended on shoulder poles.

"*Shey-shey.*" Smiling and shaking her head, Gillian wove through the milling throng. "*Shey-shey.*"

"What are you saying to them?" Hawk asked as they headed for yet another section of the moving stairs.

"Thank you. Just keep repeating it politely and forge ahead."

"*Shey-shey. Shey-shey. Shey…*"

The fluted trill of a canary sounded just off to his side. Hawk glanced around and saw a familiar pair of pink sneakers topped by a tattered pink T-shirt.

"Isn't that the kid from the promenade?"

Gillian spied the girl at the same moment the pint-size con artist lifted her head and spotted them. Her eyes rounded in recognition, then flooded with fright.

"Ai-ah!"

Spinning, she tried to run, but the crowd and the wooden cage she clutched in one grubby fist impeded her way. Frustrated by the solid wall of humanity, she darted toward the down escalator.

"Hey, kid! It's okay! I'm not looking to recoup my twenty bucks."

Obviously, she didn't understand, but the shout produced another panicky glance over her shoulder. Hawk's heart stopped dead in his chest when the violent twist threw her off balance.

"Look out!"

A high wail tore from the girl's throat. Her small arms flailing, she teetered at the top of the steep metal stairs. Her scream was still ripping across the air when Hawk lunged through the startled bystanders.

He caught her just as she started to tumble downward and swung her, cage and all, into his arms. "It's okay. It's okay, baby. I've got you."

Her small body convulsing with fright, the girl locked her arms around his neck. Wrenching sobs replaced her terror-filled wails. The canary's agitated chirping added to the din assaulting Hawk's ears.

"Don't cry, kid. You're okay." He patted her heaving back and threw Gillian a pleading look. "I could use a little help here!"

Murmuring in Chinese, she stroked the girl's hair. The sobs lost some of their piercing volume, but the canary continued to chirp its fool head off.

When Gillian tried to relieve Hawk of his burden, the girl gave a muffled shriek, tightened her stranglehold and crawled up his chest to bury her face in his neck.

"Oh, for…!" He eyed the crowd that had gathered with a touch of desperation. "See if any of these folks know the kid. They could take her home."

Gillian's queries produced only head shakes and

murmured negatives. A sudden scuffle parted the crowd. The boy who pushed his way through stumbled to a stop when he saw Hawk, then gulped and charged forward.

"Why you hurt Mei Lin? She little. I take your money, not her."

He dug several wadded bills from the pocket of his jeans and shoved them at Hawk.

"Here. Take dollars. No hurt Mei Lin. No call police."

"I don't want your money, and I have no intention of calling the police. Mei Lin's not hurt, just scared. She tripped and almost fell down the escalator."

The kid queried his sister in urgent Chinese. She answered with watery sniffles and what Hawk assumed were affirmatives.

"Okay, sweetheart." Gently, he tried to disengage. "Your brother's here."

When the girl refused to budge, Hawk patted her back again and addressed the kid. "What's your name?"

"Young Tau."

"Tell your sister you'll take her home."

"No have home."

"You must eat and sleep somewhere."

"Sometimes in street." He made a vague gesture toward the shanties. "Sometimes with Ah Chang."

"Who's Ah Chang?"

"Honorable Grandfather."

The crowd had begun to disperse, but Mei Lin still wouldn't loosen her death grip.

"Am I being conned again?" Hawk asked Gillian.

"I'm not sure." Frowning, she shifted her gaze from the boy's Nikes to the girl's pink T-shirt. "The shoes look almost new, but the T-shirts are ragged, and the air is cool enough that they should be wearing jackets."

As if to underscore the observation, Mei Lin shivered and burrowed deeper into Hawk's warmth.

Well, hell! Cradling her against his chest, he glared at the boy. "Take us to this grandfather of yours."

Young Tau hesitated, clearly trying to decide whether to comply...or how he could milk the situation, Hawk thought sardonically.

"Now, kid!"

As slums went, these weren't the most miserable Hawk had ever seen. Central America and Mexico had worse. In some of the former Russian republics, whole families lived in abandoned railcars. The U.S., too, had its share of homeless sleeping on park benches or in cardboard boxes. Yet the sheer density of the population inhabiting this jumble of tile- and tin-roofed shacks made it unique in Hawk's experience.

With Mei Lin still cradled in his arms, he and Gillian dodged wet washing and picked their way carefully over uneven ruts. Dogs sniffed at their heels. A rooster hissed and fanned his tail feathers, guarding his harem of hens. The sharp tang of burning charcoal from cooking braziers mingled with dust and incense from ceramic altars almost identical to the one Gillian had just shelled out megabucks for.

People in all shapes and sizes added their stamp to the mix. Old men with drooping mustaches sucked on long-stemmed pipes and huddled over mah-jongg boards.

Women squatted beside the glowing braziers. Youngsters who should have been in school played in the dirt.

Despite the cool temperatures, several of the toddlers showed bare bottoms through cutouts in the seat of their pajamas or overalls. The utility of that became obvious when Hawk spotted a young girl holding her baby brother over a ditch to go to the bathroom.

"You come."

Young Tau crooked an imperious finger before ducking between two shacks that leaned so close together their corrugated tin roofs almost touched. Putting a hand to the back of Mei Lin's head to protect her from the sharp edges, Hawk held out his other hand to Gillian. They made it through the narrow gap with mere inches to spare.

"How far to your grandfather's?" he asked Young Tau.

"No far. There."

He poked a finger toward the jumble of shacks clinging to the ridge directly above them, reached by a rickety set of steps.

"Gillian, can you manage the stairs in those boots?"

"I'm okay. Can *you* manage Mei Lin and her canary?"

Hawk would have jettisoned the bird a ways back if he didn't now suspect it provided a primary source of income for the kids.

"I can manage. Hang on to my arm."

Young Tau scrambled up ahead of them and ducked under a weathered lintel that must have once been painted a bright red. Hawk was hauling Gillian up the last few feet when a stooped old man hobbled out. His ankle-length, quilted cotton gown hung loosely on his thin frame. The worn hem brushed the tops of his black slippers. Even from ten or fifteen yards away, Hawk could see the cataracts clouding his eyes. The pupils were almost as white as his long, wispy beard.

Huffing a little after the climb, Gillian greeted him in Chinese. He bowed deeply and answered at some length.

"Ah Chang thanks you for saving Mei Lin from a fall," she translated for Hawk. "He says he isn't really her grandfather, and Young Tau isn't her brother. They all sort of just adopted each other. He invites us to come in and take tea."

Hawk eyed the shanty with some misgiving. The front end was supported on stilts dug into the hillside at sharp angles. The rear section looked as though it had been carved out of the dirt.

Gillian had already stooped under the lintel, however, leaving him little choice but to set Mei Lin down and follow. Once inside he had to crouch to keep from banging his head against the poles that supported the roof or bumping into dust-coated lanterns decorated with faded red tassels.

"Honorable Grandfather say, Mister please to sit here." Young Tau patted a wooden chair with curved arms. "Madam, please to take cushion."

Since the chair looked to be the only substantial piece of furniture in the two-room dwelling, Hawk started to defer to the elderly gentleman. Gillian stilled him with a warning glance and sank onto her cushion.

"Honorable Grandfather does us much honor. We are pleased to sit."

Ah Chang hobbled to another cushion. When he sat, Hawk had to hide a wince at the audible creak of his joints.

Gillian made the introductions. "This is my husband, Callahan *Shen Sheung*."

"Cal Han *Shen Sheung*," Young Tau echoed.

"Call-*a*-Han."

"Cal Han," the boy repeated.

"That's close enough. I am Gillian."

Her name was immediately shortened to Jill-An.

The introductions out of the way, the kids scrambled to brew fresh tea. They'd obviously performed the task many times before. Young Tau stirred the coals in a small brazier while little Mei Lin lifted a chipped porcelain teapot from a low shelf. From the reverent way she handled the piece, Hawk guessed it was reserved for special guests.

A murmur of polite Chinese drew his attention to Ah Chang. Gillian responded in the same lilting, sing-song dialect.

"Honorable Grandfather wishes to know why we visit Hong Kong. I told him we've come to buy antiques."

The old man stroked his beard and added another comment.

"He says we must be careful," she translated solemnly. "There are many fakes on the market."

"You don't say," Hawk drawled.

"He says that he has lived many years," she added after another colloquy. "He knows what is genuine and what is not. He offers his assistance, should we wish it. The children, too, are very knowledgeable of what happens on the streets."

Yeah, right. Hawk was still struggling with the fact that he was partnered with Gillian on this op. All he needed was to add a blind old man and a couple of junior grifters to his team.

Except...

Pretending to need their services might be a way to slip them a little extra income. God knew, they could use it. Hawk had only a restricted view of the other room, but from what he could see, it was even more sparsely furnished than this one.

"Please tell, er, Honorable Grandfather that we would be grateful for any assistance he wishes to provide. But only if he'll allow us to pay a commission on the pieces he authenticates."

The warm approval in Gillian's eyes went a long way to stilling some of Hawk's doubts about his team's unexpected expansion.

The man listened intently to the proposal and dipped his head in a nod.

"Done," Gillian said after another brief discussion. "Honorable Grandfather and the kids will take the ferry across the harbor tomorrow afternoon and meet us at the hotel to look over our potential purchases. I told him we would be honored to return his hospitality by taking them to dinner."

"That's fine. Better ask him, though, why the kids aren't in school. Isn't education mandatory throughout China?"

"It is, but some kids fall through the cracks here, just as they do at home. Mei Lin is probably still too young for school. Young Tau..."

"No time school," the boy answered for himself as he poured hot water into the porcelain teapot. "Very busy, work very hard."

Looking at the skinny kid with the jet-black hair, Hawk saw himself twenty-five or -six years ago. He'd been just as thin, just as hungry, but considerably more belligerent. Too bad he hadn't stumbled across an Honorable Grandfather to rein him in. Maybe he wouldn't have collected so many bruises or spent so many nights curled up in culverts.

He'd learned how to survive the hard way. He'd also picked up some interesting tidbits of information. So had Young Tau, he'd bet.

"Hey, kid. You know anything about animals being shipped out of Hong Kong illegally?"

The wary expression that dropped over the boy's face countered his quick negative.

"Know nothing."

"How about animal parts? Tigers' eyes or bear gall or…?"

"Young Tau see nothing, know nothing."

The denial was too quick, the glance he darted at the old man too furtive. Hawk didn't press the issue. Obviously Honorable Grandfather had drawn some lines regarding the kids' money-making ventures. Just as obviously, Young Tau knew more than he was willing to admit in front of the others. Hawk would have to get him alone and have a fistful of dollars handy.

A swish of sneakers on the dirt floor directed his attention to Mei Lin. With a shy smile and a murmur of Chinese, she offered him a thimble-size cup of steaming tea. Hawk accepted it and looked to Gillian for a translation.

"She says she thanks you for catching her before she fell. She thinks maybe you're not so big and ugly after all."

"Shey-shey," Hawk replied.

Mei Lin's rosebud mouth parted. A moment later, she burst into giggles. Young Tau snorted, and the old man raised a blue-veined hand to hide a gap-toothed smile.

"What did I say?"

"You got the tones wrong." Gillian's eyes were filled with laughter. "You just wished her a cold donkey."

Still giggling, the girl crawled into Hawk's lap and proceeded to chatter away. He didn't understand a word. He didn't have to. She didn't appear to require a response.

"Your husband very good to children," Ah Chang commented to Gillian.

"So it appears," she murmured.

Her heart turned over at the sight of Hawk's head bent attentively to Mei Lin's. She'd known him for so long, had watched him interact with both her younger sister and brother. A few moments in his company and shy, quiet Samantha would shed her natural reserve like an old coat. Even the irrepressible Tank was convinced the two of them were communicating man-to-man.

Yet until this moment, Gillian's main preoccupation with Mike Callahan had been sexual. First as a target of her teenaged crush, then as a challenge to her femininity. Only recently had she admitted to a hunger for him that grew more urgent by the hour.

Now…

Now, she realized with shattering insight, she wanted more. She wanted a future that included moments like this. A future where she and Hawk shared more than heat, indulged more than animal hunger.

"You have sons? Daughters?"

She dragged her attention from Hawk and Mei Lin to find Ah Chang studying her with those rheumy eyes.

"Not yet," she answered. "We've, uh, only been married a short time."

"Ah so." His gaze shifted to Hawk. "Your man, I think, will give you many sons, many daughters."

"That's the plan," she said softly.

Chapter 8

The image of Mei Lin cuddled in Hawk's lap stayed with Gillian throughout the ride to Kowloon's deepwater commercial port. It lingered at the back of her mind during the tour of the gigantic Ching Mai Container Facility.

Hawk had contacted Griff, who'd pulled the necessary strings to hook them up with the Port of Hong Kong's director of security. William T'ang was one of China's new breed of up-and-coming professionals. Still in his late thirties, he sported a Bluetooth phone device hooked over his right ear and two beepers clipped to his belt.

Clearly not happy about the possibility that a person or persons unknown might have breached security at his facility to smuggle animals into a shipping container, he began his briefing with visual references to the wall-size map that dominated his office in the Marine Operations Center.

"Our port has been the world's busiest for many years. We currently operate nine terminals."

He thumped various facilities scattered around Victoria Harbour.

"Our main dockages are here, at Ching Mai. On Stonecutters Island. And this is our newest facility. Altogether, we service more than forty thousand seagoing vessels a year, from supersize oil tankers to two- or three-passenger sampans."

Forty thousand ships! Gillian's gaze shifted from the map to the window. T'ang's office was in Ching Mai's Marine Operations Center, a multistory structure that gave a bird's-eye view of the sea of endless rows of shipping containers she'd spotted from the air.

"How many of those containers can a cargo ship hold?" she asked.

"That depends. As you can see, they come in varying lengths. For international shipping, we measure cargo capacity in twenty-foot equivalent units, or TEUs. Our nine-container terminals alone have a total handling capacity of eighteen million TEUs."

"Yikes! Eighteen million units! How in the world do you keep track of all those?"

"Very carefully." T'ang gave her a thin smile. "And, if I may say so, very efficiently. Our average turnaround time for a container vessel is less than ten hours."

Gillian was impressed. Even more so after he handed hard hats to her and Hawk for their ground-level tour of the operation.

"Hong Kong was one of the first facilities to comply with the International Ship and Port Facility Security Code promulgated in 2004," T'ang informed them. "The process begins at the entry gate."

Wheeling his open-sided vehicle through a canyon of containers bearing familiar labels such as Wal-Mart and Target and Tyson Foods, he pulled up at the main entrance. It reminded Gillian of an automated car wash. Side and overhead beams formed a long tunnel that container-laden trucks passed through at the blazing speed of five or six miles per hour.

"Our Integrated Container Inspection System uses gamma-ray imaging to view the contents of every container passing through the portal," T'ang informed them as he led the way into one of the buildings attached to the tunnel. "We also use radiation screening to check for explosives and optical character recognition to marry the container to its computerized log. Together, these three technologies answer the crucial question of what's inside the box."

What was inside the box presently progressing through the tunnel, Gillian saw when T'ang directed their attention to a monitor showing a three-dimensional cross-section, were flat screen TVs. Carton after carton of 'em, stacked so tightly inside the container there wasn't an inch to spare.

The imagery was incredible. So clear and precise, she expected the screens to flicker to life at any second with mind-blowing displays of color.

"We use portable screening units to check containers loaded or unloaded from ships at sea. The system isn't infallible," T'ang conceded. "Contraband *could* slip through. But the monitors would certainly pick up live animals, moving around in cages, making noise."

"Unless they weren't moving around or making noise," Hawk countered. "They could have been drugged. Or someone could have slipped the cages into a container after it went through screening."

The suggestion that his dockworkers might be engaged in smuggling clearly didn't sit well with the port's security director, but he was realistic enough to admit the possibility.

"We do full background checks on all our operators. That's not to say we can't miss something. Our best defense against the kind of tampering you suggest, however, is the container locking system. It's completely cipher-driven. Once the shipper seals his containers and certifies that they're ready for international transit, only certain officials can decode the ciphers and open the boxes enroute."

"Like who?" Gillian wanted to know.

"Like the people who work directly for me. Our Coast Guard units. Your transportation security agents."

With eighteen million units passing through Hong Kong's port facilities at any one time, Gillian remained skeptical until she got down and dirty in the midst of the terminal.

Diesel fumes belched from the trucks lined up under a massive lift that moved on rails. The lift operator sat in a booth high atop his moving, frame-shaped crane, operating his joystick with astonishing speed and accuracy. While Gillian watched in awe, he dropped a set of giant prongs, clamped them onto a container, swung the box off the truck and deposited it atop a stack of three others.

He emptied the truck within minutes. It drove off and another chugged into place. When the second truck had been unloaded, the lift slid forward on its rails and got ready to unload a third.

The speed and efficiency of the process amazed Gillian almost as much as its computerized mechanization. When she searched up and down the endless rows, the only humans she saw were the truck drivers sitting patiently in their cabs, the lift operators perched high above them, a scattering of cargo managers in hard hats and armed security guards.

After the tour of the main facilities, they jumped a high-speed patrol boat for a trip to one of the massive platforms that loaded and unloaded ships in midchannel. The process was pretty much the same. Cranes removed containers from the ships and loaded them onto marine transporters. The transporters passed through a portable scanning system before transferring the containers to other ships ferrying them back to a land terminal.

By the time Gillian and Hawk parted company with T'ang around 5:00 p.m., she was windblown and salt-sprayed and reeking of diesel fumes. She had also pretty much bought into the theory the infected animals could have been drugged and concealed in a shipping container before it went through screening at the port.

Hawk wasn't quite as convinced. "It might pay to make another visit to the terminal facilities. After dark, and without the director of security looking over our shoulder."

Gillian was mulling over the somewhat daunting prospect of dodging those giant cranes in the dark when they arrived back at their hotel. The same clerk who'd greeted them on their arrival was at the reception desk again. The young woman looked a little startled at the dock smells her guests brought with them but smiled and presented Gillian a note sealed with a red wax chop.

"This came for you. I was just going to send it up to your suite."

"Thank you."

"And thanks for the champagne you sent up yesterday," Hawk added. "We enjoyed it and the fruit tray very much."

Yesterday? Good Lord! Gillian stepped into the elevator with a slight sense of shock. Was it only yesterday they had arrived in Hong Kong? Only last night she'd slapped her champagne glass down on the coffee table and attacked the man beside her? So much had happened in the hours since that she hadn't really let herself think about the fireworks that angry kiss had set off.

She could think of nothing else as the elevator doors pinged shut. Feeling the heat, Gillian unfolded the monogrammed note. Adriana Hall's scent drifted from the thick vellum and penetrated even the eau d'diesel filling the small space. Wrinkling her nose, Gillian relayed the note's contents to Hawk.

"Our friend has just received word that one of Hong Kong's most prominent physicians is putting part of his collection of cloisonné on the market. She's wrangled an invitation for a private showing this evening at seven. With dinner afterward, if we're available. Are we?"

She lifted her gaze, saw Hawk frowning at the flashing floor buttons and waved the note in front of his face.

"Private showing at seven? Dinner afterward?"

Personally, Gillian had had enough of Ms. Hall for one day. She half hoped he would suggest a let's-keep-her-dangling strategy.

"We're available." His mouth took a wry turn. "As long as you refrain from writing out six-figure checks for items you know are fake."

"Be interesting to see if Ms. Hall tries to palm more repros off on us," Gillian agreed as the elevator doors swished open.

Hawk checked his handheld scanner before inserting his key card. Once inside the suite, Gillian tossed the note onto the black lacquer coffee table. The handwriting was as bold and distinctive as the scent.

"Hall has our cell-phone numbers," she mused. "Wonder why she didn't call instead of sending a note?"

Hawk shrugged, clearly more interested in the alignment of the porcelain ginger jars than her idle question. "They're dead center again, damn it."

"Best not to mess with Chinese notions of harmony and balance."

Unconvinced, Hawk prowled through the rest of the rooms. While he checked his other triggers, she unwrapped the package they'd left with the chauffeur. He'd had it delivered to their suite.

The altar was a pretty piece. Not worth a tenth of what she'd paid for it certainly, but the design was well executed and the glaze hand-fired. After careful consideration, she moved the bamboo plant gracing a narrow console table a few feet to the right and countered it with the altar.

Satisfied that she hadn't disturbed the balance of the room, Gillian wandered out on the terrace. The wind off the bay lifted the ends of her hair and played with the flaps of her deep blue cardigan. She had a clean view of the dock area where Adriana Hall's warehouse was located, but the tall buildings of the business district blocked most of the jam-packed Mid-levels. From this distance, she could see only a faint trace of the shacks clinging to the hills above.

Funny how that outdoor escalator had crawled upward with the weight of a thousand years of history on its back, moving from gleaming, twenty-first-century high-rises to dirt-floor shanties that had seen empires come and go. Those one- and two-room dwellings might look like a gray-brown blur from the Peninsula's lofty terrace, but the images Gillian had taken away from her visit were more vivid than any of the others she'd gathered during this jam-packed day.

One in particular stayed with her. She didn't have to close her eyes to summon the picture of Hawk with Mei Lin snuggled in his lap. She was reliving that moment—and Ah Chang's prediction that her man would give her many sons, many daughters—when Hawk joined her on the terrace.

He'd shed his blazer and some of his exasperation with the Chinese passion for neatness and order. The wind ruffled his short dark hair and flattened his tan turtleneck to his frame. Following her example, he leaned his elbows on the rail beside hers.

"Some view, isn't it?"

"Mmm."

She angled her head, debating how much of her thoughts to share with him. The decision came easy when she looked up at the stranger she'd been so certain, so arrogantly and stupidly certain, she knew.

"Speaking of views, I saw a different side of you this morning."

"How's that?"

"You were good with Young Tau."

"He reminds me of myself a few decades back."

"And Mei Lin?"

"She's a little cutie." A smile crept into his eyes. "A lot like another dark-haired beauty-in-the-making I used to know."

Gillian swallowed a sigh. This wasn't the moment to rekindle the anger from last night. Still, she couldn't let the little-girl bit pass unchallenged.

"We didn't know each other when you were Young Tau's age, and I was never as cute or as cuddly as Mei Lin."

"I doubt your father would agree with that."

She refused to debate the issue. She had a more important matter to get off her chest.

"After watching you with those two, I think I owe you an apology."

Confusion and a hint of wariness replaced the smile in Hawk's eyes. "For what?"

"I'm sorry I goaded you last night," she said quietly. "I wanted to force you to see me as I am now, not as the girl I used to be. But it turns out you weren't the only one wearing blinders."

She lifted a hand and stroked his cheek. His skin was warm against her palm, his five o'clock shadow prickly.

"I've seen only what I wanted to see, too. The unflappable Mike Callahan, as cool and in control at the firing range as he is in the field. I haven't really looked for the man under that macho exterior. I don't know him or what he went through when he was Young Tau's age."

"You don't want to know."

"You don't want to tell me," she corrected. "Any more than you want to tell me about the woman you once loved."

Hawk could feel himself stiffening. After all these years, he should have put the past behind him, should have been able to conquer the memories.

"That's okay."

The understanding and acceptance in Gillian's voice made him cringe inside.

"Right now it's enough that you want me," she said. "Almost as much as I want you. I can wait until you realize what we might have together could be as good— or better—than what you lost."

She came up on tiptoe to brush her lips over his. The kiss held none of the fury of last night's, none of the anger or the greedy desire. Yet the whisper-light touch bent Hawk's control to the breaking point.

She had it wrong, he thought savagely. She couldn't feel anywhere near the craving for him that he did for her. It was like a beast in his belly, clawing and snarling for release. He could feel the raw hunger tearing at his insides.

He'd unleashed the beast once, and listened to its

agonizing death rattle amid the roar of chopper blades and stutter of gunfire. He couldn't, he *wouldn't,* let his hunger for Jilly dull his instincts or put her in danger.

The need to protect her, to spare her the kind of agonizing death Diane suffered, went beyond thought or reason. She didn't want to hear that, though, any more than he wanted to tell her about Diane's agonizing death.

He owed her a response, however. Owed her the truth after her quiet offer to wait.

"Listen to me, Gillian." Clamping his hand over hers, he flattened it against his cheek. "You're nothing like her. You're everything that's bright and beautiful in this world. She was… She was…"

Clever. Mercurial. A fire in his blood.

"She was like me," he said finally. "Different background, different path to law enforcement, same gut-deep craving for something we never quite found together."

"What kind of something?"

"I don't know. Contentment, I guess is the best label for it. Joy in little things like reading the Sunday paper or sharing a meal we didn't have to cook over a can of Sterno."

"Or having sex that wasn't spiked by danger?"

"That, too," he admitted.

"Hmm." She thought for a few moments. "We may have a problem."

As if that was news to Hawk. Hadn't he been trying to tell her for weeks now that he wouldn't fit into her world or she into his?

"I might not give you that 'something,' either," she

said with a small frown. "The only part of the Sunday paper I read is the book-review section. I rarely cook, and when I do, it's not over a can of Sterno. As for sex…"

The frown dissolved into a smile that looped Hawk in knots from the neck down.

"I have a feeling we'll both find what we're looking for there, with or without the danger."

He almost lost it then. The woman tempting him with that smile was all Gillian. Salty and wind-tossed and more aromatic than usual but unmistakably Gillian.

A trill of ascending notes was the only thing that kept Hawk from burying both hands in her hair and covering her mouth with his. It took a second shrill ring to get him to back off completely.

With a muttered curse, Gillian went inside to retrieve her cell phone. Hawk followed in time to see her make a face when she identified the caller.

"Yes, Adriana, we received your note. It was waiting when we got back to the hotel a few minutes ago."

She listened a moment, one dark brow lifting.

"No, we didn't go antique hunting after we left you this morning. I decided to show my husband some of the city."

The term came more easily to her, Hawk noted. The knowledge pleased him in a way he wouldn't let himself think about right now.

"We're thrilled about the private showing tonight," Gillian was saying. "Thanks for arranging it. Black tie? We can do that. Good. Fine. See you then."

She flipped the phone shut. There was no explanation needed for the call, as he'd overhead the conversation, and no going back to those moments before it.

The grim business that had brought them to Hong Kong had returned to center stage.

"Adriana says she'll pick us up in forty minutes. We'd better get cleaned up."

Chapter 9

While Hawk showered in the guest bathroom, Gillian took over the dressing room in the master suite. She intended to use every one of the allotted forty minutes to arm herself for her second session of the day with Adriana Hall. She was damned if she'd go the neat and demure route this time. Not with Hall doing her exotic Suzie Wong imitation.

Field Dress hadn't included a slinky *cheongsam* in Gillian's wardrobe for this op, but they had raided one of D.C.'s trendiest boutiques. The strapless bustier was made of blonde lace and cut straight across her breasts. The matching bikini panties showed more creamy flesh than they covered. The lacy garter belt clipped on to stockings that added a lustrous sheen to her legs.

Over the decadent undergarments, she wore a slim, ankle-length skirt slit high on one side and a tuxedo-style jacket, both in tawny gold velvet. The fabric was whisper-thin and as soft as milk against her skin. The gold Guiseppe Zanotti heels that completed the ensemble roused instant lust in her heart.

Even before she strapped on one of the three-inch sandals, Gillian knew she'd have to reimburse the government for these babies. For the whole outfit, she decided as she made a slow pirouette in front of the mirror. No way was *any* of this going into Field Dress's storage vault.

She kept the jewelry simple—gold earrings, the jade charm, the wedding ring—but went all out with her makeup. Mahogany shadow, a darker shade of liner and two coats of mascara deepened her eyes to blue smoke. Pale blush with just the faintest glitter of gold dusted her cheeks. Her lip gloss was a cool sherry. To emphasize the long, straight column of skirt and jacket, she swept her hair up and anchored it in a cluster of curls atop her head. Only a few tendrils escaped to feather her nape and brush against her cheek.

Hawk's low whistle when she joined him in the sitting room more than justified the extra time in front of the mirror. He'd put some effort into his appearance, too. His tux was shadowy black, a dramatic contrast with her shimmering gold.

Darkness and light. Heaven and earth. Fire and water.

The East was weaving its spell on her, Gillian thought as Hawk did an approving walk-around. She didn't need the spark that leaped along her nerves to know deep inside they could come together eventually, yin to yang, male to female. Now all she had to do was convince Hawk of that.

"Did Field Dress come up with that outfit?"

The husky edge to his voice upped her yin level by a factor of ten. "They did."

"Remind me to give them my personal thanks when we get home."

"I intend to do better than that. I'm going to write out a check for everything you see here and one or two things you don't."

Okay, maybe she shouldn't have tacked on that provocative remark. She and Hawk had stirred so many emotions out on the terrace it probably wasn't wise to add to the mix.

She could wait, she reminded herself sternly. Sooner or later he'd bury his past. When he did, they would forge a future. Together. She could wait.

Or not.

Her carefully scripted scenario went all to hell when Hawk slid his palm around her nape and played with one of the long, loose tendrils.

"Do you remember when you tapped me to escort you to that Washington soiree? The one where I wanted to hook up with Congressman Kent?"

Like Gillian could forget? That was her first semi-official date with Hawk. True, she'd more or less coerced him into using her as entrée into the tight-knit community of Washington's elite. Also true, he'd abandoned her when he spotted his prey. Until he had, however, she'd feasted on the sheer excitement of walking into a crowded room on his arm and the smooth play of muscle and tendon under the sleeve of his tux.

"You wore your hair up that night, too."

The rough pads of his fingertips raised goose bumps on the back of her neck.

"Did I?"

"All I wanted that night was access to Kent. Yet all I could think about was the curve of your neck. The way these loose curls teased your jaw."

And how much he'd ached to spring the silky mass free of the confining hair clip and watch it tumble over her naked shoulders.

Hawk had known then Gillian-with-a-J was trouble as far as he was concerned. Only now did he realize just how serious that trouble was.

"We'll talk," he promised. "As soon as this op is over."

When he had her home.

Safe.

And in his bed.

There was something different about Mike Callahan and his pseudo bride. Adriana sensed it as soon as they joined her in the limo.

It wasn't just their physical appearance, although Gillian Ridgeway's seductive elegance produced an instant spurt of envy. Adriana tried to tell herself any woman could achieve that combination of sultriness and sophistication given enough time and money. Look at what she herself had accomplished with a few stolen millions.

With a hidden smile, she slid her fingertips along the deep, slashing V of her gown. She'd opted for Western dress tonight: a designer label she could never have afforded on her paltry government salary. The halter top bared most of her cleavage. A dog collar of sparkling crystals concealed the wound left by the bullet that pierced her larynx.

Would Mike notice? She'd make sure he did. She'd certainly noticed his attire.

Adriana had never seen him in formal dress. He'd been in Special Ops when they'd worked their first op together in Afghanistan. She'd been part of a DEA task force that was supposed to convince the United States' supposed allies to cut back on their poppy production. Sergeant Mike Callahan had been in charge of task force security. Even decked out in Kevlar and coated with dust, the man was hot.

They'd hooked up several times after that, each meeting more explosive than the last. The woman Adriana once was had convinced herself she'd found her match. Then Callahan left her to die in that sweltering green hell.

This was the same man, she reminded herself fiercely as he stretched out his long legs beside Gillian's. He might have traded his jungle BDUs for a starched white shirt and hand-tailored tux, but it was the same man.

"I'm glad you were available on such short notice," she purred.

"So are we," the Ridgeway woman replied, shifting to snap on her seat belt. The movement bared her left leg below the knee and several inches above. "Tell us about this doctor who's putting part of his collection up for sale."

"Alexander McQuade is quite a character. A hard-liner who opposed returning Hong Kong to China right up until the Union Jack came down in 1997. I didn't know him then, of course, but I've procured several items for him in recent years."

She kept her voice pleasant and her gaze on Gillian's face, but she didn't miss the hand Mike laid on his "wife's" knee. The gesture was so casual—and so possessive—that Adriana felt herself stiffening. But it wasn't until Gillian answered the gesture with a slanting sideways glance that she began to suspect there was more between these two than she'd realized. Something sour churned in her belly as she tipped Ridgeway a cool smile.

"Are you as knowledgeable about cloisonné as you are about ceramic altars, Gillian?"

The zing hit home, although the brunette tried not to show it. Ridgeway knew she'd been fleeced on the altar, and the fact that she did added another level to this cat-and-mouse game they were playing.

"More so, as it happens."

The response was as barbed as the question.

"During my stint as a Cultural Exchange officer, I convinced the Beijing Museum of Arts and Crafts to put together a traveling exhibit of antique cloisonné pieces. It toured the U.S. for eight months. Most people prefer the blue of the Jingtai era, but I have to admit I'm particularly addicted to the red and green patterns developed at the court of Emperor Jong Te."

Well, well. So the woman had claws and wasn't afraid to show them.

"Are you familiar with their spread-wing dragon patterns, Adriana?"

The pointed query necessitated a quick retreat. She'd taught herself enough about Oriental antiques to demand ridiculous prices for the pieces she hunted down for collectors, but she was no expert on any particular school.

"Not as familiar as I should be," she answered with perfect truth. "It sounds as though you and Dr. McQuade will hit it off rather well. Mike and I will have to entertain each other while you two talk colors and dynasties."

Which suited her plans perfectly. She wanted Callahan to herself so she could twist the knife a little before thrusting it home.

As Adriana had anticipated, Alexander McQuade found an instant soul mate in Gillian. He barely gave her time to take a sip of the perfectly chilled white wine his butler served before stubbing out his black cigar and thumping his own tumbler of scotch onto a side table.

"You've a liking for the Jong Te era, do you? Wait until you see my phoenix vase. It's the centerpiece of my collection."

He practically dragged her to the upstairs gallery that ran the length of his home in one of Hong Kong's older and exorbitantly expensive neighborhoods. Adriana took advantage of the opportunity to slide her arm through Callahan's. Her steps were slower going up the wide oak stairs, her smile deliberately seductive.

"Your wife is quite charming."

"I think so," Callahan answered, his gaze on the pair ahead. A seemingly accidental press of her breast against his arm jerked his attention back to Adriana.

"How did you meet?"

"Her father asked me to teach her to shoot."

Adriana would keep that in mind. If Mike Callahan had instructed Ridgeway, the woman would know which end of a weapon was which.

"Perhaps you could give me some pointers. It's been a while since I got out my gun." Particularly since she'd become so adept with a knife.

"What kind of weapon do you shoot?"

"A SIG Sauer P226."

The flicker of surprise in his hazel eyes gave Adriana a vicious satisfaction.

Did I trigger some memories, Callahan? Are you remembering that the P226 is standard issue for U.S. Drug Enforcement Agency officers?

"That's more gun than most women want to handle," he said slowly.

"Perhaps, but then I make it a point not to conform to expected standards."

She got to him. She didn't have any doubts on that score. Yet when Gillian negotiated the purchase of a cloisonné vase and a pair of candlesticks from McQuade and their host led the way back downstairs, Callahan seemed to slip away from her.

The other dinner guests arrived before Adriana could reel him back to her side. She didn't ignore the people seated on either side of her at the table groaning with silver candelabra, but her focus never left Mike or his partner on this op. By the time Adriana stuck her fork into a puffy Yorkshire pudding, she'd finally interpreted the pair's private signals.

Gillian Ridgeway was in love with Callahan. She disguised it beautifully with her new-bride patter and the frequent touches expected of a recently married woman, but Adriana had learned to interpret the most subtle signals.

She'd had to, first during her DEA days, then to survive those brutal months with a drug lord who needed to inflict pain to receive pleasure. She'd turned the tables finally and derived more pleasure than she'd ever imagined from watching the pig die. Slowly. Agonizingly. To this day, she wasn't sure whether he'd bled out from the knife she slid between his ribs or suffocated on the testicles she'd cut off and stuffed in his mouth.

Or maybe it was the shock of learning that she'd watched him through eyes swollen almost shut from his blows. That all the while she'd crouched in a corner, she'd listened to his drunken boasts about the millions he and his cohorts had reaped in profit over the years. That she'd used the codes he'd stupidly taped to the shelf above his computer to access his account and transfer those millions to a secret account she herself had set up.

Slitting Charlie Duncan's throat had given Adriana almost the same thrill. Duncan hadn't recognized her. Not until that last moment, when his blood gushed over her hand. In his last frantic seconds, he'd tried to tell her that he thought she was dead, that he'd checked her pulse.

The gutless, lying bastard! She hadn't lost consciousness. Not for a moment. She'd almost drowned in her own blood from that shot to the throat, but she hadn't blacked out. She knew Charlie Duncan hadn't come within ten feet of her, let alone checked her pulse.

Nor had Mike.

Her eyes narrowed on him across the table, so rugged, so masculine with those wide shoulders and that cool, don't-mess-with-me smile. She wouldn't have believed he'd leave her. Even now it was like a steel-toed boot to her midsection.

While the candles flickered and crystal sang, Adriana savored her imminent revenge like the other guests savored McQuade's forty-year-old Bordeaux.

She'd make her move tomorrow, she decided. She'd continue the farce, take Callahan and his "bride" on another buying expedition and torment Gillian Ridgeway by seducing the man she hungered for. The man who had once hungered for *her*.

Then she'd end the game.

Several hours later Gillian tossed her evening bag on the coffee table of their hotel suite. The beaded crystals hit with a sharp snap.

Hawk gave her a quizzical glance as he deposited the carefully wrapped cloisonné pieces beside the bag. "You haven't said a word since Adriana dropped us off. Is something bothering you?"

"No."

She dragged in a breath. Let it out with a huff.

"Okay, yes. That woman was all over you like a bad rash."

"What?"

"Adriana. She had her hands on you all night."

"No, she didn't."

"Let's just do a recap, shall we? There was that little

arm squeeze when we went upstairs at McQuade's. The palm she ran up between your shoulder blades after dinner. The hip nudge when we got into the limo for the ride back to the hotel."

"There was a hip nudge?"

"Don't play coy with me, Callahan." She folded her arms. Above them, her blue eyes flashed a warning. "If you expect to pull off this pose as a brand-new husband on a honeymoon buying spree, you'll have to at least *pretend* some interest in your bride."

"Pretend? Jesus, Gillian. We must have inhabited alternate universes tonight."

As irritated at the grilling as he was aroused by the rise and fall of her breasts above those crossed arms, Hawk yanked his white tie out of its bow.

"Couldn't you tell I spent my entire evening trying to keep *my* hands off *you?*"

"Actually, I couldn't."

The tone was still pure acid, but some of the belligerence went out of her stance. Only some. Adriana Hall had obviously sparked a temper Hawk had witnessed only in brief flashes before.

"Tell me this," she demanded, one foot tapping. "Did you or did you not pick up on the tension that crackled through the air whenever she got within ten feet of you?"

"If I felt any tension, it was because she's still our only link to Charlie Duncan and the black marketeering case he was working when he was murdered."

Gillian tapped her foot again. Every feminine instinct she possessed told her the blond bombshell wanted more than a business arrangement from Hawk. The woman oozed sex from every pore. Did Hawk honestly not see she had her claws out? Was he that zeroed in on their mission?

Had he really spent the whole evening trying to keep his hands off *her?*

The admission went a long way toward putting a cap on Gillian's simmering irritation. Still, she and Ms. Hall were going to have a serious discussion in the not so distant future. Right now she needed to make her position clear to her husband, pretend or otherwise.

With a swish of velvet and nylon, she crossed the room and caught the dangling ends of his tie. "You said earlier that we'd talk when this op was over. I'll hold you to that. In the meantime…"

She yanked on the tie and tugged him down to her level.

"Keep this in mind the next time Adriana rubs up against you."

She should have expected the sizzle. After all, she'd initiated the contact. Yet the voltage lit her up, inside and out. This was their third kiss, but who was keeping count? All Gillian knew was that she'd never get enough of his taste, his touch.

She pulled back, breathing hard. Her hunger was reflected in Hawk's narrowed eyes and the rigid set to his neck and shoulders. He'd kept his hands to himself, although his fists were balled and the knuckles showed white.

Torn between satisfaction at the sight and guilt at tempting him, she left him there in the living room.

She could wait, Gillian reminded herself. Grinding her back teeth, she changed into the negligee and cleaned off her makeup. She could wait, she repeated as she crawled into bed. She could wait until Hawk buried his past.

He'd damned well better get on with it, though.

Chapter 10

Hawk stood with his tie hanging loose and his fists bunched. He heard water splash in the bathroom. Drawers slam in the bedroom. Gillian's mutter just before she flicked off the bedroom lights.

Stillness settled over the suite. Still he didn't move. He knew damned well that if he so much as twitched a muscle, he'd storm into the bedroom and feed the savage hunger Gillian's kiss had roused.

The minutes ticked by. Five. Ten. When he was sure he had himself under control, he hit the suite's well-stocked minibar. He poured one shot and made sure it lasted until he was certain Gillian was asleep.

He cracked the bedroom door to check. She was curled on her side at the edge of the wide bed. Her black hair spilled over the pillow she'd punched up under her cheek. Her slow, regular breathing confirmed she was out for the count.

Easing the door shut, Hawk went into the dressing room and ripped off the tie. His tux jacket hit the floor. The white dress shirt followed. Moments later he was in a dark T-shirt, jeans and a black leather bomber jacket. His Glock nested in its holster, a familiar weight at the small of his back. He had to get out, had to release some of this tension before he blew. Jaw tight, he stalked back into the sitting room and activated his transmitter.

"OMEGA control, this is Hawkeye."

"Yo, Hawk. Ace here."

Griff sounded wide-awake. He must have just come back on the control desk. With all the time zone changes, it was still yesterday in D.C.

"What's happening, buddy?"

"I've decided to pay a late night visit to the container facility we toured this morning."

"You see something there that looked suspicious?"

"No, which is why I'm going back. Any operation that large and complex has to have some holes."

"Roger that. Jade providing backup?"

"Negative. She'll remain here at base. I'll brief you if I find anything."

He signed off, hoping to hell his instincts proved true. He craved action, the more physical the better. Nothing would give him greater pleasure right now than to come face-to-face with human slugs engaged in black marketeering.

* * *

Hawk slipped out the hotel's back entrance and hailed a cab. He had the driver drop him off at a dingy-looking dive he'd noted about a mile from the container terminal. The flyspecked neon sign advertised beer in both Chinese and English. The fog of cigarette smoke that rolled out when he opened the door was as noxious as the reek of stale sweat.

Inside, a motley collection of truckers, dockworkers and sailors off ships flying flags from around the world crowded small tables or stood with elbows planted on the bar. Hawk's entry turned few heads in this polyglot gathering. He wedged in at the bar and ordered a Tsingtao.

It took two of the potent brews to settle on his mark. The dockworker was big, beefy and just this side of falling-down drunk. He was Chinese but complained loudly in broken English to two sailors nursing their beers about his prick of a boss.

"Not good enough we stack containers in straight line, many, many high. No, no. The son of a turtle says wrong place. Must move all."

"Yeah, you've told us."

"Many hours to move, no extra pay. Son of a turtle."

The mariners grimaced. "Give it a rest, mate, and 'ave another beer."

"Son of a turtle."

Lurching to his feet, the dockworker stumbled to the men's room. Hawk followed. A long piss and a wad of Hong Kong dollars later, he'd convinced the man to show him how and where someone without a security pass and enough interest might access the terminal.

The dockworker sobered a little when the night closed around them. He started to get downright nervous when they approached the terminal. In keeping with its 24/7 operation, high intensity spots flooded the entire yard and lit up the front gate, where trucks were lined up to pass through screening. Cold mist seeped in off the ocean as Hawk and his now-reluctant guide skirted the gate and followed the wire-topped, fifteen-foot-high chain-link fence.

"There," the man grunted, pointing to where the fence made a ninety-degree right turn. "Hole in lights."

He was right, Hawk saw. Although video surveillance cameras and bright floodlights swept the area, the floods only overlapped at the outer rim of their arc. Closer in, at the corner of the fence, was a patch of inky blackness.

"I go now."

The dockworker took off, disappearing into the night, and Hawk settled in to wait.

He didn't wait long.

The shadows came out of the mist. Dim and shapeless at first, they gradually resolved into a string of five or six hunched figures, some carrying what looked like bundles.

As Hawk watched, the lead figure signaled the others to wait while he crept up to the fence. He crouched there for long moments, watching, listening, waiting for the accomplice that finally ducked out from behind a row of containers.

After a whispered exchange, the accomplice stood guard while the first man slipped what looked like a crowbar from under his padded jacket and used it to pry up the lower portion of the fence. Holding the fence up with one hand, he beckoned urgently to the others waiting in the shadows.

Hawk lifted his wrist to within an inch of his mouth. "OMEGA control, this is Hawkeye."

"We read you, Hawk."

"Get on the horn to Will T'ang, director of security for the Port of Hong Kong."

The crouching figures crept forward, one by one, a line of dim shadows in the mist.

"Tell T'ang he's got a perimeter penetration approximately two hundred yards west of the main gate, where the fence makes a turn to the north."

"I'm on it."

The first man had crawled through, but the chain links appeared to have snagged the second. The individual with the crowbar struggled to lift the fence higher.

"I'll stay in position until... Hell!"

The metal rod snapped out of the holder's hands and came down with a sickening thud on the trapped penetrator.

"Aieeeee!"

His agonized cry ricocheted through the night. He twisted frantically, but the chain link prongs only gouged deeper into his flesh.

"Ay! Ay!"

His screams unleashed a frenzy of activity as the others rushed to his aid. All except one. The individual who'd wielded the crowbar took off like a shot.

Hawk was up and after him in the next breath.

* * *

Dawn was just beginning to streak the night sky when Hawk deactivated the alarm and used his key card to access his hotel suite. He still reeked of stale cigarette smoke. Damp earth was smeared across his face and skinned knuckles. The bastard who'd wielded the crowbar hadn't gone down easy. Thank God!

Hawk could have prevented the brutal exchange of blows. He knew enough dirty moves to disable any opponent without breaking a sweat. His only excuse for wading in was that he'd craved the action...and the physical release that came with it.

The subsequent hours with Will T'ang and the port police had added to his satisfaction. The scum Hawk had taken down admitted to being part of a people-smuggling operation and implicated a number of others—including the VP of a shipping agency who'd provided him and his pals with the necessary codes to unlock the containers.

The downside to the night was that none of the persons interrogated admitted to involvement in the black-market animal trade. Still, Hawk thought as he moved through the darkened suite, he now had a hard link to at least one smuggling ring. If the police shook these characters hard enough—and Hawk intended to see that they did—one of them might make the connection to another....

A soft snick froze him in his tracks. He was in the gun business. He recognized the sound of a round being chambered when he heard it.

"Turn around. Very slowly."

"Jesus, Jilly!" Relief crashing through him, Hawk swung toward the sound of her voice. "It's me."

A lamp clicked on. Light chased away the predawn darkness and illuminated the woman in the high-backed wing chair. Above the distracting V of her negligee, her face was as cold and hard as the blue steel Beretta she had aimed at his chest.

"You want to point that away and engage the safety?"

"I don't think so."

"Jilly—Gillian," he corrected hastily. "Ground your weapon."

For an incredulous moment, Hawk thought she'd ignore the safety drill he'd pounded into her.

He sucked in a swift breath, and let it out again when she downed the Beretta, thumbed the safety, ejected the magazine and emptied the chamber. Even without the loaded weapon, the atmosphere in the suite was lethal.

"Where were you?"

"I paid another visit to the container terminal."

"And you didn't think it was necessary to advise me of your intentions?"

"You were asleep."

The feeble excuse only compounded his sins. Hawk recognized that even as her eyes narrowed to slits.

"From the blood on your face and hands, I have to assume you connected with someone or something."

"I connected," he confirmed. "If you'll call room service and order some hot coffee, I'll clean up and tell you what went down."

"Order your own damned coffee."

"Lighten up, Gillian. I told you when we left Ching Mai that the terminal warranted another visit."

"Yes, you did," she acknowledged icily. "But you failed to mention that you didn't consider me necessary for the return trip."

Hawk wasn't used to being grilled by a rookie...especially one with a tangle of dark hair tumbling over her bare shoulders and her skin gleaming through the lace of her gown.

"Look, I may have screwed up by going solo on this one but..."

"There's no 'may' about it, Bubba."

"...but," he continued, working hard to contain his annoyance, "I opened a lead. I'll tell you about it after I clean up."

He picked up the phone and ordered the coffee on his way to the shower.

While Hawk occupied the walk-in glass stall with its panoramic view of a city just coming awake, Gillian changed into a military-style tunic and slacks in regimental red. The jacket's high collar and elegant fit had come from the hand of an exclusive designer. The martial style highlighted by shoulder epaulets and gold piping more than matched Gillian's mood.

She'd conquered her anger by the time Hawk reemerged, but hurt and disappointment still bit at her like angry wasps. He met both head-on with an apology.

"You were right. I *did* screw up. I'm sorry."

She nodded stiffly. "Apology accepted. On one condition. I want the truth, Callahan. Why didn't you wake me and tell me what you planned? Were you playing the big, strong protector again? Making sure little Jilly didn't get her hands dirty? Or were you just worried that I'd get in your way?"

"None of the above. I had to get out of here for a few hours, Gillian. If I didn't, I would have ended up putting my fist through the wall."

"What? Why?"

She saw the answer in the hot glance that raked from her neck to her knees.

"Oh."

"Right. Oh."

Well, crud! Now she felt not only hurt but stupid. And guilty. She'd *had* to yank on his tie last night. *Had* to give him something to remember the next time Adriana Hall rubbed up against him.

"I guess I owe you an apology, too."

Hawk's grim expression lightened, and something close to a smile edged his mouth. "Not hardly, babe. There's the coffee," he added when the doorbell buzzed.

How did he do it? Gillian wondered ruefully as he headed for the door. One minute, he had her steaming. The next, she was putty in his bruised and battered hands.

Which, she thought while he tipped the waiter, might be a tad difficult to explain to Adriana Hall when they met with her for another buying expedition later.

Gillian didn't comment on that fact until he'd downed some caffeine and briefed her on his nocturnal activities.

"So," she summarized as the sun made a valiant attempt to burst through the drawn drapes, "you might have a line on a smuggling operation, but our only direct link is still Adriana Hall's export operation. Which means, unfortunately, we'll have to spend more time with the woman. How are you going to explain those?" she asked with a nod at his skinned knuckles.

The issue didn't seem to worry him. Shrugging, he inspected his hands. "We went out for a nightcap after Adriana dropped us off last night, chose the wrong section of Hong Kong and I had to muscle our way out."

There it was again. Tough, macho husband taking care of the little woman. Gillian felt her back teeth grinding.

One of these days, she vowed, she'd smash that mold for good.

"Don't forget," she reminded him, "Ah Chang and the kids are meeting us here this afternoon."

"Right."

"I wonder if Young Tau has sniffed anything out."

"He might have," Hawk said wryly, "if he's got the same nose for trouble I did at that age."

Although Gillian had *not* been looking forward to another buying expedition with Adriana Hall, the session produced unexpected results.

After purchasing an ancestor painting depicting the history of a family named Hu, several scrolls of calligraphy art and an antique snuff bottle, Gillian fell completely and utterly in love with a pair of temple dogs reported to be from the residence of a powerful, seventeenth-century courtier. They were cast in bronze, about five feet high and, in Hawk's opinion, not exactly friendly looking. Gillian, stroking a hand over the cool

bronze, tried to infuse him with some of her enthusiasm
for the pair.

"You place them outside, at the front door, to ward
off evil spirits."

"They'd probably do a pretty good job of scaring off
delivery men and mail carriers," Hawk drawled, eyeing
the snarling teeth.

"See how the male's raised left foot rests on a
rounded sphere? It represents the worldly possessions
of those who live in the house."

He duly noted the sphere. An amused Adriana stayed
in the background with the shop owner.

"This one's the female. Her right foot rests on the
belly of a baby temple dog, representing the home
and...and family."

Hawk caught the slight hesitation and had a pretty
good idea what was behind it. Despite the rings circling
their fingers, he and Gillian didn't have a home or a
family for these bizarre creatures to guard.

Something shifted inside him. He never let himself
think about the cesspool he'd come from. He was
younger than Young Tau when he'd lit out on his own—
and twice as belligerent. Thank God for the judge he'd
been hauled in front of in that grim Montana court-
house. His Honor had turned him over to the recruiter
who promised the military would kick the smart-ass
street punk out of him. And kick it had. Hawk grew up
in a hurry. In the process, he'd found a band of brothers.
Special Ops took care of their own.

So did OMEGA. Nick Jensen had recruited him
during the long convalescence after the botched op in

Central America. Hawk had needed the change, needed a new focus to numb the still-searing memories.

That was *all* he'd needed until Gillian Ridgeway had forced her way into his world. Now he couldn't think beyond getting her in bed, sliding his palms over her breasts and belly, burying himself in her heat.

The idea of making a home with her, of starting a real family, hadn't even entered the equation. Until now.

Cursing under his breath, he swung toward Adriana. "How much for the pair?"

She was in business black today. Tailored suit with a skirt cut above the knees. Spike heels. Pale blond hair swept up in a smooth twist and anchored with an ebony clip. Lifting a brow at Hawk's terse query, she consulted with the shop owner.

"His asking price is fifteen thousand dollars."

"U.S. or Hong Kong?"

"U.S."

Gillian nudged him with an elbow and issued a gentle warning. "Careful, darling. If these are the real thing, which I think they are, we'll need a certificate of authenticity and documentation that the sale conforms to Chinese laws on the export of antiquities."

Adriana gave her a cool smile. "Naturally, I would make sure those are provided." Her glance slid back to Hawk. "If you're serious, you should counter. I'd suggest twelve thousand."

"Tell him eight. Cash."

"He won't take that!"

"Tell him."

* * *

They settled on ten-five, with the heavy bronze dogs to be delivered to Adriana's warehouse for packing, crating and shipping.

"I'll need to cash a check," Hawk informed a delighted Gillian. "Why don't you take the car and our other purchases back to the hotel? I'll meet you there."

"You sure you don't need me to go to the bank with you?"

"I can handle it. And we're expecting visitors, remember?"

Adriana's pulse jumped. They'd just handed her the opening she'd been waiting for.

"I'll go with him," she told his pseudo wife. "By the time we return, the necessary documentation should be ready. I'll make sure your husband gets back to the hotel."

The offer wiped some of the delight from Gillian Ridgeway's face.

She knows, Adriana thought gleefully. She knows Callahan and I share some kind of connection she can't quite put her finger on. It isn't physical. Yet. But she's worried it could be.

And so it will.

Something dark and sexual stirred in Adriana's belly. The bastard who'd kept her chained to his bed had taught her to satisfy him in ways Gillian Ridgeway could never imagine. Ways *she'd* never imagined.

The memory of those brutal lessons fed her craving for revenge. She'd have Mike Callahan on his knees. She'd make him groan and beg for release. He wouldn't get it, but he *would* pleasure her over and over again before she sent him back to the hotel with the yeasty scent of sex clinging to his body.

She would take immense pleasure from throwing the fact that Callahan had betrayed her in Gillian Ridgeway's face. Then, at last, Adriana would exact her revenge for the betrayal that had robbed her of her soul.

Chapter 11

Gillian returned to the hotel with the day's purchases, minus the bronze temple dogs. The doorman extracted the packages from the backseat of the limo and informed her she had visitors.

"They arrived about fifteen minutes ago."

"Thank you. Would you have these packages taken up to our suite, please?"

"Certainly."

She made a concerted effort to smooth her frayed nerves as she crossed the lobby and hurried toward Ah Chang and the children. Adriana Hall could put Mother Teresa's teeth on edge, and Gillian certainly didn't qualify for sainthood. Something had to break on this op, and soon, or she would strangle the predatory blonde.

Mei Lin saw her coming and popped out of her chair. "Jill-An! *Nee hao?*"

"I'm very well, thank you."

Scooping up the girl, Gillian gave her a warm hug. Mei Lin was in her pink sneakers and grungy jeans, topped by a slightly frayed brocade jacket that Gillian guessed was probably her Sunday best. The girl returned the hug but was clearly disappointed not to see Hawk.

"Where is Cal-Han *Shen-Sheung?*"

"He'll be here shortly," Gillian promised as she hooked an arm around Young Tau's shoulders.

The boy looked startled and a little embarrassed at the contact. He, too, had spiffed up for the visit. His hair was slicked down and he wore a cable-knit sweater several sizes too large for his thin frame. Gillian hitched Mei Lin on one hip and greeted Ah Chang.

"Honorable Grandfather, I apologize most sincerely for not being here when you arrived."

He accepted the apology with a gracious nod.

"Would you like to take tea here in the lobby, or shall we have it upstairs where it's a bit more quiet?"

High tea at the Peninsula was a world-renowned institution. A string quartet played in the upper gallery, while waiters in impeccable white uniforms wheeled carts loaded with an incredible selection of tea cakes, finger sandwiches and scones with clotted cream. Because it was *the* place to see and be seen, however, it was crowded and usually required a long wait to be seated. Gillian was prepared to offer the headwaiter an exorbitant bribe for a table when Ah Chang opted for a more private setting.

"We should go upstairs, yes? So I may examine the items you intend to buy?"

"Very well. I've made a number of purchases," she told him as she escorted the group to the elevators, "pending your approval."

Gillian set Mei Lin down and offered Ah Chang her arm to the elevators. Once on her floor, she almost forgot to deactivate the intrusion-detection system Hawk had set when they left and had to fumble in her purse. The device brought a leap of avid interest to Young Tau's eyes.

"You have iPod? You listen to Chao Tsai?"

Gillian was very familiar with the first Chinese rock band to burst on the scene in the late nineties. She'd attended one of their concerts in Beijing. Despite the government's suspicion of Western-style heavy-metal rock, Chao Tsai—Overload in English—was still going strong.

"I love Chao Tsai," she told the boy. "I don't have any of their music on this device, but I have several of their CDs at home."

The naked envy on Young Tau's face spurred an instant decision to procure him an iPod loaded with songs from his favorite bands before she left Hong Kong. She'd splurge on Mei Lin, too, Gillian decided as she inserted the key card. New jeans, fuzzy pink sweaters, a warm winter coat. And hair ribbons. Or barrettes. And dolls. Maybe a stuffed bear and…

"Ai-yah!"

Young Tau followed his exclamation with a long, low whistle. His sneakers squeaking on the foyer's marble tile, he led the way inside. He stood small and thin and almost lost in the luxuriousness of the suite as he made a slow circle to take it all in.

Mei Lin wasn't particularly impressed. She skipped inside and scrambled onto the couch, making herself at home. Gillian escorted Ah Chang to a comfortable chair before shedding her jacket. The hotel's efficient staff had already delivered her packages. They waited on a side table along with her purchases from last night.

"Let's order tea first, shall we? The hotel has a fine selection. Do you have a preference, Honorable Grandfather?"

She started to hand Ah Chang the room service menu but realized the cataracts clouding his eyes must limit his sight. Maybe she could arrange to have those taken care of, too, before she left.

"May I read you the brands?"

At his nod, she ran through the extensive list. Ah Chang stroked his wispy beard and pondered his choice for several moments. Selecting tea was serious business in China. Choosing from the Peninsula's incredible medley made it a matter of grave consideration.

He settled at last on Snow Bud, a delicate white tea made from the leaves grown in the highlands of Zhejiang Province. Gillian placed the order and added an assortment of cakes, pastries and sandwiches to accompany it.

When Gillian retrieved her purse to get some money for a tip, the holstered subcompact tucked into a side pocket gave her pause. She didn't *think* either of the kids would go through her bag, but she couldn't take the chance.

The holstered gun went into the suite's safe before she showed a curious Young Tau and Mei Lin around. The wide terrace with its plants and bubbling fountain delighted the little girl. Young Tau glommed onto the brass telescope set on its wooden tripod in front of the windows.

"Look! I see the elevator to Mid-levels. It climbs the hill like silver dragon. Look, Mei Lin."

He boosted up the girl and balanced her on his knee so she could peer through the eyepiece.

Watching them, Gillian felt her heart turn over inside her chest. The boy couldn't be more than nine or ten, yet he'd become the protector of a child who, according to Ah Chang, was no relation. How would either of them survive if the man who'd taken them in succumbed to age or disability?

Ah Chang followed her gaze. As if reading her mind, he exhaled a small sigh. "I, too, worry for them."

His rheumy eyes followed the children as they explored the console that controlled the flat-screen plasma TV.

"Young Tau does much to put food on our table," Ah Chang murmured. "I fear he may pick the wrong pocket one day, however, and I will not be able to help him."

"Perhaps my, uh, husband can talk to him."

Damn! She was sure she'd progressed beyond stumbling over that word.

"Mike had it rough as a child, too. He doesn't speak of those years, but I suspect he can share his hard-earned wisdom with Young Tau."

Along with the fund the Callahans would establish. Gillian had already decided it would pay a monthly living stipend for both children's upkeep. She was still mulling over how best to go about setting it up as she unwrapped her purchases for Ah Chang's inspection.

The ancestor paintings and calligraphy art she'd picked up this morning won an approving nod, as did the antique snuff bottle with a winter scene painted on the inside with incredibly delicate brushstrokes. Ah Chang brushed a loving hand over the cloisonné vase she'd purchased from Alexander McQuade last night, but the three-foot-high candlesticks drew an exclamation of delight.

With a little grunt, he lifted one of the heavy pieces and squinted at the intertwined dragon and phoenix depicted in exquisite enamel. "Very old," he confirmed. "Very fine. How much you pay?"

He didn't so much as blink at the five figures Gillian quoted.

"Good price. You bargain well. But you must have papers to take these pieces out of China."

"They're being prepared."

Room service arrived at that point. The tall candlesticks held places of honor on the coffee table as the waiter wheeled in a cart. The assortment of cakes and tea sandwiches made Mei Lin squeal with delight and Young Tau gape in openmouthed astonishment. Both children waited to dive in, however, until Gillian had tipped the waiter and poured a cup of Snow Bud for Honorable Grandfather. The pale amber blend gave off a floral aroma with just a hint of nutty undertone.

Ah Chang's seamed face folded into lines of sheer ecstasy at his first sip. He savored the moment with eyes closed. When he opened them again, the children were quivering like greyhounds at the starting gate. At his nod, Young Tau attacked the cart. Mei Lin was more dainty in her approach but still managed to pile her plate high.

Gillian held the plate for her while she scrambled onto the sofa once again. Her stubby legs stuck straight out. Pink sneakers bobbing with impatience, she waited while Gillian spread a napkin across her lap, then reached for her plate of goodies. Her first choice was a cucumber-and-shrimp sandwich cut in the shape of a heart. Flicking off the dill sprig adorning the shrimp, she gobbled up the heart and looked to Gillian with a question in her black eyes.

"Where is Cal-Han *Shen-Sheung?*"

Good question, Gillian thought as she filled a plate for Ah Chang. Where the hell was Callahan?

"McQuade messengered over the documentation for the cloisonné pieces early this morning. I can't believe I forgot to bring them with me."

Trailing the scent that stabbed at Hawk's memory like a serrated knife, Adriana led the way across the tiled foyer of a pricey, waterfront high-rise.

"How fortunate my condo is only a few blocks from the bank. It won't take a moment to retrieve the papers."

Hawk merely nodded as she jabbed the button for the thirty-fifth floor. After an hour with Adriana, his internal alarms were pinging like hell. What he couldn't decide was whether the warning signals were due to her less-than-subtle sexual overtures or his growing conviction she was tugging on invisible strings in a determined attempt to keep him and Gillian dancing to a tune only she could hear.

Although he'd downplayed Gillian's biting criticism of Hall last night, Hawk wasn't dead from the neck down. His senses had registered every careless brush of Adriana's arm or leg, every throaty laugh.

In another time, another place, he would have jumped on her unspoken invitation. She was the kind of woman who'd once pushed every one of his buttons. Smart. Supremely self-assured. Cool on the outside, molten at the center. Yet Hawk felt only relief when the elevator disgorged them on the thirty-fifth floor.

"This is me."

She keyed the lock of a door painted dragon-red and framed by a black lacquer oval. The interior of the palatial condo reflected the owner's complex personality. The furnishings were Asian but sparse and dramatic. The floor tile, sofa and chairs were stark white. The tables and chests and desk that stretched along one wall were black lacquer. Slashes of red and thick area rugs in rich colors put Adriana's sensual stamp on the place.

Tossing her purse on a table, she headed for the intricately carved chest that dominated one wall. The doors folded back to reveal a high-tech entertainment center on one side and a bar racked with gleaming crystal decanters and glasses on the other.

"How about a drink?"

"It's a little early for me."

"It's always five o'clock somewhere."

Hawk went still. Absolutely still. As if from a

distance, he heard Diane Carr echo the title of the Alan Jackson–Jimmy Buffet classic.

She'd thrown the line out so often it had become a joke between them. Yet the DEA agent knew how to hold her booze. She never worried about the time and would toss back a shooter when and where she wanted. That last mission, before she and Hawk and Charlie Duncan went into the jungle, she'd damned near drunk them both under the table.

An ache started in Hawk's chest, squeezing his lungs, constricting his air. He could still see Diane in that smoky dive, her hair a short, shining cap of red, her gray eyes mocking as she and Charlie went at it again. They'd never clicked, she and Duncan. Hawk usually ended up having to referee arguments that too often went from friendly to downright hostile.

"I'm having a scotch on the rocks."

He dragged himself from that small, dank bar and locked on the woman who sent him an over-the-shoulder glance.

"Sure you don't want something?"

"Maybe I will. Scotch is good."

Hell! His hands were shaking. What was wrong with him?

Adriana Hall was nothing like Diane Carr. The face, the frame, the voice, the accent, the mannerisms—all different. Even their style of dress. When Diane wasn't in jungle or desert gear, she lived in jeans and tank tops. Adriana was always in silk, with high mandarin collars and side slits designed to make a man sweat. Yet...

What were the odds that the widow of a British Lord who'd spent most of her life in Asia could quote Alan Jackson and Jimmy Buffet?

His thoughts chasing after themselves, Hawk suddenly remembered the gap. After Lord Hall died, his widow dropped out of sight for almost eight months. She'd resurfaced in Hong Kong, a silent partner in Wang and Company. Griff was still digging into that gap. He would have contacted Hawk if he'd come up with anything.

Those eight months were front and center in Hawk's mind when Adriana handed him a heavy crystal tumbler.

"What shall we drink to?" she asked.

"How about old friends...and new acquaintances."

"Is that how you regard me? As a new acquaintance?"

"We don't fit the old friends category," he said slowly, tipping his glass to hers.

The scotch burned a line down the back of his throat. Hawk welcomed the kick as Adriana's green eyes challenged him over the rim of her glass.

"There *is* the possibility," she murmured, "we might become more than friends."

"I don't think so."

"So quick, so sure." Her lips curved in a mocking smile. "Too quick, perhaps?"

"Are you forgetting Gillian?"

"Ah, yes. Your bride."

She took a long swallow of scotch, making perfect semicircles of red on the tumbler, then set it on a round-topped drum table.

"Rest assured, I haven't forgotten Gillian. I simply

consider her, shall we say, extraneous. What happens here, between us, has nothing to do with her."

"Nothing's going to happen between us, Adriana."

"So quick, so sure," she repeated with that taunting smile. "Is it me you're afraid of? Or yourself?"

He couldn't get the Jimmy Buffet song out of his head. He had to know, had to kill the absurd thoughts that kept pushing at the edges of his reason. Hawk could think of only one way to deep six them.

Deliberately, he let his gaze roam from Adriana's red, glossy lips to her throat to her full breasts. When his eyes met hers again, he saw himself reflected in the dark pupils.

"Hell, yes, I'm afraid. Of you…and of how much I could want you."

She didn't try to disguise her triumph. It glowed in her face and threaded through her husky laugh. "Let's see how much that might be."

She flattened her palms on his chest, slid them upward, curved them over his shoulders. Her perfume gnawed at his senses.

Hawk banded her waist and drew her against him.

He had to know.

Her hands locked behind his neck. Their bodies fused at hip and thigh. With her three-inch heels, Adriana didn't have to stretch to reach his mouth. Her lips moved over his, seeking, demanding.

Slowly, Hawk reached up. He gripped her wrists, unlocked her hold and brought her arms down. "I can't do this, Adriana."

Her eyes narrowed. "Actually, you were doing it quite well."

"I won't do it," he amended.

"Why not?" She wrenched free of his hold. "You can't tell me you don't want me. And you certainly can't pretend you're in love with your 'wife.'"

She spit the word out, her tone every bit as acid as Gillian's when she'd warned Hawk that Adriana was putting the make on him.

"Oh, Christ," she muttered when he refused to respond to her taunt. "You *are* in love with her."

Disdain flashed in her eyes, followed by something heavy and dark. Hawk used that as his exit cue.

"I'd better go."

He swung toward the door, and the abrupt turn brought him into contact with the drum table they'd set their drinks on. He made a grab at the table before it toppled but missed. Pale gold scotch spewed, and the tumblers hit the tiles with the splinter of breaking glass.

"I'm sorry." Hawk went down on one knee to gather the sharp pieces. "Get a towel, and I'll wipe up this mess."

"Don't bother."

"You could cut yourself."

Stacking the larger pieces, Hawk carried them to the wastebasket beside her desk. A detour to a kitchen outfitted with gleaming white tile counters and black appliances produced a hand towel in hand-stitched linen.

The smaller pieces joined the larger in the wastebasket. The sopping linen went into the sink. Only then did Hawk nod to the woman who was still standing where he'd left her.

"You nailed it, Adriana. I am in love with Gillian. If

you want the truth, I didn't know what love was until she came into my life."

Her nostrils flared, but she didn't say a word as he let himself out.

The moment the elevator doors closed, Hawk signaled OMEGA control.

"Yo," Griff answered. "What can I do for you?"

"I want pictures of Lord Hall's wife. Some shots taken immediately before his death."

"We can manage that. I'll have the computer guys do a search of the Singapore social scene."

"E-mail them to me as soon as you get them."

"Will do. Anything else?"

"Yeah. Get on the horn to DEA. See if they still have the DNA profile for Special Agent Diane Carr on file."

"Special Agent Diane Carr. Got it."

Hawk reached in his pocket and carefully withdrew a glass shard. The glossy lip print looked as red as blood.

"I'm overnighting a DNA sample to you. Run it against Carr's. I need the results, like, yesterday."

"Roger that."

The glass shard was in his pocket when he exited the elevator and had the doorman hail a cab.

He still wasn't sure. Everything in him said Diane *couldn't* be alive. He'd watched her die, choking on her own blood. She *couldn't* have risen from her dank, green grave and taken on the form and face of Adriana Hall.

He might have convinced himself, if not for that kiss.

His eyes bleak, Hawk tipped the doorman who held the cab's door open for him.

"Where shall I tell the driver you wish to go?"

"The airport."

The hotel could probably arrange a courier and overnight express service. Or one of OMEGA's contacts in Hong Kong. But a grim sense of urgency drove Hawk. He had to see this glass shard get on a plane himself.

Then he needed to sit down with Gillian. He couldn't let his past destroy her.

High above, Adriana stood at the window and watched the cab cut into the bumper-to-bumper traffic.

He loved her.

He didn't know what love was until she came into his life.

The bastard! The lying bastard!

How many times had he backed *her* against a wall and yanked down her jeans or BDU pants? How many times had she locked her legs around his hips and ridden him with unrestrained greed? How many nights had they flopped down in a tangle of limbs, breathless and limp and sweaty?

And he didn't know what love was until that black-haired bitch came into his life?

Seething with a fury so raw it all but consumed her, Adriana stalked into her study. Her hand shook as she slid back a small wall panel to reveal a safe. Inside was a selection of disposable cell phones and the electronic device that disguised her voice.

She stabbed in the number she knew by heart. When a voice answered in the guttural Cantonese of the streets, she replied in kind.

"Where is the woman?"

"At the hotel."

"You're sure?"

"We've been watching both exits."

"Take her! I want it done today." Adriana's knuckles were white where she gripped the phone. "Watch yourselves. She may be armed. Just be sure you deliver her alive."

She snapped the phone shut, still shaking with fury. The game was over.

Chapter 12

Gillian caught her cell phone on its second ring.

"Mrs. Callahan."

She didn't stumble. Playing Hawk's wife not only came more easily now, it was starting to feel almost natural.

Almost being the key word, of course. There was still the slight matter of consummating the vows they hadn't exchanged.

"It's me," Hawk growled into her ear.

"Finally! Where are you?"

"Stuck in traffic. I have been for the past half hour."

"I hope you're on your way back to the hotel. We finished tea some time ago, Honorable Grandfather has inspected our purchases, and Mei Lin keeps asking for *Callahan Shen-Sheung*."

"I'll be there as soon as I can. I have to make a quick trip to the airport first."

"Huh?"

"I may have something. I'll tell you about it as soon as I get back. Right now, my priority is to get a DNA sample on a plane and on its way to the OMEGA labs."

Gillian felt her jaw sag. Where in the world had he acquired a DNA sample?

"The traffic's hell. It may take an hour or more to make the round trip to the airport. Can you keep Honorable Grandfather and the kids occupied until I get there?"

Gillian glanced at the trio. Ah Chang's hands were tucked in the sleeves of his blue jacket. His chin had sunk almost onto his chest. He was ready—more than ready—for an afternoon nap. The kids, on the other hand, had polished off the cake and most definitely needed to work off their sugar high.

"I'm sure I can convince Ah Chang to stretch out on the bed while I take the kids for a walk. We might hit a few stores while we're out."

"Sounds like a plan. Just stick to the main thoroughfares. I'll be back as soon as I can."

Gillian hung up, feeling just a tad guilty. She'd left Hawk with Adriana. He'd intended to make a quick trip to the bank and be back at the hotel in fifteen or twenty minutes. When those minutes had stretched into an hour, then into two, she'd started to wonder.

Okay, she'd done more than wonder. She'd begun to think some very nasty thoughts about a certain predatory blonde who couldn't seem to keep her hands to herself.

From the sound of it, Hawk had either dumped Adriana or used her to uncover this DNA sample he mentioned. Wondering what the heck that was all about, Gillian slipped her cell phone in the pocket of her slacks and approached Ah Chang.

"Honorable Grandfather, my husband just called. He's been delayed but hopes you and the children could wait and have dinner with us. Would you care to lie down on the bed and rest while I take the children out to visit a few shops?"

Young Tau and Mei Lin gave the plan a hearty endorsement. In the face of their eager enthusiasm, Ah Chang made only a token protest before allowing Gillian to show him to the second bedroom. She made sure he had everything he needed for his comfort, then grabbed her purse.

"All right, kids. Let's do it!"

She couldn't wait to hit Nathan Road! She'd have to curb her buying urge, though, and get them what they needed, not what she'd like them to have. Jackets, she decided. New jeans. Long-sleeved shirts and sweaters in preparation for Hong Kong's cold, damp winter. Warm socks. New underwear. A stuffed elephant or monkey for Mei Lin. An iPod for Young Tau, loaded with songs by Chao Tsai and every other Chinese rock band in existence.

So stuffed elephants and iPods didn't fall into the "need" category? What good was the fat savings account she'd built up during her years with State if she couldn't blow it on friends and family?

She and Young Tau negotiated the lobby with Mei

Lin between them. The girl clung to their hands, and
every other step was a skip or a hop. When they approached the front door, one of the Peninsula's smartly
uniformed bellmen tugged on the tall brass door handle.

"Would you like a car, madam?"

"No, thanks. We'll walk. We're just going one block,
to Nathan Road."

Young Tau's face fell a little as he took in the fleet
of Rolls-Royces parked at the ready.

"I'll send you home in one," Gillian promised. "The
driver will take you and Mei Lin and Honorable Grandfather right to the Mid-levels."

The three strolled down the hotel's curving walk.
When they hit the crowded street fronting the harbor,
the stiff breeze blew Gillian's hair into her eyes. She
tossed her head to clear her vision and caught a jerky
movement from the corner of one eye. Swinging
around, she saw only a mass of humanity behind her.
All of Hong Kong, it seemed, was out this afternoon.

With a smile of anticipation, she led the kids across
an intersection, around the corner and onto the street of
one of the world's great shopping meccas.

Gillian couldn't remember the last time she'd had so
much fun. She had four shopping bags draped over one
arm. Mei Lin and a stuffed panda occupied the other.

Young Tau strutted beside them, showing off his
American Eagle hoodie and the white wires sprouting
from his ears. An accommodating clerk at the Apple
store had used the gift card Gillian purchased to
download a hundred of the boy's favorite songs from

iTunes. The shopping bags that Young Tau carried swung to the beat of Chao Tsai's latest hit.

Her arms ached, but Gillian needed to make one more stop. She'd spotted an optometrist's sign in one of the shop-lined alcoves leading off Nathan Road. Luckily, it was only a few doors down from a Ben & Jerry's.

More sugar—what the hell.

She found an empty booth and deposited Mei Lin, her panda and the collection of shopping bags. Young Tau emerged from his music long enough to make his selection from the gargantuan menu listing flavors in English and Chinese. Mei Lin took longer. *Much* longer. After considerable debate, she settled on a scoop of Cherry Garcia.

"Wait here for me, okay? I'm going in that shop." Gillian pointed to the store at the rear of the alcove. "I'll be right back."

As expected in a Nathan Road optometrist's shop, the window displayed frames by Calvin Klein, Christie Brinkley, Donna Karan and Oakley, to name just a few of the top designers. Gillian wasn't interested in frames. What she wanted was the name of a reputable ophthalmologist who could remove the cataracts clouding Ah Chang's vision.

The optometrist was more than helpful. She left the shop a few moments later with a list of three top surgeons. She'd check out each one personally, she decided as the shop door snicked shut behind her, and...

"Excuse me, madam." The man came out of the shadows at the back of the alcove. "You want hand-tailored dress? Very elegant suit?"

"No, thanks."

"I am excellent tailor." He planted himself in front of her, smiling. "Just come. Look at my work."

"No, thank you. I have all the dresses and suits I need."

She tried to go around him, but he was persistent.

"Just come, look my shop. I sew for children, too." He nodded toward the ice-cream shop where Mei Lin was waving her spoon at Gillian. "Make very special *cheongsam* of finest silk for little girl."

Gillian hesitated, wavering. "All right, I'll look."

She held up a finger to let Mei Lin know she'd only be a moment and followed him through an arched opening. All she saw was a row of trash containers lined up along an alley.

"Where is this shop?"

"Just here, madam. Just here."

"Sorry, I don't have time to go farther."

She spun on her heel, made one step and took a crushing blow to her temple. Her knees crumpled. The world went black.

"Ai-ah!"

Mei Lin's high-pitched cry pierced Young Tau's musical haze. Jerking upright, he yanked out an ear bud.

"Why do you screech like a rooster with its tail feathers plucked?"

"Jill-An!" Mei Lin aimed her spoon like a sword. "Jill-An fall. Two men pick her up. Carry her away."

Young Tau leaped out of his seat and crashed through the front door. Her panda forgotten, Mei Lin darted after him. He skidded to a stop in the center of the alcove and spun in a circle.

"Where?" he shouted at Mei Lin.

She wielded her spoon again, her hand trembling. "There!"

"Go back to the hotel!" Young Tau raced for the alley. "Tell Honorable Grandfather!"

He didn't stop to ask if she could find her way. She'd wandered the back alleys and prowled the tourist haunts with him since the day he'd found her, huddled beside a battered suitcase in an out-of-the-way corner of the Ferry Terminal. Hungry and frightened, she didn't know how long she'd been there. Many, many hours, she thought.

Who had left her there, and what had happened to them, Young Tau never discovered. He'd taken her to Honorable Grandfather. Ah Chang had made inquiries but found no answers. When he suggested turning Mei Lin over to the authorities, the girl had cried and clung to Young Tau like a small, frightened crab.

No, he had no worry that Mei Lin would find her way back to the hotel. What scared him to the soles of his sneakers was what might have happened to Jill-An. Hong Kong presented a gleaming face to the world, but Young Tau knew all too well there were still dark, reeking dens that wise men would be well to avoid at all costs. He also knew young, beautiful women like Jill-An had been known to disappear, sucked into the sex-slave trade that flourished despite every attempt by international authorities to stamp it out.

Under his new hooded sweatshirt his heart was hammering, as he raced for the far end of the alley. The sound of an engine gunning added a kick to his step. He burst onto a narrow side street just as a truck pulled away from the curb. It was a small lorry with a roll-up rear door, the kind that made deliveries to shops all over Hong Kong.

Panting, Young Tau swung in a circle. When he saw no sign of Gillian, he started after the truck.

Thank the gods for the drunken dragon that was Hong Kong's traffic! It lumbered forward, lurched to a halt, rolled ahead again. Young Tau darted across three lanes, dodging taxis and lorries and commuters, keeping the truck in sight. His heart jumped into his throat when it edged into the lane leading to the high-speed tunnel connecting Kowloon and Hong Kong Island. Once it hit the tunnel, it would pick up speed and Young Tau would lose it.

First it had to clear the massive construction project at the west end of the Harbor Promenade!

Legs pumping, Young Tau cut left and ran for the spot he knew constituted the worst bottleneck. Four lanes of traffic merged to two as vehicles crawled under a new overpass that was still just a framework of steel girders and half-poured cement. Prominently placed signs warned that this was a construction zone with restricted entry. Ignoring the signs and the shouts from workers in hard hats, Young Tau darted onto the half-finished overpass.

He crouched behind a girder as the truck approached so the driver wouldn't see him. At the last minute he dropped like a lychee nut and spread-eagled himself across the roof of the back compartment. His acrobatics didn't go unnoticed. Horns honked and the driver of the car behind the delivery truck stuck his head out the window. But by then the truck had cleared the construction. Speeding up, it entered the lane heading for the tunnel.

Mei Lin's sneakers slapped the circular walkway leading to the hotel. Her heart was bursting inside her chest. Her breath came in ragged gasps.

She recognized ornate doors and the man in the tall hat who opened them. She knew that beyond those doors was a vast lobby filled with marble columns and potted plants where she, Young Tau and Honorable Grandfather had waited for Jill-An. She also knew they had taken an elevator to Jill-An's pretty rooms. But what elevator? What rooms?

She'd ask the man in the tall hat. He would know. He *had* to know.

She plowed through a group of businessmen strolling down the walkway and darted right into the path of a taxi pulling up the circular drive. Mei Lin froze. The taxi screeched to a halt. A door sprang open.

"Mei Lin!"

With a sob of joy and desperation, she recognized the deep voice. "Cal-Han *Shen-Sheung!* Someone take Jill-An!"

Hawk didn't understand anything except the names, but the little girl's distress plunged a knife into his gut. Swinging her into his arms, he spun toward the doorman.

"What's she saying?"

Shaking, sobbing, Mei Lin poured out a torrent of Chinese.

"She says... She says someone has taken your wife."

"Where! When!"

The doorman fired the questions at Mei Lin. Clinging to Hawk, she alternated between speech and sobs.

"A few moments ago," the doorman translated, "on Nathan Road. She says she runs right away to tell Honorable Grandfather. She says someone called Young Tau goes to look for Jill-An."

"Ask her if Honorable Grandfather is in our suite?"

"She says he is," the doorman responded a moment later.

"Take her upstairs." Hawk thrust the girl into his arms. "Tell her to wait with Honorable Grandfather. And have someone from the hotel stay with them."

There was a chance Young Tau might call the suite. If so, Hawk wanted someone there who could relay the call. Grabbing a pen from the doorman's pocket, he scribbled his cell-phone number on the closest printable surface, which happened to be the back of the man's hand.

"Here's my number. Tell them to call me immediately if they hear from Young Tau."

He sprinted for the cab that was still idling, the passenger door hanging open, and shouted to the bewildered driver.

"Let's go."

"Where?"

"Nathan Road until I tell you otherwise." Slamming into the backseat, he keyed his Rolex. "OMEGA control, this is Hawkeye. Come in."

"We read you, Hawk."

"Have you heard from Jade?"

"Negative."

"Can you get a GPS fix on her?"

"Not unless she transmits a signal."

An iron band clamped around Hawk's chest. This was what had kept him awake. This was what had gnawed at his insides. Gillian could be hurt. She could be lying in some dark alley, bleeding, choking, gurgling his name with her last...

"Why do you need a GPS fix?" Griff asked sharply. "What's going down?"

The questions yanked Hawk from the inferno of his fears. His chest so tight he had to fight for breath, he keyed the Rolex.

"Jade may have been abducted."

Gillian jolted awake on a shaft of pure agony. Gasping, she lifted a hand to her temple. For reasons she couldn't quite comprehend, both hands came up.

It took her several confused moments to realize her wrists were taped together. Several more to associate her body's seemingly uncontrolled jouncing with the fact that she was stretched out in the back of a vehicle moving over a bumpy road. A paneled van, she discerned when the agonizing pain subsided enough for her brain to resume functioning, or delivery truck of some sort.

If it was a delivery truck, she thought as the fog cleared a little more, she was the only delivery. Her heart thumping as painfully as her head, she struggled to sit up. That was when she discovered her ankles were taped, as well.

A sudden thought speared through the confusion and incipient panic. Mei Lin! Young Tau! She'd left them sitting at the ice-cream shop. They must think she'd deserted them.

Fury gave her a sudden surge of strength. If anything happened to those kids, the bastard who'd whopped her over the head would pay, and pay dearly.

Her anger conquered the pain. She rolled onto her side, searching for her purse. Her cell phone was in her bag…but not her neat little subcompact. Crap!

Only after she'd made a futile search for her purse did she remember the jade pendant. She'd tucked it inside the red tunic.

It was still there, she discovered on a rush of relief. She could feel it against her breast.

With a fervent prayer of thanks that her abductor had taped her hands in front instead of behind her back, Gillian yanked at the tunic's gold buttons. Her clumsy efforts popped the first one off. The second slipped out of its hole. Digging inside the gap, she fumbled for the pendant and felt for the right squiggle.

"OMEGA," she whispered. She didn't think the driver could hear her through the front panel, but she wasn't taking any chances. "This is Jade. Come in, please."

She waited for a response, straining to hear over the roar and thumps of road noise. With a muttered curse, she remembered she had to press twice to receive.

Griff's terse voice jumped out at her. "…from Hawk that you may be in trouble. Please advise as to your situation."

"I'm in the back of what looks like a delivery truck. My wrists and ankles are taped, and I have the mother of all headaches, but I'm otherwise okay."

"We have a fix on your signal. We're tracking you via GPS as we speak. I'll advise Hawk of your direction and notify the Hong Kong police. Can you describe the van? Make? Color?"

"All I can see is the inside of a gray box. The walls have side metal struts with loops. For cargo restraints, I guess. There's one of those roll-up metal doors at the rear."

"What about the driver? Can you see him or anyone else in the front cab?"

"No, the box doesn't have a window."

"Okay. Hang loose while I contact Hawk."

Like she could do anything else?

Then again, maybe she could. The prospect of flopping around in the back of a truck, waiting for Hawk to ride to her rescue, didn't particularly appeal to her.

Scrunching and stretching, Gillian crabbed her way to the side of the compartment and used a strut to pull herself upright. The edge wasn't very sharp, but it was the only edge available. Raising her wrists, she sawed them against the strut.

The tape was tough. That black electrical stuff. Her jaw set, Gillian dragged her wrists up and down. The friction heated the metal. The tape, as well. With a leap of excitement, she saw a tiny cut appear.

She bunched her muscles and tugged. The cut stretched into a deeper V but didn't give. She started sawing again and was concentrating so hard Griff's terse report made her jump.

"Hawk's on your tail. He's ten minutes behind, fifteen at most. I've also given the Hong Kong police your speed and direction."

"Roger that."

"You're picking up lingo. Good goin', Jade."

She knew Griff's approval stemmed less from her grasp of spy talk and more from relief she hadn't succumbed to screaming, hyperventilating hysteria. Gillian didn't rule that out as a possibility, however.

"Can you get to your weapon?" Griff wanted to know.

"Uh, negative."

She didn't really see the point in admitting she'd tucked the Beretta in the safe and waltzed out of the hotel unarmed. Biting down on her lower lip, she attacked the strut again.

"What's that noise?" Griff asked sharply.

"Me. Grunting. I'm sawing…this tape…against the… Yes!"

With a flex of her arms, she parted the bindings.

"I've got my wrists free! I'm working on my ankles."

"Better work fast," Griff advised grimly. "I'm looking at a satellite map and I think I see where you're headed. There's a dockyard dead ahead. If I'm right, the truck will slow for the gate."

She felt the deceleration even as he spoke. With a yank that took some of her skin with it, Gillian got the damned tape off her ankles. She scrambled up, grasping the struts again to steady herself as the truck made a left turn and slowed to a crawl. A few moments later, it stopped.

"I've got you, Jade." Griff was calm and steady, with none of his usual drawl. "Hawk and the cops are just minutes away. Just stay calm."

"Calm. Right."

Gillian's heart pounded. Sweat pooled on her palms.

It was too late to play possum. The shredded tape would give her away in a second.

Flattening herself against the side, she edged closer to the roll-up door. A sick feeling swirled in her stomach when the metal rattled upward.

The two thugs who peered into the compartment didn't see her right away, but Gillian spotted the club one of them wielded. It was thick and heavy and had no doubt left a permanent dent in her skull.

The sight of the billy club steadied her skittery nerves. One way or another, the sleazoid was going down!

They spotted her then. Their eyes widened when they saw she'd freed herself, but it didn't faze them for long. The larger of the two thugs hooked a hand impatiently.

"Come out, woman, or we will come in to get you."

She didn't move.

"Come out!"

The distant wail of sirens broke the standoff. The men looked at each other, startled and obviously unsure what that wail signified but galvanized into action.

"Get her!" the bigger of the two snarled. "Drag her out!"

His cohort reached for a handhold and had a leg up when something dropped from the sky. Thudding into him, it slammed him to the pavement.

"Son of a turtle!" Screaming insults, a furious Young Tau pummeled the man's head and face. "Son of a she-dog!"

Gillian and the second abductor recovered from their

astonishment at the same moment. He swore and swung his club. She leaped forward and swung her foot.

Her ankle boot clipped him right under the jaw. His head snapped back with a neck-cracking crunch. Grunting, he sank like a stone.

Chapter 13

Hawk's taxi tore into the dockyard mere seconds before a flotilla of police cars.

He leaped out of the cab, his weapon drawn and murder in his heart, and took in the scene at a glance.

One man was on the ground. Another lumbered to his feet. Young Tau was on the beefy thug's back, his skinny arms windmilling. As Hawk closed the few yards to the truck in a dead run, the man shook Young Tau off like a pesky puppy.

"Freeze!"

Hawk's shout rifled through the air at the exact moment Gillian popped into view, swinging a billy club like a baseball bat. The thug went down like a stunned ox.

His heart hammering, Hawk reached Gillian's side.

"You okay?"

Her chest heaved under her red jacket and an ugly bruise was forming on her temple, but below the bruise her eyes were alive with glee.

"I'm fine. Did you hear that whop? I gotta tell you, Hawk, it felt *good!*"

He stared at her incredulously, his adrenaline at full boil. Far from the terrified woman he'd expected, Gillian-with-a-J had swung the weighted club by its rawhide loop like a friggin' majorette twirling her baton. Hawk opened his mouth, snapped it shut and turned to Young Tau. Snagging the boy's arm, he helped him to his feet.

"How about you, kid? Are you hurt?"

"Pah!" The boy landed a swift kick in the ribs of the man Gillian had flattened with the club. "This pig no can hurt Young Tau."

Hawk should have felt nothing but relief. He should have thanked the kid for whatever crazy stunt he'd pulled to stick with Gillian. All he could do was clamp a hand on Young Tau's shoulder and squeeze it.

Later that evening, Hawk's thoughts were as gray and as stormy as the thunderclouds that had piled up above Victoria Peak.

After a long session with the Hong Kong police, he'd brought Gillian and Young Tau back to the hotel. They related their adventures to Ah Chang and Mei Lin while Hawk sent a doorman to retrieve the purchases abandoned at the ice-cream shop. After treating the trio to a sumptuous feast at the Peninsula's magnificent rooftop restaurant, they'd sent them home in a limo with promises to see them again before they left Hong Kong.

It would take more than dinner and a couple of drinks to unkink Hawk, however. His mind still churned with unanswered questions, not the least of which was who'd orchestrated Gillian's abduction.

Neither of the men who'd snatched her knew who hired them. The order came from a nameless, faceless caller who used a device to disguise his voice. The number on the thug's cell phone traced to a disposable phone that didn't return a signal. Hawk would bet it was already at the bottom of Victoria Harbour.

Nor did the men know the reason behind the abduction. After some intense interrogation, though, the big, surly one admitted he'd snatched other women for the sex trade. Some he'd picked at random off the street. Others had been selected to fit precise criteria. Gillian, he'd assumed, fell into that category, since the person who'd hired them had described a blue-eyed, black-haired Caucasian and directed them to watch her specifically.

They'd been paid half the agreed-on sum in advance. Bundles of bills had been left at various locations. The Hong Kong police had promised to check out every location in the hope someone had noticed whoever made the drop. Hawk didn't hold out much hope they'd get a break. Whoever was behind the aborted abduction had covered his tracks too well.

Then there was this business with Adriana. Gillian's kidnapping had shoved it right out of Hawk's head. Only now, with Hong Kong's spectacular light show bathing the skyscrapers across the harbor in a rainbow of brilliant colors, did he again think the unthinkable.

Which was why he was somewhat less than responsive when Gillian sashayed out of the bedroom, ready to rehash the afternoon's events. She was all warm and cuddly after a shower and wrapped in one of the hotel's plush robes. She was also still pumped by the fact that she and Young Tau had taken down two heavies.

"I just about lost it when Young Tau dropped out of the sky like that. I can't believe he jumped onto the top of the truck and rode it through the high-speed tunnel."

"Me, either," Hawk growled.

His stomach twisting at the thought of what could have happened to both Young Tau and Gillian, he shoved his hands in the pockets of the jeans he'd changed into while she was in the shower. With everything that had happened today, his mood was too edgy and his temper too close to the surface for worsted wool and cashmere.

"I have to tell you," Gillian said as she tested the purple bruise on her temple with a fingertip, "swinging that billy club gave me one intense jolt of satisfaction."

"Yeah, well, watching you swing it scared the hell out of me."

She blinked at the curt response. Hawk knew he should throttle back. She'd held her own today and then some. The mere fact that she'd *had* to still had him rattled.

"What if you'd missed?" he told her. "The goon you attacked must have weighed two-fifty or more. If your swing had gone wide, he could have slammed you against the truck and broken every bone in your body."

"Then it's a good thing my swing *didn't* go wide," she said stiffly.

"Griff told you I was right on your tail. All you had to do was stall for a few minutes."

"Oh, sure! A nine-year-old takes on two kidnappers and I'm supposed to stand there, wringing my hands and waiting for you to ride to the rescue, while they beat him to a pulp." Exasperated, she yanked on the belt to her robe. "Why don't we talk about what's really bugging you?"

"You think you know what's bugging me?"

"I've got a good idea. You still don't believe I can take care of myself—or my partner—in the field. Obviously this afternoon didn't settle any doubts."

"I might feel a little better about this afternoon if you hadn't waltzed out of here unarmed."

The sarcastic retort raised spots of red in her cheeks. She'd only admitted she'd left the Beretta at the hotel after he'd insisted she report it missing along with her purse.

"As it turned out, I didn't need the Beretta."

His answer to that was a disgusted snort.

"So what's it going to take for you to trust me, Hawk? Do I have to kill someone? Put a bullet between his eyes or strangle him with my bare hands? Rip out his heart? Eat it raw?"

"Now you're being childish."

"No, now I'm pissed."

Her eyes were as stormy as the clouds that had begun to dump sheets of rain. The drops splattered against the windows as Gillian crossed her arms.

"Let's just review the bidding here, fella. True, I let myself get snatched in broad daylight. Also true, I was weaponless at the time. But I was far from helpless. I sawed through the tape, clipped one of my kidnappers under the chin with a well-placed foot and coldcocked the other. I think I did pretty damned good. So would you, if you'd stop brooding long enough to admit it turned out to be a pretty exciting afternoon."

"Exciting? You thought getting kidnapped was exciting?"

"Terrifying and mortifying *and* exciting."

The last remnants of Hawk's self-restraint snapped. He'd done everything in his power to dissuade Gillian from getting into this business. Even here in Hong Kong he'd tried to his damndest to shield her. Yet she refused to stay in the safe, secure niche he kept shoving her into.

"You want excitement?" His fists closed around her upper arms. "I'll give you all you can handle."

Her head went back. Her astonished gaze locked with his. Hawk knew she could read his intentions in his face. He waited, giving her an out. Two seconds. Three. Then he yanked her against him and crushed her mouth with his.

Everything inside Gillian leaped with joy. At last! She wasn't sure how she'd finally broken through his defenses, but this wasn't the time to stop and analyze the situation.

Flinging her arms around his neck, she matched his violence with her own. Her mouth ground against his. Her hips thrust forward. They were belly to belly, her breasts pancaked against his chest, her breath coming in short, delighted gasps, when Hawk swung her into his arms.

He kicked the half-closed bedroom door and sent it back on its hinges. She was already tearing at his shirt as he strode across the room. The buttons parted and gave her access to his chest. Gillian swept her hand over the planes and contours, her stomach rolling in wild anticipation.

He dropped her on the bed and ripped off his shirt. His jeans hit the floor. She waited, one leg bent, her entire body screaming, until he came down beside her on the silken coverlet and unbelted her robe. The flaps parted, and Hawk's breath left on a hiss.

"You're lucky I didn't know you were naked under that thing," he said, his voice hoarse. "You would've never made it to the bed."

"I don't have any objection to floors or sofas."

Or any other surface, horizontal or vertical, that would give them the necessary leverage.

"I'll remember that," Hawk muttered.

He skimmed a hand from her throat to her breasts to her belly.

"Christ, you're beautiful. Like a porcelain figurine. Smooth and delicate and perfect."

Uh-oh. Gillian didn't like where this was headed. The *last* thing she wanted right now was for Hawk to decide she was some kind of fragile Dresden doll that required careful handling.

"Perfect, huh? I'll remind you of that when you poke me awake and tell me to roll over so I'll stop snoring."

"You snore?" he said absently, more interested in the dark triangle between her thighs.

"My sister says it's more of a snuffle."

His hand trailed over her mound. Gillian let her legs part.

"I, uh, also hate sharing my French fries," she warned

on a breathless note. "You get your own, Callahan, or you don't get any."

His fingers burrowed into the silky hair. A half smile tugged at his lips.

"I'll get my own. Anything else?"

He slipped a finger inside her, then another. His thumb pressed the sensitive bud. The exquisite sensations shot straight from her belly to her brain.

"Nothing you need to worry about right now!" she gasped.

Arching, Gillian gave herself up to his touch. He used his hands, his mouth, his teeth, driving her to a near frenzy. Amid the spiraling pleasure, one thought kept repeating.

Hawk. This was Hawk. She'd hungered for him for so long, ached to feel his body crushing hers. The sheer joy of having him in her arms, multiplied the pleasure streaking through her by a factor of ten. Twenty. A thousand.

They rolled together across the bed, legs tangled, mouths greedy, and Gillian stopping thinking altogether. She couldn't get enough of him. The taste of him. The sight of his face tight with desire. The feel of his smooth, taut muscles.

She was panting when he tore himself away and fished a condom out of his wallet, wet and eager when he kneed her legs apart. With a gasp of pure pleasure, she welcomed him into her heat.

The first time was hard and fast. The second time, so slow and incredible that Gillian discovered pleasure points she never knew she had.

The third time was just before dawn. Rain was still coming down with a steady patter when she woke. She lay quiet, enjoying the sound and the heavy weight of Hawk's arm draped across her waist.

Enjoyment soon gave way to a more pressing need. The rain reminded her she had to pee, like really bad. The longer she listened to the pinging drops, the worse she had to go. Finally she slithered out from under Hawk's arm and tiptoed to the bathroom.

As long as she was there, she might as well remove the night's fuzz from her teeth along with the sticky residue left over from their lovemaking. With both the bathroom door and the door to the shower shut tight, she figured she wouldn't disturb Hawk.

She figured wrong. She'd just worked up a nice lather when the shower door opened and Hawk muscled his way in. Dark bristles sprouted on his cheeks and chin. His hair looked as though he'd combed it with his fingers. His smile was slow and lazy and raised instant goose bumps on Gillian's naked skin.

"'Morning, Jade."

"Well, Hallelujah! I've finally made the transition." She flicked the washcloth at him. "And all it took was one night of wild sex."

He planted his palms against the tiles and caged her in. "The night's not officially over yet."

Hawk was dressed in jeans and had the international news on the flat-screen TV in the living room when Gillian emerged from the bedroom. She'd opted for casual, too. Gray slacks and a turtleneck sweater in bright, cheerful gold to combat the rain that had morphed into a torrential downpour, sheeting the windows and obscuring the cityscape outside.

"You ordered tea! Thank God!"

She made a beeline for the silver tray room service had delivered. While she'd downed a life-restoring infusion of Celestial Blossom, Hawk drummed his fingers against the table.

"I need to tell you about the DNA I took to the airport yesterday."

"Oh, Lord!" Disgusted, she shook her head. "I can't believe I let little things like a kidnapping, a long session with the Hong Kong police, dinner with the kids and three of the most explosive orgasms of my life make me forget that."

His grin slipped out. "That good, huh?"

"That good. So what's with the DNA? Whose is it?"

The grin faded. His face took on a grim cast that put a sudden damper on Gillian's lighthearted mood.

"I'm not sure," he said slowly. "I got the sample from Adriana but…"

He hesitated for several moments, prompting another question.

"Just out of curiosity, when and how did you obtain a sample of Hall's DNA?"

"Yesterday, after you came back to the hotel and Adriana and I went to the bank. She said McQuade had messengered over the documentation for the cloisonné pieces but she'd forgotten them. We went to her place to pick them up."

Stay cool, Gillian lectured sternly. Keep listening. No

need to get all itchy because Hawk made a little side trip with the Queen of Snide.

"While we were there, Adriana offered me a drink."

"Ha! I bet that's not all she offered."

The comment spilled out before she could stop it. Hawk shrugged but didn't deny the very real possibility Adriana had crawled all over him.

"When I said it was too early for a drink," he related slowly, "she tossed out the title of an old Alan Jackson–Jimmy Buffet song, 'It's Five O'clock Somewhere.'"

So Adriana liked country music? Unusual for the widow of a British lord, maybe, but the song was a classic. Gillian couldn't grasp the significance of the quote. The fact that Hawk went to stand in front of the windows, however, told her there was more to come.

It was a while coming. He stared unseeing into the rain pelting against the glass so long Gillian felt the lazy satisfaction left over from their session in the shower give way to a slow, tingling tension.

"Diane used to throw that line out, too," Hawk said at last.

"Who?"

He turned to face her. His expression was as neutral and as impenetrable as the fog shrouding the harbor.

"Diane Carr. She was an agent with the Drug Enforcement Agency."

Certainty burst inside Gillian, sucking the breath from her lungs. "The woman you once loved," she whispered.

"The woman I thought I loved."

His eyes held hers. She braced herself, not quite sure

she'd heard him correctly over the news coming through the speakers of the plasma TV.

"I realized yesterday I didn't have a clue what love was until you wormed your way into my heart."

Her breath whooshed out again. With the distinct sense that her world had just turned upside down, Gillian shoved away from the table and joined him at the windows.

"That wasn't the most romantic declaration I've ever received," she said on a shaky laugh, "but it will do. It will do very nicely. Now, please," she begged, "tell me what Adriana Hall has to do with a DEA agent named Diane Carr."

"I think..." A muscle ticked in one side of his jaw. "I think they may be the same woman."

Gillian's jaw dropped. She'd been imagining all sorts of wild possibilities. Maybe Carr had met Hall during an overseas posting. Maybe they'd become friends. Drinking buddies who crooned the same song while tossing back tequila shooters. That they might be one and the same had never even entered the realm of possibility!

"But I heard... Someone told me..." She gulped back her confusion and incomprehension. "Didn't the woman you knew as Diane Carr die?"

His eyes were bleak, his mind a thousand miles away. Her heart aching, Gillian laid a hand on his arm.

"Tell me," she said softly.

She didn't think he'd heard her. He was back in the jungle, reliving the horror.

"She took a bullet in the throat," he said at last. "I heard her choking. I tried to get to her."

The newscaster droned on in the background. His measured tones formed a counterpoint to Hawk's stark tale.

"They were still firing at us. The rounds sliced through vines, plowed into tree trunks. I took a couple of hits, too, and Charlie called in a chopper."

"Charlie?"

"Charlie Duncan. He was Special Ops then, like me."

"Wait a minute. Are you saying the agent who got his throat cut in San Francisco was there in the jungle with you and…and Diane?"

"Diane, or, as she might be going by now, Adriana."

"Good Lord!"

The implications were so staggering that Gillian couldn't process them. Her mind whirled as Hawk continued grimly.

"I went back for her after the docs dug out the bullets. I searched for weeks. I couldn't find her body or any villager who knew where it had been taken."

He stared at the sheets of rain, his shoulders rigid.

"I went back again, almost a year later. A rumor had surfaced that a gringo woman was living in the remote mountaintop stronghold of a drug lord. I led the raid that blasted into his lair, but he and his mistress escaped through a tunnel. The description of the woman given by others captured in the raid killed any hope she could be Diane."

He turned to face her then, and Gillian ached at the anguish in his face.

"I can still see her lying in that pool of blood. Still hear her choking. I couldn't save her, Jilly. I couldn't shield her."

"As you want to shield me," she murmured, heart-sick. She understood now why Hawk was so opposed to her joining OMEGA's ranks. She knew, too, that he would throw himself in front of a bullet to save her, as he tried to save the woman who might or might not be Adriana Hall.

If she *was* Diane, who would he choose?

The thought leaped into Gillian's head and stuck there, raising a host of sudden doubts.

If Adriana was the woman he'd once loved...

If she'd somehow survived...

If she'd been playing with Hawk all this time, stirring his memories, testing his bonds to his supposed wife...

Her stomach churning, Gillian tried to sort through her chaotic thoughts. The newscaster blathering on in the background didn't help. With a smothered curse, she snatched up the remote and aimed it at the big-screen TV. The next moment she went rigid with shock.

"Oh, my God!"

Hawk spun around. Horrified, Gillian pointed to the TV. "Look!"

The TV camera panned across the rows of shanties above the Mid-levels. With terrifying clarity, it zoomed in just as a solid wall of mud and debris began to slowly, inexorably slide down from above.

Chapter 14

Gillian and Hawk leaped out of the car that had whisked them through the high-speed tunnel and dropped them off as close as it could get to Hong Kong's outdoor escalator. Hawk had yanked on a jacket over his jeans, and Gillian had snatched up a raincoat to cover her slacks and sweater, but the rain hammered right through the plastic-coated fabric as she ran the remaining block and a half to the base station.

The scene that greeted them only compounded the fear that had clogged Gillian's throat since she and Hawk had watched the wall of mud descend on the shanties. Officials had reversed the escalator's direction to bring down dazed, mud-covered survivors. Frantic friends and relatives jammed the area, searching for their loved ones. Several banks and businesses near the base station had opened their doors to relief agencies for temporary shelters and processing centers.

"You check that shelter," Hawk shouted above the pounding rain. "I'll take this one."

Gillian darted up the steps and through the tall marble pillars of the Bank of China. A hundred or more bedraggled people huddled under blankets, sipping hot tea or soup.

Gillian scanned faces and feet, searching desperately for a pair of pink sneakers. Her hopes crashing, she spotted a woman with a clipboard.

"I'm looking for a boy about nine years old and a four-year-old girl," she told the relief worker. "Their names are Young Tau and Mei Lin. They'd be with an older gentleman named Ah Chang."

The woman flipped through her list. "We don't have them here, but we've set up three more shelters. There's another here at the base station, and two at the Mid-levels. You shouldn't try to get up there, though," she called as Gillian whirled. "It's a long climb. They'll be bringing people down when they can."

When she rushed out of the bank, the rain pelted her face. She blinked it out of her eyes and ran to the shelter Hawk had dashed into. She found him trying to communicate with a harried official and using hand gestures to indicate he was looking for a little girl, a taller boy and a stooped old man. Hope flared in his eyes when he spotted Gillian and died when she shook her head. In swift Cantonese, she queried the official.

"They're not here," she told Hawk, "but they've opened two more shelters at the Mid-levels."

"Let's go."

She didn't bother to repeat the first official's warning about the long climb. Hawk wouldn't heed it any more than she intended to.

The stair-stepping walkways on either side of the elevator were jammed with people surging upward while the moving stairs carried mud-covered evacuees downward. Some were sobbing, some clutched the few possessions they'd managed to save. Others were hollow-eyed with shock and disbelief. Gillian tried to search every face as she and Hawk jostled their way up level after level.

She had a stitch in her side by the tenth level and was gasping for breath by the thirteenth. Hawk practically dragged her to the sixteenth level. Forging a path through the throng, he came up against a set of sawhorse barriers and stopped dead.

"Oh, God!"

His low mutter stabbed into Gillian's heart. Flipping her wet hair out of her eyes, she blinked to clear her vision and felt her fear morph instantly into shock.

Half the hillside seemed to have given way and cut a huge brown swath through the tin-roofed shanties. Those directly in the onslaught's path had disappeared. The shanties on either side of the churned earth looked in imminent danger of going, as well. Some tipped precariously on their support poles. Others had completely collapsed. Fires, no doubt caused by overturned cooking braziers, had broken out in several places, hissing and spitting in the rain.

Rescue workers were frantically clearing everyone

out. Another section of the hillside could come roaring down at any moment, Gillian realized. Sick with fear, she searched the faces of the evacuees being led toward the barriers.

Suddenly, Hawk went stiff. "I recognize those two!"

He pointed to a young girl gripping the hand of a toddler in a quilted jacket and overalls with the seat cut out.

"Last time I saw them, the girl was holding him over a ditch to do his business. Ask her if she knows what happened to Young Tau or Mei Lin or Honorable Grandfather."

Gillian intercepted the pair and hunkered down. She sprang up a moment later with terror in her heart.

"She says she saw Young Tau and Mei Lin! They were trying to dig out Honorable Grandfather."

Cursing, Hawk leaped over the barriers. Gillian ignored the shouts of the official who tried to stop him and scuttled under.

They had to dodge evacuees and rescue workers and scattered debris. Rain and smoke obscured their vision. Twice they took a wrong turn in the maze of shanties and had to double back. Gillian had almost given up hope of finding the narrow opening that led to Ah Chang's place when Hawk spotted it.

"Here! Up here!"

He went first, ducking under tin roofs so close they almost touched. Gillian scrambled after him. When she cleared the narrow passageway, her heart dropped to her boots.

They stood at the very edge of the slide. Just a few feet ahead was a solid river of mud. Here, on the rim of that monstrous swath, houses tipped at crazy angles. So did the wooden steps leading up to Ah Chang's shanty.

"Hawk! Look! There's Mei Lin!"

They could just see the girl. She huddled at the top of the stairs, clutching a wooden cage and looking scared to death.

"Mei Lin!" Hawk shouted. "Mei Lin!"

Her head whipped up. A high, thin wail carried through the rain. "Cal-Han *Shen Sheung!*"

"We're coming," Gillian shouted, scrambling after Hawk. "Don't move, baby. Don't move."

The stairs tilted even more under Hawk's weight and for a terrified moment Gillian was sure they'd give. To her infinite relief, they made it to the top. Hawk scooped up a sobbing Mei Lin and her drenched canary. Two seconds later, he shoved them both into Gillian's arms and raced to aid Young Tau. Panting, sobbing, straining, the boy was struggling to lift the corrugated tin roof that had collapsed and opened the shanty's front room to the rain.

Hawk grabbed an edge and heaved. An ominous creak sounded from the support poles dug into the hillside beneath his feet, but the tin lifted with a loud ponging sound. Young Tau dropped to all fours and crawled inside. His panicked shout echoed out a moment later.

"Back of roof fell in, blocks Honorable Grandfather. He can't get out."

Gillian plunked Mei Lin down and propped a shoulder under the corrugated tin. "I'll hold it."

"It's too heavy for you."

"I'll hold it! Get Ah Chang."

Every moment it took to free Ah Chang felt like a thousand. Gillian refused to think about the rain slamming down or the mountain of dirt still waiting to break loose.

Young Tau scrambled out first. Hawk backed out next, his arms hooked under the old man's armpits. As soon as Ah Chang was clear of the tin, Hawk slung him up into his arms.

"Let's get the hell out of Dodge!"

They had just made it to the barriers when an ominous rumble sounded behind them. Gillian threw a look over her shoulder and felt her heart stop when the hillside above Ah Chang's shanty seemed to implode. Tons of soaked earth broke loose. Seconds later, what was left of the dwelling was buried under an avalanche of mud.

The Peninsula's doormen were too well trained to gawk, but they came close when a taxi disgorged five soaked and muddy passengers several hours later.

Gillian and Hawk had insisted on taking Honorable Grandfather to the emergency room to have him checked over. The ER doc confirmed Ah Chang's self-diagnosis that he was shaken but not hurt.

All of them were shaken. Mei Lin wouldn't let Hawk put her down. She clung to him like a burr, one arm locked around his neck. With her other, she kept a death grip on the cage containing her bedraggled canary. Young Tau tried his best to hold back his tears when he'd discovered he'd lost his iPod, but he climbed out of the cab with twin streaks down his dirty cheeks. Gillian's stomach knotted every time she thought about how close all of them had come to being buried alive.

They left a trail of muddy footprints through the Peninsula's pristine lobby. As soon as they got to the suite, Gillian pried a protesting Mei Lin out of Hawk's arms.

"It's okay, baby. We'll just wash off the mud. Yes, we'll get your birdie clean, too."

She hiked the girl higher and switched to English.

"I'll take her into the master bath. Hawk, show Young Tau and Honorable Grandfather the other bathroom. Then call down to the gift shop. Tell them to send up some clothing suitable for a four-year-old girl, a ten-year-old boy and an elderly Chinese gentleman ASAP."

Hawk made the call while Honorable Grandfather soaked in a steaming tub and Young Tau scrubbed off in the shower. With Ah Chang wrapped in one of the Peninsula's robes and the kid encased in a supersize bath towel, Hawk took his turn in the shower.

He made it quick. He knew Gillian was still pretty shook up. So were the kids. Hell, it would take *him* a long time to forget the sucking, sickening sound of a whole damned hillside coming loose.

He left his filthy clothes in a heap with Young Tau's and Ah Chang's and pulled a pair of khakis and a white shirt out of the closet. Once dressed, force of habit had him closing and locking the bedroom door so he could clean the weapon that had nested at the small of his back. He started to clip the holster onto his belt and hesitated. Better not, while the kids were here. The Glock went into the room safe alongside Gillian's Beretta.

When he strolled into the living room, a now-yellow canary was perched atop one of the porcelain ginger jars and tissue paper littered every square inch of the floor.

Gillian saw him take in the scene with a raised brow. She'd warn him later, when they were alone, that this was nothing compared to the purchases they'd have to make to help Ah Chang and the kids get back on their feet.

"You did good," she told him as a scrubbed and blow-dried Mei Lin paraded around the room in a long-sleeved yellow T-shirt trimmed with lace daisies, matching overalls and frilly socks. The shiny, white patent leather Mary Janes were too big for her tiny feet, but she absolutely refused to part with them.

Young Tau was still desolate over the loss of his iPod. Not even designer jeans and a polo shirt sporting the Peninsula's distinctive logo could console him. Ah Chang's brocaded silk robe trailed the floor a little due to his stoop, but the length wasn't his concern. His expression troubled, he fingered the rich silk.

"This is too fine for such an old man, Jill-An."

"You look very distinguished in it, Honorable Grandfather."

"I cannot accept such a gift. It is too expensive."

"It isn't a gift. We have an agreement, remember? Cal-Han and I owe you a commission for checking out our purchases."

She swept a hand toward the tall cloisonné candlesticks still holding a place of honor on the coffee table.

"The commission on those pieces alone will replace much of what you lost today."

His cloudy eyes looked from her to Hawk. Behind the old man's back, Gillian bobbed her head up and down in a vigorous motion. Hawk got the message and nodded.

With a small smile, Ah Chang turned back to Gillian. "Cal-Han understands not a word, does he?"

"No, Honorable Grandfather."

"Yet he agrees with what you say."

"Occasionally."

"You have a good man, Jill-An."

Some of the horror of the morning lifted.

"Yes," Gillian replied softly, "I do."

Hawk felt his watch begin to vibrate while everyone was feasting on a lunch of hot and sour soup, shrimp-stuffed dumplings and noodles steamed with cabbage and carrots. Excusing himself, he went into the bedroom and closed the door. Griff came on as soon as Hawk acknowledged the transmission.

"We just got the results. The DNA is a match."

Hawk stood rigid, every muscle taut, every tendon corded. The elegance of the master bedroom faded. The murmur of voices in the other room died. The rain splatting against the windows grew louder, sharper, like sniper bullets slicing through tangled vines.

"Hawk? Did you read me?"

"I read you, Ace." The reply was automatic. Empty. "Thanks."

Griff signed off, and still Hawk didn't move. Every part of him felt frozen. His arms, his legs, his mind.

He had no idea how long he stood there. It might have been seconds, minutes, hours, before he heard a loud buzz.

The door. Someone was at the main door to the suite.

His mind was still shut down, but blind instinct kicked in. Automatically, his hand went to the small of his back. The empty hollow where his weapon usually nested jerked him back to reality.

Adriana. Diane. Charlie Duncan.

An icy coldness settled in the pit of his stomach. Kids or not, he had business to take care of. The coldness spread as he punched in the code for the hotel safe and clipped on his Glock. His navy blazer covered the holster as he strode out of the bedroom.

Ah Chang and the kids were still at the table, wielding chopsticks. Gillian stood in the foyer. Her face was dead white.

"We..." She swiped her tongue over her lower lip. "We have a visitor."

Hawk's gaze locked on the woman behind her. "So I see."

Diane. How could that be Diane? The hair, the face, the voice, even the eyes were different.

Those unfamiliar eyes fixed on Hawk and hardened to glittering green glass. "You know, don't you?"

"Yes."

She let out a long, slow hiss. Then casually, so casually, she angled around enough for Hawk to see the silencer a few inches from Gillian's back.

"I didn't plan to do it here," she said with chilling nonchalance, "but the fools I hired to snatch your 'wife' and lure you to a more isolated locale bungled the job." Without shifting her gaze, she nodded to the trio at the table. "Get rid of them."

"They don't have anywhere to go," Gillian protested. "They lost everything in the mud slide and..."

She broke off, wincing as the silencer dug into her ribs.

"Get rid of them, Callahan."

"They've seen you." Hawk knew it was useless to point out the obvious but had to try. "They can describe you to the police."

"They'll describe a woman who won't exist after today." Her husky voice took on a raw edge. "Just like Diane Carr ceased to exist. She died in that stinking jungle where you and Charlie left her."

The hate spilled out, low and savage.

"Get rid of them, Callahan, unless you want them to witness what happens next. And keep your hands where I can see them! I've been waiting a long time for this moment. I don't want it to end too soon."

"Young Tau."

The boy looked up from his dumplings.

"Do me a favor, kid. Take Honorable Grandfather and Mei Lin down to the lobby."

"We still eat."

"I know. But you're almost finished. There's a bakery just off the lobby. Order any dessert you want, and tell them to charge it to our room."

"But…"

"Jill-An and I have business to conduct with this woman. Honorable Grandfather will understand."

Frowning, Young Tau laid down his chopsticks and translated the request. Ah Chang acceded with a nod. Mei Lin pursed her lips and countered with a request of her own.

"Little sister asks if she can leave canary."

"Yeah, sure."

As the three rose from the table, Diane nudged

Gillian out of the foyer and into the living room. They might have been two friends strolling side by side to admire the cloisonné candlesticks on the coffee table.

"Have one of the clerks at the desk call the room before you come up," Hawk told Young Tau, fighting to sound natural. Everything inside him cringed at the possibility the kids might return and get caught in a cross fire. "Our business may take a while."

A stark silence blanketed the suite after the door closed. Diane broke it by moving far enough across the room to give her an angle on both Gillian and Hawk. Her smile sliced into his heart.

"Charlie didn't recognize me. Not even when I had the knife to his throat. How'd you break the code, Callahan?"

"The perfume. The SIG Sauer P226. The title of that old song."

"What song?"

"'It's Five O'clock Somewhere.'"

"Hell! When did that slip out?"

"Yesterday, at your condo. Right before I knocked our glasses off the table."

Comprehension twisted her perfect features into an ugly mask. "Sunnuvabitch! You took one of those glass shards, didn't you?"

Hawk nodded. He wanted her looking in his direction, wanted her attention focused solely on him. When he made his move, Gillian would be out of the line of fire.

"Yes, I took one of the shards. And I just got word a few minutes ago the DNA was a match. They know you're alive, Diane. They'll…"

"Diane's dead!" she lashed back. "She died when you abandoned her."

The wounds had opened up. Hers. His. Hawk felt them bleed as she spewed out her rage and pain.

"The woman who survived against all odds... The woman who spread her legs for the bastard who raped and beat her to a bloody pulp for the sheer sport of it... The woman who finally killed the pig and stole his blood money... That's the woman who derived immense satisfaction from slitting Charlie Duncan's throat."

Her eyes glittered. The gun in her hand never wavered.

"I knew you'd pick up where Charlie left off and follow the leads I planted so carefully. I knew you'd want to avenge his death, although you made no effort to avenge mine."

"That's not true!"

Gillian's protest knifed across the room.

"Hawk went back for you. As soon as his wounds healed. He told me he searched for weeks. And again, a year later. He led a raid on some drug lord's mountaintop stronghold where a gringo woman was supposedly living."

The blonde's gaze whipped to Hawk. "That was you?"

For a moment, just a moment, Gillian was sure she saw regret and something that looked like despair flicker across the other woman's face.

"You were too late, Mike. By then, I'd become what they'd made me. The only thing that kept me alive was plotting and planning ways to make you and Charlie suffer as much as I did. And you handed me the perfect opportunity."

There wasn't a trace of regret in either her face or her voice now.

"You're going to watch her wallow in her own blood, Callahan. You're going to listen to her crying and moaning and sobbing your name. Then you'll die, too."

"It's not going down that way, Diane. You know it. I know it."

Gillian sensed Hawk coiling, knew he'd lunge and draw the bullet intended for her. So did the blond bitch across from them. Her aim shifted.

"Don't do it, Callahan."

With the other woman's entire being focused on Hawk, Gillian knew this was the only chance she'd get.

She didn't stop to think. Didn't calculate her chances. Acting on blind instinct, she wrapped a hand around one of the heavy candlesticks and swung it in a vicious arc.

The blonde caught the movement and ducked. Gillian didn't hear the silenced shots, only a thud as a bullet plowed into the wall behind her and the crack of a window shattering. She heard Hawk's Glock, though.

The gun flew out of the blonde's hand. She gave a cry of pain and cradled her arm.

Gillian thought it was over. She was sure it was done. Trembling all over, she sucked in a breath that carried the stink of cordite.

The flash of naked steel took her completely by surprise. She saw the blonde's other arm come up, caught a glimpse of the serrated blade, heard Hawk shout a warning.

"Don't do it, Diane!"

"It's me or her, Callahan. Make your choice. One of us is going to die."

Her arm whipped forward.

Hawk's Glock bucked in his hand.

Epilogue

The van OMEGA had sent to the airport at Hawk's request pulled into the circular drive of the Ridgeways' two-story brick residence. October winds had stripped the leaves from the maples and oaks, but the clay pots filled with white geraniums decorated the brick front steps and offered a warm welcome.

Hawk got out of the van first and went back to lift out Mei Lin and her canary. Transporting the damned bird to the States had cost him hours of paperwork and a hefty sum in bribes. Same with the temporary visas for Ah Chang and the kids. Gillian had used her pull at the U.S. Embassy, but Hawk had to grease a few palms before Chinese officials issued the necessary documentation.

Young Tau climbed out of the van next, sprouting a

new set of ear buds, while Gillian assisted Ah Chang. She'd called ahead, so the entire Ridgeway clan had been on the lookout. Including Tank, she'd learned, who was on a fall break from Harvard.

"Brace yourself," she warned in Cantonese. "My family is very large and very noisy."

Even with the warning, the chaos that erupted when her mother threw open the front door startled a small shriek from Mei Lin.

"Ai-ah!"

Radizwell raced out first, prancing and barking his fool head off. He was followed in short order by Gillian's sister, Samantha, her parents and Tank. Her jaw dropped when she spotted the tiny ape perched on her brother's shoulder.

"Radizwell! Down! Quiet!"

Gillian's exasperated commands finally penetrated the sheepdog's joy at seeing her again. She returned her mother's fierce hug, but before she made the necessary introductions, she had to ask.

"Where did Tank get the furry neckpiece?"

"Your friend Ben Nareesh dropped him off two days ago. He said you told him to claim the creature if and when it cleared quarantine."

"That isn't exactly what I told him. Er, how does Terrence the Lizard get along with the monkey?"

"He doesn't," her father drawled. "Good to see you, Hawk. We heard what happened in Hong Kong. That was some damned fine shooting."

Gillian didn't want to relive that awful instant when Hawk's shot shattered the knife in midflight. The pieces

rained down at the same instant Gillian swung the cloisonné candlestick again.

She connected the second time. Adriana Hall…Diane
Carr…now sat in a Hong Kong prison awaiting extra-
dition to the U.S. And, she thought with a spark of happiness that warmed her from the inside out, Hawk had
finally buried his past.

"Mom, Dad, this is Ah Chang." Smoothly, she
switched to Chinese. "Honorable Grandfather, these are
my parents."

Adam returned Ah Chang's bow. "Please tell him
we're honored to welcome him to our home."

Tank joined them then. The gibbon had crawled up
his neck and was now wrapped around his head like a
turban. Mei Lin gaped at the two of them from the safety
of Hawk's arms, but Tank gained an instant pal in Young
Tau when he pulled his iPod out of his jeans pocket.

"Do you like the Red Bananas?"

The boy's eyes rounded. "You have songs by Red
Bananas?"

"Every CD they've put out. C'mon, you can plug into
my computer and download the songs onto your iPod."

Gillian could have kissed him when he looped an arm
around the boy's shoulders. Her little brother was now
six-two and as broad-shouldered as their dad but a lot
more laid-back.

"And who's this sweetheart?" Gillian's sister cooed.

"This is Mei Lin."

"Hi, Mei Lin. I'm Samantha."

"She's a little unnerved by the long trip," Gillian
warned. "She won't leave Hawk's arms."

"Sure she will."

Smiling, Sam produced the object she'd tucked under one arm. The stuffed tiger was missing an eye and had had his tail sewn back on twice, but his silly grin made an instant hit with Mei Lin. Transferring her canary to Hawk, she fell into Samantha's arms.

"Let's go inside," Maggie suggested, her maternal antennae quivering. Something had happened in Hong Kong, something Gillian hadn't included in her telephone report to her family. She had a glow about her, and the smile she gave Hawk when they started up the walk was *not* the kind one field operative gave another.

She contained her impatience until the adults had gathered in the den. Adam poured Ah Chang a glass of restorative brandy and offered one to Hawk.

"I'll have one, too," Gillian said. "Mom, too. I want to make a toast."

Her father hooked a brow but dutifully splashed Courvoisier into Waterford snifters and passed them around. The brandy's aromatic fumes tickled Gillian's nose as she held up her glass.

"Here's to you," she said to her parents. "Thanks for putting us all up. We *had* to have Mei Lin, Young Tau and Honorable Grandfather at the wedding."

Her father's brows snapped together as she repeated the toast in Chinese for Ah Chang. By the time she'd finished, her mother wore a broad smile.

"I told her you'd be tough to bring down, Hawk. How did she manage it?"

"Damned if I know." With a wry grin, his arm slid around Gillian's waist. "I think it was *feng shui.*"

His grin faded as he stared down at the woman who'd turned his world upside down and, with the swing of a candlestick, had made it right again.

"Wind and water," he murmured. "Darkness and light. Male and female."

Laughter danced in her blue eyes. "You're mixing *feng shui* with yin and yang. Better get the concepts straight before we go back to Hong Kong for our honeymoon. The real one, this time."

The interested observers forgotten, Hawk tightened his hold. "I may have the concepts confused, but I know this much, Gillian-with-a-J. Whatever happens with the kids and Honorable Grandfather, however we decide to work our jobs with OMEGA, you restored balance and harmony in my life."

Harmony was good. Love was better.

Gillian saw it in his face and felt the joy of it in every corner of her heart.

"Think we can we throw together a wedding by this weekend, Mom?"

"Consider it done."

* * * * *

The World of Mills & Boon®

There's a Mills & Boon® series that's perfect for you. We publish ten series and, with new titles every month, you never have to wait long for your favourite to come along.

Blaze.
Scorching hot, sexy reads
4 new stories every month

By Request
Relive the romance with the best of the best
9 new stories every month

Cherish™
Romance to melt the heart every time
12 new stories every month

Desire™
Passionate and dramatic love stories
8 new stories every month

Visit us Online

Try something new with our Book Club offer
www.millsandboon.co.uk/freebookoffer

M&B/WOR